CASTLE SHADE

LAURIE R. KING

Allison & Busby Limited
11 Wardour Mews
London W1F 8AN
allisonandbusby.com

First published in Great Britain by Allison & Busby in 2021.
This paperback edition published by Allison & Busby in 2022.

Published by arrangement with Bantam Books,
an imprint of The Random House Publishing Group,
a division of Random House, Inc., New York., NY, USA.
All rights reserved.

A CIP catalogue record for this book is available from
the British Library.

10 9 8 7 6 5 4 3 2 1

ISBN 978-0-7490-2756-8

Typeset in 11/16 pt Adobe Garamond Pro by
Allison & Busby Ltd.

FSC
www.fsc.org
MIX
Paper from
responsible sources
FSC® C020471

The paper used for this Allison & Busby publication
has been produced from trees that have been legally sourced
from well-managed and credibly certified forests.
Printed and bound by CPI Group (UK) Ltd, Croydon, CR0 4YY

To all those who manage to keep their heads in an impossible time.
May all your stories have happy endings.

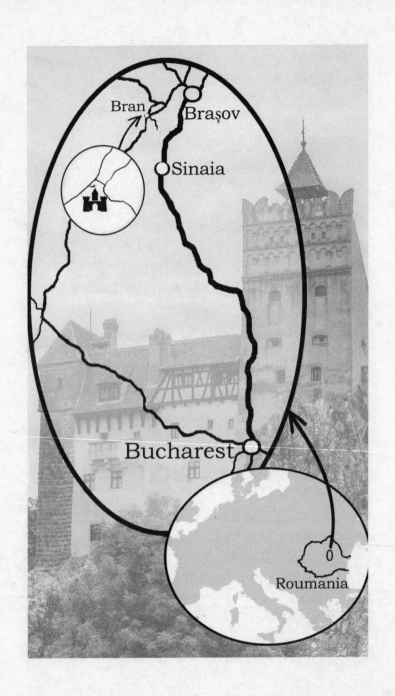

Bran

Brașov

Sinaia

Bucharest

Roumania

THE WALLS OF MY CASTLE ARE BROKEN; THE SHADOWS ARE MANY, AND THE WIND BREATHES COLD THROUGH THE BROKEN BATTLEMENTS AND CASEMENTS. I LOVE THE SHADE AND THE SHADOW . . .

— BRAM STOKER, *DRACULA*

Chapter One

I RIPPED MYSELF FROM THE fever dream somewhere west of Ljubljana.

My face was pressed up to a window, as it had been in the dream. Outside was the same mist-soaked night, the same eerie glow of a full moon.

I jerked upright and thrust out my hands, turning them over, back and front – but even in the near-dark, I could see they were perfectly clean. There were no red and dripping stains gloving the skin.

And no wolves, I thought, chasing after the smell of blood on my hands. The pack's vivid howls merged into the distant rise and fall of a passing train's whistle, while my horse-drawn carriage and its sinister driver became, reluctantly, an aged train compartment behind a steam-powered engine.

I shuddered to rid myself of the macabre sensations, then pulled the thin blanket back up around my shoulders, coughing as I patted around for my glasses. With them on my nose, menace retreated a step. Only a nightmare. Wolves and a carriage, triggered by our destination. The blood, though . . . I'd had the blood of two different dead men on my hands, these past months. Perhaps I should have anticipated the psychic toll.

I wiped ineffectually at the cracked window, trying to see where we were. Not a mysterious forest, thank goodness, but a railway station, with one dim light shining through the decorative iron braces of the platform roof. Silent and deserted.

How long had I been here? For that matter, where was here? My memories weren't entirely gone – I knew what that felt like – just . . . slow. Like pulling a boot from deep mud. Let me see: we had boarded the train in the Côte d'Azur. And we were headed to Roumania. The last station-marker I'd noticed was – Padua?

None of which helped much. I squinted at the rusty and ill-lit metal sign, decided that I had assembled as much information as I could without outside resources, tossed back the travelling rug – and only then realised that I was not alone in the compartment.

'Holmes, what are you—' I began, then dissolved into a fit of coughing, followed by an enormous sneeze. That knocked loose a recollection: the Murphy children, back in France, hacking and snuffling in all directions. 'Sorry, I seem to have picked up a head cold. And I think a fever – I had the most vivid dream, that I was in Jonathan Harker's coach at the start of Dracula. All the evil things in the world will have full sway – sorry, I'm babbling. But why are you sitting there in the dark? And where on earth are we? I can't even tell what language that sign is.' Surely Italian didn't have that pepper-pot sprinkling of accents and subscript marks?

He stirred in his dark corner. His feet came down from the seat, his features coming into view as he leant forward to look out of the window. 'I believe that is Slovenian,' he said, then retreated back into the shadows.

Slovenia. Edge of the Balkans, south of . . . everywhere. Next to Italy?

I sneezed again. This time his arm stretched out, offering a clean handkerchief. Sherlock Holmes always had a clean handkerchief. I used it, and again the pressure on my sinuses knocked forth a couple of ideas. First, that any question Holmes did *not* answer was generally more important than the one he did, and second, the fog I was looking through was not all on the outside.

'Good Lord, Holmes, are you trying to suffocate us?' I stood to wrestle with the window latch, no more able to smell the air than I could read the sign outside, but knowing that at least some of my dizziness was due to the dense smoke in my lungs. Heaven only knew how long he had been sitting there in the dark, mulling over some conundrum. By the looks of the compartment's atmosphere, it had been quite a five pipe problem.

The stuff that billowed out into the night was thick enough to summon the fire services. I dropped onto my seat, coughing now with fresh air rather than stale fug.

With an exaggerated show of patience, Holmes put down his pipe and picked up the Italian newspaper from the seat beside him. He crossed his legs and switched on a reading lamp, to disappear behind the pages.

When the coughing spate passed, I tried again. 'Slovenia is some way from Bucharest.'

My husband and partner muttered something under his breath. The exiting air had ceased to look like a chimney, so I closed the window somewhat, scowled at the station name that might have been spillage from a typesetter's tray, then turned on

11

my companion a glare strong enough to burn a hole in the pages he was pretending to read. He raised the paper a little.

'How long have we been sitting here?' Another mutter. '*How long?*'

He gave up, folding the newspaper noisily into something resembling a rectangle, and took out his watch. 'Not quite three hours.'

During which time he had not been stirring up alternate transport or threatening the engineer with bodily harm, but instead, silently poisoning us both with nicotine.

I recognised the signs. To find him curled in a corner with his filthy old pipe and a handful of the very cheapest tobacco meant he was searching for connections between a series of apparently unrelated facts. As Dr Watson said, Holmes had a positive genius for minutiae – dogs that stayed silent, dried pips from an orange. Many of his cases started with some tiny event that the rest of humanity would not even notice.

A pipe-fuelled rumination explained why he had been sitting there, oblivious to the world. However, in my current state, there was little point asking what he was working on. I would never be able to follow his thoughts without stimulation of my own.

'What are the chances of getting some tea?'

'Very slim. We left the dining car behind in Trieste.'

'Trieste?' I laboriously summoned a mental image of Europe, drawing a line between where we had started and where I'd thought we were going. Granted, I'd been both busy and distracted in the Riviera, where several much-interrupted nights (and, I suspected now, a low-grade fever) caused my brain to shut down within minutes of boarding the train. That same mental state, come to think of it, had led me to follow Holmes blindly in the first place,

12

without questioning the details of his travel plans. Never a wise thing to do.

'Holmes, why the devil are we . . . never mind. Where's the *Bradshaw's?*'

'Our *Bradshaw's Guide* appears to be somewhat out of date. Hence the siding upon which we sit.' He handed me a book that looked as if it had walked from Paris on its own.

'Holmes, this was published before the War.'

'I was assured that little had changed in this part of the Continent.'

'You were duped,' I said brutally. I dropped the thick volume onto the seat, causing several pages to shoot to the floor. When I stood, stretching my cramped limbs, I could feel the rawness in my throat and the ache in my bones.

Children: such a gift.

The passageway was dark, lit by bulbs of tiny wattage at both ends. I set off down it, glancing into the other compartments, but the train seemed as deserted as the station. Two cars back, I became aware of a noise, and followed it to the train's last car. The snores of a uniformed attendant were causing the windows to rattle. Until I walked over and kicked his feet from their rest.

He fell to the floor, snorting himself awake, then leapt upright when he beheld me looming over him. 'Madam! Yes! May I be of service?' He straightened his tie and looked surreptitiously around for his shoes.

'How do I get to Vienna?'

The answer required his cap, but that, once firmly squared on his blunt head, seemed to bring a degree of professional memory. 'Madam is going to Bucharest, is she not?'

'Madam is clearly going nowhere at the moment, and I can't

see why I should visit every tiny village in Eastern Europe on the way. Getting out of . . .' I waved towards the unpronounceable sign outside. '. . . here, in any direction will give us more of a chance of actual progress than waiting for the tides to wash us to the northeast.'

He blinked in incomprehension, and bent to retrieve the footwear he had spotted under the table.

I sighed. 'Do you have a *Bradshaw's?* Or any train schedule?'

The one he had was in German, but it was only three years out of date, rather than Holmes' fifteen. I pored over it, trying to locate a string of letters approximating those on the sign outside. I found one at last, followed its listings along the page, then consulted the clock on his wall.

'We are here?' I asked. He bent to study the name above my finger.

'Yes, madam,' he said, following that with a noise like an aged coal miner clearing his throat. I took a sharp step back, then decided he'd been pronouncing the village name.

'And this train, going west, will pass here at three-fifteen? This is Tuesday, right? And not a second or fourth Tuesday?' There did not seem to be any other tiny-print rubrics in the train schedule – assuming it was still August, and I hadn't been in a Sleeping Beauty coma on the cramped leather seat.

He looked at the calendar under the clock, his lips moving as he worked on the complicated matter of the day of the week, then nodded. 'Yes, madam.'

Now the big question: 'Can you get that train to stop?'

'But madam, your tickets are for . . .'

The gaze that had failed to ignite Holmes' newspaper worked a treat on the attendant. He did up a button on his uniform coat

14

and nodded vigorously. 'I can, madam.'

'You stop that train, and I shall reward you. You let it go by, and I shall not be pleased.'

He actually gulped, and snatched up a lantern to trot away down the corridor.

I went back, ever the optimist, to tell Holmes he should gather his things.

The approaching train seemed determined to roll on through, but our wildly gesturing attendant did catch the engineer's attention at the last moment, and the squeal of slammed-on brakes managed to stop it before it had entirely gone past the station platform.

We waited until our new attendant appeared – rumpled, unshaven, and clearly flung from his sleep by the abrupt deceleration. The two men hurled recriminations and explanations at each other, ending when Holmes shoved his valise into the new man's arms and climbed through the train's open door.

The man led us to a compartment, satisfyingly empty. When I then asked if he might possibly be able to find some warm food for two benighted travellers, either my demure fluttering of eyelashes or (more likely) the sizeable tip he had seen me hand the first attendant soon had us seated in the dim, barren dining car, while hopeful noises came from the kitchen.

What seemed like two minutes later a simple feast appeared: tea – blessedly hot and reasonably near-British. It was soon followed by fat, buttery omelettes and bread only slightly stale.

We pronounced ourselves well satisfied, and sent the cook back to his bunk.

I surfaced at the end of the omelette – which must have employed at least six eggs – and soothed my raw throat with more tea. At last, with the urgent needs of alternative travel and stoking the inner furnaces behind me, I could attempt to make sense of our longer-term issues.

Namely, what on earth we were doing here.

Chapter Two

'Aʟʟ ʀɪɢʜᴛ, Hᴏʟᴍᴇs, ᴡʜᴀᴛ's going on?'

'There is a situation of interest in Roumania.'

'You told me that some days ago.' It had seemed unlikely at the time, standing on a sun-drenched walk over the Monaco harbour. Roumania was as close as Europe got to wilderness: neither West nor East, not quite feudal yet a fair distance from a functioning democracy, a land beyond the reaches of the Cook's guides. 'And granted, it's a place where the maps have "Here be dragons", but I can't see why we needed quite such a roundabout route. Instead of the nice, luxurious Train Bleu back to Paris and a transfer to the Orient Express, you chose a long, slow meander on a rock-hard seat, with no dining car, through villages with names like Coughhackiščina and Phlegmja?'

'Are you in a hurry to get somewhere, Russell?'

'I . . . Holmes, *you're* the one with the urgent task! Aren't you? I'd have been more than happy to spend another week in the Côte d'Azur, baking out this head cold. Instead – what awaits us in Bucharest, anyway?'

'Not Bucharest.'

'No?'

'A village near the town of Braşov, in Transylvania.'

'Transyl— good God.' I stared at him. If Roumania was a realm of dragons, then the province of Transylvania would be the creature's lair: dark, mysterious, and potentially deadly. There was a reason why Bram Stoker chose it as the home of his ancient vampire – a novel that had given me nightmares even before I knew I was going there.

'It is actually quite a pleasant piece of countryside,' Holmes insisted. 'Mineral resources, rich agricultural valleys, the Carpathians for defence. A fascinating source of folkloric traditions and superstitions.'

'One assumes their farmers grow plenty of garlic. You were there, right?'

'I was, yes. A week of what might be called reconnaissance, while you were sailing from Venice to the Riviera.'

'A whole week? And you didn't solve the case?'

'My – *our* client was not there at the time.'

'Who is this client? You said in Monaco you had an interesting woman with an intriguing problem.' The other word he'd let drop that day – *vampires* – might have sparked my subconscious imagination, but I had taken it for one of his laboured witticisms, and had not dignified it with further questions.

'Our client is the Queen of Roumania.'

'Queen *Marie*? Wow.'

Granddaughter of two empires – her father was Victoria's second son, her mother the only surviving daughter of Tsar

Alexander II – Marie had been given to the crown prince of Roumania, now Ferdinand I, the second king in Roumania's young dynasty.

I was not generally impressed by inherited power, but I'd been seeing photographs of the glamourous and clever Queen Marie my entire life: Marie in Red Cross garb during the War, Marie's translucent eyes beneath a splendid Baroque crown, Marie waving to her adoring countrymen from a train, Marie in a folkloric costume, Marie taking tea in the gardens of Buckingham Palace. Theatrical, striking, and unmistakeable – and then the woman had gone on to conquer the Paris peace talks armed with little more than beauty and determination, charming Europe's leaders into remembering their promises to Roumania – promises that included the return of Transylvania. She had single-handedly doubled the size of her adopted country overnight.

'What does she need from us?' I asked. 'Another batch of missing Russian jewels? Roumania was badly plundered during the War – I imagine any royal possession that wasn't nailed down vanished into some invader's pocket.'

He rearranged his coffee spoon, straightened the handle on his cup until it was parallel with the table's edge. 'Nothing missing, no.'

'Blackmail, then? Or smuggling?' Roumania's boundaries included both the Danube and the Black Sea, making for a watery highway into the very heart of Europe.

'Their problem is with *strigoi*,' he said. I waited. He took a sip of cold coffee, replaced his cup, and adjusted it again. I frowned at the deliberate motions of his fingers, and at the way he was not meeting my eyes. He looked . . . embarrassed?

19

'I'm not familiar with that word, Holmes.'

'*Strigoi* are a kind of, er, vampire.' He sighed, then looked up. 'Russell, this corner of Transylvania appears to be having a problem with vampires.'

CHAPTER THREE

ILAUGHED. WHO WOULDN'T? But once I'd recovered from the coughing fit this set off, I noticed the distinct lack of humour on his face. 'Oh, Holmes, you can't be serious? When you mentioned Roumanian vampires, I thought it was like . . . I don't know. Switzerland having a plague of cuckoos. Do you mean to tell me that people in Roumania are dying of exsanguination?'

'Not dying, no.'

'Holmes, I absolutely refuse to believe that the dead are walking in Eastern Europe.'

'Of course not. This agency stands flat-footed—'

'—On the ground. Yes, I read Dr Watson's story. "The Sussex Vampire" turns out not to be a vampire, but a disturbed young man with some poison darts.'

'No doubt we shall uncover some similarly prosaic explanation here. However, there is a child involved in this situation as well, and I agreed to look into it.'

'An infant victim?'

'Oh no. Not an infant. By no means.'

He slid his hand into his breast pocket and came out with an envelope. From it he pulled the crisp, clear photograph of a document, on which was printed:

SA NU ADUCI FIICA TA INAPOI LA BRAŞOV

SAU VA MURI.

'Is that Roumanian?'

'Yes.'

'What does it say?'

'Russell,' he chided, '*Roumanian* is a cognate of *Romance*.'

For a split second my sluggish brain pictured a land inhabited by newlyweds and women bent over Ethel M. Dell stories – but no, he meant *Rome*, as in Ancient. Which suggested that the country's language was closer to that of Spain than of neighbouring Serbia.

Reluctantly, I focused my eyes on the photograph. '*Fiica* would be girl, or daughter. *Braşov* you said was the name of a town in Transylvania. And *muri*, well. That last phrase probably means "she's going to die."'

'"Do not bring your daughter back to Braşov or she will die."'

I tipped the glossy surface to better see the image. 'There's a smudge.'

'Blood. Human blood – our friends in the Monaco police department allowed me to use their laboratory. I believe it was placed there deliberately, for effect, since the lines of the thumbprint are too smeared to identify. I've sent the original card back to London for safekeeping.'

'When did you get it?'

'It reached me in Venice, the day after you departed. It was re-addressed from Sussex. Along with this.'

He handed me a page of expensive paper, with expensive handwriting – a woman's hand using a bold nib, the script upright, clear, and strong. Full of personality. The page itself had been torn away at the bottom with a straight edge – or more likely, I decided, the top of the page had been removed, to conceal an identifying address. But when I held it to the light, the watermark made my eyebrows go up. When I looked at Holmes, he nodded.

24 June 1925
London

Dear Mr Holmes,

I write in a hurry and in secret, with a mother's hope that this finds you, and that you are able to help me. The enclosed reached me last week. Before I left Roumania, in April, there had been two or three rather unsettling episodes and rumours in the neighbourhood of my castle, Bran, near to the town of Brașov.

I had intended to return home to Bran in August with my daughter Ileana, following some weeks in England and Germany. Now I am divided as to what I should do. I have spoken with my cousin about the matter and he has suggested that I ask you to come and see me, to give your advice as to what action I should take. Were this threat aimed at myself, I would step down from the train with my head high, daring any man to act against the wishes of the people who love me. But it concerns my daughter, and my will quivers at the thought of harm coming to her.

I shall be in London for another two weeks, and would gladly see you at any place you find convenient. Please respond to the Palace – my cousin's people will see that I receive any letter or cable.

> *Marie*
> *Queen of Roumania*

My cousin, I reflected, was King George V; *the Palace* was Buckingham, whose letterhead she had been trying to conceal.

I studied the dramatic signature of a woman who knew her own mind, and considered Holmes' response to this letter. One trip across Europe might be explained by curiosity, or even a grudging sense of responsibility to Victoria's granddaughter. But a second trip? By a man who had been known to blithely send female clients back into danger, who had insulted the King of Bohemia to his face? Why didn't he simply tell her to hire a bodyguard?

'Holmes, you turn down cases with more substance than this all the time. I accept that Marie is an intriguing person in her own right, but you can't be taking her seriously just because she's royal?'

'It was her reference to "unsettling episodes and rumours" that caught my attention. You being off on your sailing expedition, I wired back to say I would look into the matter, then took the train to Bucharest and thence to the village of Bran. Where indeed I found the air filled with rumours of mysterious figures and men risen from the dead.'

My head was starting to ache. 'This all sounds a touch . . . metaphysical, Holmes.'

'Some of my more challenging cases began with what one might call supranatural events. Ghostly dogs, a face looking in at a second-storey window.'

'If you say so.'

'The castle's major-domo knows more or less who I am, but to all the rest, I presented myself as an architectural consultant – Castle Bran is in the midst of renovations – with an interest in folklore.'

'Which allowed you to both poke into every corner and ask a bunch of odd questions. And yet, you did not manage to solve the case. Not only that, you broke off your investigation and travelled back across Europe to Monte Carlo, to find me.'

'Yes. Although I had done as much as I could in the Queen's absence, and thought I might as easily wait for her return in the South of France as in the Carpathians.'

As I studied him, I realised that he was again avoiding my eyes. What could be any more embarrassing than Transylvanian vampires? (I admit to a touch of humiliation myself, merely writing that sentence.) What possible, even more uncomfortable part of his explanation had yet to drop?

'All right, Holmes, let's have the rest of it. I imagine it has something to do with why you were in such a deep study with your pipe that you nearly asphyxiated us both.'

He reached down to pick up the loathsome object, fortunately making no move to fill it with tobacco, merely turning it over in his hands.

'The solution of a case requires two things,' he said. 'Data, and perspective. My "deep study", as you call it, was an attempt at the latter.

'Russell, when my practice was young, a governess once came to me with a question that irritated me with its triviality. My attitude nearly cost the woman her life. Some years later, I refused to board a train for Switzerland to help another woman, with catastrophic results. And yet, both of those cases came *after* the one in which I met

Irene Adler, whom I chose to overlook until she had soundly trounced me. Even now, after all this time – indeed, after having you in front of me for ten years – I suspect that again, in the South of France, I failed to understand some key elements of the matter. Elements having to do with another woman I ought to know well, Mrs Hudson.

'No,' he said, waving away my protest, 'I am aware that there are things she – and you – did not tell me, but for the moment, I merely mention the matter because it underscores an inescapable fact: that I, Sherlock Holmes, have a blind spot. I tend to overlook those problems brought to me by women.'

I blinked at this extraordinary admission.

He gave the pipe a wry smile. 'Hence, my suspicion, when the Queen's letter came, that to follow my impulse and reject this mother's plea for her daughter might be . . . unwise. Hence, too, my ruminations with the pipe, in an attempt to overcome the blindness with a closer examination of the facts.'

'Which you have not?'

'Which, as you say, I have not managed to do.'

'I see.' I was not sure I did, entirely, but it was food for thought.

'The daughter's name is Ileana. Beloved child, close companion. She is the Queen's youngest, after an infant son died during the War.'

'All right.'

'She is sixteen.'

'And?'

'And I realised . . . That is, I suspected that perhaps another, more qualified . . .'

I leant forward over the table. 'Holmes, what is it you want me to do?'

He took a deep breath, and met my gaze at last. 'I should like you to be my inside informant, into the mysterious realm of the adolescent female.'

'You want me to spy on a Roumanian Princess? Or – no: you expect me to befriend her! You think that because she and I are only nine years apart, we are sure to become good chums? Or perhaps you're looking for a nursemaid to keep her out of your—'

He cut me off before my indignation could rise. 'Russell, no, I do not imagine that you will either be assigned a young friend or handed her to care for. Although a girl in her situation – surrounded by servants, her closest relationship with a mother who has lost all her other children by marriage, death, or alienation – would no doubt benefit from meeting a person like you. A woman with abilities and a life of her own, a person habitually unimpressed by royal titles, stunning heritage, and blatant wealth.'

From him, this was a compliment. Although his next sentence was more to the point.

'My time in Bran led me to suspect that the focus of threat centres on Princess Ileana – and not merely the warning on that card. All of the "unsettling episodes" to which the Queen refers have to do with Princess Ileana's contemporaries in the village. That is, her friends. And yet, even now I cannot decide whether to treat these episodes as adult fact, or as childish imagination. In either event, you will agree, Russell, that girls of that age are more likely to confide in a slightly older woman such as yourself than they would a considerably older man.'

I was not overjoyed at the prospect of being thrown to a gaggle of young women, but I could see his point. 'I hope you're not going to tell me that the Princess is jabbing some poor infant in the neck with a poison dart.'

'Not so far as I am aware.'

'Very well, I will *provisionally* agree, to be your delegate to the

27

land of the adolescent girl. However, you also told me this case had to do with vampires. Holmes, I have to say that the idea of setting young girls alongside someone with Bram Stoker fantasies makes me distinctly uncomfortable.'

He glanced around the deserted car, and dropped his table napkin beside his plate. 'Let us adjourn to our compartment, for the remainder of this conversation.'

CHAPTER FOUR

To my pleasure, I discovered that the beds in our compartment had been made up in our absence: untold luxury after a night on a bench. My aching limbs wanted nothing but to crawl into one and disappear; however, I needed to hear what we were up to. So I compromised by wrapping myself in one of the bedcovers, but taking care to sit bolt upright, lest the call of sleep prove too loud.

'What are these "episodes and rumours" that unsettled the Queen? And where do the undead come in?'

Holmes dropped into the chair that had been pushed to the corner and took out his pipe – the amiable cherry one, with the fragrant tobacco.

'Vampires are a persistent theme across history,' he began. 'Writers like Polidori, Le Fanu, and Stoker draw from ancient myths and folk belief. And from each other, naturally – Mycroft had a well-worn penny dreadful called *Varney the Vampire* when we were growing up, which I imagine Stoker also read as a boy. The idea is found in cultures from Egypt to Ireland, of a person who rises from the grave to commit mischief and destruction.

'The Slavic countries up into the Carpathians are a particularly rich source of vampire mythology. Every region has its favourite means of identifying, repelling, and killing a member of the non-dead. Among them are the *strigoi* – cognate with the Latin *strix* and *striga*, a sort of owl that feasted on human flesh, and thence the Italian *strega*.'

'Witch.'

'Modern laboratories might diagnose porphyria from the photosensitivity, red lips, and prominent teeth. Or rabies may cause a person to bite, while catalepsy has been the cause of premature burials for as long as – what is wrong?'

He'd seen me shiver – but less from fever than from the creep of rising hair. 'I've always been horrified at the thought of being buried alive. God knows where I first came across the idea, but when my family died, I'd have nightmares that they were trapped in their coffins. I would picture my mother's fingernails clawing the . . .' I rubbed my arms and gave him an awkward laugh. 'Just a minor phobia, Holmes.'

'I shall arrange for you to be buried in a Victorian patent safety coffin. One with a large bell.'

'Very good of you. But when it comes to your Roumanian shades, I don't believe you're talking about premature burial.'

'No indeed. In the Stoker novel, vampirism is a kind of contagion, used to create more of its kind out of the living. In Roumania, a vampire is someone who dies but whose soul refuses to fully leave the body. Hence a being that is neither living nor truly dead.

'There are a thousand variations in how *strigoi* behave and what one can do about them. Some of the creatures are merely irritating, not dangerous. Others literally suck away their victim's lifeforce, be it livestock or people, and must be dealt with before they kill an entire village. Some run in packs like werewolves, others behave like witches – apparently alive, a part of the community, but secretly robbing their neighbours of life.

'Once a village have decided that their troubles are due to a *strigoi*, the solutions vary. Some areas dig up the body to burn the heart and scatter the ashes, or cut the corpse's tendons and leave it face-down in the coffin to keep it from climbing out. If the *strigoi* is one of those who appears to be alive, they solve the problem by burning the house down around them. And there is the classical spike through the creature's head or heart – I understand that ancient skeletons have been found with iron bars lodged in their ribs.

'Sometimes, when a vampire is suspected but not identified, villagers attempt to repel it by hanging up garlic or wearing a cross. Sprinkling mustard seeds over a floor or roof keeps the creature too busy counting to go further.'

I had been subsiding into the bedclothes, pushed there by the inevitable weight of a Holmesian lecture, but at this statement, I roused. 'That one has to be a joke.'

'At times,' he said, 'an outsider finds it difficult to be certain.'

'Holmes, what do vampires have to do with the threat against Princess Ileana?'

'In another country, perhaps nothing. But in Roumania, with its history and folklore, and with a Queen out of England – quite a bit. One has to travel the road of how Her Royal Highness Princess Marie of Edinburgh became the beloved mother of a nation. Marie was the product of Russian empire, British throne, and German nobility. Far too valuable a piece to waste in the chess game of nations, at the tender age of seventeen she was played into the promising new house of Roumania, a country on the border of several great powers, promised to the nephew and heir presumptive . . .'

The trickle of cool air through the train window had no chance against the warm wrap, the soft bed, and Holmes' droning voice. I slept.

My fevered state no doubt contributed to the dreamlike tints that coloured the narrative – coloured the events of subsequent days, for that matter. However, I believe the story of Queen Marie of Roumania would have ended up feeling like a fairy tale no matter how bluntly the facts of her life were presented.

CHAPTER FIVE

ONCE UPON A TIME there was a young golden-haired Princess named Marie. She and her sisters lived in a big country house in a peaceable landscape, with ponies to ride and gardens to run through and servants to watch over them. From time to time, they were taken to visit their grandmother, who was Queen of Half the World.

As Marie grew, she became a beauty, a tall, slim young woman with thick blonde hair and ice-blue eyes. She fell in love with the young man who would – although no one knew it yet – become her country's king, but being first cousins, her mother's religion forbad it. Instead, the Duchess of Edinburgh and her mother-in-law, Victoria, chose for Marie the crown prince of a new country on the other side of Europe. Prince Ferdinand, Roman Catholic nephew to the childless king, was physically awkward, socially shy, largely inarticulate, and primarily interested in plants. Had she been less beautiful, less sure of herself, less skilled a horsewoman, he might have been less awkward with her. As it was, he was no match for his bride in anything but position.

That was judged enough. The match was made.

Marie was sad, because she loved her cousin, because her new home was far from her dear sisters, and not least because she had little in common with her new husband. But the blood of the world's greatest dynasties ran in her veins, and she had been training for the job of Queen from the time she could walk.

Two months after her seventeenth birthday, the English Princess became the Roumanian crown Princess, and went to live in a barbaric place more Ottoman than European, with few railways, no telegraph, and not even a proper palace in its capital city. A country whose language the girl did not speak, whose customs she did not understand, and a husband she barely knew. And when she got there, the old king had expectations: that his heir's wife would be quiet, and obedient, and tame.

Marie was accustomed to riding out alone on the most spirited of horses, seated astride as she raced paths and jumped hedges. Now she had attendants, and a side saddle. She lived in the king's castle and rode the king's horses and travelled at the king's whim, making such friends as she was permitted.

The years passed: children, parties, ceremonies.

Not until she was thirty-one, the mother of four in a world of growing turmoil, did she encounter a man who took her seriously. Prince Barbu Ştirbey came from a family of boyars prominent since the fifteenth century. Astute, quiet, darkly handsome, and Sorbonne-educated, this high-ranking aristocrat was yet known for his interest in modernising his vast estates. He was also a fine horseman, with a house in the same hill resort the royal family occupied during the hot summers.

The two met during a time of peasant uprising, when farmers rebelled against the conditions of near slavery imposed on them by the feudal system of land ownership. Prince Barbu was a patriot to his bones – and to him, that meant a loyalty to the people of Roumania. He taught Marie about the urgent need for democracy, and for agrarian reform – and thirty-two-year-old Marie, venturing into the realm of politics for the first time, convinced her husband, and eventually the king.

It was the beginning of a formidable partnership between a prince whose family had ruled the land for centuries and a Queen who could barely speak a Roumanian sentence. Gossip flew, naturally, but since neither her husband nor the prince's wife showed any hint of offence, there was no fuel to feed scandal's flames.

The Princess had found firm ground beneath her feet at last, and began to look at Roumania as a home, rather than a place of lonely foreign exile. When she rode out, she spoke with peasants in their fields and housewives at their doors. When her husband and the old king talked, she would look up from her needlework from time to time, and venture questions. She began to wear the richly embroidered traditional clothing her people had given her – at first awkwardly, as a sort of fancy dress, but then as a way of showing her Roumanian identity. She bore her sixth child in 1913, when she was thirty-eight. War broke out in the Balkans. Cholera swept the land, and Marie left her palace each day to tend to the camps of dying soldiers, holding their hands, wiping their brows, listening to their prayers. Over their sickbeds, she fell in love with her people – and in the process, they with her.

Then an Archduke was shot, and a world of long simmering tensions erupted into the Great War.

Roumania's king was a German, chosen to establish a new nation's monarchy. When the War began, his impulse was to declare for the Kaiser, though the majority of Roumanians – along with the English-born Princess Marie – were opposed. The country chose neutrality. When the king died two months later and Ferdinand and Marie took their thrones, neutral it remained. For two years, Marie honed the traditional feminine arts of persuasion, working behind the scenes, among men who laughed at the idea of a beautiful woman with a mind for politics, to convince them that the Central Powers of Germany and Austria were going to lose, and that Roumania's future lay with the alliance of Russia, France, and England. She and the prime minister prevailed, and in August 1916, buoyed by the Allies' promise of national reunification, Roumania declared war on Austria-Hungary.

The fighting began immediately. Marie donned a Red Cross uniform and spent her days nursing the sick and wounded. In November, her three-year-old son died of typhoid. In December, Bucharest fell, and the government and royal family fled to a small, starving enclave trapped between Russia and the Central Powers. Injured soldiers came on every train; the army grew short of bullets for its German-made guns; food dwindled. In late 1917, the Bolsheviks swept across Russia, murdering Marie's cousin and all his family, lining up the army's officers for execution, leaving Roumania a tiny island surrounded by enemies who snarled over her bones and sent assassins after the royal family.

Shaky treaties were signed, to save the remnants of the country, yet still the army was slaughtered. Bucharest and the countryside were stripped bare by occupying troops. By the time Armistice was declared, half its soldiers, nearly one in ten of its citizens, were dead. The countryside was ravaged, the capital city was a husk.

And yet, when the royal family arrived back in Bucharest, the starving populace exploded in joy – and their love was directed in most part at the Queen who had nursed them, comforted them, grieved with them, and shared both their sufferings and their determination to prevail.

A year later, when Roumania's prime minister failed at the Peace Conference, Marie rode into Paris and threw all her forty-four years of royal wit and charm into the masculine business of negotiating a fair settlement. She fixed her mesmerising blue eyes on Clemenceau, Curzon, and Churchill, until all but the tight-laced American President were eating from her graceful, if work-hardened hands. When she returned to her home, she brought with her all the long lost provinces of greater Roumania, and laid them at the feet of her beloved adopted homeland.

There was one final, fairy-tale touch to the story.

On the edge of Transylvania, the biggest and richest of those returned provinces, stood a small castle beside a mountain pass. Built in the fourteenth century as a customs post and border defence, it was visible for miles, a blunt, workaday fortress rather than an aristocrat's home. As centuries passed, the Ottoman threat came and went, weapons changed, borders shifted. The castle was taken over by Hungary, then returned to the city fathers of nearby Braşov, then sold to a Transylvanian prince before returning to Braşov again. It was used to house Austrian troops, then became the headquarters of the Forestry department.

In 1920, the Braşov city fathers desperately presented it to their new country's Queen. Not that they expected much more of her than the occasional visit and a willingness to keep the walls standing. After all, her main summer residence was only thirty miles away, on the other side of the former border.

But instead of polite dismay, Queen Marie embraced their gift with all the passion in her romantic heart. Its evocative outline, its derelict state, its location in territory she herself had brought to Roumania – Castle Bran was the stuff of dreams, which came to her at a time when her daughters were marrying, her sons growing away from her, her husband ageing into himself. She had been given at last the opportunity to create a home that was not in the corners granted by any king. Castle Bran was hers, as no person or place had been since she'd married at the age of seventeen.

Renovations were gentle, gardening extensive, happiness complete. The Queen came to Bran as often as she could, to ride through the hillsides and entertain friends and spend happy hours with the gardeners. She stepped back from the international stage and worked on her writing, publishing books and articles about her homeland for American and English readers. Photographers would visit and capture this dignified figure, whose mature beauty the camera loved, posing among the flower beds in her Roumanian embroidered costumes and wimple-like headscarf that covered her middle-aged chins.

The fairy-tale Princess, born to royalty, embraced by commoners, could now retire to her mountain-top keep with her books and her triumphs and her youngest daughter, and be happy at last.

In some fairy tales, happily ever after is where things end.

In others, happiness is where the problems begin.

CHAPTER SIX

WE RODE THE TRAIN – indeed, we rode a number of trains – for what seemed like days. We passed through cities, mountains, farmland, while the restless fever rose again and pulled me into sleep. I would wake, and follow Holmes into the restaurant car, then return to my seat and my stupor. Holmes would be there, then gone, then there again.

When I woke, countryside was passing by, bright fields beneath a blazing sun. This time, the hypnotic rhythm did not lull me back to sleep. Instead, I found my mind turning over in a way that felt almost normal – although it had skipped back to the days before Marie of Roumania had entered my life, to seize on a series of odd events and innuendos, creating links and eventually presenting me with an uncomfortable conclusion.

'Holmes, you and I – what's the matter?'

He hastened to wipe the startled expression from his face, and finished using the lit match I'd nearly caused him to drop in his lap. 'Nothing is wrong, Russell. Merely that you have not spoken in nearly seven hours.'

'Really?' I looked again at the day outside: it was well after noon. 'Hm. My fever may have broken. I feel better now.'

'I am relieved to hear it.' He got his pipe going and waved out the flame. 'You were saying?'

'Oh, yes. You and I really need to discuss how much of a role Mycroft is allowed to play in our lives.'

He eyed me through the drift of smoke, then asked cautiously, 'How does this thought come to you now?'

I made an impatient gesture at the landscape. 'We're headed into the Carpathian Mountains to investigate village whispers. Either you suspect this to be the edge of some criminal enterprise, or someone other than you sees it as a series of sparks near a political powder keg. The only indication of crime I've heard is the vague threat to a young woman. However, if it's politics, that means your brother, Mycroft, has sent you here – a theory supported by your continued attempts to avoid giving me direct answers. Hence, my statement that we need to move the matter of Mycroft's influence over our lives up on our agenda.'

A deliberate puff of smoke nearly obscured the mingled look of amusement and wariness on his face. For the moment, amusement won out. 'Do you know, I now begin to understand Watson's astonishment over my thinking processes. Russell, it is true that I had a telegram from Mycroft, urging me to assist Queen Marie – but I was already in Bucharest when his wire caught up with me. Following a Queen's entreaties, not a spymaster's order. I did not feel the need to irritate you by mentioning his request.'

'Well, it is irritating, to have the sense of some invisible force—'

He overspoke me, forcibly. 'Russell, for the present, let us agree that you and I do need to develop a policy regarding my brother's . . . requests, whether or not they come from the British government. However, I do not feel that is a question we can confront without him in the room.'

After a moment, I nodded. 'When we get back to London, then.'

'Agreed.'

'Though to be fair – could the threat here actually be political? Less against the daughter than the mother?'

'I would agree, the threat is as much against Marie as it is against Ileana – perhaps more so. And in this part of the world, political unrest is a given – although at present, things seem relatively calm. There was a Bolshevik-led peasant revolt a year ago, up in Moldavia. The Communists are no doubt busily infiltrating every branch of government. And there are many Hungarian nationalists who wish to see the provinces returned to the one-time Empire.'

'What about resentment at the royal family being outsiders? Surely the fact that the king and Queen are German and English, respectively, creates tensions? Why did they do that, anyway? Didn't Roumania have its own royal families?'

'That was the trouble – there were too many of them. Choosing to elevate one prince over the others would plunge the country back into chaos. Bringing in a superfluous younger son from the other side of Europe and placing the crown on him put the native princes on equal footing.'

'And are none of those families making a bid for power? Such as the Queen's friend, Prince Whatsit?'

'There are those who believe Prince Barbu somewhere between éminence grise and outright Rasputin, but were it clear that he was positioning himself for a takeover, I have no doubt Mycroft would have told me.'

I watched some countryside go past: hay and maize, sheep and rivers. If not politics, then what was responsible for bringing this fairy-tale Queen up against cold threats and ancient superstitions?

I had seen a film the previous autumn, on a ship bound for Lisbon. Nosferatu was Stoker's novel with different character names, and had proved chilling even though one of its reels had disappeared over the side. The stark black-and-silver images reduced a number of my young, blonde actress companions to quivers and shrieks, which was probably why the film stuck with me. Nine months later, I could clearly picture that eerie pale figure, looming over the bed of a beautiful woman . . . perhaps a very young one . . .

'So tell me, Holmes, how does this beautiful, wealthy, much beloved and apparently perfect royal person come to be worried about . . .' It was hard to even say the word.

'Vampires?'

'Yes,' I said.

'In fact, it is not only vampires, but all stripes of witches, ghouls, and supernatural creatures. Remember, this is a land of peasant farmers, who cannot banish the night by switching on an electrical bulb. I suppose that is why the country is rich ground for dark stories. There's nothing like a long winter with a forest outside one's door to stir the imagination.'

'An odd place to find Victoria's granddaughter.'

'The capital city, naturally, is a different world from Transylvania; though Bucharest is more Ottoman than European, and it must have been difficult in Marie's early years. Even now the country has its share of economic and social problems. It would not be helpful to have rumours circulate about the Queen.'

'Such as?'

He eyed me, no doubt judging my fitness to participate in a discussion. But whatever he saw seemed to satisfy him, and he gave a decisive nod.

'You complain that I have avoided direct answers. Very well, I shall give you the points on which I have been meditating. Perhaps you will be able to see more of a pattern than I.

'During my week in Bran, I managed to glean details about three key events – although as you are aware, burrowing to the source of any whispered tale is never an easy task for an outsider.

'It began the second week of March, when a seventeen-year-old village girl disappeared. She worked at the castle – Bran is strictly a summer retreat for the Queen, but this year, Marie came earlier than usual, wishing to consult with her architect and gardeners before she left for her planned summer in Europe. One morning, the village girl did not show up for work. That evening, one of the other maids went to see what was wrong, and found that the girl's parents had thought she was at work.

'Alarm was raised. Some hours later, cooler minds thought to conduct a search of her room, where it was found that some of her possessions were missing as well. The next day, the Braşov police learnt that she and a young man had boarded the train to Bucharest. Some days later, a brief letter came to say she had gone off with her love – and yet, village gossip persists with the conviction that she did not go of her own will, but that someone took things from her room to make it appear that way, and sent a letter in writing that merely looks like hers.'

'What has that to do with the Queen?'

'On the surface, nothing at all. The second episode was serious,

43

but hardly out of the ordinary. It happened some ten days later, when a twelve-year-old scullery maid was preparing vegetables in the castle kitchen and sliced open her hand. Something had drawn the cook and other adults away, and it happened that the Queen was passing and heard the child cry out. She went to see what was wrong, seized a bowl to protect the child's clothing, and started to bind the injury with a dishcloth. When the others came in, they saw the child struggling against the pain in her hand and the Queen working to hold her still while she staunched the wound.'

A curiously vivid picture came to mind, attached to some dark bit of memory: a rustic kitchen, a beautiful Queen, a young girl bleeding copiously into a crockery bowl . . . But I couldn't trace my uneasiness to a specific source, and Holmes was going on.

'There was considerable alarm upon seeing a bowl apparently half-filled with blood, but as it turned out, much of it was water. However, it is worth noting that, when I heard the story some three months later, it was the bowl of blood that had become the main interest, not the royal person hastening to give care.

'In the days that followed, villagers reported a series of uncomfortable events. A shooting star, a cow's death, a broken leg, a bat trapped in a room. Then, the night before the Queen and her daughter were to set off for Paris, a child took a shortcut through some trees, and either tripped or was attacked.'

'How old a child?'

'Eight. She burst into her house crying, covered in dirt, with blood on her palms and on the neck of her blouse. She claimed that some huge, dark, winged creature had come out of the trees and flung itself at her. She fell, struggled, and got away, fleeing home. Her father and some other men took torches to go see, but found nothing except for a trampled flower from the Queen's garden. A branch of lilac. When asked the next day, the child denied that she had stolen the flower. Some time after that, she said perhaps she had taken it, and also that it was possible she'd just tripped and fallen. By the time I spoke with her, she had no idea – and the story of an attack had already taken root.'

'The lilac couldn't have come from some other garden?'

'Not this one, I am told. It is of a particularly rich shade of purple.'

'And the Queen's garden isn't public?'

'Strictly, no. It would not be difficult to pilfer the occasional blossom, but the villagers tend not to. And a child of eight would surely know that taking such a thing home to mother would be cause for a scolding, at the least.'

'What about the other things – the dead cow and the broken leg?'

'The cow may have been old, and the man's leg broke when a wheel came off a cart.'

'Meaning that both carry as much weight as a trapped bat, when it comes to evidence of wrongdoing. The interesting thing . . .'

'Mm?' he said, by way of encouragement.

'Well, it's a series of unconnected events in the life of a village. I could imagine that in the winter, when there's nothing to do but watch the snow fall, odd events would take on significance. But I'd have thought that in the springtime, everyone would be too busy to gossip.'

'And yet, the events grew in importance, taking on shadows of meaning far beyond a cut hand and a fall in a forest.'

'It suggests underlying tensions in the area. I do hope they didn't drag some old woman out of the woods and burn her as a witch?'

'No one has been burnt, hammered with a stake, or otherwise dispatched. At least, not before I left for Monaco.'

'And you found no indication of what those tensions might be? If not political unrest, then economic problems?'

'Farmers always live a precarious existence, but harvests have been good, and the country is pulling out of its post-War hardships.'

'What about after the Queen left in April? What strange events have happened since?'

There was a brief gleam in his eyes. 'None.'

'None at all? No broken arms, two-headed calves, rabies outbreaks?'

'The summer would appear to have been remarkably placid. In fact, two different people thought to remark on how the events ceased as soon as the Queen and her party departed.'

'Really. What about before they arrived – wasn't anything strange going on during the winter?'

'Only one that I heard. A village girl caught sight of a man who had died in the War.'

'Would that have been a ghost or a – what was the word? *Strigoi*?'

'The young man died in battle in 1916. One gathers that the rules of vampirism require the living dead to show up within a reasonable time.'

'Seems a bit arbitrary, but fine, let's call him a ghost. When was he seen?'

'Sometime in January. While the Queen was in Bucharest, many hours away.'

'Holmes, I don't see a reason why any of this should be attached to the Queen.'

'In another part of the world, it would not be. However, there is a complication to keep in mind here.'

'Only one?'

'A figure in the shadows that only someone from Eastern Europe would see. Have you heard of a Hungarian Countess by name of Erzabet Báthory?'

Two days earlier, retrieving the name would have been a struggle. It was a relief to have the information pop up, and make connections. 'Countess Báthory! So that's why . . .'

The name brought with it the impression of dusty tomes: an ancient library in the depths of the Black Forest. October, 1919. Trying to take my mind off recent matters and the pain in my shoulder by an escape into books – except that recent matters included a woman who'd tried to kill me, and my topic of research was history's murderous women.

'Erzabet Báthory,' I said. 'Known as the "Blood Countess." Accused of a mindboggling number of crimes.' The countess had been a remarkable beauty, which her accusers attributed to a regimen of bathing her skin with the blood of virgins. My state of turmoil as I bent over those German books explained the uneasiness attached to the image of a bowl filled with blood. I realised that I was rubbing my shoulder, and dropped my hand away.

'One of history's few women multiple-murderers,' Holmes noted. 'Accused of the torture and death of hundreds of young girls, between 1590 and 1610.'

'Accused, yes,' I said. 'Although she was an extremely wealthy woman and, as I recall, the charges were brought by those who – by complete coincidence, I am sure – happened to benefit hugely when she was stripped of her possessions.'

'There were hundreds of accusers, with an extensive list of crimes and atrocities.'

'Compiled years after the first accusations, by a religious fanatic whose help in "overseeing" her dead husband's estate had been spurned by the Countess. A man who was close friends with those due to inherit the most. Who tortured her servants into providing information, and quickly put to death the three closest to her – those who would know the truth of the matter. The Countess herself was permitted to live out her life under house arrest in a very comfortable castle. Which does rather weight the scale on the side of conspiracy.'

I remembered the details, since I'd been desperate for a retreat into the safety of research. Not something I needed to mention now. 'Holmes, you know that any wealthy or strong-willed woman in history has always been in danger of accusations. If not of sexual misconduct, then of some kind of witchcraft. When her enemies are high-ranking political and economic rivals, it is easy for a few ugly rumours to become outright atrocity.

'But that was three centuries ago. And as far as I know, no Bram Stoker has produced a work of popular fiction about the Countess Báthory. The only reason I know about her is because you abandoned me that week you spent in men's clubs and Turkish baths, going after the Stuttgart embezzler. How would a village of Roumanian peasants even have heard of her?'

'In fact, the Countess is as well known in this part of the world as Jack the Ripper is in England. A native of the Balkans would react to a bowl of blood in the same way a London resident would react to a woman found dead of savage knife wounds.'

'Ah. I begin to see the problem.'

'I thought you might. I should also mention that it is not uncommon to find a belief that Elizabeth Báthory drank the blood she shed, not just washed in it.'

'Rejuvenation internal and external,' I mused. If there was one thing the world knew about Roumania's Queen, it was her striking beauty and youthful vigour. It would not take a great deal of talk to have people seeing her as a modern version of the Blood Countess – or indeed, one of Bram Stoker's Transylvanian vampires.

CHAPTER SEVEN

THE RHYTHM OF THE train changed. A short time later, buildings grew up around us and we pulled into Braşov, climbing down into the late afternoon sun amidst the bustle of a town of some forty thousand souls. The passengers washing in and out of the train doors looked distinctly rural, with an equal balance of native dress and Western-style clothing. The men were bearded, the women's costumes demure, and as for skin colour, I was probably the darkest person in sight, apart from my sun-bleached hair.

Holmes had wired ahead with our arrival time, so we were met by the Queen's own Rolls-Royce. Its driver, a black headed, mischief-eyed fellow of around thirty, was dressed in the costume of the natives. Despite looking like someone who would be more at home with a horse cart, he greeted us in English and efficiently supervised the porter's loading of our bags. When all was stowed away, he put the car into motion and took us through a neat and prosperous-looking town surrounded by wooded hills.

His skill was reassuring, and I relaxed enough to turn my gaze to the town's high-faced buildings and broad, paved squares. Carts moved among cars, some of them a sort of modern hybrid – a traditional horse-drawn wooden cart, but built atop the axle and narrow tyres of some ancient motorcar.

The town gave way to a prosperous and fertile countryside. The road became dirt, though well maintained, and the houses farther apart. Electrical poles ceased to follow our way, although a telegraph line persisted. Another mile, and the villas turned to farmhouses, their gardens to orchards and fields. I began to catch sight of the haystacks that I had been seeing all day from the train. Nothing like the familiar piled domes of England, these were six or eight metres high with a trimmed sapling protruding from the top. The stacks marched over the countryside like a clan of enormous, shaggy creatures.

'Those haystacks look like gigantic bears,' I said to Holmes, after a while. 'Or those mythic Himalayan creatures said to live above the snow line.'

'One does wonder if the local hooligans don't occasionally adorn them with a pair of dinner plate–sized eyes.'

I laughed, then with a glance at the driver – behind a glass shield, but still – lowered my voice. 'They do rather . . . loom. I'd have thought the people would build their horror tales around those things, rather than dead folk climbing from their graves.'

'History gives us a number of reasons why these people are quick to see shades and vampires in every corner. The Countess Báthory would be one. And another—' He stretched forward to retrieve the speaking tube. 'Would you kindly pull over up ahead? Just past that hay field will do nicely.'

The driver nodded as he steered towards a wide patch, the entrance to a field.

A short way off, a family was in the process of building one of the haystacks. A young woman was balancing beside the protruding sapling, at least a dozen feet from the ground, while two men and a woman took turns throwing rake-fulls of hay up for her to arrange. Children were collecting freshly cut hay into clumps with rakes of their own – the wooden kind, handmade, with teeth whittled before a fire during long winter nights. Further out, two figures rocked back and forth, back and forth with the implacable rhythm of the scythe that looks so easy but leaves a neophyte's back in spasms. Nearby, in the deep shade of a walnut tree, two old women were gathering up their spindles and knitting, having spent the heat of the afternoon on a pair of three-legged stools watching over a baby and a tumble of small children. One of the grannies noticed me, and gave me a wide and toothless grin.

Holmes caught my elbow to redirect my attention away from the rustic scene.

I had been aware of the low mountains encircling this agricultural plain, with the occasional mouldering castle perched on their tops, but since leaving Braşov, the fruit trees and fields of tall maize lining the road had kept me from noticing how near we were to the approaching hills. From this clearer spot, I could now see the ridge that rose abruptly a few miles away, heavily wooded, its trees parting to reveal, in stark loneliness, a tall, pale castle that . . .

I thought my recent dreamlike state had given way to full-blown hallucination.

The castle seemed to ripple as I looked at it, mimicking the effect of Dracula's mist – or more likely, of the day's heat.

Mist or mirage, the structure was from the pages of a child's book. High and narrow, on the point of a hill, it was composed of mismatched towers and blunt stone walls. A bit of half-timbered construction framed its few high windows. One expected Rapunzel's hair to gleam from beneath a cupola, and long, bright, Medieval banners to ripple from the tower tops. One wondered if a troll lived in its cellars, or a Count who preyed upon the village girls . . .

I took off my glasses to rub my eyes, but when I looked again, it was unchanged. Magical, yet enigmatic.

How was it possible for a building stuck atop a bare hill to feel secretive? It should be the very opposite, open and forthright. And yet, it gave me that distinct primitive sensation of being watched, as if something was studying me from a hidden corner of its façade. Not threatening, or even unfriendly, merely . . . there.

Holmes appeared not to notice anything. And being loth to admit to another round of febrile delusions, I kept my impressions to myself.

I followed him back to the car and we set off again, pausing to avoid a trotting horse cart laden with people. From a distance, they were indistinguishable from any other cart full of Roumanians, but up close, the differences were profound – in their attitude more even than their clothing. The women stared at us openly, the standing man with the reins pretended we weren't there, and the children, who needed haircuts or shoes or both, jeered.

These would be the local Romany, or gipsies, rootless and proud and never trusted by their more settled cousins. Somewhere nearby would be a collection of lightly built houses and fences made of scrap, with glossy horses and well cared-for wagons. Nothing of value that could not be packed up and carried away within hours.

But now the more settled village began to appear, the very opposite of Romany dwellings: sturdy houses surrounded by wooden fences with high, heavily carved gates. Some of the gates had a horse's skull fastened to them, but other than that macabre touch, they were handsome entries to the dwellings within. Most of the gates stood open, showing glimpses of the gardens and yard inside. Pigs rooted, chickens scratched, children wandered – but when a boy came pelting out of one gate, a laugh on his face and a dog at his heels, our driver matched his speed and leant out of the window, saying something in a language that I did not know, but almost felt as if I understood. The boy slowed and made what was clearly a smart reply, causing the driver to raise a finger that was not threatening, but certainly admonishing. I felt that the exchange might have escalated into a confrontation, but the boy glanced into the back, saw us there, and made a wave of the hand that could have been taken as agreement. The driver took it as such, and drew his elbow in to continue on our way.

'That was something about the Queen?' I said to Holmes. '*Regina,* and *sara asta*?'

'I believe it was "The Queen is coming tonight." Although I fail to see the significance.'

I reached forward to slide the window open. 'May I ask, what was that you were telling the boy?'

'I warn him, that Queen Marie returns.' A glance in the mirror told him that I did not understand. 'Mr Florescu, he has orders to village people, when Queen is here, that dogs are inside or tied.'

'Who is Mr Florescu?' I asked.

Both men spoke simultaneously. 'The butler,' Holmes said. I did not really hear the driver's reply; however, it had looked like he said, 'God.'

'Why would – ah,' I said. 'Because she rides?'

'Yes. Mr Florescu say to Bran: if a dog frightens her horse and makes her fall, that dog will be shot and family will go to prison.'

There was once an eccentric Duke of Portland so misanthropic, he made his maids turn their faces to the wall at his approach. Requiring dogs to be tied at least had some justification.

Although perhaps not deserving of a death sentence and imprisonment.

We went past what looked like the village shop, separated from the road by an expanse of gravel. On this sat a most unexpected conveyance: a large, new motorcar, halfway between a shooting brake and an ambulance. As we went by it, I noticed a sign on the small building attached to one side of the shop: the surgery for the village doctor, with a plaque giving his hours.

It was comforting to know that we could have our vampire bites treated by Western medicine – at least, if we fell ill on a Monday, Thursday, or Saturday, between the hours of 10 a.m. and 7 p.m. Which reminded me: 'Holmes, we stopped back there to illustrate why the people here tend to see shades and vampires. Was it something to do with the castle?'

'You remember that Stoker's character bears the surname of a Roumanian ruler whose name is synonymous with brutality.'

'Vlad Dracula. Known as Vlad the Impaler.'

'In this part of the world, Vlad is something of a hero, for his long success against the Ottomans. During his career, he had any number of dealings with the rulers of Brașov, it being the town nearest the border between Transylvania and Wallachia. Vlad's grandfather owned all of the land around here. And it has to be said . . .' (Here he paused, to bend down and peer through the windscreen at something, then resumed.) '. . . that despite the novelist's trick of using shiny facts to create a façade of verisimilitude on an otherwise unconvincing farrago of nonsense, in Stoker's case there is some indication of a more specific connection; namely, that for a period of several weeks, Vlad Țepeș . . .' (The motorcar slowed to avoid three wandering hens and a goat, then turned off the road.) '. . . a man who built his reputation for brutality by impaling enemies on spikes while they were still alive, when he was finally captured by the Hungarians in 1462, may have been kept locked in a small dungeon at the base . . .' (The heavy car slowed, then shifted gears for a steep climb. The moment our bonnet tipped towards the sky, Holmes made a wide-handed voilà gesture to the front window screen.) '. . . of Castle Bran.'

The conclusion of this long, drawn-out, and meticulously timed sentence was a close-up view of a slab of rock, on which stood the high, featureless walls and towers without flags that I had seen earlier. Bending far down, its top extended out of sight.

I looked at my husband. 'Do you plan on indulging your flair for the dramatic throughout our time here?'

'I expect so,' he said complacently.

A lesser motorcar would have coughed to a halt and drifted backwards down the hill, but the Rolls flexed its muscles to deliver us through the narrow gap between the castle's trim, flat outer wall and a hacked-off outcrop of native stone. Beyond the gap lay an open area just large enough for a motorcar, with care, to turn around.

Waiting for us was a tall, black-eyed man in his forties with a melancholy face, a silver streak through his slick black hair, and a moustache so trim and pointed, it resembled a punctuation mark. This had to be the major-domo, the grand version of a butler. He, like the driver, wore native dress – the same loose trousers and blouse

I had seen in every field and village, although this man's pantaloons had never worked in a field, and his cream coloured shirt was heavy with embroidery. This appeared to be the uniform of the place, since others in similar, less heavily decorated clothing appeared from out of nowhere, tugging at their forelocks before queuing up behind the car to seize our bags. The . . . butler? – gestured, causing one of his underlings to leap forward and seize Holmes' door. At the same moment, the driver reached for mine, that we might emerge simultaneously.

Once we were standing on the ground and every spine was as rigid as could be, the butler gave a formal dip of the head and welcomed us to the castle – which, according to his attitude, was his castle, even though his words explained that the Queen sent her greetings, that she regretted that she had been delayed in Sinaia, but that she would come as soon as possible on the morrow.

This had to be the godlike Mr Florescu. He continued speaking, though mostly to Holmes, which was both typical of men and understandable, since they already knew each other. That left me free to crane my head at the sheer walls rising up from the outcrop of living rock.

Castle Bran was, I had to agree, a stage built for the dramatic. All the theatrical storybook elements were there: remote, wooded, and secretive. And yet, it was no Neuschwanstein, no picturesque home for pampered aristocrats and their art collections. This was a defensible slab built for hard use by armed men. Its towers had been designed, not for show, but for unbroken views of the two lines of approach. The small, narrow windows in its lower levels were not some coy façade, but a means of protecting the castle's defenders as they took deadly aim – both for their arrows and, if I judged that higher protrusion correctly, for the dropping of heavy objects or boiling hot liquid on enemies below.

Whoever built this castle did not intend to be driven off.

Behind it lay a valley, linked by a narrow depression in the hills with the plateau we had driven through. A cluster of houses and small fields followed the curve of a busy stream, with a road leading up to the forested ridges – an unassuming track that Holmes' maps, pored over on the train, had told me led to Bran Pass and through the southern leg of the Carpathians to the Danube, then to the Balkans and the Adriatic beyond. I would have studied the view in more detail, except the butler had taken up an expectant position at the foot of a long, steep stairway. At the top of it waited a set of sturdy wooden doors, studded with iron bolts and fitted into a stone arch.

The stairs were narrow, to make it difficult for invaders to fight their way up. The windows puncturing the walls grew larger with each level, with those at the top storeys conveniently placed for the dropping of stones or boiling liquids. Even the castle's shield wall facing the drive – a blunt, massively thick prow intended to repel siege machines – had windows at the heights, with shallow balconies that were built as machicolations. A stone eased from there to bowl its way along the sloping wall would hit those at the bottom like skittles pins.

'Russell?'

Holmes' voice called me from reverie. I gave the gathered menfolk an apologetic smile and followed him around the motor and up the stairs.

I wondered, as we started up the steep climb, if this could possibly be the only entrance. Wouldn't that mean princes and potentates rubbing shoulders with cooks, housemaids, and delivery boys?

Or perhaps this *was* the trade entrance, and Holmes and I were not quite as honoured as he had thought.

I gave a mental shrug. So long as we were not housed in the quarters used to imprison Vlad, and I was not expected to carry my own bags, I could live with being considered a hireling. I followed Holmes and the Transylvanian butler through the iron-studded doorway and into the Medieval castle of Bran.

Chapter Eight

THE ROOM AT THE top of the stairway did appear equipped for servants, with an old fireplace to keep the guards from freezing. However, the equipment on view was more geared to greetings than to defence: there was an assortment of umbrellas to keep incoming guests from the rain, but the only firearm in sight was an old shotgun. We followed Florescu – all three of us ducking to pass through the decorative archway – out of the room and down a few steps to an open-air space beside a small courtyard.

Immediately to hand were three doors on as many levels. One of them, marked with a huge terracotta pot holding a market stand's worth of cut flowers, stood open to reveal a flight of stairs with a carpeted runner. Carpet and flowers together signalled that we were not entering the servant's wing, but the living quarters of the royal family.

Which told me that royal feet did indeed trudge up and down those stairs like the rest of us. The housemaids here would have legs of iron – but then, considering the relationship between its narrow footprint and its considerable height, stairs would be a major part of life for everyone in Castle Bran. In Britain, castles were often broad-based refuges where livestock and peasants would be gathered in during times of threat. Not so Bran. Unless there was a cellar beneath us, with stables and a ceremonial entrance, Bran would not shelter anything less nimble than a goat.

It also occurred to me, catching sight of the courtyard as we started up the second or perhaps third storey, that this could not be Castle Dracula. The only way Jonathan Harker would have been driven inside was if his carriage had been hoisted bodily over the walls. And once there, it could have become a permanent fixture, since the courtyard was barely large enough for a horse to turn, its floor a madly irregular collage of stone steps, plastered walls, decorative garden beds, and raw outcrops of the native rock underneath.

The walls encircling the courtyard were similarly varied, as if to create a sampler of architectural styles – or perhaps a miniature Italian hill town, with a diminutive town square formed by three-, four-, and five-storey buildings. Stone walls, plaster archways, red tiled roofs and turrets, the whole joined at the top by zigzags of half-timbered galleries from which spilt scarlet geraniums. All over were signs of recent renovations – the galleries looked reassuringly firm on their ramparts – but the glimpses I had of the whole uneven and idiosyncratic establishment were curiously appealing, considering that the place was built as a military outpost. One hoped that its current owner did not tidy the patchwork into bland uniformity.

We climbed up and up the corkscrew stairway, passing through rooms and arched passages. In every possible corner was another pot or bowl or ancient stone urn bursting with a mix of summer blossoms. Finally, on the fourth, or perhaps fifth, storey, the stairs came to an end, and the butler ushered us with some ceremony through another low doorway and into a different era.

Crisp, clean, newly renovated, this suite of rooms might have been set down here from another place. The bones of the Medieval castle were there, but the jumble of stone arches and dark corners we had gone past were here fresh plaster and bright whitewash. Snug wood-frame windows held glass modern enough to see through; newly-tiled floors gleamed with polish between colourful rugs. The furniture, antiques all, also gleamed with polish: heavily carved four-poster bed, aged ark wooden drawers, tall iron candelabras set with candles as big around as my wrist – it would appear that the renovations did not extend to electricity. A massive tiled fireplace, thankfully unlit, held a polished copper bowl of flame-coloured roses.

I moved to one of the deep-set windows, kneeling down on its cushioned seat. We were on the northern side of the castle, overlooking the portion of village we had motored through, and the room was high enough that its openings were actual windows rather than arrow-resistant slits. The gleaming walls made the most of the late afternoon sunlight, although the room would soon grow dim.

No ghosts here.

'Velcome to Cahstle Brahn, Meesus Holmes,' said the major-domo, the pointy ends of his moustache rising and falling with the rhythm of his words. 'My name is Florescu. I hope these rooms will prove comfortable. May I ask, when would sir and madam care for dinner?'

I replied before Holmes could. 'Thank you, Mr Florescu, the rooms are lovely, and supper would be heavenly, but right now I'd appreciate a cup of tea.'

'But of course, Madam. I will have it brought immediately. Let me first give you air . . .' He walked down the row of windows, throwing them open, and reassured us that if we wished to leave our door open for a brief time, the air would cool – and we were the only guests up on this level.

'A girl will come to light the candles,' he added, and bowed himself out.

Heaven only knew what manner of beverage would be considered 'tea' in this distant part of the world, I thought with a mental sigh, and went to explore our Transylvanian quarters.

To my astonishment and joy, one of the doors opened into an actual bathroom, with a brand-new porcelain tub and gas geyser. Running water – in a Medieval castle! In disbelief, I cracked open the tap, expecting nothing but dust – but instead, after a moment, water came.

That did not guarantee that the geyser was connected, or that the device would not blow up, but it did suggest that housemaids would not have to haul steaming buckets up an Everest of stairs to indulge my wish for cleanliness.

I was humming as I scrubbed my face and arms free of heaven only knew how many days of travel. I changed my shirt, combed my hair, glanced at the mirror – definitely not the castle of Count Dracula, I thought happily, if it had a looking glass – and walked back into our sitting-room area feeling considerably more human.

I then came to a dead halt, at this latest in a day of astonishing sights. Delicate porcelain cups and plates, crisp white linen, a polished silver teapot suspended over a little blue flame – and was that . . . ?

'Good Lord, are those scones?'

The girl setting out this feast looked taken aback, but Holmes merely said, in a voice that sounded suspiciously muffled, 'Both fruit and savoury.'

I stared down at a tea tray that would not have discredited a head waiter at the Ritz, and realised that I should have trusted that an English Queen, no matter how many years she had lived in Roumania, would not abandon such a cultural tradition as afternoon tea.

The promise of a bath, a proper cup of tea – I suddenly felt much better about this venture into the hinterland. My face must have shown my relief, because the young woman stepped forward to finish arranging the spoons into a neat line.

'May I pour tea, missus?'

I listened to the same accent I had heard from the butler and the driver before him – the exaggerated diphthong of may, the tongue's tap on the end of pour, the elongated vowels that turned which and Miss into 'wheech' and 'Mees,' and the marked tonal slides up and down, compared to that of a native English speaker. 'Thank you. What is your name?'

She showed me her dimples and made a quick curtsey. 'I am Gabriela, missus.'

She was on that border between adolescence and womanhood, with a face of fifteen but the attitude of someone two or three years older – not uncommon with working-class girls, who confront reality sooner than their sheltered counterparts. This one was taller than most of her countrywomen, only two or three inches shorter than I, but she was dressed in the same costume I had seen since we arrived, with embroidered overskirt and full-sleeved blouse gathered under a wide belt. Her head, however, was uncovered, the cut of her light-brown curls suggesting that fashion magazines were not unknown here. The pious touch of a little gold cross at her throat was somewhat undermined by the mischief in her dark eyes. Charming, confident, intelligent – and if she wasn't known to all as a troublemaker, it wasn't for lack of trying.

I grinned at her. 'Thank you, Gabriela, tell the cook that she has saved my life.'

She laughed – not a giggle, a laugh – and swept out of the room.

I heaped strawberry jam onto a scone and carried it and the cup over to the colourful pillows of the window seat.

Bran stood at the spot where the Carpathian Mountains, which run from the northwest to the southeast, meet the east-west horizontal of the Transylvanian Alps, forming an arrow aimed at the mouth of the Danube on the Black Sea. The view from this window showed the agricultural plateau within the point of the arrow, with the forested wilderness on its edges.

Below Castle Bran lay a collection of roofs and roads, green gardens and tiny splashes of flower beds. Touches of white marked the presence of cows and goats, and ambling through the more distant fields were the tall figures of the haystacks. Leaning closer to the window, I saw that the base of the castle was a sort of park around a wide spot in the little river. On a map, the roads in and out of Bran described a sort of lopsided H, the upper section of which was visible here: right arm reaching up towards Braşov, left arm meandering along between the fields and the hills, joined by the crosspiece that ran through the village at the edge of the castle's park. Out of sight, the left leg of the H followed the river valley up to the mountain pass, while the right, little more than a lane, kicked up into the hills in the direction of Bucharest.

From my current godlike position, I could see the common themes of the buildings: roofs were of thatch, shingle, corrugated iron, or tile, but all were sharply angled – the winters here would see a lot of snow. Houses were of wood rather than stone or brick, and generally two-storey, often with the stairs on the outside. Windows were small, both because of the cost and to keep out the cold. Looking over those high walls and carved gates, I found that most encircled a small compound of house, sheds, and garden – some with vine-draped arbours and simple benches. Many appeared to have their own wells, washhouses, and drying lines.

From the lower right corner of my view, emerging from the lane into the hills, appeared a wagon that might have evoked a Constable painting had it not been for the surprising number of people clinging to its raised sides. I could hear their voices, then a burst of laughter. Adding to the rustic idyll, a rooster crowed, followed by the complaint of a cow. I did not have to rush to catch a train; no one was shooting at me or bleeding at my feet. I'd even been given a cup of quite decent Indian tea.

I sighed in contentment. 'Shall we take a walk?' I suggested. 'Before night falls?'

Holmes picked up his tobacco pouch, I dabbed up the last crumbs of scone, and we made our way out to the Transylvanian countryside.

We walked down the steep drive and into the small village, pausing to avoid the dust from another heavily populated cart. This one was pulled by a pale ox with wide horns, and every person in it, from tiny child to wrinkled grandmother, stared and giggled when they spotted us, two alien creatures in our Western clothing and great height. As they passed on, I noticed that the watery eyes and headache of recent days were subsiding. I could even smell the clean odours of hay and sweat that trailed behind them.

My brain seemed to be crawling back into life as well. As I watched the cart rumble along the road to Brașov, it occurred to me that the way in had been remarkably straight. 'Holmes, do you think that if an archaeological team were to dig into that road, they would find the stone slabs of a Roman highway?'

'Without a doubt. This is Trajan's Dacia Felix. The small town halfway between here and Brașov was once a Roman outpost named Comidava. I have found myself wondering if some of the symbols in the gates here originated in Rome.'

I followed his gaze to the nearby example: wide and high enough for a laden cart, its tall uprights were carved with a braided pattern, from top to bottom, while the crossbeam had a number of elements that I did not think were mere design. He pointed upward.

'That at the centre is the Eye, for protection. Those marching peaks represent a wolf's teeth, providing guidance even through dark and wild places. The braids are life unbroken, that generations of family might be protected by the house. I have seen patterns like them in ancient Roman artefacts. And I understand,' he added, 'that the women's embroidery is similarly crafted to bear meaning, blessings, and protection.'

A woman in wide skirts and a brilliant headscarf scurried past us, one hand tucked around a chicken and the other firmly pulling along her wide-eyed infant. And indeed, my eye spotted a similar shape to that at the peak of the gate arch, worked in red cotton up the length of her sleeves.

'*Buna seara*,' Holmes said politely. She giggled and hurried on.

'Roumanian sounds rather like Italian, doesn't it?' I said. 'Perhaps if I simply wrote things down, the locals would understand me. The literate ones, at any rate. How much of the language did you pick up while you were here last month, Holmes? Er, Holmes?' I looked around and saw his figure disappearing into the pathway between a small pasture and a barn. I followed, and found him leaning on a low wall surrounding an orchard, taking out his tobacco pouch.

Bees.

The hives were old-fashioned skeps, knee-high basketry domes resting on boards – like eggs from those shambling hay creatures dotting the landscape. The small openings at the bottom of each skep were thick with end-of-day traffic. The air smelt of honey. I propped my elbows against the wall, facing the opposite direction from Holmes, watching half a dozen sheep crop the stubble around the base of an amiable hay-monster. Somewhere nearby, the odours of meat and spices heralded the approach of the dinner hour. Smoke rose from many of the chimneys.

After a time, Holmes led me down a beaten path that turned out to connect with the centre line of the H of roads through Bran. Dogs barked, children shrieked. Every woman we saw wielded either a farm implement or the eternal spindle. Somewhere, a concertina was playing. We ambled along, admiring the neat houses and a few shopfronts. One could see signs of long-time poverty given a sudden boost: even the smallest and meanest of houses had repaired shingles and new front doors. One or two of the buildings here were in need of renovation – which surprised me, since I'd have thought that the closer to the castle, the greater the prosperity. On closer examination, they proved to be abandoned, and yet they backed onto the Queen's parkland. Perhaps the Queen's architect had plans for them.

We went through a vestigial crossroads and turned down the leg of the H that followed the river. More homes and small farm buildings, many of them with long strings of garlic hanging beneath their eaves, but I had seen those before, and told myself that the purpose was culinary, not for the repulsion of the undead. Indeed, there were often strings of drying peppers, onions, and maize under the eaves as well.

We came to a garage, the Queen's Rolls-Royce out in front with the driver assiduously polishing away the dust of the road. We greeted him; he tugged at his hat in response. The stables were nearby, and behind them an orchard of trees old and young, with a riot of flower beds along the edges – explaining all those bouquets in the castle.

'Have you met her? The Queen of Roumania?' It was a question I had somehow not considered before. Perhaps because the idea of knowing the granddaughter of an empress and a tsar seemed inherently unlikely.

'Not since she became Queen. I met her briefly, many years ago in Malta, when she was very young. I doubt she would remember the occasion.'

'It must be odd,' I reflected after a time, 'to grow up aware that your chief value as a person lies in who you can be married off to. There is power, and yet little self-determination.'

'Every so often, one encounters a woman of her type who reaches past the distractions of position, pleasure, and society's assumptions to become something greater. And even more rarely, one finds a woman who craves not power, but the chance to create something new.'

'And Marie is one of those?'

'As I said: an interesting woman.'

A boy came out of a nearby farmhouse with a bucket, setting off a stampede of goats that leapt and bounced in pursuit of whatever the bucket contained. He held it high, just out of their reach, to tempt the creatures into a nearby shed. There followed a series of thumps, bangs, and affectionate curses. Silence fell. We studied the goat shed door which, like almost every other wooden surface in the village, had been carved – although these shapes were crude geometry compared to the village's elaborate gates and posts. I was about to ask Holmes if he knew of any significance when the boy came leaping out, slapping the door shut behind him. He fastened the latch, noticed us watching, and tugged his hat brim as he trotted across the yard to his own supper.

The thought caused me to notice how long the shadow from a nearby hay creature was. 'We should probably head back before the sun goes down. I wouldn't want the castle to send out a search party.'

He tapped out his pipe on the ground, crushing the embers under his boot. We walked back arm in arm, up the hill to the castle, and to a very pleasant dinner, and to a most welcome bed.

CHAPTER NINE

I FELL ASLEEP THAT night as if I'd been clubbed. I woke in exactly the same position that I'd lain down in. However, the light coming into the ancient room was not the golden dawning sun, but the silver tones of the near-full moon.

I wasn't sure what had awakened me, but I had been dreaming. Dracula again, with horse-drawn carriages and dancing blue flames. I turned irritably on the pillow, pulling it down under my head – and froze.

Was that wolves?

I jerked up from the pillow, straining to hear, feeling the ghostly stickiness of drying blood on my palms. A long minute ticked by . . . then yes, it came again, a distant howl, unearthly in the night.

Russell, be honest: could you tell the difference between a wolf and a dog, from far away? It was a dog. Sure to be. And even if it was a wolf, the thing wasn't about to appear, glowing-eyed, beside my bed. I settled back against the pillows.

And waited. But I'd either gone to bed too early, or slept too many hours in various trains, because my body was telling me it was time to rise.

After a while I gave up. I donned my glasses and a light robe, padding through our rooms to the narrow window seat, where I drew my feet up onto the cushions.

I could feel the castle sleeping around me, half a millennium of stone and wood, unimpressed by the ephemeral beings that traipsed around its rooms. Change here would be slow, and hard won, with the everyday miracles of modern life laid on at the cost of much sweat and probably blood. How many generations of sleepless eyes had gazed out of this window, across the dark village? There was one light in the landscape below, one faint, warm rectangle where some citizen lay restless, or ill, or birthing a child. Other than that, the view beneath the full moon was like a film paused in a projector with a failing bulb: silent, still, and half seen.

Moonlight is always uncanny. It obscures as much as it reveals, putting every object into sharp and deceptive contrast. Here, it exaggerated the presence of those haystacks. I found myself trying to catch them move. As if they were trolls or woolly mammoths, dancing an imperceptibly slow pavane across the fields.

Even more slowly, I became aware that there was actually movement out there, somewhere. Not that I could tell what, or even where. An owl, perhaps – or a bat too small and quick for the eyes to follow? Or maybe a wisp of high cloud, gently migrating? I rose onto my knees, then took my eyes out of focus, which is generally the best way to perceive anything by half-light. And waited. Nothing disturbed the pale tracks that were the roadway. No gleam of cigarette or silhouette of wings. But after a time, I found myself watching one of the faint building shapes. There was no reason for my eyes to focus there, so why . . .

A distant dog barked at the same instant my attention snapped to a spot a thumbnail's breadth from a gleam of pale doorway. A shadow had flitted from one side of the lane to the other. I waited, then – yes, another faint smudge along the marginally paler line of the track, slipping behind a shape I knew was a barn, pausing there long enough that I thought I had missed it . . . only to have something quiver in and among the trees and flicker across an open space to merge its shadow with that of a hay-monster—

I squeaked and nearly flew head-first out of the window when something brushed my bare toes. 'Holmes! Damn it, you nearly sent me to the rocks.'

'You did seem remarkably intent,' he said. 'What is out there?'

'Nothing. I mean, something, but I couldn't tell what.'

'How large?'

'I don't know, it was never completely out in the open. It might have been a—' I caught back the word wolf. 'A large fox. In this light and at that distance – and with my eyes – all I had was an impression of motion.'

'Do you believe it was a fox?'

'Or a dog. Sorry to disturb you – I couldn't sleep, after a dog howling woke me. It sounded like a wolf.'

'It probably was a wolf.'

'Really?' I pulled back to look at his face, close to mine in the shadows, lit only by the moon.

'Was it a fox?' he persisted.

'Why does it matter?'

'Russell, please. Did it feel like a fox to you?'

'No, it "felt" like a man – or a person, at any rate.'

'Large, small, young, old?'

But at that, I had to shake my head. 'Probably someone on his way home from the pub.' Did they even have pubs in Transylvania? And if some man headed home for his bed, why had my first thought been of flitting?

'Where was it, exactly?'

I dropped into a seated position on the cushion. 'Holmes, what are you expecting to see there?'

'Tomorrow,' he said. I shrugged, and glanced back at the window.

'If you drew a line between us and that light at the far end of the village? The shadow was about eight degrees to the west, and just this side of that gleam of metal roof. It moved off, away from the road, and had just gone behind that double haystack when you startled me. I expect that whoever – or whatever – it was, it then went into the orchard rather than crossing the open field.'

Holmes' eyes might be nearly four decades older than mine, but they were better at night than mine ever were. He turned them onto the village below as if shining a narrowed searchlight into a sky filled with hovering zeppelins. Remarkably intent was not the half of it.

I slipped out from under his focused glare and moved to the other window. I, too, watched for a time. For five or six minutes, nothing stirred. When there was movement, it was only a motorcar's headlamps, starting up several miles along the road. But unless its driver had sprinted in Olympics-record time, it had nothing to do with Bran. Or with me, clearly. So I retrieved the book I had left on the bedside table and went into the adjoining room to read.

I thought I would find it difficult to sleep again. There seemed to be a great deal of life in these old walls, an accumulation of history and violence. It is not that I believe in ghosts, exactly, but I will admit that more than once in my life, I have felt some inexplicable presence, the sense of being watched. And it was always in an old building in the dark. Which made the iron latches on the insides of our doors curiously reassuring.

However, several hours later I woke with the book on my chest and the candle long burnt out. The sun shone. The brass pot overflowing with flowers – a dozen or more varieties, all of them shades of orange – filled the room with good cheer. Filled me, too, it seemed. I stretched hard, feeling almost normal for the first time since boarding the train in Nice. The mid-night episode appeared to have cleared the fur from my brain as well, restored my thoughts and perceptions to reassuringly crisp outlines. I threw back the soft woollen rug I didn't remember pulling over myself the previous night, and went in search of company and caffeinated beverages.

Holmes was missing – no surprise there – but my stirring around drew the attention of the house. As I was buttoning my shirt, a tap came at the door.

'Come? Ah, Gabriela, good morning.'

'Good morning, Missus, I bring tea.'

'You are a blessing from heaven, Gabriela.'

She grinned, and set down the tray: teapot, jug of milk, toast and jam, an English newspaper three days old, and one perfect rose that could only have been picked at first light. 'Your husband say this is what you like now, is right? Black India tea, not Queen Marie's Early Grey? And eggs in a little?'

'Perfect, thank you. So he went out already?'

'Very early. Before light. He came, he drink coffee in the kitchen, he asked Unc – Mr Florescu to show him where the builders left their things, and then he leave. Left.' she corrected herself.

'That does sound like him,' I said.

'Queen send message to say, I come tonight. Though not Ileana – Princess Ileana, yes?'

The second sentence was accompanied by a small shrug of disappointment. With my assignment in mind – to ingratiate myself into the world of the adolescent girls – I hastened to get my foot inside that door. 'I don't know the Princess, but I hear she's a lovely person. Does she come often?'

'Oh yes, Bran is home to her. To her heart, yes? She is . . . she is my friend.'

The girl's chin was up when she made the declaration, daring me to argue or to scold her presumption.

I merely smiled. 'I imagine it's difficult for someone in Ileana's position to make an honest friend. It's always hard to know when people like you for yourself, and not for what you can do for them.'

The girl nodded eagerly, heedless of any intimation that she might be among the latter.

I decided to take it a little further. 'What is she like?'

The girl's hand fiddled with the cross at her neck as she considered her reply. 'Princess is a good friend. Well, as good as possible. So many differences between us. Big, big differences. But she laughs and teases and is easy to talk with. We sneaked her to movie once in Braşov, her first time, can you believe? She works so hard.'

'Really?' Hard work wasn't something I'd have expected of a Princess. 'Doing what?'

'Oh, so much. School, dinner parties, gives speeches, Girl Reserves, Red Cross, factory girls – all sorts of help. Then she comes here and teaches, helps girls. And Girl Guides. You know Girl Guides?'

'I know of them, yes. They do much good.'

'Is not easy, being woman here in Bran. No jobs, school is mostly for boys. Ileana – Princess Ileana, she is a good person for girls here to see. Good friends to many, not just me. I think she likes here, too, because it is not . . . how do you say – formal? Not formal like her other lives. No one watching her here, she can go into the hills with friends and not guards and drivers and all. I think she is lonely, sometimes. She comes here and comes to the kitchen, just to talk. She likes that we don't treat her—'

A noise from outside snapped her attention to the door. No one came in, but it reminded her of her duties, and perhaps of her indiscretion. She gave me a nervous smile, then ducked out, leaving me with my morning tea, my out-of-date news, and my thoughts.

It was after eight o'clock when I heard the doorknob turn. Holmes sidled in, cradling what appeared to be an armful of dirt. I grabbed up the newspaper and tossed it on the table for his treasure, which turned out to be two elongated puddles of hardened plaster, containing the prints of shoes, left and right.

'Our shadow?'

'A rather substantial ghost who walked through a patch of wet ground near a horse trough.'

'But not the farmer? No, of course not, those are city shoes.'

'Men's. A foot in the neighbourhood of 290 or 300 millimetres – the settling of the mud during the night makes it hard to judge. Mud can also interfere with a determination of height, since people tend to shorten their stride when the footing is uncertain. However, he was at least as tall as you, though some three stone heavier.' He glanced at his hands, then walked off to the adjoining room, raising his voice over the splashing water. 'Florescu said that you hadn't taken breakfast yet, so he'll have it brought up.'

'About time.'

'Pardon?' He appeared in the doorway, drying his hands.

'Sounds nice,' I said.

He tossed his towel somewhere in the vicinity of the water source and came out. 'He also said that Queen Marie needs to stay in Sinaia until this afternoon, but that she should be here by evening. That gives us the day to question the villagers about recent events. Ah, I hear the approach of coffee and eggs.'

He opened the door, to save Gabriela the juggling act of knocking, and she dipped her head in thanks as she came in. She propped the tray on the table and began to lay the settings, as she had with our tea the afternoon before. I stopped her.

'Gabriela, why don't you just leave everything on the tray, and we'll pick and choose. An informal breakfast is fine. I imagine you must have plenty of work, if the Queen is returning today.'

Her dimples were both an acknowledgment of my statement's truth, and an indication that she was happy to do it. She bounced us a curtsey, and whirled away.

CHAPTER TEN

'WHY DID YOU EXPECT to find footprints, Holmes?' I asked, settling down with my laden plate. 'And why did you refuse to tell me what you were looking for last night? Or for that matter, at any time in the past few days?'

'I did not expect them, although the possibility led me to taking along the plaster of Paris. I did anticipate some sort of disruption in the village.'

'And you did not think that worth mentioning? Or was this merely a test of my mental acuity?' I paused, fork in air. 'Which, I grant you, has been somewhat less than scintillating.'

'You have not been, as they say, at the top of your game. I judged a night of rest might help restore your wits.'

'Very well, I have rested, I am no longer impaired. So why did you expect a disruption?'

'Because the Queen is back from her travels. Or nearly so, Bran being only thirty miles from Sinaia by road –

fifteen as the crow would fly.'

'Or the bat,' I murmured.

'Pardon?'

'Nothing. So we are operating under the assumption that the peculiar incidents in the night time are either aimed at the Queen, or done by the Queen – or by someone close to her.'

'You prefer the idea of coincidence?'

I looked at him; my eyebrow may even have raised a little. Granted, the head cold had rendered me less than brilliant, but there was no reason to insult my intelligence. 'Holmes, not only is there the question of causation versus correlation – the Queen is near; a man walks at night; therefore the one caused the other – but you are also making the assumption that because no one has yet mentioned seeing a shadow walking the town in the past weeks, no shadow has been there.'

He had the grace to look a touch chagrined, but only for a moment. 'Agreed, last night's incident is no basis for an hypothesis. However, as a means to confirm the ongoing evidence, it is worthy of inclusion.'

'Fair enough. And you've been working on this case longer than I. But assuming the Queen is the target of some kind of prankster – or rather, if I understand you, her reputation is the target – that raises two questions. First off, why? General troublemaking? Revenge for something she's done? Or an actual attempt to raise the rabble against her, and thus the monarchy itself? And more seriously, how does this justify making an actual threat against her daughter?'

'At this point in the investigation, it does appear that there are two separate schemes. I regard that as unlikely, although possible. I trust that further data will develop any link between the two.'

I chewed, literally and figuratively, for a minute. 'Didn't you find anything else? Other than the footprints? I can't see that merely walking around in the dark achieves anything, considering that you and I may have been the only people awake to notice.'

His face seemed to relax – was that relief? – before he reached into his pocket and drew out a handkerchief wrapped around an object no larger than a child's fist. He lay it on the table, pulling back the pristine linen to reveal a deerskin pouch with drawstrings made of silk. He pulled it open and poured the contents out onto the handkerchief.

I snatched aside my plate. 'Is that hair? And teeth – though not human, thank goodness. What do you suppose those bones are from?'

'It is human hair, yes, knotted together in a pattern – rather like the mourning brooches of my youth. The teeth could be those of a shrew, or a mole. The bones are a mix, small rodents mostly, though that broken one is more likely from a bird.'

'The leaves look like – tea?' Reluctantly, I lowered my face over the handkerchief and tried out my nasal passages. 'Is that bergamot I smell? It's Early Grey!'

'Pardon?'

'The Queen's preferred tea is Earl Grey, according to Gabriela. What's on the folded-up bit of paper?'

He pulled it apart with his fingertips: a pentagram – a five-pointed star within a circle, drawn on a scrap of thick paper using a fountain pen.

I studied the macabre little collection. 'I'd guess it's meant to be a witch's hex bag, though it has an amateur air about it. You might want to wash your hands before you finish your breakfast.' He poured the collection back into its pouch – and then he did go into the next room to wash his hands.

'Where did you find it?' I called.

'It was at the entrance to the farmer's chicken house, as if it had been accidentally dropped there.'

He came back in. 'Was it? Dropped accidentally, that is?'

'I think not.'

I slowly applied butter to a roll. 'Someone wishes to suggest that there are witches in the neighbourhood?'

'I believe it was intended to do more than suggest. Although to be certain, we shall have to take a short walk into the woods.'

'I'll get my boots.'

Twenty minutes later, the two of us stood looking down at a depressing sight. I nudged one limp body with my foot. 'Did you know there was quite so much of the stuff?'

'No, I thought perhaps it had been mixed with that left over in the feeding trough. In retrospect, I should have known that a farmer does not put out chicken feed so late in the day that it stays out overnight.'

'We probably shouldn't leave these here.'

'It would attract attention, I suppose.'

'And I'd guess the villagers would find a flock of mysteriously dead wild birds nearly as disturbing as domestic ones.'

In the end, we piled the eight small feathered corpses underneath a half-rotted log, and Holmes did his best to bury the remaining kernels of corn, to save the rest of the local wildlife from the experimental avicide.

Instead of returning to the village, we continued up into the hills.

'Holmes, would you agree that the intention was for the village to think a witch placed a curse on those chickens during the night?'

'I would.'

'A night when the Queen was expected to return – or at any rate, when she was not far away.'

'She was expected here yesterday,' he pointed out.

'Would the village know her plans?'

'Certainly. They generally ring a bell to announce her arrival, but one doesn't always hear it. And you'll have noticed that the dogs are being kept inside their gates. When I was here before, they were left to wander all over.'

'Sorry, but I'm a bit confused. First you were talking about vampires and the atrocities of the Countess Báthory. And you mentioned a girl seeing a ghost. Now witches?'

'Interesting, is it not?'

I must be better, I thought: his gnomic utterings were irritating me again. I replied in my customary way; namely, I ignored him. 'What do you suppose will happen when nothing, er, happens?'

'When the village fails to rise up in terror, after a witch curses a henhouse and accidentally drops her hex bag on the way out? Our troublemaker may assume that someone found the bag and noticed the grain, and decided it was suspect. Things do go awry, at times. I expect he – or she, granted – will spend the day waiting to hear the news, then wonder why it hasn't risen up. I expect that soon, tonight or more probably tomorrow, he will make another attempt. Not in the same place, if the intent is to frighten the village rather than a single household. And I expect it to be something more emphatic than chickens. Russell, are you familiar with the phenomenon of group hysteria?'

'Peculiar behaviour that appears contagious – an epidemic of dancing in Strasbourg, fits that looked like epilepsy in Salem. Often

83

involving women and girls – hence the term "hysteria" – and often blamed on witches. You think such a thing is starting up here?'

'One cannot overlook the number of young women and girls involved,' he pointed out.

'Well, they do make up somewhat more than half the population.'

'Yes, and because women are often kept in a position of subservience, they may prove more sensitive to unspoken tensions and threats than men.'

I was so stunned by this statement that I came to a dead halt. Half a dozen steps on, he noticed that I was behind him. 'What?' he asked.

'You did say you realised that you have a blind spot when it comes to women, but I hadn't thought . . .'

Indeed, I had not thought. I'd been so wrapped up in the turmoil of having lied to him about Mrs Hudson, I had overlooked this bedrock truth about Sherlock Holmes: once the man's attention came to focus on an inequity, all his energies would go to setting it aright – even if the problem was one in his own self.

His eyebrow rose. 'You think that, even though I have spent the past four months in a series of investigations with women at their centres, I might simply accept my relative blindness and dismiss its ramifications?'

'Well . . .'

'I hope, my dear Russell, that I am not so hidebound as to overlook the lessons life hands me. In any event, long before you and I met and my masculine sensibilities were delivered into your gentle hands, I was in fact aware that women are vulnerable in ways men are not. There were even times when I accepted a case based solely on that knowledge.'

'True.' But it was troubling. Humility was not a thing one expected from Sherlock Holmes – not even for his wife of nearly five years and partner of ten. If he was willing to reconsider . . .

I pulled my thoughts away from that tortuous pathway: this was not the time to explore such an essential matter. Instead, I would add it to the growing list of Topics in Need of Discussion that now included what to do about Mycroft, how to find a replacement for Mrs Hudson in Sussex, and how not to lie to one's spouse.

'So,' I said, 'if our troublemaker plans on increasing his efforts, once the Queen is back in Bran, should we not be getting out word to the villagers? Or at least to the farmers, if you think it's a matter of poisoning some poor animal. I'd hate for a family to lose their only milch cow because this chap wanted to make a point.'

'And give ourselves away, if it is a farmer doing this? No, Russell, I fear that the task of keeping guard belongs to us.'

'No sleep tonight, then.' I resolved to sneak off for a nap, in the afternoon. Assuming we weren't called to rescue more chickens or drop boiling oil on a storm of revolting peasants.

Speaking of peasants, we seemed to have left the castle rather far behind. Left everything far behind, come to that. 'Where are we going?'

'You need to see the woods, Russell. And some of its inhabitants.'

The track underfoot was narrow, but definite. In the winter, it would be so slick with mud that a person could easily skate all the way back to the village, but it had not rained for some time. The trees here were a mix, beech and fir with the occasional oak tree and maple. Squirrels and blackbirds were everywhere, and we startled deer several times during the day. Eagles sailed over our heads, and once a brief flash of motion, brown-and-pale, registered itself as having been a forest marten.

The air was warm and still. We walked for half an hour, in easy silence for the most part, before my wandering mind realised I was about to walk into Holmes one step before I hit his back.

'What are – good God!'

A corpse hung from a tree, skin peeled away to reveal red muscle, white sinew, bone – then my senses caught up with my eyes and reinterpreted the shape: a deer, strung up for butchering.

I gave a cough of relieved laughter. 'Is it deer season?'

'Best not to ask,' he answered. His right hand went up in a gesture of greeting. I saw nothing until the figure moved – and suddenly I was looking at an entire domestic setting. Across the clearing, a small cottage lay half buried under honeysuckle. To one side stood a small woman the same colour as the trees behind her – the first Roumanian woman I'd seen whose clothing wasn't brilliant with primary colours. She was not much over four feet tall, with the wrinkles of a centenarian but the straight back of a woman in her prime, and her blue eyes gleamed like flames from the shadows. One hand held a wickedly thin filleting knife.

'*Buna ziua, doamna,*' Holmes said.

'You again,' she replied, and turned back to her task – which had to do with the deer and at which I did not look too closely.

Holmes, however, felt no such compunction, but walked across the clearing to the rough table where she was working. I followed, eyeing the herbs that hung from hooks near her door. If I was not mistaken, a couple of those leafy bunches could poison half a village and all its livestock.

He pulled something from his pocket and held it out to her: the hex bag, its enveloping handkerchief pulled back. 'Please, *doamna*, what can you tell me of this?'

She glared at the thing, then stabbed the thin knife down into the lump of flesh she was working on and pointed at the table with her chin. He laid the bag down, working open the drawstrings, and would have poured out the contents but for her gesturing for him to stop. Instead, she leant over it to examine the leaves and bones, then pulled a twig from a nearby bush and used it to stir things around. With a grimace, she tossed the twig away and passed judgement.

'Pah. Where this from?'

'Someone left it in Bran, to make it look like a witch had done a wicked deed.'

She glared at him. 'What deed?'

'Minor troublemaking. I stopped it.'

'*Bun*,' she said. She waved a dismissive hand over the leather bag. 'Child's game,' she pronounced, then jerked the knife from the slab of meat and resumed her work. Holmes returned the bag to his pocket and thanked her, leaving a pair of coins on the table.

'Holmes,' I hissed, when we were out of earshot, 'was that an actual witch?'

'Think of her as the traditional alternative to the village doctor. Nurse, herbalist, and occasional midwife.'

'I can just imagine what Dr Watson would have to say about it.'

'Aspirin and quinine are made from bark, digitalis and cocaine come from leaves, hesperidin is—'

'Yes, yes, I know. Still, I found myself looking around for her black cat and broomstick.'

'Her cat is a tabby, and I believe Mrs Varga uses her broom to sweep the floor.'

'And she doesn't think that's a real hex bag you found.'

'I wanted it confirmed.'

'I wonder what gave it away?'

'I should think the Earl Grey tea.'

'Don't witches drink tea?'

'Not Earl Grey. It is a distinctly English beverage. I doubt there are a dozen people in Roumania who have heard of it.'

'And around here, most of those will be connected with the castle in some way.'

'It does narrow down our likely suspects.'

'And I agree with Mrs Varga. That whole hex bag, with rat's teeth and a diabolical pentagram drawn by a fountain pen, then put into a rather expensive little bag, was designed to impress the gullible.'

The day grew hot as we walked on, following the same well-beaten path along the side of the hills. Every so often, a lesser footpath would branch off to one side, with a glimpse of a dwelling at its end. None appeared made of gingerbread, although any of them might have belonged to axe-bearing woodsmen.

At the third of these lesser pathways, I stopped to examine a mark carved into a tree, just up from the main route. I had seen similar marks along the other two as well. And when I looked to say something to Holmes, I saw that he was waiting, an expectant look on his face.

'What?' I asked.

'You noticed something?'

'These are what a folklorist would call apotropaic marks – "run away" marks. Put at vulnerable places to repel witches. Like pagan versions of the mezuzah. Or . . . like the gate carvings in the village. Do they have them inside, too? On their chimneys?'

'Some do.'

This one was a sort of W with an overlap of the middle arms. I had seen them before, used as a pilgrim souvenir representing the initials of *Virgo Virginum* – both invoking the Virgin Mary and providing the sort of crosshatching thought to confuse evil spirits.

'Isn't it odd that they let your Mrs Varga live in the area, yet mark their paths and houses to drive her away?'

'Not necessarily her in particular. Although I do imagine they take care to ensure that she doesn't stray into their private area.'

'Yet they ask her to heal their goats and, I don't know – make their amulets? Help at childbirth?'

'Probably.'

'Isn't that a bit like trusting the crocodile in your moat to let you go for a swim?'

'You of all people, Russell, should not be surprised at the lack of consistent logic in a system of belief.'

'Fair enough. But tell me, honestly: how long did it take *you* to notice the marks, when you first came along this path?'

His mouth twitched. 'A little longer,' he admitted, and on we went. But it was a good ten minutes and three more scratched W marks before his finger went out and his voice drifted back to me. 'It was that one.'

Before I could react, something else did. A furious snorting and scrabbling in the bushes, alarmingly close, had me eyeing the tree trunks for reachable branches – then moments later a trio of young piglets scurried across the path ahead, in the direction of the noise. The crackle of dried leaves and snapping twigs receded down the hill, and my heart ceased trying to climb out of my throat.

Wild pigs were dangerous. Though maybe the Roumanian branch of the family was not as pugnacious as those I'd met in India.

I cleared my throat, to bring my voice under control, and asked Holmes, 'Do I need to worry about any other deadly creatures in the woods? Has the Queen decided to introduce tigers into the Carpathians, perhaps?'

'No introductions, only the natives. Such as wolves.'

'So you think that was a wolf I heard, last night?'

'Very probably. And of course, bears.'

'Bears, again? Oh, lovely.'

We saw no other large predators before we emerged from the forested area onto a narrow, rutted road. To our left lay the main road to Braşov. To the right, the lane would curve around to Bran. And just over the fields, in what was sure to be the least hospitable piece of ground for miles, we could see the Romany village.

Writers of travelogues adore sprinkling their pages with picturesque descriptions of criminal men with flashing eyes and barbaric women with flashing legs, dancing to wild music amidst the naked children, bony horses, and old crone fortune-tellers. Writers of travelogues are rarely forced to scrape a living in a place where they are not permitted to own land or hold jobs, and from which they will be driven at the least suspicion of crime, disease, witchcraft, or any trouble at all. One might imagine that a writer of travelogues would see dignity in a people who have maintained their identity since they first wandered out of India a millennium ago, but that is not the task of the writer of travelogues.

When we went past this encampment, we took care to nod at the men and smile at the children. Holmes touched his hat to the women, and we did not stop to take a photograph, point at the bright caravans, or have our fortunes told.

A little further along, we bought lunch from a farmhouse, and conversed with a beekeeper in something that might have been German. I purchased two pairs of alarmingly red socks from a hugely pregnant young woman who was knitting in her front garden, and we spent the better part of an hour watching maize being fed through an ancient watermill by her husband. We were passed by eleven carts drawn by horses and two by bullocks, one motorcycle, and two motorcars (one small and ancient, the other vast and glossy). We saw walnut trees, head-high maize, a flock of sheep, seventeen goats, more haystacks than I could count, and a priest.

Holmes and this last figure waved at each other across a field, but the other man was deep in talk with a family at their door and we did not approach.

Shortly after the priest, we were overtaken and pulled bodily up onto an empty flatbed horse cart by its cheerful, completely toothless driver, who told us all about his horses, pointed at a nearby house and revealed its attendant scandal, laughed at three boys in a field and gave us their history, then dropped us off in Bran with a cautionary finger and a long lecture about the hazards of life in the big village. We thanked him, and waved our benefactor away down the road.

'Did you understand a word he said?' I asked Holmes.

'Not one.'

CHAPTER ELEVEN

BACK AT THE CASTLE, we found the hallways alive with bustling maids, their arms filled with dust-cloths and bedsheets. Enormous displays of freshly cut flowers had sprung up in every corner, making the air heady with scent.

The Queen was on her way.

To my amusement, nervous anticipation infected me as well, driving me to the wardrobe and looking glass, that I might prove presentable to Her Majesty. Even Holmes changed his shoes.

After the long day's tramp, I craved a tea tray as substantial as that of the previous afternoon, but it was not forthcoming. The bustle outside our doors grew to a pitch – then abruptly all fell silent.

The throb of a powerful engine came through our windows, followed by another. After a moment came the distant *bang bang* of car doors closing. The stone walls of the castle seemed to gather their focus on the iron-studded doorway that was the only breach of its defences. Enough time went by to account for welcome greetings in the forecourt, a quick survey of the garden from the heights, and a dignified climb up the outer stairway. Then a murmur of voices rose from below.

The Queen had only come some thirty miles, which even at a dignified pace on dirt roads would not have taken more than three hours. She would not need to wash away the dust of travel, although I hoped that she would be as desirous for her tea as we were. A quarter hour went by, twenty minutes. I finally grumbled at Holmes, sitting with his heels propped on the window seat, reading a German text on the history of tobacco.

'Do you suppose if I went down to the kitchen, I might beg a bald mug of tea?'

He turned a page. 'I imagine Florescu had to deliver the most urgent pieces of news. Which would include the state of the garden and any new "unsettling episodes."'

I drank another glass of water from the jug on the sideboard, ate some stale nuts from a twist of paper in the corner of my travel valise, and tried to interest myself in the words of my own book.

Forty minutes after the door slams of the motorcar, we heard a tap at our door.

'Thank God,' I muttered, tossing the book onto the table and standing up. 'Come!'

But it was neither a summoning, nor a laden tray. Instead, a rather distracted-looking Florescu appeared in the doorway.

'My apologies, Her Majesty has asked me to explain that urgent business prevents her from asking you to join her for tea, but instead she will welcome you for dinner. I will come for you at twenty to eight, if that is well with you?'

'I—'

'Your tea should be here within minutes, and again, I apologise for the delay.'

There was nothing to do but thank him. He nodded and made to withdraw, then recalled another item of business. 'You will be dining in Her Majesty's flats, and she asked that you be told that dress is informal. However, if you wish to adopt traditional clothing while you are here, you will each find her small gift in your chest of drawers.'

He bowed more deeply, and backed out of the room.

I had taken a change of clothing from the wardrobe, on our return from the day's outing, but I had not looked into the chest beside it. Nor was I destined to look through it now, since I had only taken one step in that direction when another rap came from the hall.

This was our tea, brought in not by the ever-cheery Gabriela, but a sour-faced, grey-haired woman. However, the tray she set down was piled suitably high with the apologies of the kitchen, both savoury and sweet, and it was several minutes before I recalled the Queen's 'small gift.' I went to investigate the contents of the drawers, coming back with a truly magnificent garment.

'If this is "traditional clothing,"' I remarked, 'then it looks as though we're to be guests of honour at a Romany wedding.'

The resemblance to garments seen on the local citizens was clear: a blouse of fine pale linen with full, bloused sleeves, loose and long to gather inside skirt and sash – both of which were also in the drawer. Thick embroidery covered the upper body, down the sleeves, and along the front – so thick, in fact, it might have been intended as armour. Needlework was not one of my skills, but I'd seen Mrs Hudson do enough of it to know that, while the native dress might represent a dozen or so evenings of work before the

94

fire, this garment represented solid days – weeks, even – of highly skilled handiwork.

And that was just the blouse: the overskirt beside it represented months.

I draped the tunic over the back of the chair, arranged to display its block of red and blue threads, picked out in fine geometric patterns – and I smiled as I recognised the protective eye and a stylised grapevine. Then curiosity got the better of me, and I went to investigate the contents of Holmes' wardrobe.

I came back with a loose-sleeved tunic that was a masculine version of my own, made of white linen with a sumptuous band of embroidery around the hem, cuffs, shoulders, and neck. With it was a waistcoat so solidly embroidered it might have been tapestry. Holmes looked at the garments. One eyebrow rose, just a little.

'So, that's a no, then?' I asked cheerfully. 'The man who does not hesitate to disguise himself as a drunken street corner lout, elderly cleric, or opium addict puts his foot down at Roumanian peasant?'

He turned his lifted eyebrow towards the teapot and set about refilling his cup. I returned the pieces of womanly art to their former resting place.

A little after seven-thirty, I heard a motorcar engine start up, and glanced out of the window in time to see a sporty little Citroën buzz down the drive into the dusk.

When the knock came, Holmes was dressed in a plain, dark suit, while I compromised by tying the embroidered sash around the waist of a more traditional frock – demonstrating my appreciation, without fully committing myself to fancy dress.

Florescu led us down a level and around the courtyard to the round, pointed tower on the other side. He knocked at the door, opened it, waited until a pair of black dogs had shot through and disappeared in the direction of the cooking smells, then stepped inside, drew himself up, and formally declared our names.

And thus we were welcomed into the presence of Marie, Queen of Roumania.

Chapter Twelve

I HAVE MET A wide number of aristocratic and royal personages over the years, both before and after this. Some are charming, a few have been delightful, while a handful caused my hackles to rise – but all have been expert wielders of the professional warmth characteristic of a race surrounded by those they consider, to some degree or another, inferior.

I have never met one who wielded her warmth more graciously than the Queen of Roumania.

She rose when we came in, crossing the room to greet us, and although I did feel that her outstretched hand was meant to be pressed to our bowed foreheads rather than shaken, any royal faux pas I may have committed, then or in the days to follow, went firmly unacknowledged by Her Majesty.

Holmes she greeted as an old acquaintance, although his salutation was a formal, heels-together bow over her hand. Her own first words gave lie to the impression of familiarity.

'My dear Mr Holmes, I feel that we have known each other for years, although I admit, I cannot recall ever having been formally introduced. I first met you, as it were, when I was fifteen and some cousins were discussing a story they had secretly read concerning a royal scandal. Debate was fierce over whether the "King of Bohemia" was really meant to be our distant cousin, the Emperor. A few months later, I discovered there were more such stories, and that the servants read them religiously. I would borrow each new copy of *The Strand* when it came out. So exciting – and now here you are! Although I trust that Dr Watson will not be writing this little adventure for his reading public.'

'I believe that Watson is at home in London,' he assured her, although that did not quite answer her question.

'And Mrs Holmes – or rather, being a modern woman, Miss Russell. So very pleased to meet you. I understand you have had an exciting time in Monaco? Such a charming place, a piquant blend of flower gardens and wickedness.'

Her accent was cut-glass English with a trace of German, her laugh a throaty ripple that made me smile in response. She held out her fingers to me, and although I stifled the impulse to bow or even curtsey, I discovered that my knees had betrayed me just a touch, and given her a brief dip of honour.

'Your Majesty, thank you for making us welcome.'

She swept us into her rooms and settled us on rug-strewn divans near what in the wintertime would have been a cosy fire, but was now a setting for a fiery display of dahlias, equally welcoming. She leant forward to ask Holmes something about London, leaving me to study the woman and her singular surroundings.

Fancy dress or no, Marie's clothing paid no mind to the skimpy fashion of the twentieth century. Instead, it flowed: loose linen blouse, calf-length skirt, and sash belt, all thick with the same embroidery that I had found in my chest of drawers. Her head was wrapped in a sort of turban with a long descending tail, an elaborate version of the women's headscarves I had seen. The pearl drops in her ears were as large as the end joint of my thumb, and around her neck was a long rope of pearls, each one brilliant white and the size of a cooking cherry.

And her face – I had known she was handsome, this much-photographed woman, but I had expected that her pictures would deceive, or at least exaggerate. If anything, they had not done her justice. She was tall and graceful and extraordinarily beautiful, even her skin young for a woman of fifty years. Her gaze was both direct and compelling, her eyes a pale, almost translucent blue, as if the open windows to an open soul. Her features were perfect, her spine erect, and yet, far from a languid beauty, there was strength in her, and her fingers were not those of a coddled showpiece.

She'd been an ardent horsewoman, I remembered. Her hands suggested she still was.

Her voice broke into my thoughts. 'And you, Miss Russell, I am told you are a noted academic. At Oxford, no less.'

Told by whom, I wondered? 'If I ever managed to spend more than a few weeks at a time there, my studies might have progressed more rapidly,' I told her. 'As it is, ma'am, my books gather more dust than they do margin notes.'

'I often wonder what I might have been, had Mother believed in the education of women. I have lamentably little book learning, and what I do read these days is mostly fiction.'

'Your Majesty does not appear to have suffered under a lack of Greek and Latin tutoring.'

'Yes, nothing classical, I am afraid, only English and Roumanian. And French, naturally. German. A little Russian. Some of which are easier to read than to speak, although for simple relaxation at the end of the day, I tend to reach first for a story in English. Do you know Aldous Huxley?'

'Not personally,' I replied, 'although I've read some of his writing.'

'I was not sure what to make of *Crome Yellow* – how much was satire and how much simple biography. The Bloomsbury set as a whole is most intriguing – I regret my time in England is invariably much taken up with matters of state, since I should enjoy inviting the entire lot of them to tea and listening to them carry on. Though perhaps not while my daughter is present.'

I laughed. 'I met F. Scott Fitzgerald and his wife, down in the Riviera.'

'Oh, I did enjoy his early *Jazz* stories, although I'm not sure *Gatsby* was a success. I was also pleased, while in London this summer, to discover a number of new detective-story writers. A woman named Christie seems most promising – do you know her? No? She's quite clever. Although my daughter Ileana is devoted to Bulldog Drummond, more a man of action than a detective. Ah, heavens, where are my manners – what will you take by way of *aperitif*?'

Florescu, who had been hovering behind us as we talked, took a step forward, but seemed disappointed when we both opted for wine.

'I understand you have some excellent wines here,' I told him, then wondered where I had picked up that bit of information.

His lugubrious face was transformed by pride. 'Roumanian wines have been famous for thousands of years.'

'Although most of the vines died from phylloxera forty years ago, to be replaced by French stock,' Holmes commented, which was a touch ungracious of him.

'And I'm sure they've already taken on the distinctive qualities of their terroir,' I hastened to add, earning a grateful glance from the Transylvanian butler as he turned away from the waiting drinks cabinet and went in search of our wine.

When he returned, I noted that while the liquid in our glasses had a faintly amber tint, the one he set before his Queen looked more like mineral water. We toasted – 'Roumania!' – and took a sip of the crisp summer wine, waiting for the Queen to choose our topics of conversation.

Those began with the events of her recent trip to England and Germany, mostly along the lines of the health of the British royal family and how fast children grew. Our dinner arrived, brought by a footman and a kitchen maid I had not seen before, younger than Gabriela and less sure of herself. She laid out the dinner service as if consulting an inner checklist, and when she succeeded in getting it all right and the Queen thanked her, she blushed with pleasure and automatically seized the royal hand to press against her brow.

After which she blushed in consternation, and began to apologise. The Queen laughed, Florescu shooed her out, and she bobbed her way out the door like a cork in a pond.

She, too, had been wearing a small gold cross around her neck.

Over food, talk moved on to the arts and theatre. Over dessert it was outdoor sports – and when riding and shooting failed to spark our passions (I considered offering her my thoughts on the sport of pig-sticking, but decided I did not know her well enough to judge her response) she tried sailing. That, at least, I could reply to, having done my share of actual labour during a three week voyage from Venice to Antibes the previous month.

'Ah,' she exclaimed, 'Ileana adores sailing. And it explains the fashionable brownness of your face and the paleness of your hair.'

Also the calluses on my hands and the straw-like texture of that sunburnt hair, but she was too polite to mention that. She questioned me on the nature of the yacht, and asked about the people we had met in recent weeks, identifying several mutual friends (though none of the various royal families whose names she ventured had come our way, and she quickly set those to one side).

At last, plates were cleared, coffee brought, along with a platter laden with figs, grapes, peaches, and tiny chocolates, lest a corner of appetite remain – and then Florescu and the various footmen and maids swept out, leaving us alone.

The Queen's demeanour shifted, just a fraction, when the door had shut behind them. Many of those whose servants see to their every need, be it producing a meal or buttoning up a gown, grow to treat them as part of the furniture, and make less of an attempt to curb their speech than if the servants were of no more concern than the family dogs. But this woman, who had probably never been out of a servant's earshot since the day of her birth, was very aware of the meaning of actual privacy.

The quick smile she gave us was genuine, an admission of the need for honesty. 'Florescu is a treasure,' she said, 'but one is aware that he has definite opinions when it comes to Bran.'

'He is from here originally, I believe?' Holmes asked.

'Indeed, his family have cared for Castle Bran for generations. When the city fathers of Brașov presented me with the keys, Mr Florescu was the man who held them – literally, that is, although without the full authority of a castellan. It had been a long time since anyone actually lived here, but Florescu knew everything my people needed to know: where the pans were kept, which sections of roof needed repair, which chimneys could be trusted to draw. He knows the castle better than anyone else – he told me once that the only time in his life he went more than a month without coming inside was during the War.'

'You were fortunate he's young enough to carry out what must be a demanding schedule, here. Particularly when there have been builders in.'

'I honestly do not know how we should have managed without him. He arranges guides during the hunting season and tours of Brașov for my foreign guests, he tracks down unusual foods and helps me locate sources of flower bulbs for the gardens. He can do an emergency repair on the castle's bits of ancient plumbing, produce a roast chicken when the cook has been taken ill, and stop the bleeding in a cut hand until a doctor can be found. He's even hired most of those who work here, half of whom are related to him, I think. A true gem, is our Florescu.'

The Queen took a sip of coffee, and settled into her chair with as much ease as a woman of her stiff-backed generation and class ever showed. Her pale, compelling gaze rested first on Holmes, then on me, before returning to Holmes.

'How much do you know of what has been happening here?'

'When I came last month, Mr Florescu described the incidents that took place in the spring. He was quite thorough.'

'I am glad. He was not pleased at sharing our problems with a stranger.'

'Understandable. But I believe that things have been quiet since then?' I shot Holmes a quick glance. Did he not intend to mention last night's adventures?

'So I understand. Florescu says there were a few odd happenings, but nothing the people have found too troubling. A cow dies, an old man becomes ill, a tree fails to set fruit. Witchcraft, perhaps, but nothing worse.'

'I am sorry to hear that.'

She looked up sharply. 'What do you mean?'

'I mean that if the disturbing episodes do start up again, now that you are back, there will be even more blame attached.'

The pale eyes blazed. 'Sir, do you suggest that "blame" turned against the Queen is of more concern than outright assaults on her citizens?'

'No, I am not,' he said, although to some degree, he had been. 'I am suggesting that, if trouble starts again, it indicates that the threat may be larger than mere local resentments. And that could mean that political unrest follows. Madam, I do not think any of us wish for Roumania to experience the sort of unrest common to the recent past.'

She nodded – but I liked her the more, for this instantaneous defence of those beneath her on the social scale.

'I am loved here,' she said, in that aristocratic voice that brooks no disagreement. 'Have no doubt of that. My work during the War years, my refusal to flee or to even send my children into safety, my willingness to undertake unseemly manoeuvrings during the Paris peace talks and the victories I won there – they have made me the people's Queen as no coronation could have done. Any rumour that attaches to me will soon wither and die, as they have in the past. No, sir, the fears that drove me to send for you, Mr Holmes, are not the fears of a Queen. They are the fears of a mother.'

'So you said in your initial letter,' he replied.

'Open threats are not unusual. The world is full of mad people. But I have never before had one directed against my children. That is why I left Ileana at Peleş – our castle in Sinaia. She wanted to come – she loves Bran as much as I do – but I ordered her to stay there with her father who . . . is not well. She is guarded there, as she could not be here. I left my lady-in-waiting there by way of support.'

'Why do you think that note was sent?' Holmes asked. 'And why against her, rather than you personally?'

'Whoever sent it no doubt knows that I would never be swayed by a threat to myself. It is a coward's way to come under my guard, by attacking my daughter. And here in Bran, of all places, where she and I are accustomed to ride, even to walk about, completely on our own.'

'Tell us about the Princess. If the threat is against her – against her presence here, at the very least – why might that be? Why would someone not wish her to be here in Bran?'

'Other than that Ileana's absence would guarantee mine? I cannot think. Her life here is perfectly innocent and without event. She rides, she visits with the village girls, she joins me in the garden and helps entertain our visitors. Foreign visitors adore Bran, despite its remoteness – particularly journalists with cameras.'

I took the opportunity to inject a question. 'So the Princess has friends and interests of her own here?'

'Of course! She invites friends from the city, but she also has a group of village girls she helps with schoolwork and such. She . . .' The Queen paused, then gave a short sigh and a long answer. 'You must understand, to be the child of royalty is not a comfortable thing. One's physical needs are met, certainly, but there is a cost. And in these modern times – oh, the cost can be heavy. When I grew up, I had sisters all around me, parents who loved me, a country that honoured and respected what we were. It was idyllic, in many ways. But Ileana . . . my daughter's childhood has been hard.'

She rose, causing us to shoot to our feet as well, and walked over to a collection of silver-framed photographs on a side table. She brought back two, handing one to each of us. We sat down again, studying them.

Mine was a studio photographic portrait of a girl who looked vaguely like young Gabriela. Formally posed, then hand-tinted, it was not entirely a success, with the subject's innate solemnity coloured by pinks and blues more suited to a porcelain doll. It showed a girl at the end of adolescence, whose face retained some childhood roundness, but whose eyes – those unnaturally blue eyes beneath the heavy brows – were direct, unflinching, and older than her years. It was the expression of a person who had been wounded, and left with the expectation that life was going to require all the strength she could summon.

Holmes held out the other photograph, so I traded him. This second one – untinted – showed a more informal gathering of men and women in a summer before the War: men in uniform, women in long white skirts and broad-brimmed hats, two boys in sailor suits seated at the front. A woman at the side dandled an infant, and one at the centre held a young girl on her lap, the child's blonde curls gathered in a big white bow.

Then a face at the back came into focus, and I realised what I was looking at: the Romanovs – Tsar, Tsarina, and children. And that was Queen Marie, seated beside the woman with the girl.

'The photograph was taken during my cousin's visit to us in 1914, just before the War began. We'd hoped that Carol and Olga might . . . well. But instead, Ileana and Alexei simply adored each other. The Tsarevitch is the boy sitting down at the front, next to my son Nicholas. Ileana was five – that's her with the bow. In a better world, Alix and I might now be discussing an upcoming engagement between Ileana and Alexei. Instead, the whole family lie in their graves somewhere in Russia, and Ileana was made to witness things during the War that no young girl should see. She has nightmares, still, of carts filled with naked bodies.

'Since the War, Ileana has lived a somewhat solitary life. Her nearest sister is nine years older, which makes for a wide gap between playmates – and then Mignon married and Ileana was left with me. It's one of the reasons I agreed that she might spend a year at home in boarding school. She needs to make friends from that world, as she will not here. One might wish she was not so shy. Still, she and I are very close. In many ways she is the daughter of my heart. Nonetheless, a girl needs someone her age to confide in. In the city, she has friends more suited to her position, but out here, the choice becomes servants, or loneliness.'

'You say servants. Is one of her friends the kitchen girl? Gabriela?'

'Florescu's niece, yes. A most dependable young person. And through Gabriela, as I said, Ileana has come to befriend certain of the nicer girls of the village.'

I considered that. Where there were young girls, there would be factions and rivalries – and considering the vastly unequal positions involved, there was sure to be a jockeying for favour.

Were Holmes and I searching too high for our culprit? Could it be something as simple as a girl taking her petty revenge for some affront or snub? Most of the events did involve girls or young women, and all would have been quickly forgotten but for the gossip that followed: the young woman who ran off to Bucharest (but maybe really hadn't), then the kitchen maid's cut hand (which interested the Queen strangely), and finally the child who tripped in the woods (or was it an attack?). A particularly determined young person could have been responsible for stirring up village talk, aiming it not at Ileana herself, but at the authoritative figure behind her: the Queen.

Holmes would be unhappy if it all came down to a resentful adolescent.

At present, he was not interested in girls, even those who were royal intimates. Instead, he asked, 'Who else would wish to discourage you from Bran?'

'From Bran? No one but me cares a fig about Bran. The castle was derelict when I received it, as you can no doubt see. The land it stands upon is small, and would not justify so much as a resentful letter, much less a campaign of threats. No doubt there are many who resent my happiness – not here in Bran, but those in Bucharest and elsewhere. But to organise against me and menace my daughter? Who would be so cruel?'

Who indeed? I had known husbands who relished tormenting their wives, but I had no reason to think King Ferdinand was one of those – even if he could contrive to build peasant rumours in a village he rarely visited. To say nothing of his current illness.

The wife of one of Marie's rumoured lovers? Chief among those was Prince Barbu Ştirbey, a man who lived much of the time in the summer capital of Sinaia, not far from the royal castle of Peleş: intimidating Queen Marie into leaving Bran would cause her to spend more time near Prince Barbu, not less.

What about another lover, one we did not know about? Marie was a remarkably attractive woman, but she was fifty years old, growing thick around the middle. Her great passions appeared to be riding horses, growing dahlias, and building a literary reputation.

Was there someone else who resented her presence here? I'd lived in the English countryside long enough to know that a sudden influx of royalty – bringing with it the royal purse – would make the local residents grumble about new-fangled inventions, motorcars racing through the lanes, and the way that foreign visitors leant on the fences and frightened the livestock. To say nothing of forcing the local residents to keep their dogs, goats, and presumably children from straying across the roads.

At the same time, this was a poor corner of a backward nation. One would have to be a remarkably devout Socialist to spurn a job on the castle repair crews, a market for milk and cheese, and a chance to sell embroidered goods to the castle's wealthy guests.

I was depressed to think that, of all the possibilities, the one thing I had not disproved was the thing that Holmes swore had not brought us here: international politics.

CHAPTER THIRTEEN

W E MADE OUR WAY through the winding passages of the castle by the light of dancing flame, and found our rooms aglow with fragrant candlelight. I went to change out of my dress. Holmes, however, did little more than exchange his jacket for a dressing gown.

He poured himself a glass from the crystal decanter, then snuffed the candles as he passed, to join me at the window. As my eyes adjusted to the dark, traces of village life came into view: a few faintly-lit windows, a swinging lantern winking in and out between the trees. The headlamps of a motorcar wound back and forth for a time, then turned in to a lane and were swallowed by darkness.

'You still anticipate another . . . episode, now that the Queen is back?' It seemed unlikely, after that warm, sunlit breeze that was Queen Marie. Surely her presence in Bran would drive the haunts away, not attract them?

Holmes set his glass on the deep stone window sill and reached for his tobacco. I closed my eyes against the flare of the match.

'If one does take place,' he said at last, 'it will tell us a great deal.'

'When shall we go down to the village and keep an eye on things?'

'It is too early, the residents are still astir.'

'Midnight, then? Although let's hope no one notices us, wandering about the village. They'll get out their pitchforks and stakes, then and there.'

At midnight, dressed in dark clothing, we crept from our rooms and through the unlit passageways. The night was still, the moon three days after full. Just outside the door to the guard's room, which would have men on duty at all hours while the Queen was in residence, I took up position behind a terracotta vase the size of a baby elephant. I listened to the low grumble of their conversation, and braced myself against the coming noise.

At the count of sixty, Holmes sent a bronze pot full of flowers clattering down the stone stairs. As the guards shouted and ran to confront this noisy intruder, I slipped around behind them, and had the outer door open when Holmes appeared. We shut it silently, and left the guards puzzling over what resident cat might have pushed the pot over.

Holmes was at the bottom of the stairway by the time I'd felt my way down it, but my eyes were adjusting to the moonlight, and I could move off with him into the drive without feeling utterly blind.

I had been over the central roads of Bran village during the daylight, but Holmes' previous stay here had taught him which houses had noisy dogs or sleepless old ladies, and which corners had conveniently long views. He now steered us around the former to a convenient position with the latter, and there he abandoned me. We could not know where a disturbance might come from; therefore, I would watch over the upper section of village from the Braşov road, while he took up a position overlooking the side along the river.

I listened to his retreating footsteps, and he was gone. I was alone, in the dark, in a place where some evil was stirring . . . In Transylvania. Which, between Polidori (winner of the Most Melodramatic Final Line in Fiction award) and Vlad Ţepeş (there being no melodrama in his battlefield 'forest of the impaled') made a person all too susceptible to Stoker's dark shapes creeping head first down a tower wall, or the repugnant intimacy of an undead Count, whose cold, red lips sought to nuzzle into the warmth of a woman's neck—

Oh, for heaven's sake, Russell, don't be a child! I scrubbed at my apprehension with cold scorn, and stepped inside the small roofed structure that we had seen earlier. In a proper town, it might have been a shelter for those awaiting an omnibus. Here, it had probably been a pig shed whose walls had rotted away. Or a home for all the local pigeons and bats. The night felt cool, after weeks of Mediterranean summer, so I pulled my coat up for the warmth and my cap down for bat protection, took a slow breath to calm my thoughts, and prepared for a long night of doing nothing at all.

The village slept. The moonlight rendered a mosaic of half-familiar shapes. The metal roof of a house up the way shone clear, as did the white-painted trim of the village shop and a line of whitewashed stones some houseproud citizen had arranged along their front garden. Everything else was rendered in tones of grey:

dark grey doorways and recessed windows, shimmering grey willow leaves catching a drift of air, pale grey chimneys and window frames. I could even make out the tessellations of plaster triangles on the ancient half-timbered building in need of renovations.

Many ancient peoples believed in a land of shade, where the dead dwell in a twilight underworld. In Hebrew, it is tsalmaveth, the death shadow. In one of the more peculiar Biblical passages, King Saul, who is in desperate need of advice, orders the witch of Endor to summon the prophet Samuel from the shadows. Samuel appears, but he is vexed at being disturbed and angry at Saul's lack of faith. Things don't go at all well for the king, implying that summoning the dead is not the best way to reach a decision.

Fairy tales often contain similar lessons. I remembered a story from one of my mother's books, read when I was far too young for it, about a couple who were given three wishes. The first inadvertently causes the death of their beloved son; the second brings the son back – but when the young man's father realises that what is being returned to them is the very corpse that lay, rotting and mutilated, in the graveyard, he uses the third wish to banish the nightmare crawling towards their cottage door. I did not sleep well for weeks after reading the story – but I also spent hours trying to come up with commands that might be specific enough to avoid the loophole repercussions of horror.

My father said this proved I would grow up to be a lawyer. My mother took to storing some of her books on higher shelves.

I could also remember lying in my lonely hospital bed many years later, knowing that I, too, would ask for my family reanimated, no matter the result.

As I sat there amongst the sleeping innocents of Bran, twenty years after reading 'The Monkey's Paw' and eleven years after the hospital, I became aware of a sound. Faint, still far away, but coming closer.

The hair rose down the back of my neck. My breath stopped, my ears strained, my eyes stared into the grey shapes outside the shelter – all equally futile. Nothing moved, yet there was sound. As if some creature was laboriously dragging itself along. Scrape; pause. Scrape; pause.

I eased my hand down to pull the knife from my boot top, and stood—

The noise stopped. A minute, two. I put all my perception to my ears, but it was hard to hear over the pounding of my heart.

Finally it started up again, more rapidly now: scrape/pause, scrape/pause, scrape/pause. Another, slightly longer pause, then it resumed. It seemed to be getting closer, but . . . wasn't the sound a little . . . unsubstantial, for a crawling corpse?

Then my eyes caught motion, at last. A shadow moved out from one patch of darkness to the next, but the size of it calmed my heart even as the shape piqued my curiosity.

The next time it emerged, out of the dappled print at the base of a bush, I realised what it was: a small cat dragging its large prey.

The tension of the past minutes came out in a loud snort. The cat froze, staring in my direction, then adjusted its jaws around the rat or rabbit and staggered away with it.

I hugged myself, laughing soundlessly, and slid my knife away, shivering a little as the sweat cooled on my skin.

The night settled back into a study of greys. I heard all sorts of things – owls, bats, a child waking and being soothed, a reassuringly distant chorus of dogs-or-perhaps-wolves, but the only motion I perceived, in the hours that followed, was an owl, two mice, and the near-imperceptible shift of shadows from the moon.

I sat on the log all that night, eyes open and ears ready, waiting for witches, cats, or Transylvanian vampires, and thinking of the superstitions of darkness. Nothing moved until the stars were fading, and Holmes came up the road.

I tried to feel pleased that no trouble had disturbed the sleepers of Bran during the night, but mostly I felt tired and cold.

'How do we get back in?' I asked Holmes. 'I'll need to limber up a bit if we plan on scaling the walls.'

'The watch changes at six each morning. When I was here before, I took care to establish myself as a man who enjoys an early morning perambulation. The morning guards will assume that you and I walked out openly during the night watch.'

'I hope you also established yourself as a man who enjoys an afternoon nap?'

'I would often take to my room and ask that my study not be disturbed.'

'Excellent plan,' I said.

In the meantime, a cold bath and strong coffee would have to suffice. I went to run the former while Holmes set about the latter. When I came out, still shivering but wide awake, I found him shaving before the mirror. 'I suggested that we would omit the tea phase of the morning and go straight to coffee and eggs,' he told me in pauses around the moving blade. 'The fires were already going, so the girl should be here soon.'

Indeed, he had just begun to wipe away the shaving cream when the knock came. I opened the door and greeted Gabriela as she walked past me. She returned my greeting with a mere nod, and set about unloading the tray, head down, moving in a brisk and business-like fashion. Perhaps the Queen's presence put everyone on their best behaviour, I thought, rather regretting the change from the ebullient serving girl to this silent one.

'Thank you, Gabriela, it's good of you to bring this so early, we have to be—'

She had been moving a plate from tray to table when it caught the edge of the milk jug and fell from her grasp, falling to the table with a clatter. No harm was done, but the girl jumped back with a startled cry.

No, not business-like: deeply troubled. 'Gabriela, what's wrong?'

'No, no – nothing, I sorry for the noise, *sunt proasta*, my hands they—'

I touched her arm to stop her. 'Gabriela, don't worry about the plates, what has happened? Is someone bothering you? Shall I ring for Mr Florescu?'

'No!' She pulled away, twisting her hands together, then burst out, 'My friend Vera, she is meeting *strigoi*!'

And with that she spun and darted from the room.

I followed as far as the empty hallway, but did not pursue her into the labyrinth. A serving girl as proud as she would be humiliated at knowing she had troubled one of the castle's guests, and in any event, that particular trouble did not seem to require our immediate intervention.

I closed the door and went to take the cup of coffee Holmes held out.

We ate a rapid and subdued breakfast, and went in search of information from a higher power.

CHAPTER FOURTEEN

THE BUTLER'S PANTRY OF Castle Bran was instantly recognisable as such, despite being in a Transylvanian fortress with an occupant wearing sumptuous peasant garb instead of the customary high-collared formal suit. It even had the right smell: silver polish, old paperwork, and a trace of ironing from a nearby room.

Also typical, the man whose realm this was – the tyrant whose word hired or fired the help, whose mere footstep on the stairs sent maids to scurrying – disapproved of this invasion by guests from 'upstairs.' Or perhaps his discomfort was entirely to do with the questions Holmes confronted him with, and his determination to convince us that all was well and there were no problems in the village. Certainly nothing involving vampires.

Holmes lifted one eyebrow in rebuke. 'Mr Florescu, you are aware that I was hired by your employer – by the Queen of your country – to make some enquiries into Bran's troubles. I trust that

I do not have to inform her that I have failed to make any progress due to a lack of cooperation from within her own house.'

The butler turned pale, and I became aware that he was older than I'd thought – his fine wrinkles suggested he was in his fifties, although his straight back and the very few silver strands in his dark hair had made him look younger. The man's pride and dignity turned his traditional clothing into a uniform, and looking more closely, I found that his shirt had been starched, his loose trousers held a knife's edge down their front – and I had to look away when I saw that his moustache bore the tracks of a comb.

'Sir, I have fully cooperated with you. If any of the other staff have not, please tell me their names.'

'No, the other servants have been most helpful, it is you I need to address. Mr Florescu, your niece seemed quite upset just now. Gabriela is your niece, I think? She said a friend of hers had met a *strigoi*. A fact that I should have been informed of immediately.'

'It . . . She is not . . . I don't . . .' He stopped, and drew himself up, a royal butler to his bones. 'I apologise, madam, sir, for the girl's troubling of you. It is true, there appears to be some difficulty in the village. A friend of hers has fallen ill, that is all.'

'Ill, how?'

'She has an active imagination.'

'In that she thought she spoke with a dead person?'

'Pah! Girls.'

Holmes and I looked at him, wordless indication that we were not going away. The man's jaw twitched, but he gestured us to the two hard chairs more commonly used for long and uncomfortable conversations with underlings.

'Girls of their age, you know,' he began. 'They enjoy stories. They read books, go to cinema in Braşov, they gather and try to

118

outdo each other's tales of love and fear. One of them will hear a thing, the next will build the details, the third says she may have met the person in question, then the first must go back to find a bigger tale. It is a, how do you say? Spiral? Yes?'

'And this *strigoi* that Gabriela's friend saw is the bigger tale?' I asked.

'Of course.'

'Tell us about the "things" and "details" that have gone before.'

'The events that made the Queen ask me here in the first place,' Holmes pointedly added.

The butler looked away, the closest he could get to actually putting distance between himself and us – or perhaps between himself and what he was saying. 'You know of the book by your Mr Stoker, I believe. A silly story, by a man who knows nothing of the country but for what strangers say about it, who brings in folktales and superstitions and says they are the same as a long-ago ruler, a man of huge violence and evil deeds. Well, there are other tales among my people, about a noblewoman whose great beauty concealed a great corruption of soul. A woman who maintained her beauty and youth by bathing in . . .' His words ran dry, and he looked at his hands as if hoping a newspaper clipping might appear there that he could simply hand us.

Holmes finished his sentence. 'Bathing in the blood of young virgins, yes. You speak of the Countess Erzabet Báthory.'

Florescu looked up in surprise, and in relief at not having to say those words. 'Exactly, sir. Terrible stories, told by silly girls and ignorant peasants to put fear into one another. I did not think the countess was known to the world outside.'

'Some of us have wide-ranging habits when it comes to research. Why are the village girls spreading stories about Countess

Báthory? I understand that the incident in the spring might have brought the Countess to mind – the kitchen maid's cut hand – but what does that have to do with a girl and a *strigoi*?'

'Nothing! Exactly – you see?'

'No, in fact I do not see. I asked about the *strigoi*; you brought up the countess. How are they related?'

The butler looked taken aback. Clearly, he hadn't considered the problem. 'They are not. You are right. Or should not be. But sir, madam – you know, strange things are happening in Bran, in recent times,' the butler admitted. 'It is why you are here. No doubt there are explanations, but still, the ignorant talk. A cow dies in a family having troubles with a neighbour – that enemy must have done it. A man goes into the forest and does not come out, evil is thought, not accident. Strange marks appear on walls, girls walking home hear noises in the night, dogs bark at nothing – sir, madam, you are educated people. I do not need to tell you that the simple person's imagination picks up the unknown and builds a mountain of it. And the talk feeds itself.'

'What kind of talk?' Holmes pressed.

The butler was practically squirming in his chair. 'Wicked talk. Irresponsible talk.'

'Saying what?'

'Evil things! Things she would never permit to enter her mind! I have served her since the day she first came to Bran, five years ago. If anything . . . like that was entering this castle, I would know.'

I could feel Holmes settle, a reflection of my own thought: *At last, we arrive at the core of the matter.* 'You are saying that gossip has started up around Queen Marie? Rumours of evil and corrupt doings, of her . . . taking advantage of the young women of the vicinity?'

'Her Majesty is beautiful in her own person! She rides out for the joy of riding this countryside that she loves, she stops to talk to the people in their cottages because she cares for them, not because she . . .' Again, his tongue froze rather than finish the sentence.

'Because she is looking the place over with an eye to victims?'

Florescu looked ashamed, perhaps for having permitted the words to have been pronounced within this place.

'Tell us about these "strange marks" on the walls,' Holmes said.

'I have only seen some. Most are scrubbed away quickly. By the fathers, you know? They fear they may be words their daughters should not see, and their sons should not learn.'

'So these are obscenities?'

'Some. When they started, in the spring, nobody knew – until a person who knew that word noticed and told the others. Now, when they appear, some may be bad, others not, but it is better to be safe and wash them away. They come at night, they are in simple chalk so a bucket of water deals with them, but they are disturbing. Some threaten girls – all girls, no names. "Girls here are not safe." Which is very much not true. Others are not, er . . .' His eyes flicked sideways at me, and he changed what he had been going to say. 'They are not *normal*? Not the kind of words boys teach each other. They talk of pain, and power over the weak, using words many villagers have never heard. Words that are in no dictionary.'

'And these words and threats are aimed at the Queen?'

'No. The other way. It is as if . . . as if she is the one saying them.'

'What, you mean they're signed with her name? Or, I suppose, title?'

'That is not necessary. Not when they are written in her own tongue.'

'Ah. They're in English, then, these "strange marks."'

'Some of the marks are words, yes, and English. Others just marks.'

'Obscene drawings?'

'Some, I heard. The two I saw were symbols, of some kind. I took those down myself, as the villagers would not.'

He was clearly hiding something, and when Holmes spoke, his voice was crisp with irritation. 'Mr Florescu, I would appreciate your help in this matter. I cannot work without cold, hard facts. I see that this causes you discomfort, but we are adults, and we both wish to present Her Majesty with a solution to her problem. Do we not?'

The man flushed, his very moustache quivering with indignation at the thought that he might not wish to serve his Queen. He jerked open the top drawer of his desk and slapped a pad of paper down on the blotter, snatched up a pencil and threw a few lines on the page.

The first was a star inside a circle. The second was the overlapping W we had seen marked into the forest trees. 'Those are just apotropaic – just marks meant to turn away witches,' I said.

'Yes. Superstition – pah! My village is small, but we are educated. The people here know better.' His shame was palpable.

Holmes nodded thoughtfully. 'So to be clear: the chalk marks that have been appearing are either rude words in English or obscene sketches. The residents take those down. But others are the marks meant to repel witches, and they sometimes leave those up. Is that right?'

'I wash them, when I see,' he declared.

'Yes. Is it possible the villagers themselves are putting those up?'

He looked away. 'Some are paint,' he said, admission enough.

We had exhausted the question of the mysterious marks, I thought, and to rescue him from the embarrassment of his people's gullibility, I returned to the question that had brought us here. 'Before we go – Gabriela's friend, the girl with the "active imagination"? What does she say happened to her?'

Before, Florescu had been uncomfortable, reluctant. Now his face shut down entirely. 'Nothing happened.'

Holmes' gaze snapped onto him. 'That is not what we have heard, Mr Florescu.'

'Nothing happened to the girl.'

Silence fell. We let it lie there.

After a moment, the moustache twitched. 'The girl was walking home last night.'

'From . . . ?'

'Here. She works in the kitchen – a new girl. Vera Dumitru. They finished cleaning later than usual.'

'What time was it?'

'Near to midnight.'

Not long before Holmes and I went out. I did not look at him, but I knew his expression would be as chagrined as my own.

'Was she alone?

'Three girls left together. Two live on the other side of the village, Vera on this. They stopped at the road – probably smoking a cigarette, if I know them – and then the two went left and Vera to the right.'

'The road to Braşov?'

'The small road, past the churchyard. She says she was passing the church and heard a voice call to her. She was surprised, but not afraid, or so she says. This is a quiet village, you understand? Things that happen in cities are not found here. And there are houses all around, to hear if a girl . . .'

'Is being attacked,' I supplied.

'Exactly! So she looked to see who it was, thinking maybe one of her brother's friends was teasing at her, and she kept her voice small so as not to wake those sleeping. She said, who was there.' He paused, noticed the pad still sitting on the desk and returned it to the drawer. 'Who is there? The voice says, "Andrei." This is a common name, so she says, which Andrei? And the voice says, "The one killed near Fagaraş during the War." This was a boy she knew, a boy we buried. His body came here.' Florescu looked up, the moustache lifted in an awkward smile. 'She ran. Down the road to her home.'

Holmes, clearly not as disturbed by what that smile had revealed as I was, asked him for the boy's name, and whether the girl Vera was generally flighty, and I think some other question that went past me, and Holmes may have asked to speak with the girl and Florescu replied that he would ask her father, and then perhaps some other conversation happened but not much, because we were on our feet and out into what seemed to be a beautiful spring morning, and I turned to Holmes and hissed, low, so as not to be overheard.

'Holmes, did you see that?'

'I saw that the man was hiding something, yes.'

'No – I mean his teeth. When he smiled? The Queen's butler has fangs!'

CHAPTER FIFTEEN

HOLMES REARED BACK HIS head to stare at me – and then he began to laugh, so hard he had to lean against the wall behind him.

It was, I realised belatedly, quite a ridiculous thing to say. Loads of people had bad teeth. The character in that *Nosferatu* film hadn't even been given the fangs described in *Dracula*, but instead had the dental arrangement of a rat. Though, come to think of it, those would be easier on an actor than long, pointed incisors: less risk of stabbing through one's lower lip.

'Yes, all right, I'm a bit low on sleep. And I'm sorry we didn't go out earlier last night, when we might have given chase.' He wiped the laughter from his eyes, and my lethargic brain grabbed at a passing thought. 'Still, I don't see how a returned-from-the-dead soldier serves to blacken the reputation of the Queen.'

'Nor do I,' admitted Holmes, to my relief. 'And Florescu's reluctance to speak about it may have been a general wish to keep me from thinking the villagers simple-minded. I suspect this particular event may be a mere jape among the village youth, rather than someone wishing to play up tensions in the village. Father Constantin will know.'

'Is that the priest you waved to across the field yesterday?'

'Priests can be remarkably useful people,' he said by way of answer. 'If nothing else, one generally has some liturgical language or other in common with them.'

'Is that where we're headed?'

'I wish a word with the village doctor first. He should be at the surgery today.'

I'd seen the surgery from the road, a small, neat outhouse attached to the kind of village shop that sold everything from rat traps to collar starch. As we walked up the road, a motorcar approached from the direction of Brașov. As it came closer, I saw that it was the large, new English shooting brake that had been parked before the shop the afternoon we arrived. And indeed, the driver steered it into the wide gravel pad and shut off the motor. His door swung open, and a handsome, clean-shaven man in his late forties stepped out and trotted around to the passenger side.

I could see no passenger – but to my surprise, he opened the rear door to reveal a long, well-padded bench seat running front to back. On it lay a young woman, whom he helped upright and down to the runningboard as a crowd began to pour from the shop, greeting the new arrivals with cries of joy and the offer of supporting hands to help her down to the ground. Their focus, I saw, was less on her than on the blankets she cradled: a new mother, returning to her family. The flock of people started to move away down the road, only to come to a halt when a young man and an older version of the patient turned back. The young man, grinning

126

hugely, seized the doctor's hand to pump it furiously. The older woman added her thanks by reaching up to pat the doctor's cheek with one hand, pulling his head down to her level so as to deliver a kiss to the other side.

The happy family moved off. Only when they had disappeared down a side lane did the doctor turn, revealing the proud smile on his aristocratic features, and move back towards the car, running a quick diagnostic eye on the two of us as he did so.

I gave him a smile and nodded towards his motor. 'You appear to be both doctor and ambulance service.' It was a clever job, converting a long-bedded motorcar designed for rifles and game into safe transport for the ill and feeble. The pad on the long box even had a sort of bumper, to keep the patient in place during turns.

'A difficult birth,' he replied, lifting his leather bag from the floor at the front end of the padded bed. 'We nearly lost both mother and son. I was happy to bring her back, since I was coming to Bran.'

His English was accented but fluent, his features those of Transylvania – a narrow face with high Slavic cheekbones and bright blue eyes, his fine-textured skin gone ruddy with the summer. His hair was going grey; his strong, slender hands might have been designed to wield a scalpel. He wore a tan coloured suit of lightweight wool, bespoke in Paris by the looks of it, rather than native dress. His tie was perfect, his shoes glossy, and he would have been more than a little intimidating were it not for the layer of dust on the motorcar and the fact that he'd gone out his door that morning without his wife or housekeeper noticing the need for a fresh collar, visible as he moved to pull the doors shut.

At last, he turned to face us directly.

Holmes held out a hand. 'Sheldon Holmes. My wife, Mary.'

'How d'you do? The name is Mikó. Come in, you are early for surgery but I can fit you in before others arrive. Which one of you am I seeing today, and what is the problem? *Salut, Casimir – cum esti?*' he called to the man standing in the shop doorway.

Casimir the shopkeeper replied and the two men exchanged rapid-fire conversation – which, to judge by the gestures, had to do with the woman the doctor had brought to town – as the doctor continued moving towards the door of the outbuilding. The door looked new – certainly its paint was pristine – and the shiny lock surprisingly robust. Its key was on the end of his watch chain. The bolt it slid back was substantial. By way of contrast to this daunting security, a friendly little shop bell tinkled overhead as the door came open, and we were ushered into Bran's medical centre.

The first room was where patients waited to be seen, with a few worn chairs, some bright watercolours, and a basket of children's blocks. Beyond it lay the surgery itself, with three chairs, a desk, a curtain in one corner if privacy was required, and three tall, glass-fronted storage cabinets. The space was well maintained and scrupulously clean, with enough modern equipment on the shelves to be reassuring. When I spotted the steam steriliser tucked behind one of the cabinets, it was a relief to know that any treatment we might require here would be linked to the twentieth century, not the nineteenth.

Holmes, however, was interested in a different piece of technology. 'That's quite a safe you have there, Doctor.'

I leant over the desk to see, and yes, it was an unexpected addition to a rural doctor's offices. Not large, but absolutely solid, and planted into the wall. And so recently, the plastered seam had yet to be painted.

The doctor gave a rueful shake of the head. 'Someone broke into the surgery during the spring. They took some money, and a few pieces of equipment that I suppose looked saleable. But they also took the drugs that I keep here – phenobarbital for fits, morphine derivatives in case of emergency surgery, that sort of thing. Sad, to find the problems of the city showing up here.'

He waved us towards the two chairs set on the other side of the desk from his. 'Now, what can I do for you?'

'Doctor Mikó, we do not require medical attention,' Holmes replied, 'merely a few minutes of your time. One of the girls who works in the castle was menaced last night.'

'Menaced?'

'Threatened.'

'I know what "menaced" means,' the doctor said, 'but I know nothing about it. I've only now arrived in Bran. What happened?'

'Just a fright, apparently. But what I wish to ask you about is the other girls, injured during the spring. A kitchen maid who cut her hand, and a child who tripped in the woods.'

The doctor sat back in his chair, fingers threaded together over his stomach as he studied us. 'You are staying up at the castle, I think. I heard there were English visitors up there.'

'We are, yes.'

'You are friends of the Queen?'

'We are acquaintances.'

'Her "acquaintances" do not generally take an interest in the welfare of village girls.'

'The Queen has become aware of some problems in the village. She is concerned, and asked me to see what I could find out.'

'Why you?'

'Why not? You think she should come down and ask, herself?

Or perhaps have the police come?'

The doctor thought for a time, although I had no clue about what. He had given the excited family an honest, open smile, but to us he showed a perfect poker face, handsome and without the least expression. However, in the end, he nodded. 'The child was nothing – some scratches, was all.'

'Where?' I asked.

'Where did she fall? Coming through the woods near the customs—'

'No, where were her scratches?'

'Her hands and knees, naturally. Nothing that some soap and a kiss from her Mama wouldn't treat. A scrape up her right arm that we kept an eye on – children who live on farms are sturdy, but they are also around a lot of germs. A scratch near her eye that could have been serious if it had been two inches over. Some scratches on her neck. Nothing serious, merely a jumble.'

Jumble? 'A "tumble," you mean?' asked Holmes.

'Yes, sorry – a tumble. Little fall.'

'The scratches on her neck. What were those like?'

The doctor sat back in his chair again. 'Are you asking if the marks on the child's neck were puncture wounds?'

I don't know about Holmes, but I was surprised at the question. 'Were they?'

'There is no such thing as a vampire, sir.'

'Of course not. But were they?'

He ran his tongue back and forth across his teeth, as if contemplating the process Holmes was suggesting. 'There were two or three spots where the skin was broken rather than . . . what is the word? *Braided*?'

'*A*-braded.'

'Yes. Sorry, my English is out of practice.'

I stepped in. 'On the contrary, your English is excellent. Where did you study?'

'I began in Vienna, then went to London – Barts. Before the War, naturally.'

'You must enjoy having the Queen to speak with, revisiting the language a little.'

His face went expressionless again. 'I do not see Her Majesty. She has her own physician, who comes when she requires him.'

'Her loss and the area's gain,' I said smoothly. 'The villagers seemed about to strew roses at your feet.'

He relaxed, pushing away the insult of not being thought good enough to attend royalty. 'And I will find a fat, nicely plucked chicken in the motor when I leave this afternoon – perhaps two.'

Holmes took us back to the topic at hand. 'The other girl, the one who cut herself in the castle kitchen. Did you attend her?'

'I did. That was a nasty slice, down the centre of the palm. I had to stitch it. It went bad for a time. The infection finally did heal, but she will never have as much flexibility in that hand as before. The Queen happened to be nearby, and her fast thinking kept the girl from losing too much blood – she grabbed up a clean onion and wrapped the girl's hand around it, hard, to keep on the pressure. She was lucky it was one of my days here in Bran.'

'There is no other doctor in the area?'

'Râşnov has one, four days a week.'

'So they would have sent for him?'

'They would have sent for me. I come when I am needed, no matter the time. I can be here in an hour – half that if I hurry.'

'Your wife must resent the disturbed nights.'

'I have no wife. And the people here are healthy and self-reliant. I am rarely called upon more than once in a month.'

Holmes picked up the questioning again. 'There were no other incidents, while the Queen was away?'

'None. And now this menaced girl last night. What happened?'

'One of the kitchen girls, by name of Vera, was walking home late last night when a voice from the graveyard greeted her and said it was a soldier named Andrei who died in a nearby battle in 1916.'

'Andrei Costea. A hard-working boy, not even seventeen when he died. But Vera Dumitru? I would have thought her one of the more sensible village girls. Thank you for letting me know, I will see her today, before I leave.'

'You live in Braşov?'

'Just north of the town, the family house is there. Convenient for the hospital, but I feel it is important to serve where I am needed as well.'

'A noble commitment,' Holmes said dutifully. 'This young soldier, Andrei. Was his body recovered?'

'I believe so. Yes, I'm sure I have seen his sister visiting him in the graveyard.'

'But you personally did not identify him.'

'I was in uniform myself then. Serving the other country, of course – during those years, Roumania was the enemy.' His wry smile spoke volumes of the changes of fortune in this part of the world – and then his gaze went past us to the adjoining doorway, and we heard the melodious tinkle of the bell. He pulled out his watch, pushed it away. 'I am afraid, Mr and Mrs Holmes, that the surgery is now open and my first patient is here. If you need me for anything else, do not hesitate to have the castle get a message to me. I am here three days a week – and, as I said, other times, *pro re nata.*' He smiled as we shook hands, then turned to his first patient of the day, a young boy cradling his left elbow while his worried mother let loose an incomprehensible flood of words.

CHAPTER SIXTEEN

OUTSIDE, A PAIR OF lads the same age as the one inside were perched on a low wall, trying to look unconcerned over the fate of their friend. I gave them a smile meant to be reassuring, and followed Holmes, who had gone into the shop.

Holmes is over six feet tall. When he plants himself in a room, people tend to edge away, particularly women who do not come up to his chin. Casimir the shopkeeper was somewhat taken aback at the parting of the customers, but as he focused on Holmes, then on me, he rallied enough to say, 'English, yes? How may help?'

I murmured to Holmes, 'Buy some peppermints.'

'I – yes, my good man. Peppermints.' One long finger jabbed in the direction of the glass jar filled with sweets of startling hues. Casimir reached for a scoop and a sheet of paper, and Holmes continued. 'The doctor. He was burgled.'

Casimir looked blank.

'Someone robbed him? Stole?'

'Ah, yes. Stole. Ver' bad. How much you like?'

It was Holmes' turn to give an uncomprehending look, so I answered. 'Two scoops. Please.'

The scoop descended into the jar, and I turned my attention to the shelves, always a fascinating insight into a village's life. The usual sacks of rice and flour were interspersed with ground maize. Tins of foods familiar and not – could those actually be red peppers, rather than tomatoes? – and boxes of everything from candles to laundry soap. Hanging from the rafters were an assortment of dried sausages and cheeses, and the highest shelves, reachable by ladder, held oversized cook pots and paraffin lanterns.

'When was it?'

The scoop stopped moving. 'When. When.' Followed by an address in Roumanian to the audience, who chimed in for a time before consensus was reached. '*Iunie.*'

'June. Does anyone know who did it?'

No hesitation: '*Tigani.*'

A chorus of voices arose, apparently in agreement. Arms were raised, pointing in the direction of Braşov. I held out some coins, letting Casimir choose his payment for the sweets. But while he was doing so, my gaze wandered up . . .

'Earl Grey!'

He looked up from his task, then cast a glance over his shoulder and laughed. Several of our audience joined in. 'You want buy?' He stretched up and took the packet down from its solitary splendour on the shelf. When he placed it on the counter, a puff of dust flew up from its surface.

'No thank you. But you sell it?'

'Sell this, you want. Hey, maybe give it to you free, you buy something else.'

'Is there not much of a market for Earl Grey here, then?'

'You ever taste that?'

'I don't care for it, no. But I believe Queen Marie does.'

'Oh yes. Her Majesty came five years ago, I put that box up maybe next year. Sat there ever since. Should be "Queen Marie Tea" not Earl of Grey.'

Chuckles from the others in the shop told me that this was a local jest. I finished paying for our sweets, and had to be reminded to take them with me as I followed Holmes out.

'So,' I said. 'Everyone in Bran knows the Queen's odd taste in tea, not just those who work in the castle.'

'Given that the packet has been a local gag for several years, that no doubt includes the nearby community of *Tigani*.'

Tigani was a word I recognised, from its European cognates, although they call themselves *Roma*, which simply means people. In England, they are called gipsies, though they migrated not from Egypt, but from northern India, over a thousand years ago. Like any nomads, they do not mix well with the settled peoples. And like my own Jewish people, they tend to be blamed for any problems in a neighbourhood.

Wherever the Roma lived, they would be well familiar with villages rising up with cudgels and flames to drive them out. I thought it unlikely that the local Romany encampment would risk breaking down the door of a doctor's surgery to steal medical equipment and drugs.

The two boys were still on their wall. I fished a mint from the twist of paper and tucked it into my cheek, then passed the remainder to them. From their reaction, you'd have thought the packet contained golden guineas.

Holmes was standing beside the doctor's new-looking motorcar.

I paused at its back window to peer inside.

Shooting brakes are designed as transport for hunting, and generally only have a front seat. Sometimes there is a bench or fold-down seat in the back, but more often, the back is open, a space to transport dogs to a shoot or birds and game home. In this one, the passenger side of the front seat was missing. Instead, seven feet of padded wooden bench ran from dashboard to back door, long enough for the tallest man to stretch out on. The wood was simple pine, bashed about and marked by heels, but the pad was covered with leather, and sturdy brass hinges suggested that the box was used for the doctor's storage as well as transporting pregnant women and injured farmers. Across from it, on the driver's side of the back area, was a shorter, unpadded bench. Gouges and oil stains on the floor suggested that the car was used to shift all manner of things. Including, by the looks of it, his patients' gifts of chickens that were still alive.

'It would make a fine rural omnibus,' I said to Holmes. Who did not hear me, because he was already out of earshot.

I jogged down the road to catch him up, and asked him what he'd thought of the doctor.

He was silent so long, I thought perhaps he hadn't heard, but he'd only been thinking. 'Doctors are a class I find difficult to see with an objective eye. My experience with them has been of polar opposites, with Watson at one end and a handful of perfectly vile individuals at the other. Whenever I encounter a doctor who appears as noble and generous of heart as Watson – well, my impulse is to mistrust the evidence of my eyes.'

'Has that impulse been wrong, ever?'

'It has, unfortunately. Those who raised the most suspicions turned out to be saints, one and all.' He gave a wry laugh.

'And speaking of saints, are we headed to see your priest?' It was far too early for those hours of uninterrupted 'study' that he had promised me, although I could already feel my energies flagging. 'You must have met him last month.'

'I sought him out. As I said, there is nothing quite so useful as a village priest for translating, though generally through a filter of Latin or Greek. Although in fact, Father Constantin speaks English fairly well.'

'I'm glad to know I won't have to struggle with my Latin declensions.'

'Today we require his memory, not his linguistic skills. If, however, it stretches back that far.'

We found Father Constantin in the small garden behind the presbytery, or whatever the Greek Orthodox called their priest's home – although until Holmes greeted him by name, I assumed him to be the gardener.

'*Kaleméra, Patéra Konstantinos.*'

The figure turned, revealing a handsome bearded individual who could not have been much more than forty. He straightened, and beamed. 'Good morning, my English friend,' he boomed, his words heavily accented but quite clear. 'You still here, eh?'

'I am here *again*,' Holmes replied, picking his way through the pepper plants to shake the man's grubby hand. 'And I have brought my wife.'

'Ah! Good morning, Missus! Wife? No – too pretty and young for this old man!' He roared with laughter as he saw me go both pink and speechless.

'Costel,' came a woman's chiding voice from the house. '*Nepoliticos.*'

'Sorry, sorry,' he said, looking not in the least abashed. 'So

138

rude. My wife, she is always reminding me. I tell her when we married, man with my tongue will never make a bishop, yet still, me she marries.'

I'd forgot that Orthodox priests could wed – as clearly this one had. His wife shook her head, then stepped back into the house as the priest crossed the garden, favouring his left foot somewhat, to trade his hoe for the dusty, once-black cassock lying across the back of a bench. He dropped the garment over his head, fished out his beard, and ran a hand down the back of a slim tortoiseshell cat that appeared from between the rows, before gesturing us towards a rustic arbour propped against the side of the house. It had been built out of sapling trunks and large branches, and planted with grapevines – which explained the exaggerated height, since its entire leafy ceiling was covered with long clusters of nearly ripe grapes.

Father Constantin paused on the way in to sluice off his hands. At the entrance to this simple gazebo, he looked over the fruit that was in the full sun, then reached up to snap a heavy stem against his thumbnail.

He held it out to me, dropping it in my cradled palms. The warm fruit, dark globes frosted with the bloom of ripeness, smelt like summer. I pulled off a few, handed the half-cluster to Holmes, and he in turn gave them back to the priest. Father Constantin murmured a blessing and popped a pair of them into his mouth.

For some reason, the fruit in my hand called to mind Persephone and her six pomegranate seeds, that tied her forever to the Underworld. I smiled at my fancy, put a grape in my mouth, and bit down.

What happened next was one of those odd moments that carve themselves into one's memory, an unexpected melding of sensation and thought that, even as it is happening, seems destined to stay in place forever. The crack of the firm grape between my molars, the flood of rich juice with a slight tang in the sweetness. The odour of the priest, an earthy smell of sweat and sunlight, comforting and real. The cool dapple of shade, the deliberation of Holmes' long fingers on the fruit, the cat, eyes half-shut and tail gently encircling its feet in the sun . . .

Like a photograph, the moment was captured. Then I swallowed the grape, followed it up with another, and the three of us ate in silent communion until the stem was stripped bare. And if I was now permanently condemned to return to Roumania because of the snack, well, there could be worse places to spend eternity.

Father Constantin brushed off his hands and laced them over his stomach, a gesture that in the doctor had raised a symbolic barrier, but in this man seemed to do the opposite. 'So my friend and wife, what do you come today for?'

'As you know,' Holmes began, 'I came here to assist the Queen's architect with his plans for the castle's renovations, but I am also quite interested in the ancient traditions of the country.'

'We spoke of many fairy tales, yes. It is a thing our Queens seem to enjoy – the other Queen, too, liked to write book of fairies.'

'Although Queen Marie is less . . . flamboyant than Carmen Sylva ever was.'

Princess Elisabeth of Wied, known by her nom de plume Carmen Sylva, had been a strong candidate for the position of wife to Edward, Prince of Wales, until Bertie decided he didn't care for her looks. Instead, she was passed on to Carol I, Roumania's inaugural king – whom she alienated first by failing to bear a son, then by showing more interest in her eccentric literary and musical salons than the work of royalty, and finally by encouraging an affair between their adopted son and an unmarriageable lady-in-waiting – topping it off, or so rumour had it, by expressing an opinion that elected governments were better than royalties. Marie, first as Crown Princess and then as Queen, had done somewhat better in carrying out her role as Queen Consort without scandal.

The priest cocked an eyebrow at the word *flamboyant*, but when Holmes gave him a few synonyms, the priest nodded. 'A good thing, that our Queen is not like the earlier. Her Majesty was not born Roumanian, but she has been made so.'

'And because of that, and because the people of Bran hold a special place in her heart, she is concerned about the fairy tales they are telling themselves now. The dark ones.'

The priest leant forward to fiddle with the bare grape stem. 'It is . . . troubling, yes.'

'You heard what happened last night? To Vera Dumitru?'

'I went to her, this morning, when I heard.'

'Is she all right?' I asked.

'She will be. Vera has a . . . what do you say – a straight head?'

'Level-headed?'

'Level-headed, yes. Not one to believe in ghosts.'

'Dr Mikó would agree with you.'

'Ah – you saw our doctor, then?'

'He'd just arrived, so he hadn't heard what happened. But he said he'd go by and check on her.'

'He will. To the doctor, all of Bran are his nestlings. Fierce like a mother hawk, you know? Since his wife and small son die of the *gripa*.'

'The flu?'

'My first winter here. Terrible time. So many funerals, chopping holes in frozen earth. I would weep at night.'

141

'I can see that an epidemic would make a doctor very protective.'

Holmes brought us back to the main track. 'What did you learn from Miss Dumitru about the incident? I should like to tell the Queen.'

I expected the priest to claim the sanctity of the confessional or something, but either it did not count as a confession to his mind, or the sacrality of the Queen trumped his own, because after a moment, he started talking.

Just before Christmas, Vera Dumitru, then seventeen, had lost her fiancé in an industrial accident in Braşov. She had loved the boy deeply, and the past months had been very hard on her. (Something in the priest's careful phrases made me wonder if Vera had been pregnant when the boy died – but if so, she must have lost the baby. Or that could have been my imagination.)

Our young friend Gabriela – 'such a responsible girl, keeps house for her father since the mother died' – had recommended Vera at the castle this past spring, when the Queen was expected to take up residence. In Father Constantin's opinion, the friendship and the work helped Vera as much as the income did. She had been looking more cheerful, of late, and she had even been seen batting her eyes at one of the village boys.

'*Şi acum asta*,' he murmured, and shook his head with a sigh. She had set off from the castle with friends last night. They stopped to gossip a little, then split up for their homes, a safe thing in this quiet place. Not like the city, he said, where fathers had to guard their daughters. Here, everyone saw everything, and any sin was sure to be overheard.

The words he used for what Vera heard from the churchyard were nearly identical to those Mr Florescu had given us: Andrei, who was killed near Fagaraş during the War.

'That would have been during the opening months of the Roumanian War, is that right?' Holmes asked.

'Roumania declared war in August 1916, after England and France said, yes, we will give you Transylvania. Andrei joined then – on the Austrian side, of course – and was killed early, in September or October. Almost no training, they were given a uniform and a gun and sent out.'

'Was he brought home then? Or much after?'

'I think not right away. Families suffered, not knowing, but armies had other things to worry about than sending home the dead.'

'You weren't here then, in Bran?'

'No, I was just finished with seminary when War broke out. I joined. In 1916 – Hungary was fighting for two years by then, and I was a captain – I was wounded.' He stuck out his left boot, by way of illustration. 'My foot was no good for rough ground, so I ended up in offices, but I wanted to help people so they later made me medic. I came to Bran six years past, when the old priest died. My wife was born in Braşov. She has family here, cousins, which is good.'

'How old are the cousins?'

'Thirties, forties. An uncle is near to sixty.'

'Would you ask the uncle to talk to me, about when Andrei Costea was buried?'

The blue eyes fixed on Holmes. 'What are you looking for, with these questions?'

'I am looking for answers, Father Constantin. To questions such as: how certain can we be that the man who lies in the graveyard is in fact Andrei Costea? And, did Vera Dumitru know the young man? What made her think the voice was actually him, rather than some lad playing a trick on her? And from there, I have to wonder if there is any link between this young soldier and Queen Marie, or her friends, or her servants.'

Constantin went over this in his mind, frown deepening. 'You think the boy was a deserter?'

'If a few weeks went by between the death in battle and his body arriving here, I doubt anyone opened the casket to examine him. Were there identity tags?'

Constantin shook his head. 'By that time in the War, who knows? There was a letter – his sister has it. And with so many dead men, on a battlefield, mistakes can be made. But if so, why would he not return? Everyone says he was a good boy who loved his brother and sister. He would at least have sent word.

'As for Vera – yes, she knew him. A small village, who does not know everyone? She was young, maybe nine or ten, when he went off to war, but Andrei's house was not far from hers. He would have been friends with her sister and brother.'

'Do the two of them still live here?'

'The sister is in Bucharest. The brother – well, there is an answer to your last question. Vera's brother is our Queen's driver.'

Chapter Seventeen

O UR INTERROGATION OF THE priest was broken up by his wife, coming to take us in, despite our protests, for an early luncheon, since the Father had broken his fast at dawn. As it was not even midday, I anticipated light snacks meant to sustain until the dinner hour. Instead, we were ushered in to a working man's primary meal.

It started with a small glass of *tuica*, the eye-blinkingly powerful plum brandy that Roumanians take before every meal. On top of that went soup and cabbage rolls and the local version of polenta called *mamaliga* and a chicken gone red with paprika, and halfway through it I could see why the good Father put in the hours of physical work in his garden. When we escaped at last, I was all but comatose with the combination of sleeplessness, slivovitz, and stodge. I staggered up the hill, blinking owlishly at the guards, the butler, and the housemaid as I made an unerring line for my bed, only dimly aware of Holmes giving instructions that we intended to immerse ourselves in quiet study and were not to be disturbed until we called.

I passed out, face-down on the covers.

Voices. My face pressed against bedclothes. I had at least managed to take off my spectacles before collapsing, then. Good. It was always inconvenient to reshape the frames.

Unwillingly, I shifted, then dragged myself upright. Stockinged feet – so I'd got my shoes off, too, it seemed.

My ears finally got a message through to my brain: someone was bumping and banging about in the next room. I had been married to the man long enough to recognise the sounds of irritation, and when I went to look, indeed, there was Holmes, on his feet, not napping.

I yawned. 'Did I hear voices? What time – heavens, it's barely one-thirty, I only lay down at one.'

Finally, my eyes joined my ears: he was yanking clothes from his drawers and shoving them with his customary brusque neatness into a valise.

'Are you going somewhere, Holmes?'

Walking past me to the bathroom, he thrust an envelope into my hand.

FAMILY FRIENDS AT ATHENEE PALACE BUCHAREST STOP.

URGENT BUSINESS DEALINGS YOUR PRESENCE NEEDED STOP.

BROTHER M

I sighed, folding the telegram back into its envelope as he came through with shaving kit and toothbrush. 'Holmes, you specifically told me that our presence in Roumania had nothing to do with Mycroft.'

'No, I said that I was already here investigating matters when he wrote, urging me to assist the Queen. It would appear that he now has what he judges pertinent information.'

'About what? Vampires and graveyard voices?'

'About the political situation.'

'I should have known that politics would rear its ugly head.'

'We both acknowledged the possibility from the start, although as you made it clear that you were not interested in politics, I have not required you to consider that aspect.' He jammed the shaving kit into the valise with more emphasis than was required.

'Holmes, I'm sorry, you are absolutely right. The Bolsheviks killed her cousin's entire family, and if they're after this branch as well, we need to know. Give me a minute to wash my face and pack a bag, I'll come with you.'

'That is not necessary. There is plenty for you to do here in Bran.'

'Such as what? Interview Vera's brother – the Queen's driver?'

'I had just finished doing so when Florescu waylaid me with that telegram. The young man knows nothing about Andrei Costea's death other than that a coffin arrived in the last weeks of 1916, with the young soldier's name on it. So far as he remembers, no one looked inside.'

'Another dead end, then. So to speak.' He did not reply, merely scowled at the bag before yanking the top shut and reaching for the buckle. I had to protest. 'Holmes, come now, sulking is beneath you.'

He looked up in surprise. 'You misunderstood, Russell. My irritation is not with you, but with my brother. My instincts are that the answer to our mystery lies here in Bran, not in the capital city. But it would be irresponsible to push away the very real threat of international intrigue simply because it does not fit into some highly incomplete data. We need that information; we cannot expect Mycroft to send his informants here; therefore, I must go to them. I see no reason for both of us to go. I shall return tomorrow on the earliest possible train. See what you can find in the meantime. And if you need me before that, wire the Athenee. I will steal a motor, if I have to, and be here before noon.'

He stepped to the wardrobe to fetch his tightly furled umbrella, picked up the bag, and left.

But as he went past me, he paused to rest his lips in a brief and apologetic kiss against the side of my head.

CHAPTER EIGHTEEN

WHEN HE HAD GONE, I rubbed at my face, then went to run some water into the basin and try to wash away the sleep. I did eye the bed, longing to crawl back into its softness. But if a man more than twice my age could keep moving on no sleep, so could I.

The voices that roused me had apparently been accompanied by a tray of coffee. The dregs remained, tepid and stale but no worse than some things I had drunk in recent travels. And it helped kick my brain into life, reminding me of the morning's conversations with the doctor and the priest.

Bran was like an English village, in that everyone would either be related, or friends, or related to friends. This was an advantage when one was looking for common knowledge that people didn't mind talking about, but if one sought information that people wanted hidden, no gangland snitch would be less of an outcast than a neighbour who gave it away.

There are various ways around the reluctance of witnesses. An amiable face can encourage a loosening of mistrust. A clever interrogator can convince a witness that she knows all about it already, and is only looking for confirmation. Occasionally, one finds a would-be informant just panting to show off his inside knowledge.

Other times, you just have to go looking.

But before I sought out people to question, I needed to take a closer look at my surroundings. Holmes had spent a week here already, and got to know the ground then. Time I caught him up.

And yes, he would probably sleep all the way from Braşov to Bucharest – then have a lovely quiet bed at the Athenee Palace Hotel – but I wanted something to show when he got back, to prove that I, too, had been on my feet and active.

I drained my cold, bitter cup and laced up my boots.

Near our top-floor rooms was a gallery overlooking the courtyard. I went there now, propping my elbows under one of the arched openings as I tried to make sense of the jumble of towers, roofs, and angles before me. This main block of the castle, its eastern tower, had five storeys, beginning with its 'ground' floor entrance and central courtyard – which were actually one flight of stairs up from the true ground level outside. On my right, forming the northern wall, was the donjon, whose flat roof angled sharply down towards the castle interior. The donjon was the highest tower by at least a couple of storeys, turning its blunt north face over the broad agricultural lands in the direction of Braşov. Beyond it, and half its height, were the castle kitchens, outside which stood the courtyard's well.

The far corner of the castle was a round tower with a pointy witch's hat of a roof – the Queen's quarters were there, two storeys below where I stood, framed in my view by the high, wooded hills immediately across the narrow river valley. The round tower was linked in both directions by open-sided galleries, strung along the ramparts and towers that encircled the courtyard. For a woman brought up in English palaces, a woman whose jewels had been worn by Tsarinas, this frontier citadel in a dirt-road village with no electricity made for an unlikely retreat. Even Marie Antoinette had put comfort at the fore, when she played milkmaid in Versailles.

I walked to the far end of the gallery and discovered a very pleasant, sun-soaked terrace, set with two chairs and a small table. It gave a view over the flower gardens and the narrow river valley, and looked a most pleasant spot for morning coffee or sunset drinks.

Although, in the company of Sherlock Holmes, I did not anticipate too many leisurely interludes of sitting and gazing at the scenery.

Nor would I do so now. Instead, I walked through the other rooms on this level, and found that our bright, modern suite – running water *and* a geyser – was the only fully renovated portion. Other rooms were clearly on the schedule, to judge by the neatly stacked builders' materials and equipment. Not that I saw any indication of the builders themselves. Perhaps work was suspended while the Queen was in residence.

But the general abandonment left me free to poke about, trying to make sense of the original purposes of these spaces.

The further one got from our suite of rooms, the fewer signs of renovation. The room beside ours smelt of damp plaster, its walls still dark in places. The next room had new windows, with clear glass and shiny brass hardware, from hinges to latch – but in the room after that, the plaster was crumbling and the worm-eaten, glassless window frames were propped against the corner.

In worst condition were two long, extremely narrow rooms, face to face along the back of the shield wall. Both had lost their ceilings entirely, to gravity or vibrations from the builder's hammer. Their floors were ankle-deep in ancient plaster, revealing the naked, hand-hewn roof beams, thicker than a weightlifter's thigh. There were tiny windows, but no sign of frames or glass.

I made my way back to the stairway, and heard voices just below. I hesitated. Not that I wished to hide my presence, exactly. It was simply easier to explore without the offer of help. So I retreated, and came across another set of stairs, these silent and dark, blockaded by what appeared to be props bracing the walls. However, I could see neither crack nor bulge, and the steps seemed whole, so I ducked under the props and down I went.

This level had a similar maze of oddly shaped rooms, but here, civilisation had taken control. The first room had wide, arched windows overlooking the courtyard, making the space pleasantly bright.

The next room was large, spanning the entire width of this tower, and clearly often used for gatherings small and large. It was scattered with comfortable chairs and massive iron candelabras, bright woven fabrics thrown across the furniture and bearskins on the floor, and bowls of the inevitable flowers. On the white walls hung folk-carvings and ikons. A piano stood against the long back wall – not a grand piano, but still, I had to speculate on how they had got it up here. Next to it stood a fireplace surrounded by a sort of inglenook shelter, suitable for hours of reading in cold weather – and yes, just beyond it was a small library alcove, its wooden shelves well stocked with books. On the north wall, deep windows allowed light inside, although those on the other end of the room were brighter. Armchairs had been placed beneath them, to encourage a reader.

I went down another flight of the blockaded stairway, and found rooms that were perceptibly smaller, with thicker walls and more deeply set windows testifying to the growing tonnage of stones overhead. This second storey appeared to be the family living quarters, linked by those open galleries to the Queen's round-tower flats. Unlike her rooms, however, these had the distinct air of a London men's club: a four-poster bed that looked like something Henry VIII might have pontificated from, dark Turkish carpets that cost more than the Queen's Rolls-Royce, and furniture so massive it would keep the entire castle heated for a winter, were siege engines to draw up outside the door. The rooms were thoroughly, even overly, furnished, but despite the overall dark clutter of a Victorian sitting room, they seemed more staged than lived in, as if chosen to please a person who had yet to arrive.

These, I thought, would be the rooms of King Ferdinand, awaiting his royal return during the hunting season. There was a fine layer of dust over the less obvious surfaces, and I wondered if he would, in fact, return. I had been told that he was ill.

Distracted by the thought, I opened a door and encountered at last another person, a plump and bustling housemaid who gave out a squeak of surprise and tossed half her armful of bedding into the air.

Her Roumanian was unintelligible to me, but I did not need a translation to know that she was expressing surprise, disapproval – and then, catching herself, apology, at having troubled one of the Queen's guests.

I smiled, reassured her that no apology was necessary, helped her retrieve the freshly ironed sheets, and sent her on her way – the transaction having required not a single word of the other's native tongue.

Down, again. On this first floor above the courtyard, one could feel the growing thickness of the walls and the increasing mass of the entire castle: doorways and passages set into a considerable depth of stone, with small, heavily recessed windows. The rooms were dimmer, as a result, and perhaps to compensate, more colourfully furnished. The two rooms built against the shield wall were a dining room and a sort of parlour. The latter, with three deep-set windows facing south, had at some point been saddled with a remarkably ugly set of shelves built into one corner. Across from it stood another of the inglenook fireplaces, this one covered in bright tiles that might have been designed to distract from the embarrassment across the room.

As I turned to leave, I felt a feather's touch of sensation brushing the nape of my neck. I whirled, all senses alert . . . but there was nothing. No sound, no movement of air, just an uneasy feeling, as if something were watching me from the dark.

On the ugly wooden shelf stood an ikon, a Virgin with her wide-eyed, enigmatic gaze. I gave my namesake a respectful nod, then left the room to descend to the ground floor.

These rooms felt like the castle cellars. Walls that were two feet thick on the level of our rooms had grown to ten feet or more, reducing the rooms to half the size of those at the top. The south-facing windows were little more than arched tunnels with glass at the ends. The north wall had no openings at all. The eastern side revealed the single tiny window I had noticed piercing the shield wall, but it seemed that the architect had been happy enough to delay the work down here, ceding it to the builders for their stacks of tiles, plaster, folded tarpaulins, and the like.

I left the dark confines and stepped out into the courtyard. This time of year, the sun reflected warmth and brightness off the high façades, although in the wintertime, it would be dank and uninviting. As with the rest of the castle, steps connected its various levels, paved in wide stones. Behind the well, a massive ivy vine rose up the wall of the kitchen block, with trunks thicker around than my arm and leaves framing an arched entrance. Through it, stone steps ascended, bowed with centuries of wear. I heard a door close. A young housemaid scurried out of the Queen's rooms and along the gallery, then moments later popped out from the ivy-covered archway. She stopped to fetch a bucket of water from the well, and, bent over against the weight, vanished through a doorway.

I had the odd sensation of being inside a living creature made of stone and brick, its veins filled with scurrying workers, its lungs breathing in life and beauty, exhaling decision and calm.

Castle Bran was the creation of one woman. Queen Marie had received it as a gift, an unloved, abandoned building, and was bringing it to life. The rest of the country might be ruled by her husband and the men of the government, but in this small corner, she was the absolute Queen, as her grandmother Victoria had been of an empire. Marie seemed to fill every corner, touch every room – even those that were derelict and deserted. Castle Bran was coming to manifest the mind and heart of Queen Marie, from the exuberant dahlias to the dusty corners of her husband's rooms. Underneath the bright rugs and ornate ikons – and certainly while standing in the close, oppressive darkness of the ground-floor cellar – one could sense Bran's long, cold, brutal history, those generations of soldiers and border guards, bored and angry and occasionally afraid, but such was the force of the Queen's personality, Castle Bran now turned its face resolutely to the sun, and would not hear any suggestion of death or war or discomfort.

I watched as another maid, an older one, walked with more deliberate steps towards the Queen's rooms, and disappeared inside them.

Enough meandering: there was work to be done, citizens to be questioned. I turned away – then tripped and nearly went sprawling over a calf-high ball of white fluff.

The creature yelped, I cursed, and jammed my arm hard against a stone pillar. I didn't quite go down, but waved my hand around to cool the scrape on my palm, looking down to see if I had flattened the animated fluff.

In the corner of my eye, I saw Gabriela, moving forward to retrieve the creature.

'Sorry,' I said, 'I didn't see it – ah, pardon.'

Not Gabriela, rounding up the Queen's wayward pet, but a young woman very like her.

A face as solemn as it had been in the studio portrait, blue eyes nearly as dark as its paint, in a round face that was not quite beautiful. She was shorter than I by a couple of inches, but equally tan with the sun, and wore a costume very like the Queen's at dinner – embroidered blouse with full sleeves, pale underskirt under a dark overskirt, her short hair sticking out from under a silken bandanna with a bright floral pattern. But though she was dressed like a native and looked like the castle maid, down to the little gold crucifix at her neck, I had not a moment's doubt as to her identity.

The daughter, Ileana.

CHAPTER NINETEEN

SHERLOCK HOLMES SCOWLED OUT at the Roumanian countryside passing slowly by. He had not been impressed with the country's train system last month, and today's journey was doing nothing to change his mind. In Braşov, he had managed to claim a corner of what purported to be a first-class compartment, but if things grew worse when they reached Sinaia – as they had on his earlier such trip – he would have to consider some means of taking revenge on his brother.

The engine had managed to clear the Predeal pass without actually breaking down, and would soon pull into the tumult of Sinaia, summer capital and resort town for the wealthy and unemployable. After that would follow four hours of loud voices, unwashed bodies, and endless maize fields all the way to Bucharest. He did not imagine he was going to sleep.

Not that he was going to sleep even before reaching Sinaia. There were matters on his mind, matters that called for decision.

Sherlock Holmes did not at all care for the sensation of being undecided.

Four and a half years of being married to Mary Judith Russell, and he was still finding the adjustment difficult.

For his entire adult life, until the night he signed his full name upon a church register, Sherlock Holmes had been accountable to no one. All decisions were his alone, all secrets his to be kept or shared. Any loyalties owed – to monarch, client, or even brother – were entirely secondary to his unflinching pursuit of the case at hand. When he judged it necessary, he had bullied, ignored, and lied, even to his friend Watson, without hesitation.

But not to a wife. A wife meant a contract of a different sort, one that stood before him and demanded an honest reply.

Serving the needs of brother and Britain had become increasingly incompatible with his partnership with Russell. He had already forced her uncomfortably close to a lie regarding Mrs Hudson's situation – forced her to prevaricate to *him* – and he could not avoid an open confrontation forever. Oh, husbands and wives deceived each other all the time – a detective learnt that early in his career – but a lie here would fester and spread, deadly as a case of blood poisoning.

Almost as deadly as an agreement to leave matters undiscussed.

Four and a half years ago, Russell had come to him with a charade that a casual and convenient partnership might be an option. He had known the proposal was coming, had even anticipated its timing to the approach of her twenty-first birthday. So he had been prepared, and had taken care to meet her hopeful fairy-tale ending with a cold, brutal message: pretence was not a thing that could survive between them. It had to be the truth in all its manifestations, or nothing.

That was one of the few times he'd been aware of their difference in age: one life new enough to retain some wishful fantasies, the other having survived half a century of hard experience.

He had made it clear, on that cold London night, that the decision was entirely hers. He occasionally wondered what would have become of him – of them both – if she had not found a path to their particularly colourful wedding, some weeks later.

Amusing, and ironic, that a man known to the world as a cold thinking machine could be more clear-sighted than a woman when it came to emotional truths. But just because emotion interfered with rational decision did not mean a person could dismiss its effects. He was quite clear that the problem of Mycroft's demands would have to be dealt with, very soon.

In the meantime, his brother had a point: Roumania was both vulnerable and essential, and required all the help Britain could offer. If Queen Marie's reputation was being attacked, whether by a personal rival or some political enemy out to split the country, he might be in a position to do something about it.

He only wished that he did not feel the same danger to his partnership with Russell. He'd spent years learning to bite his tongue when she put herself at risk, and even more years learning to accept the value of her occasionally opposing views. He enjoyed . . . well, he enjoyed a great deal about Russell, including the occasional rivalry, but only because of their deeper singularity of purpose.

So, no: he was not at all pleased to have another sharp wedge poised over their relationship – a wedge by name of Mycroft Holmes.

His mind circled around and around the matter. He may have slept, for a time, before he noticed that the train was approaching

Bucharest. He folded away his unread newspaper, tucked the cigarette case back into his pocket. He would meet with Mycroft's collection of Communist agitators, spies, and possible traitors, then escape as soon as he could, back into the clean mountain air.

He wondered how Russell was getting on with the Queen. Two strong-willed women being polite over the dinner table. Rather unfortunate the daughter could not be there, too – it would be interesting to see how the next generation of Victoria's heirs was turning out.

Chapter Twenty

'No, I'm the one who should apologise,' Princess Ileana protested. She bent to gather up an armful of fluffy white dog, her deep blue eyes studying me over the creature's pointed ears. 'Frost is so small, people are forever tripping over him. You are Mrs Holmes, I believe? Florescu told me you were here. He said that Mother had a meeting then went for a ride, but she should be back soon. Welcome to Bran.' Her voice was low for a girl her age, her accent a combination of crystalline English royalty heavily woven with threads of German and Roumanian.

'Thank you, Your Royal Highness. And it's no problem, I should have been watching where I was walking. I simply . . . didn't expect to see you here.'

It sounded accusing – but then, it was. The Queen was not going to be pleased at seeing her baby in Bran.

'I had to come. I have responsibilities here – and in any event, Father hasn't been well, so he's staying at Peleş rather than our actual house, and Peleş is so big and formal, and everyone is tiptoeing around the halls so they don't wake him, and though I'm a good nurse, all he really needs is rest. So I had the car bring me here.'

My face must have shown surprise, although it was more at the idea of a sixteen-year-old claiming 'responsibilities' than the rest of her sentence. But she took it as a reaction to palace servants going against the wishes of their Queen, because her face suddenly shed its solemnity. 'I told them that if they didn't bring me over, I'd saddle one of the horses and ride here. I think they believed me.' She put down the dog, which promptly took off after a sparrow.

It might be fifteen miles as the bat flew to Sinaia, but it had to be thirty miles by road – a long ride on the back of a horse. But for a sixteen-year-old girl with a sturdy mount? Not impossible. And there were probably back ways over the hills.

None of that mattered: she was here, and I seemed to be not only Holmes' spy, but the designated adult in the room. So I gave in – vowing to fade briskly into the background when the Queen returned.

'I can see why you wouldn't want to keep away from Bran. I've just been exploring the castle – what a fascinating place.'

Her posture shifted, betraying relief – she was not quite as self-assured as she would have me think. 'Isn't it, though? I wish we'd had Bran when I was little – I'd have led my governess a merry hunt through all the nooks and crannies.'

'Some of which do appear to be falling down, just a bit.'

'I know – my first summer here, Mother wouldn't let me explore without a footman. I still live in hope that I'll spot the hidden passages.'

'Are there any?'

'There's sure to be at least one, don't you think? This was a fortress – and what commander would hole up in a castle with no back door?'

It was a valid thought. And who would know castle architecture better than a granddaughter of kings?

'I shall keep my eye out for hidden doorways,' I assured her.

'Have you seen any of the ghosts? How long have you been here?'

Ghosts inside the castle, as well as out? 'We came on Thursday. Which ghosts are those?'

'I've never actually seen one, but I've heard them, and Gabi says – do you know Gabi?'

'Gabriela? The kitchen maid?'

'Right. I call her my almost-sister – she's a year younger but she looks more like me than 'Lisabeta or Mignon do. Gabi tells me everything that's going on here, and she says that Bran is haunted.'

'Has she seen them?'

'She hasn't, no. But she says others have. When Mother and I were here in the spring, I kept poking around in hopes of seeing one, but I never did. I heard some peculiar noises, but that was all. Probably something falling apart. Bran is pretty old – it's loads better now than when we first saw it, five years ago. In fact,' she confided, 'the city had been trying to give it away for a while, to save them the expense of pulling it down. They'd actually given it to the Germans during the War, but when the Germans lost and Transylvania was returned to Roumania, they dusted off the documents and gave it to Mother instead.' She paused, thinking over what she'd told me. 'She doesn't like people to know, so probably you shouldn't say anything.'

'I promise.'

The blue eyes twinkled, and she stepped forward to tuck her arm through mine. 'Oh, Mrs Holmes, you and I are going to be great friends, I can tell.'

'Call me Mary,' I said.

'Aunt Mary it is. Let's go liberate some biscuits from the kitchen and I'll show you the best place in the castle to sit. When I was down here earlier, Cook was making my favourite walnut biscuits – they're usually for Christmas, but we're never here then and I love them so, Cook bakes some whenever I come. Can you smell them? Divine!'

The odour of biscuits was imperceptible beneath those of onions and roasting chicken, and the kitchen was intent on the coming dinner hour. As we entered the kitchen, I let the Princess and her fluffy little dog go ahead, both to be well clear of any explosion from the commander of the kitchen's army – I knew cooks and their ways all too well – but also to watch her interactions with the servants.

Those born to the purple are brought up to assume that the world loves them. They expect bent necks and doffed caps, interpreting deference as respect and obedience as agreement. Ileana called Gabriela her sister, but it would never occur to her that while Cinderella's half-sisters went off to the ball, that less favoured sibling had been scrubbing the fireplace.

On the other hand, Ileana's youth appeared to have created a degree of actual, rather than symbolic affection. Instead of bristling at the invasion, Cook gave Ileana an indulgent smile, as she would a child – while the girl, on entering this servants' realm, made it clear that she knew she had no rights here. There was respect on both sides.

In another year, I thought, the Princess would no longer be

treated as a child of the castle. In two years, all those spines would go formal and the word *ma'am* would enter the conversation. But for now, she would be permitted the same freedom underfoot as her dog.

And be provided with the same ungrudging treats: in the dog's case a scrap of browned pastry dough, in Ileana's a little basket of fat, round biscuits oozing a dark filling.

She gave a little squeal and kissed the cook's cheek, took a bite of one of the rounds, made a sound of appreciation, waved to Gabriela, elbow-deep in potatoes, then gathered up the dog and led me out.

Within a few steps, her bouncing gait had slowed to a more adult pace and she'd fed the uneaten half of her treat to the dog.

She glanced at me. 'I do adore them, but if I ate everything Cook gives me, I wouldn't be able to waddle up the stairs.'

And stairs were clearly on the agenda. I wasn't sure how many storeys we climbed, but we came out at the top of the tower, with a view that would have satisfied the most diligent of Saxon watchmen.

Even then, she was not finished, but climbed up onto a view portal – a window that had never held glass – and settled down with her feet dangling over the side.

A long, *very* long way above the ground.

'Up here, one is the first to know when a visitor is coming. When Mama has been away, I watch for the sparkles of her motor to let me know she's returning.' She realised that I was not pressed up against her shoulder, and scrunched aside on the stone ledge, patting the space beside her. 'There's plenty of room. Come on up. One can see forever.'

'Thank you, I'm fine here.' *Where I have a chance to grab that nice sturdy sash you're wearing, as you go flying down the roof tiles.*

She gave me an encouraging smile. 'That's all right, my sisters don't like heights, either. Here, have a biscuit.' She held out the basket of treats. When I had taken one, she carefully made her own selection based on some quality I could not guess, then set the basket down beside her. She pulled hers apart, again dropping one half into the waiting mouth of the small dog.

This seemed to be a practised ritual, since once the morsel was swallowed, the dog did not continue to beg but instead trotted over to paw at a dust-coloured cloth against the wall, then curled up, nose to tail.

I leant a shoulder gingerly against the stones, taking care to come nowhere near touching the precariously balanced royal princess.

'*I* have seen a ghost,' she declared. 'Just not here.' She examined the crisp brown shape in her hand, and bit off a neat corner.

'Where was it?'

'At Windsor. After nine hundred years, I suppose it's bound to have a few.'

'Do you know whose ghost it was?'

The question surprised her into craning around to look at me. 'You don't doubt that I saw it?'

I made a gesture with my hand to indicate that there were more things in heaven and earth than were dreamt of in my philosophy. She turned away, satisfied with my response – and, apparently, with my question.

'I think ghosts are those who died dissatisfied. I think people who are happy when they die, or at least fulfilled, simply pass on. But people who are not finished with life – because they died too soon, or there was something on their minds – they linger on in hopes of finding an answer.' She glanced back again, to see how I was taking this.

I was less troubled by her imagination than by her balance, so I nodded. She turned back to her meditations.

'The ghost I saw in Windsor was a little boy. I think he died in one of the chimneys. Did you know that when great-granny came to the throne, they used to send children up to clean the chimneys? *Inside* them? And they would sometimes get stuck?'

'I have heard that, yes.'

'I think the boy I saw was one of those. Mother said I was dreaming it, but I'm sure I was there in the room, walking around at night.'

'How awful,' was all I could think of to say.

'Isn't it? When I become a Queen, I will never allow that kind of thing to happen.'

I choked a little on my sugary mouthful – and on the girl's flat assumption that 'Her Majesty' lay in her future. But then, royalty was the family business: both sisters and grandmothers were Queens, along with various aunts. Her mother's first cousins had occupied the thrones of six different European countries. Why not this tomboyish figure?

'Did you ever read Charles Kingsley's book?' she asked.

'*The Water-Babies*? A long time ago, yes.'

'Mother says the story helped change things. They'd had a law against it for years, but everyone ignored it until *The Water-Babies*. People were so upset at the idea of a boy forced to climb up chimneys, how he could never get clean, that the practice was banned. Mother and I read a lot of stories. She writes them, too, did you know? She gives them to me to read first, to see if I like them. Fiction can make people think. Not always, of course –

sometimes they're just for fun. I like those, too.'

'Your mother says you like detective stories.'

'I do. They're so clever, people like Sherlock Holmes and Father Brown. However, I have to tell you, my heart belongs to Bulldog Drummond,' said the future Queen.

'Good choice.'

'Though one does wish there were *some* girls in those stories. I tell Mother she ought to write tales where girls get into adventures, rather than fairy stories and romances, but she just says that nobody would believe them. Girls never get to have any adventures, do they?'

'Oh, you'd be surprised. But tell me about the ghosts in Bran Castle. The ones you've heard.'

'I don't know that one can hear a ghost, there's another name for that.'

'Poltergeist?'

'That's it – a spirit that knocks things about.' Which, though I would not tell her, generally appear in the vicinity of an adolescent girl who feels that not enough attention is being paid her. 'Not that I've seen things moving, just heard things. Mother says it's timbers settling, but once or twice things have gone missing. And I thought once I heard a voice speaking.'

'Saying what?'

'I couldn't hear the words, and it was just for a few seconds. And,' she admitted, 'it was at night, so it could have been rats. But the ghost the kitchen girl saw, that was during the day. And Gabi says it was someone she knew – someone Vera knew, that is.'

'Vera Dumitru?'

'Is that her last name? The new girl in the kitchen.'

'Why didn't anyone tell me?' She looked surprised, and I hastily felt around for an explanation. 'My husband is an ardent folklorist. He will be thrilled to hear that Castle Bran has a ghost.'

'You can tell him, but it's best not to talk about it too openly. Vera didn't tell anyone but Gabi and me – and Florescu, of course, he knows everything. But if Cook finds out, she'll want to fire Vera for drinking, or being mental.'

'Whose ghost was it?'

'I don't know his name, just that he was a soldier who died in the War.'

I stared at the back of her head. The girl who'd heard the voice from the cemetery was the girl who had seen the very same ghost back in the winter? Why hadn't Florescu told us this? Vera Dumitru moved to the top of my list of people to see.

Ileana had not noticed my preoccupation. 'There she is,' she said now. I followed her gaze, wondering which distant shape might possibly be recognisable as a young woman she'd known briefly four months earlier – and then I saw the approaching figure on the horse. 'She' was not the girl servant visited by ghosts, but the Queen.

People came from their houses to greet her. They ran along the road, held up their babies, clustered around her horse. Progress slowed, then halted, amidst a crowd of men and women who pushed forward to kiss the royal hand and receive the royal blessing.

'They love her so.' Ileana seemed to be speaking to herself.

'One can see why,' I replied.

'She is worthy of them, isn't she? Do you know, I'm nearly the same age that Mother was at her engagement.'

Thinking of this girl's position – and particularly, how near she came to having been wed to the Tsar's haemophiliac son – I could think of no response beyond a noncommittal noise. She glanced over her shoulder at me. 'Florescu says your husband is considerably older than you.'

'That is true.'

'Was it arranged?'

'The marriage? Good Lord, no! I mean, no, Your Highness, we chose each other.'

The solemn eyes studied me. 'Do you love him?'

'I . . .' That bluntness had to be from the Roumanian part of her heritage. Or perhaps it was the prerogative of royalty. Still, the child deserved honesty. 'I do, yes. I also like him, and learn from him, and am challenged by him. All those things are important.'

She gave a little sigh, and turned back to watch her mother's progress through the village. 'I hope I get *some* say in who I marry. People seem to, these days. I met some of the girls at the school I shall be going to in England next month, and they talked about nothing but marriage. I don't think they liked me much. Gabi said she should go in my place, since nobody there could tell the difference. I told her that her English isn't good enough, but she just said she'd keep her mouth shut and look down her nose at them all, and nobody would know.'

I laughed, glad enough to move away from the topic of marital relations. Not that school rivalries were much easier. 'School is easier for those whose lives are small,' I told her. 'Most often, happy and successful adults went through miserable times when they were younger.'

'Then I ought to be the happiest adult imaginable.'

I was not quite sure how to address this statement – but the search for mild reassurance vanished with what she did next.

She leant forward. My hand shot out, fingertips poised to dig into her sash, not quite making contact. She was looking at something, far below. I craned around to see past her, but all I saw was the little green park at the base of the castle, where the stream had been encouraged to form a small lake.

'There's only one thing Bran is missing,' she said in a dreamy voice. 'Sailing. Mother is building a house down on the Black Sea. Entirely different from Bran – open and new and filled with sunlight. She's going to leave it to me in her will. And the very best thing is the sailing. One can step off the land and into a boat, and put up the sail and fly, just fly. When I am older, I shall sail to Istanbul and through the Straits and out into the Mediterranean, and only stop when I have friends to visit or want my dinner on the land.'

The girl gave a small sigh at the inadequate little puddle below, then reached for the basket and upended the contents over the abyss. She looked over her shoulder again, her face transformed by a look of mischief. 'You won't tell Cook, will you? That I fed the birds with her special nut biscuits?'

'Not a word.'

She grinned, and handed me the basket, swinging her legs into the room. Her feet hit the floor, and I took my first full breath since we'd arrived in the room. She brushed off her skirt.

'I should get down to the stables before someone tells Mama I'm here. Do you want to come?'

'I was heading for the village, so I'll go with you as far as the road.'

'Wise of you to be headed the other way,' she said with a grin as mischievous as anything Gabriela could produce. 'Mother's going to be so irritated that I didn't stay in Sinaia. As if I can do anything for Father other than read aloud to him while he snores.'

As we wound our way through the castle and out of the door,

servants and guards snapping to attention at every turn, I asked her about the 'responsibilities' that had brought her to Bran.

'Oh, the girls,' she said in surprise. 'I promised them I'd be back, to see if they need anything. You see, without me – without someone like me – the girls here are a little trapped. For some girls, Bran is fine, they want nothing but to marry and have children. But for others, that's not enough. They need school and training and someone who can give them a hand. Girls can be doctors and teachers and innkeepers and, well, everything boys can, really. It's just that the first steps are harder for them, without help.'

'That is very generous of you.' And perhaps she wasn't as oblivious to the lives of the Cinderellas around her as I'd thought.

'I have more than any of them can imagine. Befriending them and helping them out is the least I can do.'

'Is that – I noticed the little cross you wear.' It was heavier and more intricately decorated than those I'd seen on Gabi and the other young maid, but similar from a distance.

'Oh, yes,' she said, brushing it with a finger. 'One of them admired it last summer, so I had some made to give to them. Each is a little different – only Gabi's has dogwood flowers like mine – but they're also the same. Like a membership token. Or promise, I suppose.'

Noblesse oblige, in its purest form.

The guard held the door for us to exit, clicking his soft-soled heels and coming to attention. As we walked down the outer stairs, I thought of another question.

'You said you'd heard noises, inside. Your poltergeist. Where was it?'

She gestured at the wall beside us. 'In the music room once. It sounded like someone dropped a cup, but there was no one there.

The other time was the dining room. I was looking for a book I'd left somewhere, and heard a kind of a scraping noise. It stopped before I had got far enough into the room to see.'

'Was this recently, or last summer?'

'I only really noticed it in the spring when we came. Though as Mother says, there are always creaking sounds in a house this old.'

'So, in April.'

'That's right. Why? Does it matter?'

'Just curiosity. I haven't heard anything yet.'

'I insist that you tell me if you do. I should like nothing better than to go hunting ghosts with you.'

I might need to enlist the help of Bulldog Drummond, I reflected. If for no other reason than to keep this vigorous and sharp-minded young lady from getting into trouble.

CHAPTER TWENTY-ONE

HOLMES FOUND BUCHAREST EVEN more sweltering than it had been on his previous visit. The taxi from the station panted and stank through the streets. The people on the pavements sought out any available scrap of shade. The Athenee Palace, little more than a decade old, was a blunt block of a building separated from a busy street by an equally crowded pavement. Around the streetcars and motorcars dodged pedestrians and horse-drawn carts, a reminder that busy cities had creatures other than pigs, chickens, and naked infants in their roads.

Inside the hotel, all was dignity and welcome and cool. The doormen and inside staff greeted him with a promise of calm and comfort. One young man took his bag, a slightly older one welcomed him – in English, recognising some faint hotelier's clues – and the most dignified yet murmured his own welcome and proffered the book and a pen.

However:

'Mr – Holmes, is it? Sir, there is a . . . person. With a message. We suggested that he leave it with us but . . .'

Holmes turned to follow the disapproving eyebrow. There in a discreet corner, half-hidden from view, was indeed a *person*, a young man, getting to his feet. They met halfway across the lobby, the stranger drawing an envelope from an inner pocket. 'Mr Holmes?'

'Sometimes.'

'Your brother asked me to give you this. He told me to put it into your hand.'

Holmes took it – then shot out the other hand to seize the boy's arm, propelling him back to the chair.

'Sir! I'm sorry – I don't know what – just a little lightheaded. The heat, you know.'

'You came by aeroplane,' Holmes said. 'And your stomach didn't care for it.'

'How did you – oh, right. You're like your brother.'

'Stay there,' Holmes ordered, and strode back to the hotel desk. 'That young man is quite exhausted and no doubt dehydrated. Give him a room, and food when he wants it, add it to my bill. Oh – and have his clothing cleaned.'

He ripped open the envelope, and read Mycroft's handwriting. Three names, three brief descriptions, two telephone numbers. Nothing, in fact, that could not have been sent by cable, saving the poor boy a trip. He shook his head and went back to the green-looking lad, who bore the stink of a long and queasy trip about him. 'What is your name?'

'Warburton. Bill.'

'Mr Warburton, this gentleman will see you to your room upstairs. Sleep. Eat when you can. And give him your clothes. The maids will return them to you in the morning.'

The boy looked down at his woollen sleeves, which showed every one of the 1,300 miles they had travelled since leaving London, and stammered his thanks, but Holmes had already turned away, to demand a map of the city and a means of exchanging his francs for lei.

In his own room, Holmes ordered a pot of coffee and picked up the telephone to hunt down his brother's short list of informants. The first, an Anarchist known to favour the Hungarian cause, proved to be in hospital – with, bizarrely enough, a harsh case of the gout. The second, a Communist named Mihai Dalca, was in Moscow, although it seemed that there was a secretary by name of Ivanov who was acting in his place. The third was an Englishman, whose job description gave Holmes pause.

Deep in thought, he set the bathwater running, shaved, and donned a fresh shirt, heading down the stairs to beard a Bolshevik agitator in his den – or at least, in his outdoor café.

Chapter Twenty-two

I WALKED WITH Princess Ileana down the hill to the stables. The Queen was just arriving, and I watched her dismount to greet the villagers pressing up to be near her. It was a startlingly feudal scene, in this modern era when crowds were things to be kept back from royalty and handshakes were indications of honour. Caps were doffed, forelocks tugged, the Queen's outstretched hand seized and kissed, over and over again.

The gleaming horse was led away by a stable hand. The Queen continued her gracious benedictions – until she happened to glance up and see us, over the heads of the short villagers.

An expression of astonishment and horror opened up on the Queen's beautiful features. She dropped her hand and her royal dignity to march forward, villagers parting like the Red Sea. But two of the men who had come out of the stables were moving forward to sort out matters, so I let Ileana go forward without me.

Cowardice? No doubt. But I was here as an investigator, not a counsellor, and I had no wish to be drawn into that battle. Much better to spend my evening out of the way, until the tears had dried and nerves settled.

Which was why I had already asked one of the guards to inform Florescu that I would not be there for dinner.

It took me time and trickery to locate the house of Vera Dumitru. Doors closed in my face, literally and figuratively, until I slipped into the village shop just as it was closing and came out with a quantity of boiled sweets. I found a low wall to sit on, making a show of choosing the very best one and inserting it into my blissful mouth.

I sucked, rattling the thing around my teeth, and though I had been afraid it was too near to the dinner hour for my purposes, I soon felt eyes upon me – and on the brown paper twist at my side. I sat, intently studying the sign with hours for the doctor's surgery: Monday, Thursday, Saturday, 10.00 a.m. to 7.00 p.m. Meaning that he should have been here, but his shooting brake was not in its space. No doubt if he was off with another patient, the village would know where to find him.

At last, a small, grubby child wandered up, kicking a rock and all but whistling his nonchalance. I could hear giggles and whispers in the background.

I nodded to him, and picked up the bag to choose another sweet, deftly palming the first sticky ball as I did so.

'Allo,' he said.

'Good afternoon, sir.'

More giggles from behind the hedge. The urchin eyed me for any signs of mockery. I gave him none.

'Where you from?' he demanded. Clearly, he already knew, having addressed me in sounds that resembled English.

'London,' I replied, figuring that the words *East Dean, Sussex* would not mean much to him.

'Why you come?'

'To see the Queen.'

'Why?'

Our conversation was deteriorating, somewhat. 'I wanted to see Bran. Good place. Good haystacks.' He looked blank, so I turned to point at one of the shaggy green monsters looming nearby. 'Haystack.'

He made a sound that resembled *cabbage*, which seemed doubtful – perhaps I'd have recognised its Latin cognates had it been on a page rather than in a throat. I nodded. 'Great cabbages, here in Bran.'

He goggled at me, and his companions started rolling about laughing. We both ignored the shaking branches.

'Do you know Bran?' I asked, tossing the bag of sweets up and down in my palm to reinforce his attention.

'Yes of course.'

'No, I don't think so. You are too small.'

Our audience went still at this insult. The urchin stared daggers at me. 'I not small,' he snapped, ending the sentence with a phrase that I was afraid I could guess at, all too well.

'Prove it,' I said, then simplified it to, 'show me.'

He planted his feet, put his fists on his hips, and raised his chin, accepting the challenge. I narrowed my eyes, then deliberately reached into the bag and held up one sweet between thumb and forefinger. 'There is a black rooster in Bran. Show me.'

I had seen the rooster not twenty minutes before, and indeed, he led me straight to it. I handed him the sweet, then held up another. 'The house of the man who plays the concertina.' The word stumped him, until I demonstrated the pushing-pulling action, and off we went, trailing a company of small boys.

Next came: the house of the driver of the Queen's big car. This proved to be a tiny, spotlessly clean place on the other side of town. Then: the postal box (which I had seen across from the church the day before). When there were six sweets bulging the sides of his face out, I shook my head, as if to say these were too easy, and challenged him with 'The house of Vera, who works in the castle.'

When I had that one, I threw up my hands, admitting defeat, and handed over what was left of the sweets. I watched him march proudly away to our audience, where he started plucking half-sucked sweets from his mouth and presenting them to chosen others.

The untouched ones vanished into some grubby fold of his clothing.

And I walked up to the door of the Dumitru house.

Chapter Twenty-three

Sherlock Holmes knew the kind of Bolshevik he would encounter the moment the voice on the telephone informed him that *Tovarisch* Ivanov, the secretary in charge while *Tovarisch* Dalca was off in Moscow, would be taking an early dinner with friends at La Cina, before an evening political rally.

La Cina was one of the most fashionable restaurants in Bucharest, a brief walk from the Athenee Palace, and despite the heat and the early hour, its terrace was crowded with bureaucrats in no hurry to set off for their homes.

Many of the men here were clean-shaven. Most of the women had short hair, although their skirts were several inches longer than was the fashion in Paris, or even London. Holmes ignored the maître d' who had stepped forward to greet him, running his eye over the men with beards – only to catch on an unexpected but familiar face. After a moment, he smiled. He might have known.

He dodged La Cina's greeter and wound through the tables,

waiting for his target to notice him. An expression of horror came onto the man's face – satisfying confirmation that Sherlock Holmes still held some sway in the underworld.

Also satisfying, to think that there were some things Mycroft did not know.

The man's requisite beard did not conceal the sick look that came over his face as Holmes approached. His three companions, two men and a woman, broke off to look up at the approaching Englishman.

'Good evening, Comrade . . . "Ivanov",' Holmes said. 'Or should I say, Mr—'

'Hah!' The man's loud exclamation of joviality brought nearby conversation to a halt. 'My old friend from London. Vat you doing here?'

'We need to speak,' Holmes said. 'Your friends are welcome to remain. Shall I have the waiter bring another . . . ?'

'No, we just are finishing, eh, *tovarischi*? I see you later, we finish business then, yes?'

The other three, startled at the abrupt dismissal, nonetheless rose and made their rather confused way out of the restaurant. The bearded man left behind, meanwhile, scowled at Holmes and lowered his voice, the heavy Russian accent disappearing along with the bonhomie.

'What the devil are you doing here?'

'Good to see you, too, Johnston. I had no idea there was money to be had in the Roumanian Communist Party.'

'Tell me what you want and—' He broke off, seeing the approach of two heavy-laden waiters, who began to distribute plates. The waiter paused when he noticed that Holmes was not the man who had been in that chair when the dinners were ordered, but the Bolshevik secretary gestured impatiently, and down the plate went.

'You might as well eat that,' he told Holmes, sourly.

Holmes surveyed the ownerless plates. Did he want to break bread with a man like Ernie Johnston? The man was a criminal. On the other hand, he'd always been more rogue than thug, and had been known to return a portion of his larcenous takings to the widows and orphans left behind. Under some urging. And one assumed that the Communist Party was paying for the meal: even Russell would agree that an English gentleman had the moral obligation to make whatever inroads possible into the Party's finances.

So he traded the mass of food before him for the more manageable quantity that the woman had ordered, helped himself to an untouched glass, and picked up his utensils.

'The beard is new,' he remarked.

'Itches like billy-o, but it's part of the job.'

'What are you up to, Johnston?'

The man looked at the surrounding tables, then sighed, and swung his backside over to the chair next to Holmes, taking the plate with him. When he spoke, his voice was barely audible amidst the chatter.

'It fell smack into my lap, I tell you. And say what you will, Mr 'Olmes, I'm a loyal subject of the King – I had an obligation, don't you know? So, four, five months past, I was down the pub when in strolls this bearded lot of ruffians. They was up to no good, anyone could see, and the barman wasn't keen on serving them, but I says, oi, nuffin's wrong with their bees n' honey, and so he gave 'em their pints and they bought me one and we got to talking. And they were practically drippin' notes out of their pockets so I just sort of . . . stuck.'

'And you ended up in Bucharest?'

'Funny old world, innit?'

'How long have you been here?'

'Seven weeks. Godawful place. I sometimes put a block of ice in the tub, just to cool off.'

'And how long do you plan on staying?'

Another sigh, and the man's fork went down. 'Was going to be three weeks. But if you're here, maybe you should tell me.'

'I'm not after you, Johnston.'

'No?'

'Not unless you give me a reason.'

The bearded man resumed his meal, but he was clearly paying more attention to his thoughts than the food. 'You're not here after me?'

'I didn't know you were in Roumania until I spotted you across the terrace.'

''Cause if the Bolshies think I'm a grass, I'll turn up in the river.'

'I seriously doubt that my business here has any aspect in common with yours, but if the two turn out to be related, I promise to give you time to get clear before the axe falls.'

Johnston nodded. 'Can't ask for more, I don't suppose. So, what's your business?'

'Tell me what you have heard of any plots against the royal family.'

'The *King*?' He'd raised his voice enough to be heard at nearby tables, and when he realised, he glared at his fellow diners.

'Not ours, you fool,' Holmes murmured. 'King Ferdinand. And his wife and daughter.'

The outrage turned to confusion. 'Him? Who'd plot against him?'

'The Queen is very popular. I'd have thought your Bolshevik friends would want to overturn her, at the very least. They must find it difficult to foment a peasant uprising with her in the hearts of her countrymen.'

'Maybe. But I hear tell Ferdinand's sick, and they don't believe in real Queens here like Victoria, God bless 'er. And that son of theirs is a right pillock – give the country two-three years of him, and they'll be queuing up to join the Party.'

'And until then, your Bolshevik friends will bide their time and dine at La Cina.'

'Could be worse places,' he said, and raised his glass of Tokay at Holmes.

CHAPTER TWENTY-FOUR

I WAS NOT SURPRISED when the woman who came to the Dumitru door spoke no English. It actually made things easier – and her clearly being in the late stages of cooking dinner made it easier yet. I simply kept smiling and repeating her daughter's name, until she was forced to go and fetch the girl.

She left the door ajar. And I was standing right there, so I gently reached past the long strings of garlic and drying peppers to encourage the door to drift open a little further . . .

Inside was the most colourful room I have ever seen. Even a palace in India makes use of some neutral shades to set off the brilliant fabrics and paintings – but here, the only scraps of relief were some minor patches of whitewashed plaster and portions of the wooden ceiling. Everything was ablaze with the same colours as the embroidered clothing – although whoever lived in this house had a true adoration for German synthetic dyes. If I lived here, I should have to wear tinted lenses.

The main furniture, draped under all those rugs, blankets, and stuffed pillows, was wooden: A long bench with arms and high back was clearly the family settee, laid with a long green-and-blue woven rectangle. Before it stood a long, narrow trestle table with a cloth of predominantly red and yellow, from under which peeped legs resembling branches, stripped of bark and polished to within an inch of their lives. In the far corner stood a structure like a child-sized bunk bed, its lower levels nearly hidden by the achingly bright red-and-pink geometrical weaving draped from the top. Carpets were scattered across the pristine beaten-earth floor, embroidered scarves were displayed from pairs of pegs set into the walls, needlework curtains were drawn back from the polished windows. Even the collection of family photographs on a sideboard had vibrant little samplers draped over their frames.

The only clear space my eyes could find was a small shelf just inside the door. It was the sort of spot a city-dweller would put the keys, or leave a note for another inhabitant of the house.

In this case, it held six freshly whittled stakes, similar to the teeth of the handmade hay rakes – except that these were nearly a foot long, as thick as my thumb, and sharpened to a point.

Behind them on the shelf lay a heavy mallet.

I had lived on a farm for several years. I could think of no farm-related task that required a sharpened stake and a mallet.

My horrified thoughts were interrupted by the return of the woman who had answered the door, trailing behind her a young woman, and talking all the while.

I'm not sure what I expected of Miss Vera Dumitru. The doctor had described her as sensible, the priest as level-headed; on the other hand, she had recently lost her fiancé (and possibly, if I had read between the priest's lines correctly, a baby) and had been visited twice by ghosts. I anticipated red eyes and a case of the trembles, at the very least. What I got was someone who made Gabriela look shy.

She was as tall as I was, to begin with, and stood straight-backed to look over her mother's kerchief-wrapped head at me. At the maternal gush of Roumanian, she gave a roll of the eyes that would have looked at home on a London flapper and elbowed her mother aside – politely, but without hesitation – to lead me down the steps to a bench in the front garden. The protests of the mother grew more urgent, until at last the girl gave her what was very clearly a 'Mother, please!'

With a final despairing phrase, the door banged shut. Vera raised her beautifully plucked eyebrows at me. 'Sorry at that.'

'I do understand. She is worried about you.'

'She worries of everything. Mothers.'

I joined her in a what-can-you-do? shake of the head, then watched as she fished a packet of cigarettes from the pocket of her traditional embroidered apron and stuck one in her mouth. She offered me one, I declined, and she got it going with a gesture so insouciant, I knew that here was another girl familiar with the cinema in Braşov. She tugged off her flowered kerchief and stuffed it into the same pocket, shaking out her modern, if somewhat crumpled, haircut.

'I am staying at the castle,' I told her, speaking slowly since her English seemed a bit piecemeal. 'I heard of your, er, ghost? In the cemetery.'

'Pah,' she said, waving the idea away with her cigarette.

'Not a ghost, then? Or a, what do you call them – *strigoi*?'

'Was some stupid boy, playing big for his friends.'

'Vera, I saw wooden stakes on the shelf inside your house.'

She looked embarrassed. 'My father. So old fashion. This 1925 – day of telephones, motorcar. Even in Bran, two people have fridgerator, make ice in summer. In Bran! No place for *strigoi*, vampire, wheetch.'

'But it sounded frightening.'

'Oh, yais, I frightened then. Leetle bit. Nighttime, yes? Dark, quiet, lone . . . lonesome? Lonely?'

'Either one.'

'All alone. I walk home, thinking thoughts and a voice, little voice, whus . . . whus?'

'Whisper.'

'Yes, whisper.' She dropped her own voice in imitation, a scratchy sound in the air. '"You, Vera," it say. "Come talk me." Not in English, you understand? He say, "Come talk me" and I say, "Who that?" and he say Andrei. Lots of Andreis, right? So I stay out on road, well away from bushes and wall, and say, "Andrei who?" and he say – idiot boy – "Andrei who die in Fagaraş." Big battle there, yes? Nineteen six.'

'Sixteen,' I corrected. 'Nineteen sixteen.'

'Yes, thank you. Big battle, many die, wounded walking through Bran even, I remember. Nine years old, I was, but remember well. Too well.'

'I understand that you saw that same . . . ghost earlier this year, too?'

'That was why boys tease me now about Andrei, because of earlier story.'

'Tell me about the earlier time.'

'It was almost night then. I was new in castle, everything there seem strange, you know? I walk across courtyard and look up and see man looking down at me. Make me . . . surprise? Fear?'

'Er, startled?'

'Yes, it startled me. Because he look like a boy I knew long ago, before the War. He became soldier and died. Funeral and everything, I remember. Anyway, he looked down, saw me, goes away fast. So I go ask footman if a worker was in, someone with raggedy shirt and needing haircut. He said no, so we went and looked through all the rooms, and no boy. Especially no Andrei Costea. They tease me a little, Vera is seeing ghosts, boy walking through walls.'

'When was that?'

'*Februarie*? No – *Martie*.'

'March. Was the Queen here yet?'

'No, just getting things ready for her.'

'How did you know Andrei?'

'He was a friend of my sister, Magda. Older sister.'

'Just a friend, or a boyfriend?'

'Hah – Andrei, boyfriend of Magda Dumitru? No bloody likely.'

I was surprised – both by the colloquial oath and the emphasis behind it. 'Why?'

'My sister, she wild. Little bit – not bad girl, you know? Just, she like her fun. City girl, yes? Now in Bucharest, works in office, makes good money, says I need to come, we can go dancing, people think we twins sisters. But Andrei, he . . .' She tried out a couple of words in Roumanian before venturing back into English. 'He simple, yes? Village boy – good boy, nice boy, but simple. Not smart.'

'Do you mean he just wasn't very bright, or was his brain *damaged* in some way?' It took us a few synonyms to work out the concept of damaged, but in the end, she shook her head.

'Could be, "dahmaged." But if so, was early. He was always like that, when I knew him. Strong, simple, nice boy. Handsome. Terrible father – used to hit mother, even the boys, too. Father went away at last, just before War started, and never came back. Everyone glad. Except the mother, she only lived two years more, then died, too. First year of War. So maybe yes, father hit Andrei when he was small and made his brain go scrumpled, I don't know. But Andrei, he adore my sister Magda. He not really understand that he was too young for her – only two, three years, but that age, it matters, yes? But she like him, let him follow her around. Like pet, you know? Like Princess Ileana little white dog, feed bits, tease a little, give pats.'

'He doesn't sound like someone who would enlist in the army.'

'Big, strong, stupid? Sound just like.'

I laughed, and admitted that she was right.

'But no,' she said. 'I not telling this right. I liked Andrei. I was child, of course, too young for him, but he was always sweet to me. Andrei not . . . not clever, but not stupid like – numbskull? Is numbskull word?'

'It is indeed.'

'He good with machines, okay with reading, shy with most girls except for Magda, Andrei just – dreamy. That is him: dreamy.'

'And dead.'

'We cried at his funeral,' she said, as simple and as heartfelt an epitaph as any young man could ask.

I thought over what she had told me, and wondered at one detail. 'Your sister Magda, she said you could go dancing like twin sisters. You look alike?'

'Oh yes – nine years different but same tall, same hair, same . . . well,' she looked down at her chest and gave a little moue. 'Mostly same.'

'And when you went past the graveyard the other night, the voice called to you. Did he actually use your name?' She'd said the voice did, although the other two versions I'd been given left that detail out.

But she nodded vigorously. 'Yes. "Vera," he say. "Come here." As if I some child walking up to strange bull in field.'

'Can you show me exactly where this was?'

She scraped off the last burning end of her cigarette and dropped it into a pocket, marching me down the road until we were standing outside of the graveyard.

She looked up and down a few times, adjusted her position, and said, 'I here. I *was* here, in road, like this. And whusper comes from back there, *Buna seara, Vera.*'

'And after he said he was Andrei who died in the War, you turned and ran home.'

'I throw rock at him. Then I walk home. Little fast, maybe, but not run. *Baieti prosti* – I not run from those type boy.'

'Well, thank you for explaining. It's all clearer now.' Which was a lie, because I did not understand the situation any better than I had an hour before – but I did know more details, which can be nearly as good. I reached in my pocket for some Roumanian lei, then hesitated. Would she be pleased, or offended? 'Vera, do you have a . . . a savings fund, maybe for a trip to Bucharest to see your sister? Can I give you a few lei to add to it, by way of thanks for your time?'

She demurred – it had been her pleasure to talk to me, after being locked inside with her mother all day – but after a time, when I made it clear this was merely thanks and not payment, she accepted, tucking the bills casually into her cigarette pocket.

But when I looked back, I saw her bent over the bills, looking

192

closely at the denominations. I had probably overpaid her, not knowing the local economy, but I had no doubt that Miss Vera Dumitru was a young woman who would make the most of every leu and ban that came her way.

I glanced at the sky, then my wristwatch. The Queen and her daughter would soon be sitting down to dinner – without, I hoped, too much frosty anger crackling across the table between the icy blue eyes and the darker blue. Having met the young Princess, I would not at all choose to wager on the victor here, and it was best to keep clear until matters cooled.

In addition, my massive noontime dinner was still with me, and the last thing I wanted was another hearty meal.

Instead, I headed out the southern leg of Bran's lopsided H of roadways, to look at what lay on the other side of the castle, along the road to the all-important Bran Pass.

CHAPTER TWENTY-FIVE

HOLMES FINISHED HIS MEAL while interrogating the fake Bolshevik about his boss – the man Mycroft had intended him to see – but it was clear that Tovarisch Dalca had never expressed any interest in a rural Transylvanian village. When the pudding course arrived, Holmes rose to thread his way out of the crowded terrace of tables filled with polyglot diners out to enjoy the first cool breath of the day. On the pavement outside, a quartet of Italians were descending from a white-and-gilt landau pulled by two geldings the colour of summer honey. He lit a cigarette, and walked a meandering route back to the Athenee Palace.

There he settled into the English bar, scandalising the waiter with a request for Turkish coffee. The man was somewhat mollified when he followed that up with an order for the most expensive whisky he could see on the shelf.

An hour later, the third man on Mycroft's list came in.

Middle thirties, good clothes, clean fingernails, wire-rimmed glasses. He was shaved, but overdue for a haircut. Probably habitual. English, without a doubt. Educated, certainly. And just as clearly, a regular in the Athenee's English Bar, watering hole for the high-ranking, the influential, and the stinking rich, foreign or domestic. The barman tucked the newcomer into a table both prominent and discreet. When the young man drew out a small notebook and silver pencil, Holmes was certain.

The Roumania correspondent for *The Times*.

The barman brought the man a glass of dark amber liquid with a small carafe of water. Holmes watched from the side of his eyes as the correspondent took a mouthful, savouring it before he swallowed, then pouring in a splash of the water.

A figure appeared in the doorway, a man who had paused there twice in the past twenty minutes. This time he walked in, straight to the corner table, pulling out the other chair. He leant forward onto his elbows and started talking. The barman was aware of the newcomer, and watched the table, but made no move to approach. Less than three minutes later, the conversation was over and the newcomer left. The correspondent picked up his pencil and wrote a few lines, then returned to his glass.

Ten minutes later, a similar scene took place. And five minutes after that, another, this time a woman.

When the chair cleared after her, Holmes picked up his glass and crossed the room.

'Mr Alan Broder?'

'Yes.' The man's eyes studied Holmes, taking in the details of clothing and stance, much as Holmes had done for him when he came in.

Holmes smiled to himself and sat down. He reached deliberately into his breast pocket, pulled out his leather notecase, and took out an engraved card, laying it on the table face-down. He nodded towards the man's propelling pencil.

'May I?'

A small gesture of the correspondent's fingers – ink-stained, a smudge of typewriter ribbon.

Holmes printed a word and some numbers on the back of the white card. He returned the pencil, placed his forefinger on the card, and slid it across the table to Mr Broder.

'That is a telephone number, in London, where someone always knows where to reach me. At the end of this conversation, I may owe you a favour.'

Broder studied him some more, then pulled away his gaze and turned the card over to its engraved side. All it said was:

Sherlock Holmes

Broder tapped the card on the table two, three times, then got out his own wallet and put it inside. 'I imagine most people, seeing that card, take it as a joke.'

'I do not give that card to many people, Mr Broder.'

'I can understand that. I met your brother, once. He . . . clarified the situation for me.'

'I imagine he did.'

'What can I do for you, Mr Holmes?'

'First, you can agree that you will not make use of this conversation, in any way. I am not here. You have not spoken with me, or learnt anything from me.'

'I rather suspected as much. I agree.'

'Next you can tell me what you may have heard of any threat

against Queen Marie.'

'Queen—' Broder's face was a study: first alarm, then eagerness, followed by chagrin as he remembered that he could never have heard the question. 'I knew I'd regret saying yes. What kind of a threat?'

'The actual threat was directed against her daughter, Ileana, but it would appear that the intention was to drive the Queen away from Castle Bran.'

'That old place up beyond Sinaia – on the edges of Transylvania?'

'Yes.'

'Why would anyone care? I saw it once, a year ago. It's a wreck. There are castles all over, most of them far nicer than that one.'

'And yet, Bran is the place the Queen loves.'

'I know. One would almost—'

His mouth snapped shut, the newsman's instinctive reaction to the sin of giving away information.

Holmes waited while the man considered his options, and the promise in his pocket. 'One would almost think . . . ?' he prompted.

'That she had reasons for keeping a hideaway,' Broder said. 'Private reasons.'

'Are the rumours true, then? About the Queen and Prince Barbu Ştirbey?'

'How should I know?'

Holmes let one eyebrow climb. Favours would only be owed for actual contributions.

Broder gave a crooked smile. 'If so, they are discreet. And since the Queen is generally looked upon fondly, the people are not as eager for scandal as they would be for a less likeable person. I understand there has always been talk about her. However, I have to say that her first four children do resemble their father. Two sons, two daughters. And generally speaking, here as in England, once a line of succession is clearly established, questions are not asked.'

'The second son – Nicholas – is the King's?'

Broder's voice, low to begin with, fell still more. 'The boy was born in 1903. If he is someone else's it's not Prince Barbu. As far as I know, they did not meet until the summer of 1907 – although it's hard to credit that, considering the size of the country. At any rate, there was a peasant uprising across Moldavia and into Wallachia. Thousands were killed, thousands more arrested. The government were terrified, but the farmers did have valid claims. Prince Barbu was among those who advised the king – this is the old king, Carol – that instead of turning the army loose on the revolt, perhaps he could extend a hand of friendship to them, and offer a few reforms. That is when the prince and Marie are said to have met. And certainly, that was when they began to see something of each other.'

'And the girl Ileana . . .'

'Was born eighteen months later. January, 1909.'

'I see.'

'The Queen's last child, an infant who died before the War, was said to be his. The prince barely left the boy's side during his illness, which would be remarkably attentive for a mere family friend. And yet, relations are amiable between him and the King, as they are between Marie and the Prince's wife.'

'A façade?'

'If so, it's an enduring one, and to all indications comfortable. Nadèje Știrbey is seen in the Queen's company both with and without her husband present, and the two women seem remarkably affectionate for rivals. As for the King, he could easily avoid the Prince, yet he shows no reluctance to work or dine with him. The prince's official position is that of managing the royal estates, but his position in Roumanian society is high, his family has been prominent for centuries. Both King and Queen find him indispensable, when it comes to the smooth functioning of government. For a time, his house was in effect the centre of government, since it allowed the Queen to casually drop in for conversations with visiting dignitaries.'

'Yet you seemed to think that Prince Barbu was somehow related to a threat against Princess Ileana and driving the Queen from Bran Castle. Why?'

'Had you considered that the threat could be aimed at *him*? Look, the royal family lives in Sinaia much of the year. If they were, well, lovers, it would be impossible for them to meet either there or in Bucharest without coming to the attention of all the spies and half the gossips in Eastern Europe. But by road, in a fast car, it is less than three hours to Castle Bran, a remote spot entirely peopled by the Queen's servants. By horse over the hills, I shouldn't think it takes much longer. And Prince Barbu and the Queen both spend a lot of time on horseback.'

'What kind of motor does the Prince have?'

'Probably a Rolls. Don't they all use a Rolls-Royce?'

'Even in the mountains?'

'You're right, I did see him in something else one time, up in Sinaia. I noticed because he was driving himself – something that's capable of more than ten miles an hour over those roads. A Citroën, I think it was.'

'Is it common knowledge that the Prince and the Queen employ Castle Bran for private meetings?'

Broder fiddled with his glass, and Holmes began to suspect that the man's hesitation was due not to a journalist's innate reluctance to give away hard-won information – or, not only because of it – but because of a respect for the people under scrutiny. On the other hand, there was the obligation of that telephone number . . .

'I was told of a joke, made at a dinner party a while ago. The sort of bitter jest that hides deep envy. No doubt variations of this one have been made for years, but things said in private are easy to deny, and easy for the targets to overlook. Not, however, when they appear in print. It seems a visiting photographer – a German-born Englishman – came through Roumania with his camera. As often happens here, he was invited to the royal palace and to a number of royal functions. The King sat for a photograph, the Queen motored with him to Bran. Both of them are generous with visitors – particularly those who have some audience in the outer world – and the Queen wrote a kind foreword to his travel memoir. Although she couldn't possibly have read the book first.

'In between the fellow's descriptions of exotic gipsies and romantic Carpathian vistas, the photographer describes a dinner with certain important men in Bucharest. These are men who, you understand, may have been slightly miffed about the failure of some business or social affair. At any rate, food was eaten and drinks were downed. Then one of them made a joking toast to Prince Barbu – as the "Prince Consort." And the others laughed.'

Holmes winced. It was a remarkably efficient taunt, implying a cuckold King, a Queen who wears the pants, and a Prince who was her true partner. 'It's a rare insult that drives a blade into three targets at once. The photographer could not have realised the weight of that joking title. He'd never have published it.'

'Certainly a born Englishman would not. And it did take some time for his memoir to make it across Europe – I heard a rumour that the Queen only saw a copy of it when she was in London this summer. Once it gets around, the man will find cool greetings from half the kingdoms in Europe.'

'So the love affair—'

'The *possible* love affair,' Broder put in.

'The purported affair is now public, and all parties realise it. Possibly including Princess Ileana. If this is the case, who would be driven by it into making threats, driving the Queen from Bran, and trying to ruin her reputation? Prince Barbu's wife, perhaps?'

'Good Lord, no. Although I wouldn't put it past the crown prince.'

'Prince Carol, yes. There's trouble brewing there.'

'Even the Roumanians are getting tired of the scandals and irresponsibility, and the King and Queen have given him about all the free rein they can. Rumour has it that, now the Queen has returned, matters will come to a head – the bookmakers are leaning towards their stripping Carol of the title and giving it to his little son. And Carol, who has always hated Prince Barbu and long been alienated from his mother, will no doubt see the two of them as siding against the King.'

'Would he make threats against his sister?'

'His sister? Which one?'

'The young one. Ileana.'

'The two of them have always got along fairly well. Although, he might, if he could use her against his mother in some way.'

'Which returns us to my original question: Are you aware of any overt and credible threats against Queen Marie?'

'Nothing open. And credible? Most of what I hear are grumbles, not open threats.'

'What about Prince Barbu? Not from him, but someone wishing to use him?'

'Ştirbey? He's from the wealthiest, most powerful family in the country. In partnership with the Queen, his authority is immense. And he seems quite happy with that. But I will admit, if I wanted things to change here – if I wanted to rid the country of its current king, his overly assertive wife, and an impossible crown prince – I'd want someone like Prince Barbu to offer the people instead. Stable, clever, able to move easily on the international scene, and a patriot to his core. Yes, he would do nicely.

'And to go back to your original question: I have not got wind of any overt threat against Queen Marie, but if I did, I might take a closer look at the people around Prince Barbu Ştirbey.'

Chapter Twenty-six

I FOUND THE MOST interesting thing about the section of village built along the river was the road that left it behind as it headed into the Carpathians. I walked along it for a time, seeing little but more farms, more looming hay-monsters, a few barking dogs, and labourers headed home after their long day. The air was thick with cooking smoke, and the fragrances – meat and onion and paprika, overall – were making me question my choice to skip dinner.

The little river at the base of the valley was strewn with rocks, and showed signs of torrential rains repeatedly sweeping through. The fields here looked marginally less fertile than the other side of the castle – the gardens not quite so lush, the hay-monsters a foot or two shorter. But the houses were equally neat, the people I saw every bit as amiable to a wave and a nod. The road was clear and well-marked, so I felt no great need to reach the castle before darkness fell. In any event, I had my pocket torch.

Though if I planned to walk around Transylvania alone in the dark, I thought, I should steal a head of garlic from a garden as I went by, in case of vampires. I did not spot any garlic, but I did notice, growing up against the roadway, the flower of some related member of the *allium* family. In a fit of whimsy, I stretched out a hand to break it off, tucking it into a buttonhole in my shirt.

I came to a bit of tumbledown wall and clambered across it to a high spot, settling onto an inviting slab of rock to study Castle Bran, sentinel atop the cliffs. The face it presented on this side lacked the looming, flat-faced donjon. Instead, the castle seemed an untidy collection of roofs, walls, and chimneys, dominated by the Queen's round tower with its droll pointed cap.

Perhaps the exaggerated cap was what made this side seem friendlier, less blunt and foreboding. It was still a fortress perched on a raw rockface, but from this side, a gentle hill rose up to support it. The buildings of the old customs house stretched along the road, and beyond them the Queen's extensive flower gardens, with a new-looking greenhouse and bed after bed of roses, lilies, dahlias, and the like, a riot of colour waiting to fill all those pots and bowls.

One of the Queen's high windows began to glint with the final rays of the sun. Nearby, a cow complained that it was milking time. A horse cart trotted past, its driver urging it on, in a hurry to get home before the shadows took over completely. In the distance, I caught a quick glimpse of motorcar headlamps, swinging through the crossroads and briefly illuminating a long, black shape – Father Constantin, headed to his evening meal. At least, I hoped it was. The window of a nearby farmhouse began to glow with a candle's warm light. In its neighbour, two chattering children made for their own hearth and home.

In the final moments of dusk, I brushed myself off and hiked back down to the road. True darkness came down, but I was in no hurry and the road surface was dependable, so I left the torch in my pocket, letting my boots find their way on the dry surface. Up in the castle, the maids had lit some of the candles in the Queen's tower, windows beginning to glow as the tower itself faded into a black silhouette against a near-black sky. As I went on, several more came alight, a fairyland effect.

I came to the crossroads, and turned onto the centre line of the of roads. Village houses on my left, the Queen's park and a couple of empty houses on my right. Fewer windows shone from this side – though yes, someone had lit the candles in my room right up at the top, assuming my return. The village had fallen quiet, all its life focused around the table. My feet knew the road, but there were also gentle columns of light escaping from some of the houses along the way. I decided that I would not need my torch until I turned up the castle drive.

Then my eyes caught on something pale, coiled on the road at the edge of a beam of light from an upper-storey room. Gleaming white, looped back on itself. Very like the Queen's fabulous pearls. I came closer, and saw that it was indeed a loop of gleaming white rounds. I bent to pick it up . . .

There was a sound – one quiet footstep, alarmingly close. I whirled, to be met by a cloud of black through that stray beam, a billowing shape that wrapped itself over me and clung to my outstretched arms. I hit out, leapt back, fell—

Then a blow, and the night was gone.

CHAPTER TWENTY-SEVEN

I T WAS LATE WHEN Holmes finished with the *Times* correspondent, but if Roumania was like other countries that sweltered through the day, its hours of business would extend past the usual. Broder had given him a telephone number, before they shook hands and the next informant slipped into his chair; however, Holmes took off his jacket and tie before settling down to the telephone. He expected his pursuit to be long, convoluted, and possibly fruitless until the next morning.

To his surprise, a woman's voice answered the number on the third ring.

He cast about for the Roumanian words he needed, then decided to try English. 'Please, I am looking for Prince Barbu Ştirbey.'

'Moment please,' she said, followed by murmuring in the background.

'This is Ştirbey,' said a man.

'Good evening, sir, I apologise for disturbing you at this hour. My name is Holmes, I was asked by Queen Marie to look into some—'

'The troubles at Castle Bran, yes. What can I do for you?'

'I should like to speak with you, if you are available.'

'Is it urgent that we speak tonight? If not, perhaps you would join me on the train to Sinaia in the morning. We would have privacy, and plenty of time.' And just as Holmes was about to point out that privacy was exactly the last thing they would be given on the train to Sinaia, the prince added, 'I have a private car.'

'I see. It is true that I intended to return to Braşov, but I need to be on the first possible train.'

'The earliest trains make many stops. The 7.20 a.m. leaves later but arrives earlier, particularly if you are continuing on to Braşov. Tell the attendant you want the royal waiting room, or my car if it is closer to the time. We can take our breakfast on board.'

'Thank you, sir, I will. And again, my apologies to you and the lady for telephoning so late.'

Holmes went to bed, well satisfied, yet he did not sleep. Which was odd. Granted, it was hot and there was noise from the street, but to a disciplined mind, those counted for naught. And it had been hot and noisy when he was here last month, with a bed far less comfortable than this one, but sleep he had. To the faint ticking of his watch on the bedside table, he found his thoughts returning to Russell, time and again. What had she learnt, during her afternoon? Would she decide to go into the village tonight and keep watch on her own?

Very possibly. He had left the revolver in their rooms, so she would take that with her.

Surely she would take it.

He rose early, bathed and shaved and drank a pot of coffee before dawn. He walked through the cool morning streets to the station, but did not go to the royal waiting room. Instead, he bought a platform ticket and, once through the barrier, asked for Prince Barbu's car. The attendant touched his hat brim, said he was expected, and took his bag, escorting him towards the front of the train.

The Prince was already on board, with coffee and a newspaper. He put both aside when the compartment door came open, and rose to greet his guest.

Prince Barbu Ştirbey was a slim, polished aristocrat with a full moustache, intense dark eyes, and impeccable manners. Holmes knew about him – knew that the man's knowledge of international politics was profound and his patriotism without question. Educated at the Sorbonne, fluent in half a dozen languages, with a practical understanding of modern agriculture that changed the way his vast family estates were run, Prince Barbu was a primary reason why Roumania had a chance of surviving to the end of the century.

He was also, Holmes quickly discovered, profoundly dedicated to Queen Marie, and wished to help in any way possible.

Unfortunately, he could shed almost no light on the problem.

Two things he did tell Holmes: King Ferdinand's illness had been more serious than the press knew – perhaps even the Queen, since she'd been away during the worst of it. He was recovering, but until it was easier to move back and forth, he was staying in

Sinaia's main royal castle, rather than the family's more comfortable dwelling on the grounds. In Prince Barbu's opinion, the king's recovery was not helped by the behaviour of his eldest son, Carol, which coupled personal irresponsibility with a complete lack of interest in the governance of Roumania.

He also told Holmes that, because it was almost impossible to have a private conversation with Marie at Castle Peleş, with servants underfoot at every moment, he had followed her to Bran and spent a quiet hour with her before motoring back to Sinaia.

Yes, Prince Barbu had been the urgent business – and his had been the Citroën in the castle drive – that had delayed Friday's dinner with the Queen.

CHAPTER TWENTY-EIGHT

I WOKE BLIND. THE blackness smelt of dust and dankness. And . . . onions. I lay without moving, feeling my thoughts bubble up through the sludge. Onions? There hadn't been onions the last time I woke in a black hole after being abduct— and with that word, a bolt of cold panic shot through me. *I picked an onion flower and walked through the village and oh God I'm locked in a coffin buried alive my fingernails clawing at the—*

I jerked up . . . and drew a shuddering breath in relief. I could sit up. I was not in a pine box no larger than my body.

The relief was short-lived. I'd been abducted once before, taken and drugged and dumped into a hole. I was trapped there for day after endless day, until Holmes managed to track me across the south of England.

At least this blackness did not stink of vomit.

Yet . . .

I forced myself to keep very, very still, paying attention to the air going in through my nose, feeling the same air pass out through my half-parted lips. In. Out. I willed my breathing to slow, told my heart to settle. Things hurt – scraped hand, bruised arm, an ache in my ankle and sharp jabs coming from my face and neck – but nothing seemed broken, no major loss of blood. I was absolutely blind – but that was just the dark. I had other senses. Breathe in, breathe out. Slowly. Listen; touch; smell – and *think*.

Sound. My breathing came back muffled rather than echoing, and the air was stuffy rather than cold: not a large space? I made a few clicking noises with my tongue, and that confirmed it: walls soft or uneven rather than hard and reflective; and not vast.

Touch. I stretched out my left arm to feel – promptly jamming the little finger against a wall. I snatched back the hand with a curse, cradling it until the pain subsided, then put out the hand more slowly. Wood: rough rather than finished, too old to smell of anything but dust – dust, and something else. The onion smell of the *allium* flower, yes, but also a musty odour, vaguely reminiscent of rotted vegetables. And something sharper, a chemical, pervading everything . . .

Chloroform? Yes, that would explain matters.

I patted around, finding the floorboards similar to the walls, though with a thicker layer of dust and a lot of chips and debris. Another wall to my right, running some ninety degrees from the first: I was sitting in a corner.

Then I gingerly raised my left arm – and hit wood less than a foot above my head.

At the size of the room, my heart began to race again and a whimper escaped my throat. *Buried alive – clawing – fists beating at the lid—*

Stop! All it meant was that I was in a box too small to stand upright in. I got to my knees and patted along the first wall until I found another corner, an alarmingly brief distance away. The third and fourth corners were not much more distant.

I was buried in – no: I was *inside* a compartment some eight feet square and four feet tall. As coffins went, this was roomy, but I could feel the sides close in on me. *Keep calm*, I ordered myself – *the air in here is not going to last long as it is* – and how long had I been here breathing already?

Think.

First: what did I have? Clothes, all of them except my boots. And while I was grateful not to be nude, it did mean that my knife was gone. And my pockets had been emptied, so no torch. Spectacles gone, too.

Had I been left food and drink? My survey of the edges had given me nothing: time for a detailed search.

First, the walls. *You're going to feel really stupid, Russell, if after all that panic you find a simple door.* But a methodical survey up and down all four walls gave me no recesses, no latches, no rotted soft spots – nothing but palms so filthy I could feel the clotted dirt, and half a dozen splinters whose hot pains matched those at the back of my head, my left cheek, the side of my neck – all over, really.

I sat, making sure my breathing was under control, then returned to my knees for a deliberate and methodical sweep of the floor. *You will not panic, not throw yourself at the ceiling and scream* – but I found nothing but dirt and debris.

I had been left neither food nor drink.

Breathe. In. Out. When my racing pulse had slowed, I turned to the ceiling. Starting at a corner, ignoring the feel of tears creeping down my face, I worked my way along one wall, floor to ceiling, then along the boards overhead as far as my arms would reach, then inched forward and did it again, fingertips searching for a break, a latch, a hole of any kind wider than the seams between the boards. Shuffling along, turning the corners, feeling the knees of my trousers give way, pausing to shake the circulation back into my hands. All the way around and across, every inch of it.

I found nothing. No access door, no latch. No bread and water for this prisoner. Would I be taken out – or left here to die, *weaker and weaker and flailing and alone . . .*

No! I was Mary Russell, daughter of Judith and partner of Holmes. There *had* to be a weakness. Every prison had a weak spot, and the persistent prisoner could find it. Here, perhaps it was the height. There was just enough room that I could stand at a squat. That would give me the full strength of my legs. If there was a padlock, holding the top down, I could force it open.

(*But if the lid is nailed down, if there is a foot – two feet – of soil, like a grave on top – and maybe that dust smell is from outside the coffin – no, the BOX – and I'm in the Bran cemetery . . .*)

The darkness that had been pressing in, the fear I kept tamping down had not bled away, but continued to build. It was a mix of fury and panic and shame and abject terror, and I could feel the whimpers building in the bottom of my throat, until it was either scream aloud or pound on whatever came within reach – so I did both. Trembling with the effort of control, I got into a crouch, rising slightly to let my back find the roof, then dropping again. I drew a pair of deep, deliberate breaths.

And then I let it all out, in a guttural growl that built from heels to throat as I exploded upward with all my strength.

Chapter Twenty-nine

The train reached Sinaia without mishap, breakdown, or even a cow on the line. The trip passed in an agreeable manner, as the prince proved to be a man of wide interests and deep curiosity. Their conversation ranged from opera to agriculture. Winemaking was of particular interest, famous on the Ştirbey estates since the seventeenth century, and beekeeping kept them going for a good twenty miles.

More to the point, Prince Barbu proved a wealth of information when it came to the political situation on this end of Europe. As he was providing some unexpected insight into the history of the peasant revolts, Holmes made a mental note to introduce the man to Mycroft, who clearly needed a better source of information among the Balkan states.

Holmes had hoped to stay in the Prince's car after Sinaia, since the train would continue on to Braşov, but it appeared that the car itself would come off, to be shunted onto a siding, there to await the prince's needs.

He resigned himself to elbowing the crowds for a corner seat, preferably in a compartment without too many bawling infants, but it turned out that Prince Barbu had other plans for him.

'You must come with me, my wife would enjoy meeting you.'

'I regret, sir, my own wife was expecting me before midday. Perhaps we might come when our business in Bran is over.'

'Certainly – but I cannot permit you to remain with the train. It will be faster and infinitely more comfortable for my driver to take you. I won't be needing the motor today.'

He would not take a refusal – not that Holmes tried hard. Instead, they dodged the crowds on the station, were whisked away in the waiting car – it was a Duesenberg, not a Rolls-Royce – and wound through the villas and gardens of Roumania's summer capital.

The stately pace of the motorcar was an irritation. He should have stayed on the train despite the company. But as if the prince had been reading his mind, he said, 'When we get to the villa, I'll have the Citroën brought round. Taking this motor to Bran is like sailing an ocean liner up the Danube.'

The delay in fetching the other motor meant that Holmes must come in for a brief refreshment, and that brief refreshment led to a conversation with Nadèje Ştirbey, and although he was glad to have met the woman, to put a face on the purported lover's wife, he ended up having to rudely pull out his watch in front of his host.

The Ştirbeys escorted him out to the waiting Citroën. The driver bundled him away, and drove off nearly as sedately as they had arrived. But when they reached the main road, Holmes leant forward, holding out a denomination of lei that would keep the driver in beer for some time.

'Young man, speed is of greater importance to me than comfort. All I ask is that you avoid running over any children.'

The driver looked from the note to his passenger, and broke into a wide grin.

'We go fast, yes?'

'We go fast,' Holmes agreed – and scarcely got the words out before acceleration shoved him back in the seat. At this speed, he would arrive in Bran less than an hour after the midday he had promised Russell.

He decided that he might as well be comfortable, and in any event, keeping his head below the view would make it easier to imagine that all was well. So he arranged his valise and a travelling rug into one corner, wedged his legs against the back of the seats to keep from being thrown about, and retreated into his thoughts.

Mycroft was going to be ashamed at the failure of his Roumanian Intelligence: one informant off in Moscow, another away taking a cure for the gout – all in all, the Communist threat looked to be a damp squib. Even the assistance of the *Times* correspondent had been less enlightening than problematic. Was Prince Barbu the intended target, or was he a man playing a very long game to oust the king and take control? There seemed no evidence for the former. Yet Holmes would have sworn that Prince Barbu was a gentleman of honour, committed to his country.

The Prince would not be the first likeable scoundrel he'd encountered. But he would be the one Holmes had liked the most.

He could only hope that Russell had dug up some fact that would send them on the right path through the land of women. Though it would rankle if she'd managed to solve the entire case in his absence.

Chapter Thirty

The aftermath of terror is either collapse, or rage. Needless to say, I was in a proper fury by the time I had stormed along the road and up the castle drive, knife in hand and murder in heart.

Just whom I planned to slice into pieces was unclear, but there would be *someone*.

My forceful explosion out of the box that held me had added a contusion on my skull to the other bangs and bruises. I had burst upward with all my strength against the heavy lid of my oversized coffin, expecting nothing but the faintest of results. Except it turned out that the lid had not been screwed, nailed, or buried shut. Instead, it had hinges, and had shot upward with no more resistance than the weight of its boards – then dropped down on my head, nearly knocking me unconscious for a second time.

When I had shoved it up again and rolled out onto the ground, I found I was in a derelict room with a dirt floor. Right in front of me, placed neatly side by side, stood my boots, the knife and pocket torch resting in the left one, my glasses, rather lopsided, in the other.

What the hell?

Something about the tidy arrangement lit the fuse to anger. Was that neatness meant to be an apology? *Terribly sorry, I didn't mean to whack you in the head and dump you in a hole, here's your shoes?*

I was going to murder him. I was going to find him and kick him for a while with my boots and then murder him dead.

I snatched up my glasses and shoved them on my ears, pushed the torch into my pocket, stepped into the boots, and yanked the ties snug.

And before I stood upright, I drew my knife. If the bastards who did this were sitting outside, they were going to bleed.

There were no bastards sitting outside. There was no one outside, though I heard voices. I stalked out of the deserted farm building and across its weed-covered yard. The sagging gate I passed through seemed vaguely familiar – and as I stepped out onto the road, I realised why.

I'd been stashed inside that abandoned building between the castle's park and the crosspiece of the roads. Straight inside from where I'd been attacked – indeed, I could see the marks from my dragging heels leading in, which someone had attempted to scuff out. Why hadn't Holmes . . . ? Oh yes, he'd gone to Bucharest. But why wasn't he back yet? The sun said it was past noon. And come to that, why hadn't the castle raised a hue and cry last night? Surely someone was meant to notice when a guest of the Queen vanished?

I glared up at Castle Bran. I'd been admiring its fairy-tale look, those lighted windows against the dark. Now the castle just looked sharp, its many roof lines and cupolas stabbing into the sky.

A sound drew my attention, a little further along the road. Two women stood staring at me. Onions rolled from a dropped basket at their feet. I raised a hand, to greet them, but before I could come up with the Roumanian phrase, they turned and fled.

I looked down at my clothing. It did seem to belong to a creature that had just crawled out of its grave.

'Oh, great,' I said aloud. I'd just managed to add another element of horror to the village hauntings.

I limped down the road and up the drive. One ankle ached and my head hurt and my skin crawled with filth and a dozen splinters were working their way into my flesh, and I'd been *used* and I'd been careless and I didn't know what I was going to do with the knife in my hand, but there had to be *someone* I could turn it on.

The Citroën I'd seen the other evening was back at the top of the drive. Its driver, who'd been leaning on the car and speaking with one of the castle guards, spotted me first. His jaw dropped. The guard turned, and gaped. Then a guard who'd been standing on the stairs came down to see what had drawn their interest.

I approached the top of the drive under the scandalised gaze of three tidy, clean, and idiotically handsome young men. That was *it*. I drew breath and began to shout.

'Who the hell owns that bloody decrepit old house down in the village? I don't know who thinks it clever to dump a guest into . . .'

Through the red filter of my rage, I dimly became aware that the guards' alarm had begun to divide, between me and something at the top of the stairs. My voice cut off – not that the guard had understood a word of it to begin with – as I stormed to the bottom of the stairway and glared up.

The iron-studded door was open. Florescu, two steps down from the top, stood frozen in shock.

Shock at my state – or at my escape? Did the servants know – had they been in on it? Or just Florescu?

And then Holmes appeared – only to freeze into an identical position, his face travelling from worry to relief to unbridled horror.

I looked down at myself: black with filth, trousers out at both knees, boots scraped, spectacles awry. There was a knife in my left hand and blood on my right, and I couldn't begin to guess what my face looked like – no need to, with that expression on his.

With a sudden rush, my bubble of fury collapsed. I closed my eyes for a moment to think. No: the butler's shock was clean, unmarred by apprehension or guilt. I sighed, then bent to slide the vicious little knife away into my boot-top. When I straightened, I held Holmes' gaze for a moment, then lowered my head and trudged up the stairs.

At the top, I found a small crowd, torn between pressing forward and keeping far back. I arranged my features – if indeed they could be seen at all – into an apology.

'Mr Florescu, I'm sorry, I shall need to trail dust through your clean hallways to my bath. I seem to have . . . had something of a turn, and woke to find myself in a rather grubby situation. Pardon me.'

He and the guards stood well clear as I walked past them into the castle, but Holmes caught me up before I had reached the staircase.

'Russell!' he began.

'I was attacked, Holmes,' I hissed over my shoulder. 'A blanket over my head followed by chloroform. I woke up hours later in an old root cellar. But I'm fine.'

I was not *fine*: my eyes burnt, my head pounded, and my stomach roiled, in addition to a body aching from scalp to toes, both generally and in specific places where I had been bruised, scraped, bashed, pricked, or otherwise abused. Most of that external damage I would not be able to identify until I had scrubbed away the filth. But I was *fine* in that I was walking, speaking with apparent coherence, and beginning to feel thoughts lining themselves up inside my tender skull. 'I'll be better when I've bathed. And had some tea.'

I was careful not to look into the mirror as I went past it.

I thanked the gods of Transylvania and the deep resources of its Queen as I turned the tap in the modern bathtub. Within seconds of lowering myself in, I was sitting in what appeared to be mud. I pulled the plug and poured water along the sides to sluice away the tidal line, and let the second bath run deep and hot. By which time there was tea as well, and I felt like weeping with gratitude, at the slow return of a normal world.

I scrubbed, gingerly, and submerged to rinse the soap from my hair. For the third tub-full, I poured in some fragrant bubbling soap, and when it was filled, I lay back in the foam with the flowered porcelain teacup on my sternum, and listened to the minuscule pop of bubbles around my ears.

A rap sounded at the door. Holmes came in. He had changed from city suit to country tweeds, though his collar was unfastened and his shirt sleeves rolled up. He laid his cigarette case on the dressing table and pulled up a stool, sitting down with my misshapen spectacles, addressing their bends with his strong fingers.

'Do you know,' he said in a mild voice, 'that may have been the most accelerated two minutes in my long and tumultuous life. I arrive, I walk up the stairs, I am told that the servants have only just discovered that my wife's bed has not been slept in. An absence that was overlooked at the time because the Queen was angry – with the Princess, and with them. It would seem that the Queen has never been angry with them before, so you can imagine the effect that had in the servants' quarters.' He paused to stare off into space for a moment. 'I will say, I regret that I was not privileged to witness the Queen of Roumania in full majestic wroth.' I chuckled, in spite of the discomfort of doing so, and he looked pleased before he returned to his task. 'I then am informed that not until late into the morning did the Princess grow impatient, wishing to be attended by the English visitor by whom she had been so charmed, and send a servant to take morning tea to the slug-a-bed's rooms. That is when the terrible fact dawned upon all that said visitor was missing, that she did not in fact set off to Bucharest with her husband (as some thought) or take to her bed early (as the others assumed). Florescu immediately sent out his minions to beat the bounds of the castle, and is on the verge of telephoning for the police when first, up motors the woman's husband, followed by the young woman herself, looking as if she has fought off a landslide single-handed.'

I took another swallow of the tea, and tried to find a position that was both comfortable and above the water line. When that proved impossible, I settled for above the water line, and started to talk. 'After you left for the train, I went exploring the castle, and came across Princess Ileana. She'd got tired of Castle Peleş and wrangled the driver into bringing her here, but the Queen was out riding so Princess Ileana and I went up in one of the towers and had a long conversation about ghosts. She had heard them, some others had seen them – including Vera Dumitru, not once but twice.

'After our discussion of . . . what is the study of ghosts? Fantasmology? Anyway, we saw her mother returning, and I found an excuse to get well out of earshot. I went to talk with Miss Dumitru, who was every bit as sensible as both the doctor and the priest said. She told me all about the young soldier who died . . . ah.' I had noticed his closed face and the rigid clench of his jaw. 'Perhaps I can give you that conversation later.

'At any rate, we finished well before dark, but I had no wish to sit at table between a feuding mother and daughter, so I took a walk up the river road. It was dark by the time I returned, but I could see the road, and I had my torch.'

I frowned down at my toes, protruding from the foam. 'There was something on the road – a necklace, like the Queen's pearls. I thought perhaps the string had broken while she was riding . . . but it wasn't broken.' That had been my last clear thought: *How could she lose this if the thread is whole?* 'I was bending to pick it up when something went over me, and then the chloroform.' I thought for a moment, trying to reconstruct what had happened. 'It was a blanket, or cape, or something. But wide, and I think it must have had some means of gathering the edges together because as I was fighting to throw it off, I tried to take a step and went down, as if my knees were tied together. Once I was on the ground, he clocked me on the head, though not hard enough to knock me out. Then he dragged me off – behind a wall, where no one could see. There he sat or knelt on me and must have simply poured chloroform over my head until I stopped struggling.

And woke up in a pitch-black root cellar.'

I shuddered, and reached for the tea. Silence poured off Holmes. His knuckles had gone white, working on my spectacles, but he abruptly laid them down and walked out of the room, coming back with a bottle of brandy – Holmes' standard remedy for any physical or emotional ailment. He poured me a dose, waited until I had dashed it back, then set the bottle on the floor and resumed his work on the spectacles. I sat for a moment, relishing the warm internal burn, then returned to the story.

'It was difficult not to panic, waking up like that. There were no doors or latches on the inside, no food or drink. And the roof was too low to stand. However, as soon as I shoved up at the lid, I found that it wasn't locked, and I wasn't actually buried. It turned out to be a sort of storage bin for vegetables, with earth packed around it and a heavy wooden top, to keep things from freezing. It was in that derelict house down in the village, the one with the falling-down gate. Anyway, I found my torch, spectacles, and boots arranged on the floor outside. If I'd just tried standing up first thing, I'd have saved myself a lot of scrapes and grubbiness.' I raised one of my knees out of the water, making a face at the ingrained dirt and a trickle of fresh blood. 'You might want to ring down for a first-aid kit.'

He handed me the now-straight glasses. I set them on my nose, wincing a touch as they settled onto the bruises, then noticed him rolling up his sleeves a little more. He moved my empty teacup to the stool, and gestured me to rise. 'Let us check the damage,' he said.

'Oh heavens, Holmes, it's just scrapes and dirt.'

'Russell, you were unconscious for some sixteen hours. One

dose of chloroform would not do that.'

Inadvertently, I jerked both arms out of the water to check the inner veins – and nothing. But he was right, the effects of chloroform tended to be brief, unless continuously applied, and although I had definitely breathed in that cloying odour, and it was no doubt the cause of both nausea and stinging eyes, it would not account for that many hours of unconsciousness. And yes, I'd been tired, but I'd not just been sleeping, there in that coffin.

So I pulled the plug and, allowing him to offer me his hand, climbed onto the mat.

He found the injection mark on my right biceps. I raised the elbow to peer down at the tiny red welt amidst a mess of bruises.

'You're sure?'

'Yes.'

But that did not stop him from going over the rest of my epidermis, attaching plasters to any spots that seemed to be leaking, plucking splinters and general debris from others.

I eyed the distant bottle of brandy, but at least I was not looking at him. I took a breath and forced myself to voice the thought neither of us had yet brought into the room. 'So, why did he not strip me and carry out a further assault, while I was – Holmes?'

My partner and husband had made an odd sound and rose so abruptly, the stool went over. He retrieved his cigarette case, took out tobacco, got it lit. I studied his back – and belatedly realised that perhaps at the beginning I ought to have said that the man had not . . .

Nor, I decided, should I say it now, not in so many words.

'I mean, granted,' I continued, 'the fellow may have expected someone more voluptuous, but I'm not entirely unpresentable.

And in any event, he doesn't seem to have so much as looked – in fact, it did not seem like that kind of assault at all. Which leaves us with the question of, what was his purpose? Why abduct me, knock me out for half a day, and stick me in a box? One that, in the end, took an embarrassingly small effort to escape from?'

It was absurd to mistake assault for desire, but he knew that. I went on speculating for a time, while Holmes laid his cigarette down and returned wordlessly to his examination.

Down my back and right side, up my front and left, though I had to take over his stool by the time he had finished the repairs to my knees, and I was growing impatient for food as his fingertips moved up my left arm.

'Holmes, thank you for acting the medic here, let me just put on a dressing gown and when I've sat still for a bit, we can ask for some lunch. Holmes? What is it?'

He had gone very still, his eyes on the side of my neck. I pulled away, and saw that utter lack of expression that is so worrying on his face. 'What?' I demanded. 'What's the problem?'

I felt around the skin where he had been looking, but it hurt no worse than a dozen other places, so I climbed upright and staggered over to the looking glass to see what had so troubled him.

Ignoring the livid bruise on my cheek, the inflamed red of my eyes, and the sunburnt look from the chemical, I tipped my chin towards the light from the window. Some straggles of wet hair lay down my neck, reminding me that I needed a haircut, but I brushed them aside and saw—

Two angry puncture marks, resting in the hollow above my left collarbone.

'Russell,' said my husband, in the most phlegmatic manner imaginable. 'I believe we see now what he was after.'

Her throat was bare, I thought, idiotically, *showing the two little wounds* . . .

At which point I was rescued by a flood of good, healthy rage.

'God damn it!' I shouted. 'Who the *hell* is playing silly buggers here?'

CHAPTER THIRTY-ONE

As always, food and drink helped settle the nerves. Looking back, Holmes' standard remedy might have been a touch generous that day. Halfway through the sandwiches he had requested, I found tears of laughter running down my face.

'Enough,' he chided, the second time I asked him to check if my incisors were growing.

'No, truly Holmes, you'd best not sleep near me tonight, you might never wake up. And you know, I'm feeling a touch phobic about sunlight – and yet strangely tempted to creep out of the window head-first to clamber down the stones to the ground.' I giggled, ending in a hiccough.

He stood and put away the bottle, returning with coffee.

After a few more terrible jokes and obscure literary references, I let the humour subside, although I did find myself chuckling about nothing much, from time to time.

He waited until the reactions had spent themselves – fear, fury, and laughter in order – before trying to get any sense out of me.

'What impressions do you have regarding your attacker?'

'Other than being someone who can lay hands on chloroform and some injectable sedative? It was a man.' The attack had, I realised, roundly eliminated the possibility that some troublemaking village lass was behind these attacks. The person who laid hands on me was no girl. 'He was at least as tall as I am, maybe taller. Heavier, though not heavy – when I elbowed him in the chest, there was not much extra flesh. Strong, although he had to drag me off the road, so perhaps not strong enough to lift me. Oh – and I wrapped my handkerchief around the torch, in case he left fingerprints. We mustn't forget to retrieve it before the maid takes the laundry.' I noticed a flicker of surprise cross his face. 'What, you didn't expect me to think of the evidence?'

'I am gratified that your mind was sufficiently clear.'

'Yes, well. Other than that, the attack was as anonymous as could be. Silence, cloth that muffled my shouts and was too tough to tear, and a building that stands open to the elements. He was sure of himself – no particular fumbling around, no reaction when I fought back. And he was big enough to keep me down once I'd fallen. He didn't speak – didn't make any noise, not that I remember.'

'Would you say this was a practised assault?'

I was not fooled by his controlled, dispassionate quest for information. I could feel the rage simmering below the surface, that some person had dared to attack his wife. But I was grateful for the pretence of normality, and shook my head, as if we were discussing some impersonal case. 'Not necessarily – it could simply have been carefully rehearsed. But there was no moment of hesitation or doubt, not even when I fought back.'

We considered the implications. It was bad either way: a man willing and able to waylay a strong, competent woman would find few challenges to another attack. And Holmes and I both knew that assaults tended to escalate, as confidence grew.

'Even if his motivation is the creation of rumours, rather than some sexual impulse, it does create a worrying scenario. His assaults have grown from whispering at a girl from a cemetery to jabbing one in the neck with a carving fork and tossing her into a nearby root cellar. What comes next? A full-fledged exsanguination?'

'Would you say the assault was aimed at you, specifically? Or simply any person, man or woman, who was walking down the road alone?'

'The housemaids do seem to wander around at all hours, don't they? Though few of them are my height. If someone saw me leave the castle, they'd have known I would come back along that road at some point. But to plan an encounter, specifically with me, at that precise spot, at a time no one else was nearby? That leaves a great deal to chance. The villagers tend to shut their doors at dark, but there is still a certain amount of traffic that early at night.'

'How long since you had seen anyone else?'

I thought back. 'When I came along the other road, there were some children and a farmer on a cart. A motorcar drove through the crossroads, and someone with the outline of Father Constantin was headed in the direction of his home. But it's true, when I reached the crossroads and turned in to the village, I hadn't seen anyone in five or six minutes.'

'Considering the unrest in the village, the man may have anticipated that a benighted pedestrian would more likely be a visitor than a resident.'

I couldn't help thinking of those impromptu weapons I had

seen in Vera Dumitru's house. 'It's true that the villagers are hunkering down inside their gates, but they also appear to be preparing their wooden stakes.' I described what I had seen, placed conveniently near the door.

A thought then came to me. 'It does rather raise the question of how, if you and I are caught wandering the village at night, we are to prove to an angry Roumanian that we are not *strigoi*.'

He shook his head. 'We must end this before the mobs form.'

'Or before one of the girls is attacked.'

'That, too. But I would think that, whether you were a chosen target or an inadvertent one, it is the timing that matters.'

'When the Queen is here, yes. To give the impression that the acts are committed, if not by the Queen herself, then by someone in her immediate entourage. Though come to that, could it be one of them?'

'It would seem unlikely. The handful of attendants – a secretary, a lady-in-waiting, two or three others – do not strike me as valid suspects, being either far too fragile to commit that assault, or too intelligent to do so the instant the Queen returns to Bran.'

'It is puzzling,' I said. 'We're dealing with a methodical and, I should say, educated mind. The drugs suggest a person with some degree of medical training – otherwise, he'd have just bashed me and trussed me up. That's a limited pool of suspects, here.'

'You mean, the doctor, the priest, and the major-domo.'

'You include Florescu?'

'You heard Her Majesty: the man is a jack of all trades, including the medical.'

'Dear me,' I said. 'Another butler who may have done it. Although I will say, he looked honestly astonished when I walked up the road just now.'

'It is not necessarily he. There are five people in the village who attended at least one term in university, including Casimir the shopkeeper and Vera's brother, the driver. The former was present when the doctor performed an emergency amputation last year, the latter watched him anaesthetise the kitchen maid with the cut hand this past spring. There are even a handful of would-be Communists – two men, one woman – known to have attended demonstrations in the city. The woman is Casimir's sister-in-law, who has worked as a cleaner in the Braşov hospital. And one of the men is the driver's closest friend.'

'Thus, local hotheads who know all the village habits and back alleyways, and witnessed the use of chloroform and perhaps morphia. When did you learn those little facts?'

'When I was here before. It is extraordinary how much one can pick up from the head cook in a house like this.'

'Does this take us back to the proposal that the motivation is political?' I tried not to sigh. 'Perhaps you should tell me what you learnt in Bucharest.'

He came back from his place at the window at last, to settle onto the chair across from me. A certain deliberation to his movements, a degree of lightness in his voice, were the only signs that his equanimity was not entirely real.

'In fact,' he began, 'I learnt far less than I anticipated. One goes into a series of interrogations hoping for clear clues to follow, or failing that, for clear indication that one hypothesis is unfounded, leaving one to explore the next. In this case, well . . .

'When I arrived at the Athenee Palace, I was given a packet of information sent by my brother from London, a basic dossier on three men with whom he had arranged appointments for the following day.

233

'I saw no reason to wait until morning, and instead began to ring around after them. The first is in a hospital halfway across the country, and has been for some time. The second was out of town, but has an indiscreet colleague who told me where the man's secretary would be dining. The third was known to the hotel staff as a regular in the bar. My brother will not be happy to learn that his sources of information in this part of the world are not as precise as he imagines.'

That thought cheered us both up for a moment.

'The first name in Mycroft's notes was an Anarchist currently laid up by the gout. The second was the head of Roumania's Communist Party – a fifty-eight-year-old Russian named Dalca, who may have much metaphorical blood on his hands, but very little actual. Officer class, who gives the orders to the execution squad without ever holding the rifle himself.'

'Not exactly a natural-born Bolshevik.'

'No, but precisely what they often end up with, since this kind of man knows how to organise and direct the rabble.'

'Isn't directing rabble what we're seeing, here in Bran?'

'Not according to the man's secretary. Who, you will be amused to hear, is a West End confidence trickster by name of Ernie Johnston, whose habit is to bilk men with shady business practices. So far as he is aware, Comrade Dalca has never heard of Bran, or even Braşov. And although the Party would no doubt happily take credit for any plot against the Queen, and encourage any revolt that might come out of it, it does not appear that the Communist Party is attached to this.

'Last was the Roumanian correspondent from *The Times*, who employs the hotel bar as his personal information centre. Mostly for the gathering thereof, but he was also willing to provide me with knowledge about Her Majesty's relationships with her eldest son, with Prince Barbu Ştirbey, who manages the royal estates, and with Ştirbey's wife. However, whether by knowledge or rumour, he has heard no indication of rising discontent or plot aimed at Queen Marie.'

'Was it wise to hand a newspaper man a bit of juicy gossip like that?' If word got out that Sherlock Holmes was looking at Queen Marie's Transylvanian vampires, the village would be knee-deep in cameras and eager newsmen.

'I believe he will keep the matter to himself.'

'Really? What did you have to threaten him with?'

'I owe him a favour.'

'A *favour*? Holmes, I hope it was worth it.'

'Since he also gave me a telephone number for the Prince, I believe it was.'

'You talked with Prince Barbu as well? Roumania's very own Grey Eminence? Possible—' I caught myself, and lowered my voice. 'Reputed father of various children of Queen Marie?'

'None other. We travelled from Bucharest to Sinaia in his private railway car, so we had nearly four hours together, during which time we talked about the Dacians and Huns, the Hapsburg rule, and the Austro-Hungarian empire. He agreed that, though Transylvania has not been independent since the seventeenth century, there are nationalists who live in hope – and there is no doubt that they see the current situation of the royal family a golden opportunity to break away.'

'The King is ill, his daughter said.'

'The King is ill, his heir is a libertine with no interest in ruling, and the next in line is a boy of four. Queen Marie may be the strongest man in the royal family and a much-loved source of national pride, but legally she holds little authority beyond that of advisor.'

'So this would be a time for Transylvanian Nationalists to strike?'

'It would be. Except that, so far as Prince Barbu can see, there is no sign that they are actively doing so. Which was also the judgement of the *Times* correspondent, who has little idea why the Roumanian people are so amiable about the shortcomings of their royal family, and would be pleased to catch word of a nice scandal to justify the employment of a man far from home and limited to the three hundred words of an Eastern European by-line.'

'Could it be Prince Barbu himself? Not that he personally would have waylaid me on the road, but could he be creating problems for the royal family? If he's an ambitious man, he could have his eye on founding a second Roumanian dynasty.'

'The man I spoke with demonstrated nothing but unwavering loyalty, to both Queen *and* King. He was largely responsible for the land reforms that kept the country from rising up in revolt, he administers the Queen's estates, he remains a close advisor to the king. And,' he added, seeing my dubious expression, 'Barbu's wife is a close confidante of Queen Marie as well.'

Which could mean the wife was exceedingly stupid – or remarkably modern – but Holmes was right: it was also possible that the purported lover was indeed merely a close and trusted friend.

'It sounds as if you liked him.'

'I found him a remarkably subtle mind. Quiet, unassuming, and able to listen. His knowledge is both broad and detailed, and demonstrates a habit of dedicated research, not merely cocktail hour chat. He is a patriot. He loves his Queen, but more than that, he respects her. And I should say that he respects his King as well. Which is a less easy task.'

'So either Count Barbu is immensely skilled at the art of deception, or he has no personal ambitions beyond service – to his country in general and the royal family in particular.'

'I would not say he has *no* personal ambitions. But I saw none that would drive him to betray his Queen and actively work to sully her reputation among the people.'

'So if it's not the Communists, nor the Nationalists, nor even her closest advisor, where does that leave us?'

'It leaves us closer to home.'

'The personal, not the political.'

Well, at least that got us out from under Mycroft's influence. The first good news I'd had today.

CHAPTER THIRTY-TWO

I T HAD BEEN MORE than two hours since I'd stormed up the castle drive, and I became aware of an odd sensation within my brain, like a drain when the plug had been removed. I fought its pull by getting to my feet and circling the room, thinking aloud. "'Closer to home" means evidence and interviews. More interviews. Not more people interviewed necessarily, but people more reinterviewed.' *Stop babbling, Russell.* 'Not that we have a great deal of actual evidence: those plaster casts you made, and possibly fingerprints on my torch. Have you been examining the feet of every man you pass? Most of the local footwear has little resemblance to the smooth, sophisticated plaster of your casts. A farmer wearing those would risk skating across a barnyard like an old woman on ice. Half the people wear what looks like handsewn moccasins. Where was I? Right – evidence. Can you find the equipment to raise prints off the torch, Holmes? Lamp-black and a soft brush would help.'

I had come to a halt near the recessed window frame. My shoulder was propped against it. Also my head. In the silence, some thought was trying to push itself to the surface. Some evidence that had been placed directly beneath my nose. Mice?

I tore myself away from supportive stonework to make another circuit of the room. 'I'm guessing we'll need to set up watch again tonight. And you'd think I had plenty of sleep last night, what with one thing and another, but I rather think I ought to close my eyes, just for a little time. You might want to do so, too, Holmes – you don't look very well rested. Not that you will, heaven forbid you should take my advice. Never mind, if I don't go now, you'll have to summon the footmen to carry me. But there was something I wanted to tell you. That I discovered. About mice? Damn, it's gone.'

And so was I.

Holmes woke me by the gentle urging of a poke in the ribs.

'Ow,' I protested.

'Unless you are crippled, Russell, you may want to rise.'

I turned over, cautiously. Although I was definitely aware of various pains, they were not as urgent as they had been. Holmes was looking less drawn, too – I would not ask what he had discovered while I had slept, lest he be forced to admit to that he, too, had napped.

'What time is it?'

'Just gone half-four. We are summoned to tea – substantial, I am told, in the place of a proper meal – at five, which will permit the Princess Ileana to be past the worst of the road before dark.'

My fingertips were exploring the pair of welts on my throat. 'If we don't want to stir up gossip, I'm going to need heavy

239

make-up, or a high-collared shirt.'

'Before you slept, you were trying to remember something about mice.'

Yes, there had been some thought, scurrying around the corner of my brain. What was it?

'Rats!'

Holmes raised his eyebrows.

'Not slang – memory. I think I told you that Ileana heard ghosts in the walls? Granted, even a Queen's castle has rats, but the girl insisted that once it was a scraping sound, another time a dropped cup. And each time, it was in a room up against the shield wall. That very thick shield wall.'

His eyes went out of focus as he pictured the castle floor plan. He nodded. 'A military post might well have one or more hidden passages, in case defences are breached.'

'Ileana also thinks there should be a back door somewhere, although she has yet to find it.'

'It might have been blocked off at some point, to keep the villagers from stripping away the fittings. If anyone knows, it will be Florescu.'

'Perhaps it's marked on the architect's plans?'

'If the architect had found a secret passage, everyone in the castle would know of it.'

'True. Well, at some point you and I ought to knock on the walls, see if we can find any hollow places. And speaking of hollow, if, as I anticipate, you plan to spend the night watching for vampires and/or witches in the village, do you suppose I might beg for a tray instead of presenting myself in the Queen's quarters? I don't think I could bear a thousand sympathetic questions from those two.'

'I let it be known that you took a walk and got lost in the woods. Everyone seems more concerned with how no one came to notice your absence than with the apparently minor injuries you sustained.'

'So not only am I a mess, it's my own fault.'

'You did find your way out on your own.'

'Better than nothing, I suppose. However, I'm not sure I have the energy to step in between Marie and her daughter. When I left them yesterday, the term "battle royale" came to mind.'

'I believe that negotiations are completed and a truce agreement signed, stipulating that Ileana will be driven back to Castle Peleş as soon as our meal is over, and that she will stay there for at least three days.'

'What did the Queen have to give in return?'

'Ileana then comes back to Bran, and is permitted to stay until the end of the month.'

'Well, if they managed to suspend hostilities, the least I can do is allow them to feel sorry for me. And I suppose we'd best get to work, if we only have seventy-two hours. Although I would very much like to ask the kitchen maids not to walk around at night without company.'

'That is done. I had a word with Florescu – not that I told him what you had encountered, merely said that we were concerned to keep other girls from being harassed by voices from the graveyard, and that until we could uncover the culprit, we wished to hire a cart to take them home each night.'

'Thank you, Holmes, for putting my mind at rest. Oh heavens, I must dress!'

But when I went to stand before the looking glass, I saw a problem. My eyes were less inflamed, the sunburnt effect had faded, and make-up would hide the bruise – but any Roumanian seeing those two vivid marks on my neck was going to be alarmed. Wearing a bandage would be worse. I did have high-necked shirts, but nothing sufficiently formal.

So I dug out the costume that had been left for me, and as I'd thought, in addition to the skirt, over-apron, blouse, and sash belt, it included one of the snug headpieces that the Queen had worn at dinner. More wimple than headscarf, and pale rather than the colourful squares worn by the local women, it covered everything but the face itself. She had probably first worn such a garment during her wartime nursing days, but now I suspected it was a bow to vanity, hiding every potential wrinkle and sag.

At the age of twenty-five, I was a long way from worrying about facial sags, which made it an absurd garment for me, but it might merely look as if I were attempting to flatter Her Majesty by imitation.

I worked the earpieces of my spectacles between flesh and fabric, then stretched my jaw a few times, to make sure I would be able to speak, and perhaps take nourishment. I felt a bit like a child's doll in a souvenir shop, but I could move.

When I went into the next room, Holmes – dressed in his normal suit – was waiting. He ran his eye over me, taking in the snug hair covering, the flamboyant colours of the blouse and sash, the wide hips of the skirt and apron. 'Come along, Coppélia,' he said. I toddled after Holmes to join the royal ladies.

Gentle affection was in full view between Queen and Princess, with no indication of the day's furious bargaining and compromise. Both wore clothing similar to mine, though without the headgear (which, I found as the meal progressed, attracted soup dribbles and breadcrumbs as efficiently as an infant's bib). And yes, both wanted to know about my misadventures of the night before.

There was no hiding that I'd had some kind of a mishap – storming bruised and filthy up the stairs had taken care of that. But my furious, English-language outburst had stopped before I'd given away the attack, and nothing in my appearance went counter to Holmes' story, that I'd spent the night tripping around a pitch-black forest before crawling under the bushes to sleep.

Fortunately, I remembered the Queen's fondness for fairy tales, and diverted the conversation into a light-hearted retelling of the Babes in the Wood (leaving out the tale's dead parents and homicidal uncle), after which Holmes joined in with an anecdote about Cole Porter in Venice, and the songwriter's version of the story that involved the rescue of the 'babes' – in his case not infants, but well-endowed young women – by a rich old man in a big sedan.

From there we travelled into the Venetian lagoon and my attempt at rowing a gondola, followed by a description of the newly-invented sport of water-skiing and Ileana's love of sailing, by which time we were safely past any abduction and wounding of a guest.

Before either of them could remember unaddressed questions, I popped in with a bright change of topic.

'I had a look around the castle yesterday, before meeting the Princess. What a marvellous place. However did you come to own it?' The Queen had touched on the story before, but I thought she might like to tell it more fully, and indeed she did: How she'd glimpsed the towers from horseback one day, long ago, and wished she knew more about it. How the city fathers of Braşov, their hearts bursting with pride at being reunited with Roumania and with love for their new Queen (I took care not to meet Ileana's eyes) came to her and begged her to accept their humble gift – not as tribute to the royal family, but as a gift to her, the Queen, alone.

How the first time she'd arrived, ink scarcely dry on the deed, she'd expected to find it overgrown with bramble, locked into a time long past, like some Sleeping Beauty castle. And indeed, parts of it were derelict and there were rooms into which the good men of Brașov would not let her walk (due to the floors in some, the ceilings in others), but nonetheless, she had found it surprisingly tidy and well maintained, for a structure that had so long stood empty.

'And when I discovered that the city had been paying a stipend, to ensure that the roof stayed whole and no local boys got in and accidentally burnt it to the ground, I asked to speak with the family in charge. That is when I met Mr Florescu. I hired him on the spot, to teach me about the castle and help me bring it back to life. He does not always like what my architect, Mr Liman, proposes to do,' she confided, 'but the two men have learnt that working together makes me happy, and so they do try.'

She laughed, that rich sound of pleasure, and Ileana joined in.

'I gather that a number of Mr Florescu's family are working here, too,' I said. 'Gabriela is his niece, I believe you said?'

'Yes, his sister's daughter, the poor man has no children of his own. He was married, but his wife—' The Queen's pale eyes darted sideways to her daughter, and she adjusted what she had been about to say. 'His wife was ill for a considerable time before she died, and spent many years in a sort of hospital in Brașov. In her absence, Florescu began to take an avuncular interest in a number of the village youngsters – helping them in school, or to set up businesses. Several of them work here, in the kitchen and stables. I am told one of his nephews is a magician when it comes to maintaining a motorcar engine. There's also a most promising new boy in the gardens this summer, who is one of his protégées.'

'Very useful indeed.'

'And Gabi,' Ileana put in.

'I do like to feel that I am returning their castle to life for them as well. Isn't that one of the responsibilities of royalty, after all? To care for the great houses and not only make them productive, but fill them with beauty. The people are proud when their betters are lifted up in the eyes of the rest of the world.'

I had to bite my tongue against the words of protest. A woman bred and born to be Queen, with Victoria on one side and Alexander II on the other, whose elder daughters both sat on Europe's thrones – it was too much to expect her to understand, much less hold, any faintly republican sentiments. Ileana might, with her peasant friendships – but it was not my task to turn the girl's young mind to the benefits of a democratic system.

I solemnly told Her Majesty that I hoped I might return to see the end product of her endeavours, some years down the line. 'But tell me about your own hand in things,' I urged. 'I saw the garden, which I believe is your own work? And the decoration of the rooms is a compelling mix of folklore and sophistication. Such as the ikons and statues, which I see in most of the rooms. I hope a question about this is not out of place – I have a particular interest in religion – but you are not of the Orthodox faith yourself, are you?'

'No, I remain an Anglican. The King is Roman Catholic, while the country is, as you say, Orthodox. This has created problems, but nothing that cannot be solved. For example, during the coronation, my husband could not bow to the priest of another faith, so he simply placed the crown on his own head, then did the same with me. And yet, the people's faith has great beauty and truth. I hope, some day before I die, that I might be allowed to grow closer to its great churches and rituals.'

'We had an interesting conversation with Father Constantin in his garden the other day.'

Her face lit up. 'Such a charming man. He has been of such enormous help in my own garden, a person who truly understands the needs of the local soil and what kind of flower will do well here. Although he tries to convince me to grow something other than flowers – and if I did, who would the local farmers sell their product to?'

'Is he a local man, too?' I asked, knowing the answer.

'I don't believe so,' the Queen began.

Ileana spoke up. 'Gabi told me that Father Constantin came just after the War, when the old priest died of the influenza. I think his wife was born here.'

The wife, according to the good Father, had been born in Braşov, but I did not correct her.

'You have some good men, here in Bran,' I commented. 'Mr Florescu, Father Constantin, and Dr Mikó.'

'If only the entire country was as fortunate as this small corner of it. I must get to know the doctor, I hear he is most devoted to the wellbeing of his people. One sees him bustling about at all times, day or night.'

'He seems to be quite a good doctor. His training goes beyond what one would expect of a village medic.'

'Really? That is good to know. Certainly when we had to call him in to attend to a kitchen girl's cut hand in the spring, he seemed more than competent. I shall not hesitate to call him in

246

when one of the people here needs attention.'

Although perhaps not for anyone who really mattered . . .

The smile I gave her may have been a bit thin, and Holmes rather pointedly changed the subject. 'Is your architect coming any time soon? I should be interested in asking him about the castle.'

'Next week, I believe.'

Neither of us looked at Ileana, who would be back under our feet by then. We finished our meal, and our business, and faded into the castle's upper reaches.

CHAPTER THIRTY-THREE

THE QUEEN'S ROLLS-ROYCE WENT down the drive twenty minutes later, with Ileana and her white dog in the back seat. I changed out of the Roumanian needlework and into a dark, high-necked blouse. Within the hour, we were in the village, watching several of the girls scurry down the drive and climb onto the back of a waiting horse cart, lanterns swinging at the front and back. Vera Dumitru had returned to work, I saw. She did not appear unduly fearful – indeed, she seemed determined to show how unintimidated she was by the night, lighting a nonchalant cigarette before she climbed up onto the cart, laughing perhaps a touch loudly at something one of the other girls said.

I was happy to see her spirited response to events, but also concerned. What if Holmes and I failed to uncover the voice from the graveyard? Would she forever be looking over her shoulder?

The driver snapped his whip over the horse's back to get the cart moving, and the girls laughed and called out protests at the sharp motion. To my surprise, its progress was not marked by the usual sound of iron-clad wheels, and I realised it was one of the hybrid adaptations I had seen, with the axle and tyres from an old motorcar. We could hear their voices, fading as the cart retreated down the road that circled the castle and headed south.

Silence settled over the village. Twelve minutes later, we heard the faint jingle of the harness, followed soon by the sound of hooves and the smooth purr of the rubber tyres. The cart turned up the road to Braşov, then reappeared a few minutes later, with only Vera and the driver. As the horse trotted briskly by, Vera had got to her feet, and was climbing over the driver's seat to join him. They seemed to know each other – not that everyone didn't know everyone else in Bran, but these two seemed close, she calling some laughing insult, he swerving as a threat to toss her over the edge. She gained the seat beside him and punched him on the arm, and then they were around the corner and gone.

This time, the cart did not reappear. The driver's home must be down that road – which would explain both Vera being his last passenger, and her easy familiarity with the man.

Quiet returned. And with it, a tickle of unease.

'Holmes, shouldn't Gabriela have been with them?'

A brief pause, then: 'I last saw her when she came to the door, at a quarter past four.'

'She seems to be on duty in the morning, not at night.' That statement was less reassuring than I had intended. I'd seen her as late as . . . five o'clock? Nearly six, one day. And in August, six o'clock was broad daylight, hardly a vulnerable time for a girl walking home through a busy village. Still.

'I'd like to check with Vera Dumitru, before their lights go out. She'll know if Gabriela left.'

'I will come with you.'

I rested a hand on his sleeve. 'Holmes, you cannot both watch over me and over your half of the village. I was careless last night. It will not happen again.'

I could feel him wrestling with himself, but in the end, he knew I was right.

However, he compromised by seizing my hand and – just as I thought he was going to startle me with some statement that would embarrass him later – pressed a cold, heavy object into it. 'Take the gun.'

So I took the gun, and jogged off to pound on the Dumitru door before the lanterns were extinguished.

Or, as it turned out, to stand in the road outside of the wooden gates and listen to the dogs clamour until someone came out to see what they were barking at.

I went on tiptoes to peer over the wood, letting the lantern light hit my face. 'Hullo, I need to have a brief word with Vera.'

The response was a torrent of Roumanian, so I just repeated her name, loudly and firmly, until the girl herself appeared at the door. She shouted at the dogs, who subsided into grumbles, and came to look over the gates at me.

'Meesus Holmes! What is wrong?'

'Nothing, Vera, I only wanted to check – did Gabi go home before the rest of you?'

'Yes, at seven. Or maybe bit later. But before dark. She come in early to get the breakfast started, makes for long day to work dinner, too. And her father need to eat, he at home, not too well. Drunk man, yes? You need her?'

'Oh no, thank you, we just happened to notice that she didn't go down the hill with the rest of you.'

'Yes, she gone home. She does stay, sometime, in the castle, but only if someone watching her father. And not often when Queen is there, too many people then – no beds.'

'I understand. And she probably is happy to be home before dark – didn't she tell me that she lives up near Râşnov?' Râşnov was on the road to Braşov.

'Râşnov? No, no – other side, halfway to Predelut.'

'Really? I must have misunderstood. Well, thank you, Vera, I won't keep you and your dogs up any longer, sleep well.'

The look on her face suggested that my concern about Gabriela had awakened hers, and that with one more iota of doubt, she would set off – with or without me – to check on her friend. So I took care to distract her, with a string of idiotic explanations that I'd been writing a letter home and that Gabriela had promised to get me the recipe for those delicious walnut biscuits I'd tasted the other day and I forgot to get it from her and so when I was staring out the window and noticed Vera go past I thought . . .

Nonsensical, all of it, but it deflated the girl's growing concern quite nicely, and she was looking a touch superior by the time I dithered to an end and told her that my husband was waiting to walk me to the castle, and let her shut the gates and cross the yard to her door.

The dogs gruffed to themselves a few times, and the village settled down.

The moon was not much more than half-full, and had there been any haze in the sky, I would have been blindly feeling my way down the road with a stick. As it was, I moved with caution, but I'd been over these roads several times now, so I knew more or less where I was and what obstacles to avoid.

When I reached the crossroads, I looked up at the black shape against the sky. Had there been any lights showing, I would have been tempted to continue on and check, just to be sure. But Vera said that her friend had gone home before dark – which here was half past seven – and I had little taste for causing a second castle-wide panic of the day.

The shed where I had sat the other night was as good a place as any to watch the confluence of roads through this half of the village. I felt around until I located the log, adjusted the large torch I'd borrowed from the castle guardroom, and settled my aches for a long night.

It could not have been twenty minutes later that I heard motion. A faint rumour of sound, considerably less than the scrape/pause of my feline companion from the other night. I moved out of the shed to listen . . . it came from the direction of the castle. Footsteps, heels in a steady pace.

Had it not been for the sound that proceeded it, I would have missed the figure entirely. With the warning, my eyes detected a motion of darkness against the dark, some tall cloud of a shape travelling from right to left on the road that led towards the church and cemetery. Indistinct, with the outline of a hay-monster but the dimension of a person.

My own crepe soles made less noise than a breeze against the road as I hurried to follow: down to the join of roads, where to my relief the figure was still visible. I rounded the corner and fell in behind, keeping my distance, trying to guess where he was going. He passed the Dumitru house without so much as a bark from the dogs – but as he went past the gates, a beam of lantern glow gave him the brief outline of a man in a cloak, and in an instant, my heart was in my throat.

. . . face-down with his cloak spreading out around him like great wings.

I could feel that tough fabric flung around me, the ties around my knees and the choking stink of chloroform filling the world, the terror and hopelessness, and waking up to the sure knowledge that I'd been buried alive.

The figure swept on, implacable, assured, passing the entrance to the cemetery and on to—

But I'd lost him. Did he hear my footsteps, and duck aside to wait? I bent to pull out my knife – and when I straightened, I saw the figure of Father Constantin, outlined in the light of his own front door. I heard his wife's voice, calling a question, and the door closed on his easy reply.

Not a hay-monster or vampire, but the village priest attending to his flock.

Not a cloak, but a cassock.

I stood motionless, there in the centre of the road. A cassock was made of tough, dark fabric. Could it have been he, enveloping me in cloth and knocking me out? He was all over the village, at all times, intimate with the people and their ways. Who better to plant rumours in their midst? And he'd been a medic, during the War: training enough to pour a vial of stolen chloroform over a captive.

But the seed of suspicion refused to grow. The affection in his wife's voice, and his simple ease with us. His garden, his grapes – his cat. That memorable moment, disparate parts melding into a whole, lodging in my memory: the taste of the juice and the sound of the skins breaking between my teeth; the smell of the garden and images of a thousand hanging grapes over a cat in the sun, tail curled.

Wait. Smell . . .

The reek of chloroform had washed over me, but before that. Had there been any hint of sweat, any brief, evocative moment of a man's hard work beneath a hot sun? Would I remember, a thing that would only have been a quick impression before the chemical hit?

Yes, I would.

And no, the man who attacked me, the cloth that closed in on me, had no such odour. My assailant had smelt . . . stale, perhaps? Or was that just the cloth? In either case, he had not been working in the sun, and the cloth had not covered a man who strode up and down the village a dozen times a day.

It was not Father Constantin.

I was glad. I went back to my shed, and my night watch.

All was peaceful for a long time. The occasional dog and over-vigilant rooster. The silent texture of owl's wings passing overhead.

The tiny thread of sound from hunting bats.

And then the peaceful world ended.

CHAPTER THIRTY-FOUR

THE FIRST SIGN OF the pending disaster was an odd rhythm to the sky over the village. I squinted, cursing my poor night vision, and moved into the road, staring for a full minute before I identified it: an approaching lantern on the far side of the village, the rhythm from the bounce of a person's walk.

It was coming up the centre line in the H. I retreated, ready to duck back into the shed if the lantern turned towards Braşov, but it did not. And yet it did not head for the cemetery road, either – which meant the castle.

I moved down to the village centre to watch the drive – and yes, the lantern was climbing up it, illuminating a pair of baggy trousers.

I was not startled by my name whispered out of the night, since I'd expected Holmes to follow the lantern. I felt him move closer.

'Did you see who that is?' I asked.

'No. He must have come from outside of the village, from the upper road that circles along the base of the hills to Râșnov. He is unsteady on his feet.'

'Oh Lord,' I said. 'Gabi. She lives up that road, and her father is a drunk.'

'What did Miss Dumitru say?'

'She thought Gabriela left at her usual time, just before dark, although she'd have been too busy at the time to notice for sure.' I looked at the pale shape that was Holmes' face.

'Holmes, the girl looks a lot like Ileana. At night, if they didn't realise that the Princess had left . . .'

We watched the man disappear around the top of the castle drive.

'Shall I follow him? To see what's happened?'

'No. If the girl was given a bed there, all will be well. If not, we must try to locate the place of her – the place she's gone to before others do.'

The word *abduction* stood between us, as we waited for the girl's drunken father to return. He did not. Instead, one of the castle's low windows grew light – but from moving lamplight, not a stationary candle.

The kind of light that would indicate a search of the rooms.

We hurried away, across and up the H of roads. The cluster of houses that formed the village soon gave way to small farms.

We had come along this farm track the other day, on our way back from the witch-inhabited forest. Its surface was pitted and carved with the occasional rut, and would be difficult in the winter months, but for now it was dust rather than mud. Once we were free to pull out our torches, we got to work. Holmes took the side with the larger fields, I the side with the hills rising behind the dwellings. We went slowly, playing our muffled beams over any patch of softer ground, looking for an indication of recent disturbance. Here a cow had strayed into the bushes. There a discarded tin, its label long nibbled away. A fresh crack in a fence attracted Holmes' attention, but the scuffs and debris below it testified to a log bounced from a cart.

Half a mile along the track, a glowing window down a side lane indicated a night time disturbance. (An illness, perhaps? Father Constantin's parishioner?) We clasped our fists around the ends of the torches to narrow the beams, lest the occupants be gazing out of their window.

Something caught at my attention. I paused. Nothing visible, but an ineffable breath that raised the hair on the back of my neck. Faint, but unmistakeable. 'Holmes, do you smell . . . ?' But before I could pronounce the word *chloroform*, we were spotted. Light abruptly spilt out of the open doorway and a woman's voice called, '*Tata?*' followed by a phrase that ended in a familiar name.

'I think she just asked if her father had found Gabi,' I muttered at Holmes.

'Then it can't have been much further on.' His torch light began to move more rapidly.

I turned back to my side, pulling my obscuring hand away so as to let the beam go wide. The woman called again, and then I heard her speaking to someone else.

This time, the shout came from a man.

Damn.

The man, inevitably, came to investigate what a woman might not have, his lantern marching down the road accompanied by a string of Roumanian that sounded first irritated, then aggressive.

At the corner of my eye, I noticed another window go light as a neighbour woke. 'Holmes, you slip away. They'll be so confused by finding a woman out here they won't go looking for you, and one of us ought to go up to the castle and see what's—'

I stopped. Was that . . .

The man reached the road, Holmes' torch went off, a neighbour's voice called out – and I stamped my foot down on one of the two things that had caught my eye.

I would have grabbed up the other one, had I been given two more seconds – but at least it provided a convenient distraction.

For everyone recognised the little golden cross engraved with dogwood flowers, lying broken-chained on the roadside. No one paid me any mind, or remembered that there had been two torches. Instead, the moment the woman saw the necklace, she began to wail. This would be Gabi's sister, I thought, and the sister's husband – perhaps turned from their beds by her drunken father, and thus watching the road for his return. In moments, lights sprang up in every nearby window.

And on the road. Neighbours in various stages of undress milled and queued to exclaim over Gabi's necklace. And as if the cry had been heard a mile away, powerful torches appeared, from the direction of Bran. At their head strode a middle-aged farmer, rapidly sobering, along with Mr Florescu, striped pyjamas peeking out between a formal black overcoat and a pair of well-shined shoes.

His moustache, however, bore its customary sharp points.

The woman ignored her father to turn to her uncle, resting one hand on the butler's sleeve and directing a torrent of explanation at him. The only recognition she gave her father was to jab an accusing thumb in his direction, but then, that was a common attitude from the families of chronic drunks. She held up the necklace to show Florescu, her voice wavering, and when he put his arm around her, she broke down into sobs.

Standing there, patting her heaving shoulders, he noticed me at last. It was hard to judge his reaction, what with the constant shift of light and shadow along the road, but I did see his spine go straight, so I patted the air, to reassure him that I did not require his attention.

The woman's sobs began to slow. He caught the eye of a thin, grey woman in a dressing gown, and turned his niece over to her. The crowd separated, the women heading towards the house with the sister, the men waiting for orders.

But first, there was the Queen's guest to be dealt with. 'Mrs Holmes, why are you here?'

It was a very brusque question, considering our relative positions, but his emotion was understandable. 'We saw Gabi's father walking up the drive to the castle, and slipped out to see if we might be able to help.'

A thin version of the truth, but to judge by the darting lights through the castle windows, in the first minutes of searching through its rooms, a pair of oxen might have walked through the doors and Florescu would not have known.

'Are you out here by yourself?'

'My husband went up one of the side lanes,' I said, looking vaguely into the darkness.

'I will have Dmitri walk you back.' He lifted his hand and a large young man leapt to attention. Florescu snapped out an order, his voice overriding my protests in a way that would never have happened within the castle precincts. I did not push matters. What, after all, could I do here?

Except for one thing.

I fumbled and dropped my torch. As I knelt to retrieve it, I moved my boot and used my finger to scoop up the hidden object. I then used the beam to dazzle the eyes of the two men, so they did not notice me dropping my find into a pocket.

Florescu delivered a lecture to Dmitri, either a series of tasks or a detailed warning of what to do with me. And considering Florescu's attitude, which was more that of consulting a mental checklist than of trying not to look too pointedly at a troublesome English guest, I thought the young man was being told what Florescu wanted from the castle. My suspicions were confirmed when Florescu, looking reluctant, tacked on a final command that included the words *telefon*, *politie*, and *Brașov*.

My escort and I met Holmes a short distance along the road, before the village itself. I thanked Dmitri and told him we would be along. He looked dubiously at Holmes, as if thinking him a bit on the mature side for a bodyguard, but then accepted my husband's wave of dismissal and set off to the castle at a trot. Within a few steps, it turned into a run.

Gabriela was loved, in Bran Castle.

I checked down the road to make sure we were alone, then handed Holmes my torch. 'Shine that on my hands.'

I rubbed the object free of clinging soil, then opened my hand.

It was as big as my thumbnail. Perfectly round. With a lustrous gleam even beneath the dust.

'There can be only one person in Bran with a necklace like this,' I said. 'Possibly in all of Transylvania.'

He picked the spectacular pearl off my palm, turning it about under the torch. 'The wear on the hole is almost non-existent. And I believe this one will prove to be marginally smaller than those in the string we have seen her wearing.'

'Do either of those things matter? A dramatic lie is better than a humdrum truth, when it comes to rumours. The point being that it was lying four feet away from a small gold crucifix. It was Gabriela's, I saw it close enough to be sure – although from a distance, or at night, the one Ileana wears would look the same. As indeed, Ileana herself would look the same.'

'A cross,' he noted. 'As if the person who took her could not bear the presence of a religious artefact.'

'And as I was about to tell you when we were interrupted – that was Gabriela's sister, by the way, and her husband – I could smell chloroform.'

'Did anyone else smell it?'

'No, and I didn't mention it. Gabi's cross is what sent the guard running back to the castle, under Mr Florescu's orders. They're calling in the police, from Brașov.'

He rolled the beautiful pearl around between finger and thumb, then handed it back to me. 'The police will send a detective, rather than mere constables. We can only hope that he has a modicum of brains, and can at least act as witness.'

'Holmes, we've been lucky. We've managed to foil several of his efforts before they could come to light and create a panic. Even if his target tonight was in fact Gabriela, not Ileana, I am afraid for the girl. His frustration must be enormous. If it reaches the breaking point, he may take it out on Gabriela.'

'True. Although I cannot see any solution to the matter

save laying hands on him and getting the girl back.'

'As soon as possible. But, Holmes? I don't think we should point out that the two girls and their crosses would look alike, in the dark.'

Chapter Thirty-five

When we reached the village crossroads, the castle came into view – a startling sight, with lights beaming from most of the windows.

The dark houses around us would not remain that way for long. A man with a lamp was hurrying up the path to the village telegraph office.

My feet slowed to a halt outside the sagging gate of the derelict house. 'Holmes, I . . . we need to check.'

He stayed with me as I crossed its weed-grown yard, walked across the room, and lifted the lid of the large storage bin.

It was empty, but for a crushed *allium* flower and the visceral sweep of memories raised by the smell of dust and dank. I shivered; Holmes touched my arm, and we left.

The castle was like an ants' nest. Alarmed footmen poured down the stairway with electric torches, paraffin lanterns, and enough makeshift truncheons for a small war. When we had successfully navigated against this tide, we found the female staff milling about the courtyard, hastily dressed and not far from panic. The cook had seized a rolling pin as she came through her domain, and looked more than competent to put down a revolt all on her own.

The men who had poured past us were more or less oblivious to our presence, but here we were seized upon by the women, who demanded information, reassurance, and most of all, instruction.

I pulled myself up to my full height and held up one placating hand. They subsided. 'As you all no doubt know, Gabriela . . . I'm sorry, what is her last name?'

'Stoica,' said a chorus of voices, showing me which of my audience understood English.

'Thank you. Miss Stoica seems to have disappeared on her way home. The little gold cross she wears was found on the road near her house.' I took care to use the present tense, and waited until the murmur of translation died away. 'Her family is there. The Queen's men are out looking for her. The police have been called from Braşov. I am sure all the village will join the search. You might want to have food and drink when they return.'

This time, the translation was done on the move, as the gathering of women moved as one in the direction of the kitchen. I caught back one of them who had understood my words.

'We need to speak with the Queen. Would you take us, please?'

We followed her across and up to the Queen's rooms. She slipped inside, but was back in moments to show us in. We found the Queen fully dressed, regal and in control. In front of her was a cup of tea. It was three o'clock in the morning.

I eyed the tray longingly, and suggested to the woman that coffee would be a lovely thing, once the kitchen had some brewing.

The moment the door shut, the Queen's assured posture went stiff, her icy blue eyes locking on Holmes. 'What is going on here? I wake to find the castle in turmoil and one of the girls gone missing. Is this in any way connected to why I brought you here?'

Holmes, pulling out a chair to indicate that the reply was going to be a long one, started things off. 'Ma'am, since you returned to the vicinity on Thursday, beginning the night you were in Sinaia, Russell and I have been witness to a series of events designed to slander Your Majesty's reputation. They are—'

'What events? Why have you not kept me informed?'

'Madam, it requires a series to shape a pattern, and at the beginning we did not have that. Later, we did not think you would wish to discuss matters in front of your daughter.'

'You should have come to me. That is why I hired you.'

The idea of Sherlock Holmes as a hireling raised an eyebrow. 'Madam, I can either investigate, or I can deliver reports. I was under the impression that you wanted a rapid solution to the case, rather than ongoing chapters to a story.'

A lesser man would have grovelled, or perhaps melted down, under the force of her gaze – but Sherlock Holmes had turned that mildly amused face on kings, marshals, and imperial governors. It worked as well on this imperious woman as it had on every person I'd ever seen, with the possible exception of Mrs Hudson.

The Queen reached for her cup, and when she had given it an unnecessary stir, her outrage had been packed away.

He nodded, and explained that we had found indications that someone wanted to stoke rumours that the Queen of Roumania was engaging in unsavoury acts.

'"Unsavoury acts"?' she said sharply. 'Of what sort?'

'You know of the Countess Erzabet Báthory?'

The Queen's face went pale. Clearly she had heard of the woman – and I was glad that Holmes did not have to go into details, particularly regarding the episode of the kitchen maid's cut and the suggestive bowl of blood. This proud English aristocrat did not need to dwell on the idea that her people might believe her capable of bathing her skin in a virgin's blood.

'Yes,' he said, 'along those lines, although it would appear that here, your would-be antagonist is willing to seize on any convenient sin, from witchcraft to summoning the dead to having vampiric tendencies.'

She blinked. I knew how she felt.

'I say "would-be" because in at least two of these episodes, Russell and I have intervened before the damning evidence could come to light.'

The coffee arrived, and with it a platter of hastily made but hearty sandwiches, equally welcome. The Queen took the opportunity to ask how the castle was faring, and asked her maid to convey her thanks to the kitchen, and assure them that they would hear any news as soon as the Queen did.

We waited until the door was closed before resuming.

'The first item appeared to be a witch's hex bag.'

'That's a little bag containing herbs and talismans,' I explained. 'that witches are said to use when laying a curse.'

'It was left at the door to a chicken coop,' Holmes continued, 'with a scoop of poisoned grain. Had the farmer let his hens out as usual, they'd have died. The hex bag would have pointed to a witch – and, more specifically, to you.'

'How?'

'The herbs this one contained were Earl Grey tea.'

She did not quite laugh, not with a missing girl at the fore of everyone's mind, but the impulse was clear. Instead, she waved for him to go on.

'We then took a walk up into the hills to consult with an old witch-woman I came across there.'

'Mrs Varga?'

'You know her?'

'I ride all over these hills, so naturally I've met her. An odd woman, but harmless.'

I hoped she was right. I could not help remembering some of the old woman's herbs, drying against her front door.

'Mrs Varga agreed that the bag was a sham, not something a real witch might have made.'

'Aimed, as you say, at creating rumours. Why did it not do so?'

Holmes glanced over at me. 'Because a sleepless young woman noticed movement in the night. Then her husband followed some footprints to the chickens.'

'How fortunate.'

'Indeed.'

I picked up the story from there. 'Then the next night, when you returned, one of the kitchen maids spoke to a dead man as she went home after dark. He claimed to be a local soldier, who was killed in the War. That of course was a long time before you came here, although he has family in the village and was one of Mr Florescu's young protégées.'

'I believe this was one bit of gossip that did reach village ears,' she said.

'It did.'

'But what does any of it have to do with me? Ghosts, witches. The "Blood Countess".'

'We haven't yet figured that out,' I admitted. 'Logic suggests it will be tied to you somehow, but we haven't yet seen how, in anything but the most general of ways.'

'I trust this invisible adversary is not about to build a case that the soldier was my secret lover,' she said in a dry voice. 'I am credited with rather too many of those as it is.'

'Um, well, no. Not that I'm aware. But since the boy was only sixteen, and he died four years before you came here, that would be a difficult claim to establish.'

'Mildly reassuring,' she murmured.

Holmes took us back on track. 'Now, however, we have the disappearance of a young woman who has worked for you for some years. Madam, may we examine that pearl necklace you often wear?'

'My pearls? Certainly, though I do not know what they have to do with matters.'

She went out, returning a few minutes later with a sumptuous double handful of lustrous balls. 'I don't often bring my real jewels to Bran,' she noted. 'Both because I rarely hold formal parties here, but also because I prefer this place to be free of ceremony. Pearls are quite enough, for the most part.'

Holmes and I did not remark that these unreal jewels would pay for a very nice house in London. Instead, he laid them out on the table, close enough together that their marked similarity was displayed. When he sat back, I took out the pearl I had found on the ground and set it beside them.

It was duller, less perfect in shape, and though large in itself, decidedly smaller than any other one on the table.

'I found that a few feet away from Gabriela's necklace,' I told her.

She did not protest, did not point out that it was nothing like hers. She did not need to. All three of us could see that, if a villager had found it first, any proof would have been as effective as a small boulder against a raging torrent.

A knock came at the door. I snatched up the stray pearl and Marie swept away the ropes, settling everything under our garments as the maid stepped in with a bob.

'Ma'am, there is a policeman here to see you. Inspector Dragomir? He says Mr Florescu sent for him.'

'Yes, thank you, Christina, bring him up.' When the door had closed, she turned to us. 'Will you stay? To help me decide how much Mr Dragomir needs to know about all . . . this?' 'We would be happy to,' Holmes lied.

Personally, I was interested to see what a Transylvanian police inspector would look like. In fact . . . 'Would you prefer that Holmes and I speak to him? Give him some of the same information we've given you?'

'Some of it?'

'Nothing personal, nothing touching on your daughter. But a plot against you, from within the village? It is a thing he should be aware of, as he organises the search for Gabriela.'

'I suppose you are right. And I have met this policeman, once or twice. He seemed to me a responsible sort, not like some. I have known policemen to sell information to the gossip papers, if you can believe that.'

We shook our heads at the sad decline of common decency, and went to divert the inspector from Braşov.

In my pocket – barely – was the Queen's pearl necklace.

CHAPTER THIRTY-SIX

Inspector Dragomir was a small, nondescript man in his fifties with excellent manners and fluid English. Beneath his inexpensive suit was the body of a man who went for strolls over mountains, and above his starched collar was a noncommittal mouth and a pair of black eyes that had seen everything, and been surprised by nothing.

Although the two of us were not what he had been expecting. His gaze passed over me and stopped on Holmes. 'I was asked to see Her Majesty.'

'She sent us to see you first. We have information that you may need.'

'Who are you?'

'We are private detectives, hired by Queen Marie to look into a series of incidents that may or may not be related to the disappearance of Gabriela Stoica.'

'Private detective?'

Holmes extended his hand. 'My name is Holmes. This is my wife.'

Often, especially with those for whom English was not a native tongue, the surname did not rouse any attention, even if it was coupled with the description of *private detective*. Dragomir, however, paused over the name as if it had been prefaced by *Sherlock*. I saw him waver, then decide not to ask. Instead, he pointed out that his men were waiting for him.

Holmes assured him that it would not take long, and indicated the chairs in the small reception room adjacent to the Queen's quarters. Dragomir shrugged, but illustrated his impatience by perching on the very edge of his chair.

'Inspector, before we begin, I need to eliminate one possibility in this situation. Have you had other women disappear, in the area? Other attacks, other—'

'No! This is a quiet place. We have no . . . predators.'

His use of the word showed that he well knew what Holmes meant.

'Would you have heard, if there was one in the wider areas – Cluj, Sinaia, Bucharest, perhaps?'

'I would know.'

I watched Holmes, waiting for his decision. Honesty is a risk, and we had promised not to betray the Queen's secrets. But at a certain point, one must choose between trusting a man of obvious intelligence, and crippling him with inadequate knowledge.

In any case, we needed an impartial witness to the pearl.

Holmes nodded, as if I had spoken aloud. 'Russell, I believe the Inspector needs to see our evidence. Will you show him the pearl? I shall go and fetch the hex bag.'

At the final term, Dragomir started to speak, but Holmes

waved him off. 'Inspector, in the interests of time, listen to my wife first, then I will show you our other evidence. After that, we will fill you in on as much of the background as you need to know.'

A somewhat ambiguous promise. But perhaps the man's English was not quite up to that degree of subtlety, because he merely watched Holmes leave, then turned to me.

'My husband and I have been trying to solve a number of night time disturbances by standing watch in the village, hoping to catch the person responsible. Tonight, around midnight, we saw a man come up the road to the castle. It turned out to be the father of Gabriela Stoica, one of the kitchen maids. He was worried because she had not come home when she left work, around seven o'clock. We knew approximately where she lived, and we went up that road looking for indications that she was abducted. And we did that,' I interrupted, as he'd been about to ask me why on earth we might jump to that conclusion, 'because I myself was attacked some twenty-four hours earlier. I was knocked out with chloroform, put into a root cellar in the town, and left there to find my way out. However, I am an English citizen and a guest of the Queen. Either he knew who I was and arranged matters so I would be free as soon as I woke, or he took the first woman available, then realised who I was and decided that kidnapping me would create an enormous problem.

'Gabriela Stoica, on the other hand, is a maid and the daughter of a farmer. That the royal Princess is fond of her may be her only claim to influence. But because she works in Castle Bran, and because it is clear that Queen Marie is familiar with her, she made for an ideal target. And this is why.'

I had to stand up to work the pearls out of my pocket. I stretched them out on the table and sat. 'We came here to investigate a threatening letter, aimed against the Princess Ileana. What we found, however, is a wider threat against the Queen herself. Not physical harm, but an attempt to tie her name with some troublesome, even despicable acts. That is why I'd like you to compare those pearls to this one.'

I placed it in front of Dragomir. He admired it, then looked down at the string composed of dozens of similar examples. 'They look the same from a distance, don't they? Anyone who had seen the Queen's necklace, which she wears all the time, then found that single pearl on the ground, would connect the two. Do you agree?' He gestured his acceptance. 'Well, that pearl was on the road four feet away from a little gold crucifix necklace belonging to Gabriela Stoica.'

His eyes snapped up. I nodded. 'It is possible that there are two purposes in the necklace being left there. Primarily, it is something known to be Gabi's. But second, it is a cross. A holy object said to be offensive to the demonic and even the corrupt and sinful.'

I could see this straining his understanding, and waved it aside.

'In any event, even without the cross, we believe the pearl was intended to create a picture, of the Queen's necklace breaking in a struggle, letting this one roll away, unnoticed. Anyone finding it would think it odd, then think it suspicious, then begin to remember all kinds of strange and sinister events and rumours about the woman who had come to live in the castle. Except that I was the one to find it, not a villager. And I took it away before anyone saw it.

'The reason we are giving you that pearl, Inspector, is for you to examine it and the necklace itself, and judge if the one could possibly have come from the other.'

Holmes had returned during my explanation. He now held out

his pocket magnifying glass, and pulled the candelabra closer to the table. Dragomir started the way we had, by laying the pearl beside the others, then moving it here and there to see if other pearls on the string were a match in size or colour. He then took up the rope and the magnifying glass and worked his way methodically along it, looking for any signs of recent re-stringing or repair. He found what we had found: the silk thread was uniform, and all along it were tiny frays that betrayed many hours of wear.

Eventually, he let the long rope spool down to the table, and nodded.

'Inspector,' Holmes said, 'if you hear any trace of a rumour that a pearl was found at the scene of Miss Stoica's abduction, would you be so good as to let us know? And – would you be prepared to step on it immediately? If anything . . . permanent has happened to Gabi Stoica, this is the kind of talk that would fester beneath the Queen's name.'

'I don't know that I could use that pearl as evidence,' he said. 'It is your word alone that it was found there.'

'I couldn't very well leave it there for all to see,' I protested.

'I understand. But still.'

Holmes stepped in. 'Inspector, its strength as evidence matters less than our wish to convince you. If you hear talk of the Queen being responsible in any way for that girl's disappearance, remember it. And this as well.'

He showed Dragomir the hex bag, describing when and where it had been found. He explained that we had other pieces of evidence, from the plaster shoe-casts to the torch with its possible prints. 'But none of those will help you find Miss Stoica, and that should be of primary concern now.'

'Do you have anything else to tell me?' he asked.

'Nothing that should keep you from your investigation.'

Dragomir took note of the evasive reply, but either he could tell that pushing would have no effect, or he did not want to waste any more time with us. In any event, our gamble, which had rested on a policeman with brains and integrity, appeared to have paid off.

Holmes and I watched him go, our worry about Gabi lightened somewhat, or at least shared.

We had also bought the Queen some time.

The windows were finally showing signs of light. Unfortunately, I could not see an opportunity for any sleep for some time yet, at the end of what promised to be a very long day. 'We need to know what Father Constantin was doing, walking through the village so late.'

'We should also interview Gabriela's colleagues in the kitchen, who may know more about her movements than they have yet mentioned.'

'I'll return the Queen her pearls, and talk to the kitchen,' I said, 'You go chat with the priest.'

Tasks divided, we went our separate ways.

Chapter Thirty-seven

SHERLOCK HOLMES LET GO of the brass knocker and waited for the sound of footsteps. And waited. The priest's house did not appear to believe in an early breakfast hour.

He was about to bang again, more assertively, when a sound came from within. The door opened, and the man's wife looked out. Her initial disapproval – parishioners should have the manners to wait until coffee was drunk – gave way to surprise.

'Good morning, I need to speak with Father Constantin.'

'Yes yes, come,' she said, stepping back to invite him in.

Politely ignoring her dressing gown and bed-slippers, he shook his head. 'I will wait here.'

She smiled and closed the door, and Holmes heard the trail of her voice, calling, 'Costel!' followed by a rapid string of Roumanian that included the words for *Englishman* and *young wife*. He smiled, and took a seat on the bench among the roses.

Father Constantin had put on his cassock, but pyjama sleeves peeped from the wrists. 'My friend, what can I do for you so early in the day? And you do not look fresh from your bed.'

'No, I am not. Before I tell you, I need to ask you about last night. Why were you out so late?'

'I am often out late. A priest is called at all hours.'

'But last night, where were you?'

The priest ran a hand through his hair, to generate thought. 'An old woman is dying. She was restless. The doctor was there earlier, but he can only treat her pain. So, the family sent for me. I gave her holy unction, then sat until she slept. I prayed with the family for a time, and came away.'

'Where does she live?'

'In the village. Up the Fagaraş road three, four houses.'

'Did you see anything as you were coming through the town?'

'What kind of anything?'

'Another person? A cart or motorcar, perhaps?'

'Not a soul. I walked and prayed, and saw no person until I come in my door.'

'How long had you been there?'

'Hmm, hmm. Was after dinner when the boy came. I stayed two, three hours. So maybe ten of the clock? But please, my friend, tell me why you are out from your bed so early?'

'A young woman who works in the castle disappeared on her way home last night. Gabriela Stoica.'

'Gabi? No!'

'She left the castle just before dark, and around midnight, her father noticed that she had not returned. He had, as I understand it, been drinking.'

'Too often, yes. I must go, her sister will want me.'

'The police are organising a search. I will walk with you for a bit, Father, if I may?'

The priest nodded brusquely and hurried inside. Holmes could hear his voice, in long explanation to the wife. When he came out a few minutes later, his hair and beard were combed, the pyjama-stripes gone, and he carried two tin mugs and a pair of napkin-wrapped rolls. He handed one of each to Holmes.

'My wife thinks you need feeding.'

The mug was coffee. The roll held a thick slice of some cold egg pancake dish with bits of ham and onions, savoury and sustaining. When the contents of both cups had gone down enough to permit motion without spillage, the men set off down the road.

'Father Constantin, you must know everyone in the village.'

'A priest does, yes.'

'Who in Bran hates the Queen?'

The priest stopped abruptly, then held his dripping cup away from his garments. 'The Queen? Why? What happened to Her Majesty?'

'Nothing directly. But strange events follow people who work for her. Miss Stoica, for example. She works at the castle, and is a friend of Princess Ileana.'

Progress down the road resumed while the priest tried to see any pattern in the village oddities, then decided simply to answer the question. 'No one hates the Queen. In the cities, you will find young – heat heads, is that the word?'

'Hot-heads.'

'Hot-heads, who see the King as bad and want to bring in greater democracy. "Bad," not evil, you understand – someone who costs the country lots of money and does nothing useful.'

'My country has republicans as well. We fought a war over the monarchy, and tried it for a while, but having made their point, the monarchy was soon restored.'

'Oliver Cromwell, yes.'

'And others. But I don't think here the problem is political. There is something more personal at work.'

Father Constantin took a bite of the roll and chewed absently.

'There are minor . . . *resentimente*?'

'Resentments.'

'Minor resentments, yes. The Queen hires one man and not another – or, not the Queen herself, but her men. Her kitchen buys milk from one farmer, the one left out feels it an insult. But big enough to capture a maid off the road? No.'

'There seems to be some rivalry between her butler, Florescu, and the village doctor. I am not saying that either man has anything to do with the girl's disappearance, but perhaps it could be a part of a larger issue I do not know? Some animosity that might surface elsewhere?'

'Oh, the rivalries in a village are deep, you are right there, my friend. And to be honest, because I am a man from outside, some things I do not always understand. Yes, Florescu and Dr Mikó are like two boy-dogs with each other, polite but hair a little standing up, you know? And yes, I think there was something from long ago that is at the bottom, but could be from when they were boys. Maybe one took the girl of the other, or one lost a football game and thinks the other cheated. Boyhood feelings stay, yes? Like a splinter in the skin?'

'They fester.'

'Yes, that.'

'But I thought the doctor's family was from Braşov, not from Bran?'

280

'Yes – and as a big-town boy, always a little bit more important, you know? That I think adds to the problem. He comes here to visit family, plays lord of manor, Florescu become irritate, yes? And Florescu family hold keys of actual Castle Bran – as watchmen, yes? So their boy can come and go there when Mikó cannot. It – how you say? Rubs nose in the matter?'

'Florescu's family never owned the castle, did they? They were only the caretakers?'

'No no, they never own anything. But they hold the key. Big responsibility in small village, power to keep anyone out, or let anyone in.'

'And any time young Mikó started to act the big man,' Holmes mused, 'all Florescu had to do was invite all the other boys to come play in *his* castle. Yes, I can see that would build a grudge. Who actually owned Castle Bran, before it was handed over to the Queen? The records I have seen are spotty.'

'City fathers of Braşov, I think? Built by them, long, long ago, then given to princes – different princes, of Transylvania. When the border moved to Pajura, a hundred years ago, was no more customs income, so no more reason to want Bran. Was damaged, repaired. Austrian army used it, fifty years ago. And until the War, was used by forestry people. Woodsmen, inspectors. After the War, it needed a lot of repair again, and Braşov was happy to give it to Queen Marie. Here, you finished your coffee?'

Holmes handed the priest his empty cup. Constantin placed it alongside his atop a low stone wall, tucked the napkins inside, and went on unencumbered.

'When I came here six years ago, the village was poor. No telegraph, children barefoot in winter, Dr Mikó only comes from Braşov one day a week. Mr Florescu held keys to a castle about to fall down, where bats lived and squirrels nested. Then five years ago, Queen Marie came, and was like putting water on a dying flower. Telegraph line, roads smooth, children fat and happy. Florescu suddenly the most powerful man in town, you see? She depends on him to hire maids, gardeners, carpenters.'

'And doctors.'

'I do not *know*, you understand, if Florescu or Marie was choosing doctors to come to Bran. Castle Peleş is not far, no problem to call her own doctor from there, if needed. But I think, if Florescu had wanted, he could have said, ma'am, we have an excellent doctor here in Bran, if you need him. And to be honest, I think it started that way. I remember she had Mikó come to castle for some small thing, early on – maybe three, four years ago? But maybe she did not like him, because that was all.'

'Does Mikó treat them anyway? Even villagers who work for her?'

'Oh yes. Just not up at the castle – except in March, when a girl cut her hand, very bad. But yes, he cares for all. And maybe a year ago, he came into money – so he begins to come three, four days a week. Buys new car, new equipment in his surgery. He feels that Bran is home, and is happy now to serve.'

'He no longer needs to keep up his practice in Braşov?'

'Oh, he is still there, works at hospital mostly. But money means he can choose. It is to Bran's good luck that he chooses to come here. He is a good doctor. Gentle hands, good eyes. And con . . . conscience?'

'Conscientious.'

'That, yes. Now injured men, women with birth problems, can get message to his home and he will come or send ambulance. He only charges what they can afford. Makes a huge difference in the town.'

And also makes the doctor hugely important, Holmes reflected. In contrast to his old rival Florescu, who, after all, was still just a glorified caretaker.

Ahead of them on the road was a gathering of men that could only be the search party, heading in their assigned directions. Father Constantin sped up, leaving his companion behind.

Sherlock Holmes stood in the road for a time, not seeing the figures milling about, trampling underfoot any possible sign of a struggle.

Evidence. *Evidentia*. Something that was obvious, to the eye or to the mind. It was also a piece in the machinery of the Law, a fact that went to support a proposition – but that was later on. In the beginning, a proposition would be too formless for proof.

To give a theory form, Sherlock Holmes had been known to beat a corpse and harpoon a pig. He'd come alarmingly close to a murder-suicide, in pursuit of evidence. He'd talked to unlikely individuals, travelled to distant places, and stretched out on a lot of cold, wet ground in order to gather data first to build, then confirm, his theories.

In the early stages, facts and ideas spun past like leaves on a fast-flowing stream, piling up on a protrusion, sailing on when whatever the load had caught against proved inadequate to hold it.

It helped, to be familiar with the patch of stream in question. As it helped, here in Bran, to have learnt that this village house he was standing outside had a rheumatic old woman who rarely slept (and who would have heard an abduction outside her door); and that the one down there held a man who had spent time in prison (but for burglary, not an act of violence); and that the dog there ignored passers-by on the main road (but raised holy hell if anyone went down the lane).

He had the sensation of leaves catching on some hidden impediment. Something that he had been told, or seen, or overheard, was causing the facts to collect.

But what? He patted at his jacket pockets, and made a little sound of exasperation. What he needed was his pipe and a handful of shag, and some time to stare at nothing.

Chapter Thirty-eight

I RETURNED THE QUEEN her necklace, told her that we had spoken with Inspector Dragomir, and ended up repeating virtually the entire conversation.

When I escaped at last, I came face to face with the butler.

'Mr Florescu! I didn't expect – that is, I thought you'd be helping with the search.'

'They have many people. I am needed here.'

'I understand. Please let me know if there is anything I can do.'

He gave me a distracted little bow, and continued on his way.

The kitchen was the hub of all activity. Not that everyone in the room had their hands occupied, but the room was crowded, mostly women, with a few of the younger boys. Half of the servants scattered in embarrassment when I walked in, despite my protest, leaving the women who actually worked in the kitchen turning back to their jobs, although they watched me out of the corners of their eyes. Their expressions ranged from fear to resentment.

'I am sorry,' I said. Always good to start with an apology. 'The policeman went to look for Gabriela, my husband went to talk to Father Constantin, and I . . . I didn't want to be alone. I'm a terrible cook, but is there anything I can do? Peel carrots, fold napkins, polish the teaspoons?'

They did not know what to make of this. A guest, of their Queen, doing scullery tasks? Unthinkable. However, this was an unthinkable day, and they felt sorry for me. Plus, I was a foreigner – who knew what bizarre habits foreign women had? In the end, female solidarity edged out class structure, and I was given some very clean carrots and a very clean apron, and settled into the best chair in the room to scrape.

Absolute silence held for a solid five minutes, broken only by my asking for reassurance that I was doing an adequate job. Hackles subsided, attention slipped away from me, and a couple of stilted, task-related exchanges broke the ice. In fits and starts, conversation resumed. I scraped industriously away, head down, producing the slowest but tidiest carrots that kitchen had ever seen.

Naturally, I could only follow the vaguest gist of what the women were talking about, with the occasional key word emerging from the flow. Gabi, castle, father, sister, home, dog, motorcar – they were reviewing what facts they had: that Gabi had left and her father had come after her, with speculations over why the dogs had not barked and whether any strange motorcar might have come through Bran.

I waited until I had become quite invisible, and then spoke

into a brief lull in the talk.

'They found her necklace,' I said.

Every head there swivelled to look at me, even the women who spoke no English. I diligently scraped for a bit, then looked up in surprise. 'Sorry, I was just saying. The husband of Gabriela's sister – I don't know his name?'

'Radu,' someone provided.

'Radu found Gabi's necklace. With the pretty little cross?' My fingers went to the high neck of my shirt, by way of illustration. 'It was on the side of the road. Near her house.'

Five of the women demanded to know what I had just said. Two of the others provided translation. I kept scraping my carrots.

The cook herself abandoned her ladle and came to sit across the table from me.

'Gabi was taken?' she asked, her English heavily accented but clear enough.

'I think so. Inspector Dragomir thinks so.'

She shook her head in despair. When the Greek chorus in the background had subsided, I asked, 'Do you know Dragomir? Is he good?'

A low burst of conversation, both translating and exchanging opinions, but the cook did not require them. 'He is good man. I have sister in Brașov, husband bad, Dragomir send him to prison.' Some of the others nodded their agreement.

'I am glad. He seems . . .' The word *competent* would go over their heads. '. . . good at his job.'

She nodded. 'He very . . .' but the word she used sounded like *incapacity*, which did not go with the nod. When I frowned, she searched for an English alternative. 'Stubborn?'

'Ah, yes. Stubborn is a good thing, in a policeman.'

287

'Sometimes,' she said with an unexpected twinkle.

'I know that a village girl went away, in the spring. In March, with her boyfriend. What about Gabi? Does she have a boyfriend?'

'Friends, no boyfriends.'

'Girls? That she is close to? A sister in Bucharest, or something?' I asked, thinking of Vera Dumitru.

'Just sister here, and most friends here in Bran.'

'Still, she can't be too happy at home, with a father who drinks.'

An eloquent shrug. 'Men drink. Her papa not bad drunk. Not *bruta*.'

'He doesn't hit her?'

'No, no. Just . . . sad? Sad. Wife die, son die, hurt leg, so drink.'

I had to agree: if Gabriela Stoica had wanted to get away from her father, it would have been a planned escape, not one that left her necklace on the side of the road.

'Have there been women in the area, maybe even Brașov, who have been attacked?'

This caused considerable discussion, but from the thoughtful looks and lack of exclamations, I could tell what the answer was going to be.

'Not in some time. After War, was crazy soldier, attack three girls. Not since then.'

'Was that a local man? Could he have got out of prison?'

'No. Other man kill him there.'

So a literal dead end.

The next bit would be tricky, since I did not want the castle staff to imagine that I was suggesting their master as a suspect. Though of course, he was. 'What about Mr Florescu's other . . .' I searched for an alternative to *protégées*. 'Nieces, nephews, young friends? Any of them 'specially good friends with Gabi? Someone she would go to if she had a problem?'

In other words, someone she would not mistrust along the road until it was too late.

I tried to follow the discussion, which involved names that I did not recognise.

'We think of none,' the cook said.

'Maybe someone who has now moved away? I understand Mr Florescu has helped some village boys and girls, perhaps he helped them find jobs in Braşov or outside?'

But it sparked no speculation, Florescu's help appeared limited to Bran. And if that was the case, any wrongdoing on his part towards the young people would be common knowledge by now.

'What about Andrei Costea? The one Vera thought whispered to her from the cemetery the other night?'

The reaction was both subtle and startling. Everyone in the room clearly knew the young man I was talking about, since he had been a village boy, but to most of them, his recent reappearance in their lives was merely an odd puzzle, and probably some kind of a joke.

But to three of the women, he meant something more. The cook's face turned to stone. Two of the women near her looked at each other, then moved away, one going to stir a dish on the stove, the other muttering something about beds and leaving the kitchen entirely.

The cook, her oldest assistant, and the castle's chief housekeeper.

The woman across the table from me knew she had given something away, but her tight lips told me that nothing more would cross them. I gave her a tiny smile, and picked up my scraper. A moment later, she returned to her stove.

I finished the carrots I had been given, thanked the room for its company, and left.

It was not a simple matter to avoid a person sitting in the courtyard of Castle Bran, but the servants managed. I sat, reviewing what I knew and what I did not, and was dimly aware of women and girls flitting along the upper walkways and ducking into stairways. I did not think they knew whatever it was that had caused the three oldest women to go silent, but they were aware of the unease their superiors felt, and would avoid me as long as they could.

I hadn't expected Holmes to do the same. He came out of the guardroom door, not ten feet away, and walked straight past me to the stairway, saying not a word.

Then I noticed the set of his shoulders: someone had given him food for thought, and he was off to chew on it for a while. Talking with him now would be a bit like conversing with the doorknocker.

At least two hours, by the looks of him.

I'd tried helping out in the kitchen, and there was little point in my attempting to assist with the search on unfamiliar ground.

Perhaps I should go have a conversation with a witch.

Chapter Thirty-nine

I BEGAN AT THE village shop, for yet another packet of hard sweets, along with two tins of milk and a packet of biscuits. I wasn't sure what a witch would consider a treat, but if nothing else, she could feed them to her familiar.

The doctor's fine car was just pulling up as I came out of the shop. A handful of would-be patients, who had been waiting on the bench and in his entrance garden, surged forward, clearly intent on delivering the village news. Had he been alone, I might have stuck my face in his and pointedly asked where he'd been last night, just to see what happened, but I was too late. He was already encircled by half a dozen informants, and any reaction would be wrapped up in his response to them. I merely nodded as I went around them.

I started by walking along the road past the Stoica house, but as I'd expected, if there had been any tracks, dropped clues, or even spilt blood on the roadside, they were thoroughly ground into invisibility now. Half a mile further on was a much-used lane into the fields, beside which stood the ruins of a stone barn. Heavy vegetation along the entrance made the place hard to see, so I went to poke around it. I did find signs of life – crushed weeds, a scrap of tyre print in the dust, a padlock on the door – but when I got it open, the light pouring through the missing section of its roof made it clear that although it was an occasional refuge for the neighbourhood youth, none of them were being kept here against their will at the moment. Indeed, nothing was being kept here, and any root cellars it might have held were long tidied away. I pushed the door shut and the padlock closed, and went back along the road to where the footpath set off into the hills.

Under the growing heat of the afternoon, I was happy to enter the forest shade. The path was rough but clear, the birds busy all around. I could hear the occasional faraway voices of search parties, and I kept a close eye for any sign of unusual activity along the path – the print of a city shoe or a dropped handkerchief with the letters GS, perhaps. But with every passing hour, it became less likely that Gabi Stoica would be found a short walk away from Bran.

However, she, too, would be no shrinking victim, to be marched off into the forest. She was smart, strong, and full of life. She might have been abducted in the same way I was, but if she had not yet been discovered in the equivalent of an abandoned root cellar, it suggested she was beyond reach of an easy search. That left two possibilities: by road, or into the hills. A motorcar could be anywhere by now, and a cart almost as far. But if her abductor had slung her across a horse and ridden up into the hills, I might still have a chance.

Because the hills have eyes.

There was no sign of the deer at Mrs Varga's house, although smoke in the air suggested a nearby curing shed. I walked out into the middle of the clearing, and paused, unsure of the local etiquette. A cat wandered down the vestigial footpath, stopping ten feet away to take its midday bath. 'Is your mistress here?' I asked.

It paused, then went back to its task – b ut when I glanced back at the house, she was standing at the front door, motionless as the wood itself. Had she been there all along?

I raised a hand, and walked up the path, circling a polite distance around the cat.

'Hello again, Mrs Varga,' I said, keeping my words slow. 'I wish you a good day.' I held out the string bag – also bought from the shop – to offer her my gifts. She took it, glanced at the contents, dropped the handles over the door's latch, and turned back, waiting for me to state my business.

'A girl is missing from the village. Gabriela Stoica. Could be by road. Could be into the hills. Would you know, Mrs Varga, if someone came this way?'

She chewed, either on the idea or on something at the back of her teeth. 'Stoica,' she said at last.

'Yes, Gabriela. Brown hair, this tall, brown eyes—'

'Gabriela good girl. I birthed her. Mother die six, seven years ago. Father all right?'

'Um, I think so. Distraught – I mean, angry. Sad. Afraid. The men of the village are all out looking. None have come this way, yet?'

'No. I been out.' She gave a small jerk of the head towards the higher reaches, away from the searching men.

'Have you seen anything? Heard anything?'

'Lots of voices, down there.'

'That'll be them. I don't think she is lost. I think she was taken.'

'By?'

'Don't know yet.' I noticed that I was adopting the English of the natives. Soon I would be dropping my articles and rolling my Rs. 'It will take the men a while to get up here. Maybe tomorrow. So I thought I would come, and ask you.'

'Not seen her.'

'Well, thank you, maybe if you do—'

I was talking to her backside while she bent to paw through the bag. She pulled out a tin of milk and thrust it towards me.

'Oh, no, that's fine, you can keep it. Your cat would like it, if you don't.'

'You take.'

I took. She hadn't given me back the string bag, so I worked the tin into a pocket, hoping the seam didn't split before I found someone to give the milk to.

She caught up a twisted walking stick as tall as she was and marched past me. By the looks of her, she intended a considerable hike.

But at the edge of the clearing, she stopped to look back, holding out one hand in the gesture that means, *Well, aren't you coming?*

So I came.

I can't say we walked together during the next half hour, not even where the path was wide enough for us to be side by side. She led, I followed, and precisely no words were exchanged until we dropped down out of the hills, in a place I had been before, although by a different, and slower, route.

The Roma encampment, on the back road that led to Bran in one direction and the Brașov road in the other.

Holmes and I had walked past it, giving the residents a polite nod, or in his case, a tip of the hat to the women. Mrs Varga marched straight in, past the playing children and through the chickens and dogs to a sturdy little house at the centre of the encampment.

A man and a woman stood in front of the door, either because they were just leaving or because they had somehow intuited our arrival. Mrs Varga held out her hand at me. I stared at her outstretched palm for a moment, then worked the can of milk from my pocket and tentatively held it out. She grabbed it, thrust it at the woman, and started to talk.

I could tell, from the richness of their clothing, the angle of their chins, and Mrs Varga's attitude of respectful camaraderie, that these two were important people. When she came to a halt and gestured at me, I took care to dip my head in recognition.

'*Buna ziua*,' I said.

They murmured greetings, then the man spoke up, in fluent English with an unexpectedly American accent. 'Our friend tells us that a girl from the village is missing.'

'Yes, Gabriela Stoica. She walked home after work last night, and did not get there. We found her necklace by the side of the road.'

The woman asked something, and the man explained, translating what I had told him. 'We know the Stoica family,' he said.

'The mother was a good woman. She raised her daughters well.'

'Did you see anything last night that might help us find Gabi?' I asked, since that could be the only reason Mrs Varga had brought me here.

The two looked at each other, then walked off in separate

directions. I raised my eyebrow at Mrs Varga, but the old woman seemed to think this a valid response, and walked over to some chairs around a low-burning fire. After a moment, I joined her.

Ten minutes later, half the camp was gathered before me.

More to the point, a girl and a boy, each with an adult hand on their shoulder, had been pushed to the fore. It would be hard to say which of the quartet looked more abashed.

The man started things off with a shake to the lad's shoulder. 'Tell her,' he said.

The boy flicked his eyes over at the girl, then winced as the fingers tightened and began to push out words. 'A motorcycle. Yesterday. In afternoon. Coming from Râşnov, going to Bran. We didn't . . . look.'

The woman gave the girl a push forward, but unlike her beau, the young lady needed little encouragement. A stream of words poured out of her, in a tone of voice that declared her utter innocence and willingness to assist.

Fortunately, the man provided a running translation, although without the drama of the original.

The two young people had been sitting in a quiet place beneath a tree – merely sitting, talking about life – when the motorcycle came quietly along the road, left to right, and although they expected the man to turn up for Fagaraş – why else come along that road, if not for Fagaraş? – instead he kept on the lane towards Bran. Such a beautiful machine, so shiny and new – nothing is shiny for long on these roads, unlike the cities, filled with gleaming motorcars, had I ever been to – (the man cleared his throat). Well, it was beautiful. And the engine was so smooth, they hadn't even heard it until the machine was nearly on top of them, but they were just a bit hidden and the man on it didn't see them, just kept on around the corner.

I managed to wedge a question into the flow. 'Did you see what he looked like?'

Both of them shook their heads, and the girl answered. He was wearing a jacket, gloves, leather helmet, and goggles: his own sister would not have recognised him. Average size, neither thin nor fat. Not young, she thought. And probably a *gadje*, from the little skin that showed.

Not a Romany.

I thanked the two, thanked the man and woman, thanked Mrs Varga – and made haste to escape before the wrath of the heavens fell upon the young lovers.

CHAPTER FORTY

As I walked up the castle drive, my body was rebuking me for not spending the afternoon in bed. My head ached, the scrapes on my knees and holes in my neck burnt, and I was favouring my wrenched ankle. I made no attempt at concealing any of it, since I expected the place to be deserted, with the servants either in the hills searching or in the park setting up a canteen. But as I reached the top of the drive, I was surprised to see a dozen people gathered out front – including Holmes and Queen Marie.

Her Majesty had shed her peasant garb and was wearing a simple silk dress that probably cost no more than an office worker's monthly salary. She was carrying a hat, although as I approached, she bent and tossed it into the back seat of the Rolls.

Holmes had an odd expression on his face, disapproving and undecided. Both he and Marie were listening to Florescu.

'. . . Dragomir and tell him that he can reach you at any time, Your Majesty. And if he needs to speak with you in person, rather than the telephone, I will put the motorcar at his service.'

'And you will tell him that he may telephone to Peleş at any time, day or night,' came the royal command.

'Madam,' he said, bowing.

I sidled up beside Holmes. 'What is going on?'

'Mr Florescu and I convinced Her Majesty that matters would be simplified, and servants freed to search for Miss Stoica, were she to return to Sinaia. Unfortunately, she rejected our offer to recall one of the footmen to accompany her.'

'They can be of more assistance here,' said Her Majesty, in no uncertain terms.

'Perhaps Mr Florescu . . . ?' I began.

'He is needed to coordinate efforts.' Head up, eyes flashing, she looked like a general marshalling her troops to battle. 'If they will not permit me to mount up and join the search, then the best way I can serve the effort is to remove myself from Castle Bran. I shall also dispatch servants from Peleş. I shall be in Sinaia before dark. Unless you continue to delay me.'

She turned to Florescu to deliver last-minute instructions, that he was to open the castle's pantry to the search teams, and send for beer from Râşnov if need be.

I spoke in Holmes' ear. 'We can't let her go alone, with no one but the driver.' A driver who had cropped up on our list of suspects because of dubious connections.

'I agree.'

'Shall I go?'

He ran his eye over me, head to ankle, and saw through my attempt at nonchalance. 'Russell, you do not look entirely fit.'

'I'm fine, Holmes. Anyway, how much effort is it to sit in a motorcar and prepare to fend off pirates?'

He was not convinced – he had seen me coming up the drive, and knew me too well to take my protestations at face value. However, he had to weigh the risk of me falling asleep while guarding the Queen against me getting into mischief while his back was turned.

'Motoring there and back will take at least four hours, even if the driver is urged to hurry. If I leave you here, will you promise to take some rest so I can count on you being fit for duty later on?'

'Holmes, a nap is at the top of my list of requirements.'

He did not look convinced, but he had made up his mind. He turned his head to snap out a command to the Queen of Roumania. 'Do not leave. I will be back momentarily.'

She was so startled at the tone of his voice, a tone she probably hadn't heard since her nursery days, that her mouth did not shut until he had disappeared through the iron-studded doors. When her outraged gaze turned on me, I screwed up my face in apology. 'He doesn't mean to be impertinent, ma'am. Merely . . . efficient.' That, it appeared, was not sufficient excuse.

I tried again. 'Both of us feel at a loss. Because we do not know the ground, we would merely impede the search – your servants would feel duty bound to watch over us. He is not accustomed to being useless. The least he can do is provide some limited assistance to your driver.'

She allowed herself to be placated, and let the driver hand her into the back of the car. He then got behind the wheel and shut his door – but he did not start the motor until Holmes came trotting down the stairway, the hang of his coat pocket betraying the presence of the revolver.

Hand resting on the motorcar door, he addressed me with the same commanding attitude he had turned on the Queen. 'Is there anything you learnt today that I should know now?'

'A man on a motorcycle was seen yesterday afternoon, but that's all I have so far. I thought I'd ask Florescu who that might be.'

'Can it wait until I return?'

'It can.'

'I will return immediately once the Queen is inside the royal castle. I shall attempt to hasten our return journey. Do not venture into any dubious situations.'

'Holmes, you know me better than that,' I assured him.

His grey eyes drilled into me. 'I require more than an ambiguous answer.'

'I plan on tea, and sleep. I shall try my best not to be abducted, assaulted, or even misled. But before you go – w hat about you? You looked very preoccupied, when you came through the castle earlier.'

'Mr Holmes,' came the sharp command. 'We should like to leave, now.'

The royal *We* demanded obedience, even from Sherlock Holmes. He put his hand on the side of the motor, and leant forward to murmur, 'We need to know what Florescu is hiding. We will look into it when I return.'

And with that, he folded himself inside. Doors slammed and the motorcar eased away. No doubt, icy silence would hold for much of the way.

I did in fact intend to soak my aches in that luxurious bathtub while he was away, and definitely indulge in some sleep – he was sure to find something to keep us up for much of the night. And I performed my duty as a responsible guest by dispatching a servant down to the police to say that they should seek out a man with a very new motorcycle. After that, I aimed myself at the stairs.

However, halfway up the first flight, my feet stopped, and descended again. The entire house was busy elsewhere. I could just take a quick look . . .

I put my head out to check the inner courtyard. Empty at the moment – so I slipped into the main 'ground floor' room, pressed about by its thick walls and currently used as a builders' store.

Ileana had heard her ghosts in two rooms, both on the eastern side behind the immensely thick shield wall. If there was some kind of hidden passage inside it, how many of the tower's levels did it span? To link all five storeys would require a vertical shaft with a ladder, rather than stairs. The walls on this ground floor room were massively thick, more foundation than wall. The three south windows brought in enough light to show the stacks of builders' equipment, half-covered with dusty tarpaulins. The single window piercing the shield wall was tiny, and sat at the end of a long, narrow arch.

I went over every inch of the tunnel windows, and found no breaks or seams that could hide a doorway. I even examined the windowless wall on the north side, and raised the tarpaulins to look at the floor, in case the pile was concealing a trapdoor. All I saw was some workman's half-eaten meal, left there for the mice to discover.

Short of tearing down stones or shifting the entire builders' store, I had to accept that there was nothing here.

I went back into the courtyard, nodding at a maid who was raising a bucket from the well, and trudged up the four flights of stairs to the top. It was uncomfortable to think that a hidden passage might open up near to our rooms, but here, too, I found nothing – nothing but this floor's marginally less-tidy heap of plaster and tile. And unless those buckets, bales, and crates hid an opening in the floorboards – and unless the person using it had been able to restore the dust to its original thickness – there was no trapdoor.

I turned with a light heart to my rooms, relishing the idea of four or five hours without interruption. I intended to nap, truly I did. But my hand rested on the handle and would not turn. Ileana had not heard her unlikely rats on the ground and top storeys. She had been on the first floor, and the third.

But, surely the point of any secret passage was to provide unseen escape, in case of entrapment? Perhaps not in the most luxurious of pseudo castles, where the greatest danger was of a guest laying eyes on a maidservant emptying the night waste. But here, in a military outpost between two often-warring provinces?

No, it was almost certain that what she had heard were rats.

I turned the handle and walked into the room. Someone had found the time, despite the morning's turmoil, to tidy and dust. They had even plumped the pillows of the window seat, arranging them invitingly against the wall, should one wish to sit and gaze out of the window. I was grateful, yet again, for this room – not only for its plumbing, but its airiness and light. Well worth all those stairs to be given these windows, so noticeably larger and less deeply set than those below. Directly under the roof as we were, the walls did not need to be as massive as those two or three floors down.

Less massive.

That explained why, on this top level, there were two long, narrow rooms along the back of the shield wall, the rooms whose ceilings had collapsed and given me a view of the ancient tree trunks supporting the roof.

Up this high, there was no need to cut, transport, and lift enough stones to fill the shield wall. Whereas on the ground floor, thin walls like those of the two long rooms would have caused the tower to collapse before its first troops moved in.

While in between . . .

My mind's eye created an isosceles triangle: the length of the shield wall, the angle of a length of stairs, and the height of a room – or should it be two?

I trotted down one flight of stairs to the large music room.

The lower levels all had two or more rooms, to bear the weight from overhead. The long room's south end had comfortable chairs gathered under the windows; its north side had a sort of library corner; in between were a piano and the protruding inglenook fireplace with its built-in benches, ideal for keeping warm on a winter's day. Is that what Mr Florescu did, I wondered? Light a few of Her Majesty's thick beeswax candles, drink her port, read her books? When a castle is occupied for less than half the year, do the servants begin to feel it is their own? And perhaps allow events to take place that its new, outsider owner – a woman, at that – does not need to know?

The floorboards talked to themselves as I crossed them, north to south. They were mostly covered with thick carpets and the skins of large furry creatures – a bear that measured more than nine feet from nose to tail took up most of the inglenook floor; something smaller but equally thick between the two armchairs at the south-facing windows. One's toes longed to shed their footwear.

The book on the table beneath the window was the Aldous Huxley novel Queen Marie had mentioned the other night. A length of silk marked her page.

The windows and walls on this side were smooth plaster, freshly painted, and unlikely to be hiding anything larger than one of the ikons that turned their enigmatic gazes upon my search. The eastern wall was also recently decorated, and the upright piano pushed against it did not hide a doorway. The inglenook fireplace held no secrets. The only way in through its plaster and tiles would be via the chimney, a manoeuvre suitable only to a small monkey.

But the room's northern corner was a sort of library alcove, where wooden shelves held books ancient and modern. And I'd seen enough country house priest's holes and secret passageways to know where to look for an unnecessary seam in a board, or a patch of wear in an unexpected spot.

Yes, there it was: a cunningly hidden panel set into its middle section.

And that small knot-hole above the top of the books? It would make for a logical viewing port.

I stepped to one side to consider matters. There would be a trigger device to open the door, of that I had no doubt. I could find it with my torch.

But when I worked the lock, it would make a noise.

When a rat-catcher sends his dog down a hole, he first blocks the other entrances to the den, just as a London copper only kicks down a front door when his partner is at the back. I did not want to bring in one of the castle's servants – that glance shared by the three women in the kitchen warned me against putting my trust in them. Holmes would be back, in just a few hours . . .

But somewhere, Gabriela lay in the dark.

I went back upstairs for a torch (and fresh batteries, just in case) and a couple of scraps from the builders' waste pile, which I left in the music room.

Now to locate the other end of my rat-run. The second

floor had a pair of rooms belonging to King Ferdinand, with an immense, heavily carved four-poster bed, a matching wardrobe, and tapestries on the walls (Ferdinand, I remembered – unlike his wife – enjoyed hunting, so used Bran in the winter). Any of those could conceal a passage large enough for a mounted knight, but none of them appeared to. Similarly, the room next door: heavy furniture, few decorations, a light layer of dust.

But no hidden door.

I started for the stairway, then retreated at the sound of quick feet coming up. The footsteps continued on, and I scurried down silently to the first floor.

There were essentially five rooms on this level, one of those above the guardroom. The other four had a sort of intermediate quality, somewhere between family and public use. The eastern side, against the shield wall, held a dining room on the north, with two windows overlooking the village, and a drawing room to the south, its three windows looking up the river valley and the Queen's orchard and flower gardens.

Unless the passageway was a vertical tube, negotiated by ladder or handholds nailed into the rock, the lower end of my rat's run would be on the far side of the shield wall from the third-storey library alcove.

Renovations in this room had been the work of decorators rather than builders: patch the plaster, slap on whitewash, replace the pitted and cracked window glass with clear panes, and cover as much of the floor as possible with thick carpets. Soon, I imagined, the Queen's architect would have his way with the substance of this level, and launch into arguments over whether to rip out those time-black doors between the rooms, the wood kicked about by every soldier that had lodged here for three centuries, and replace them with fresh oak and teak from Africa.

Until then, the builders had clearly been instructed to work around the existing features rather than setting their crowbars to them. Even the massively ugly wooden shelf unit beside the south-facing windows.

I took the time to study all sides of this monstrosity. Had no one noticed that the shelves only accounted for half its thickness? Or was it such a difficult piece, everyone simply agreed not to see it, and cover it over with decorative objects and framed photographs?

Mr Florescu, I thought, had paid it some attention. As, I suspected, had the cook, her oldest assistant, and the housekeeper.

Around the back, I found what I was looking for. I knelt, and got to work with my heaviest picklocks. I kept as quiet as I could, for the sake of surprise, but when I worked the mechanism, it gave a *click*.

I would not have heard anything through stone, but this was wood, and it did not block the sound of movement from within. I worked my fingernails into the wood and pulled – it gave a scraping sound, like the one Ileana had heard – but I ducked down, in case of attack, or falling plaster, or a torrent of rats.

No rats came, no man leapt at me, no gun went off or club descended. Instead, I heard the sound of a panicked scramble. I turned on my pocket torch.

Just inside the narrow doorway lay a thick pile of blankets and rugs, currently unoccupied. *Slap-slap-slap* echoed from the darkness up to my left. It stopped. Letting as little of myself into the doorway as possible, I extended the torch inside with my right hand, pointing the beam up in the direction of the sounds. Nothing lethal came crashing down, so I let my head follow.

The tunnel went up, and up, a black shaft of rough stones

not much wider than a man's shoulders. Its steps were worn from centuries of booted feet – suggesting that it was built as a mere shortcut, and later turned into a secret passage by the addition of the library and wooden unit. The man at the top was barefoot, not booted, and did not appear to hold any arms other than the two he had been born with. Both of which were currently wrestling with the back side of the library door, now firmly shut with the wedge I had jammed into its base. Eventually, he realised that it was not going to move, and he turned, lifting a hand against the light.

Tousled hair, bare feet, untrimmed beard, mismatched clothing with patches and frays. No weapon appeared, so I lowered the light a few degrees, taking it out of his eyes.

'Andrei Costea, I presume?'

CHAPTER FORTY-ONE

A T HIS NAME, THE young man stood away from the unresponsive door.

'Who that?' he demanded.

'My name is Mary Russell. Please come down.'

While he considered his options, I returned the torch beam to what lay at my feet: multiple layers of rugs and blankets, possibly with boards underneath, creating a surprisingly tidy nest. Two narrow shelves and half a dozen twenty-penny nails driven between stones held his possessions – on one shelf, a basket of candle stubs, kitchen matches, a Roumanian Bible, an English children's story, a soldier's wash kit, and a corked bottle filled with what I sincerely hoped was water, since *tiuca* would be explosive around open flame. The other shelf was his pantry: a stub of cheese, some fruit, a wheaten roll . . . and two walnut biscuits oozing their dark filling, which made me smile.

I checked his progress down the stairs, then looked at the army haversacks hanging from two of the nails. Those might hold any manner of deadly object, from bayonet to revolver. On the other hand, he might also have a gun under his pillow, so to speak, and catch it up as he went past. Though if he hadn't done so when he was first disturbed . . .

Holmes would be furious if he found out, but I decided to trust the man, and left everything where it lay, to back down the stairs and into the room beyond.

Though I did move far enough back to dive for the adjacent doorway, should he emerge with blade or firearm in hand.

He did not.

Andrei Costea, Great War deserter and ostensibly long-buried citizen of Bran – and more recently, cemetery *strigoi* and castle ghost – was a man of about my height and precisely my own age, twenty-five. Brown eyes, a mop of curly hair in need of a trim, a dark bruise on his forehead, and a nose that had been broken and thus given personality. His skin, once tan, had that washed-out look of someone who had been indoors for a very long time. It had also been some time since he had use of a bath: his moustache was so long it covered his mouth, and his cheeks bore two or three weeks of stubble. I took care not to stand too close to him.

He automatically pressed the hidden door shut, wincing at the click of the latch. He'd paused to catch up a pair of much-mended woollen stockings, and pulled them on now, eyeing the room as if expecting a wolf to come leaping out at him. I held up my empty hands.

'Mr Costea, I do not want to hurt you. But we need to talk.'

'I not to stay here. Come.'

His stockinged feet padded noiselessly across the boards. I followed, keeping well back. However, it appeared that he merely wanted to be away from the civilised portion of the castle, and scurried down the lesser stairs, ducking nimbly under the props.

When I emerged warily on the ground floor, he had closed the room's other door and settled onto a folded tarpaulin atop a stack of bags labelled Plaster. He picked up the plate of stale food and placed it on his knee, absently picking at the contents.

He was living under the noses of the castle residents – or at least, some of them.

I found an empty pail, overturned it, and sat, watching him apply his attention to the bread and apple, as if he had forgot I was there.

If Vera had not already told me about Andrei, I might have thought him slow by nature. But her word – *simple* – seemed more appropriate. He was not stupid, and any brain damage had been done early, not during the War. He was good-looking under the tousle and stubble, with a direct gaze that seemed to notice a great deal.

He reminded me of the men who spent their lives with dogs or horses: for them, most human beings did not quite claim their attention – although the few who did would win their complete and utter devotion.

I adjusted my assumptions, from brain-damaged to merely unfocused, and ventured a question. 'How long have you been here?'

He did understand basic English, probably about the level of that children's book I had seen. Speaking was, as always with a foreign language, a different matter. 'Seex month.'

'You came in February?'

His reply had four or five syllables and a diphthong, but I took it to be 'January' in Roumanian. Before I could ask him for the details, he flung out a beseeching hand. 'Please, Mees, what happen? In castle, today, all . . . confuse.'

'They're all out looking – wait. How do you know that?' He must stay behind his doors during the daylight hours, and the two peep-holes looking into the first- and third-floor rooms couldn't have told him much.

'Is holes. In stones. Tiny-tiny windows, to see out.'

'In the stones? Not just in the doors?'

'In doors and also in stones.'

'Really. How many?'

'One this end, three that end, two at side.' His gestures illustrated one hole in the wall at the foot of his makeshift bed, thus overlooking the river valley, then two over the castle's drive, and three at the top of the stairs, looking out across the wider plateau towards Braşov. I supposed it made sense: a secret staircase would be a trap without spy-holes. No doubt each tiny hole would be tucked beneath a protruding stone, invisible so long as the person inside took care not to light a lamp after dark. And a bored young man might spend much of his day circulating from one peep-hole to the next.

'Mees, please, what happen?'

'Do you know Gabi? Gabriela Stoica?'

'Gabi, yes – she good?'

'No, she has disappeared.' He looked blank. 'She is gone. Someone took her.'

This brought him to his feet with a torrent of Roumanian. I held up a pacifying hand. 'All the village is looking for her. We will find her.' He sat down, not to relax but to better see my face.

'When she go?'

'When did she disappear? Yesterday. Some time between

seven and eight. You understand?'

'Eight of the clock, yes – just dark.'

'Yes, it was probably dark. She was walking home, and did not get there. I don't suppose you were looking out north at the time?'

'Dark I was looking other way, over village. Lights come on,' he explained. 'Families, people, nice to see.'

I looked at him, hearing the longing in his voice. 'You go out sometimes, don't you? Into the town.'

'After dark only. Not often.'

'When was the last time?'

'Three night ago.'

'Ah. So it was you, who spoke to Vera Dumitru from the graveyard.'

He flushed bright red. 'Stupid, stupid thing to do. I thought maybe, so nice to talk to somebody – instead she throw rock and run away.' He touched the bruise on his forehead. 'I don't mean to scare her. Stupid Andrei.'

'She has good aim,' I said. He gave a rueful nod. 'Don't worry about Vera – she just thought it was one of the boys teasing her. Because she told people that she saw you earlier in the year, from the courtyard.'

'*Baiat prost*,' he muttered. 'I will leave here. I am too stupid, I will get people in trouble.'

That was probably true. However, I did not wish to be the cause of his hasty departure into the night. 'We will see if we can find some way to help you. Something that doesn't mean living inside the walls.'

'Is not all that bad. Only when Queen is here, I have to stay inside more. Other times I go out two, three nights a week.'

I wanted to ask him about the other nights, if he had by chance seen a man in city shoes on Thursday, or a man in a full cloak on Saturday, but my bones were aching, and I knew that Holmes would want to go over it all again. All I needed to do was return Andrei to his bolthole for a few hours, and make sure he did not sneak off before Holmes got back from Sinaia.

'Well, I'm sorry you didn't happen to be out last night, but I wonder if you'd mind—'

'You ask *medic*?'

'Sorry?'

'*Medic*. Doctor. You ask what he see?'

'I haven't talked with him today, no, though his car is here.'

'Car, yes – big, like *ambulanţă*?'

'Yes, it looks like an ambulance.'

'Was in old barn on road to Fagaraş yesterday night. Barn with no roof, you know?'

'Sorry, are you saying that the doctor hid his shooting brake – his motorcar – in a barn last night?'

'Hid? I don't know. And could have been someone else. But he goes sometimes. Think he keeps a motorcycle there. Car comes, motorcycle goes – then motorcycle comes, car goes. Not far from Gabi house – maybe he saw her?'

It was hard to focus, over the clamour in my brain. 'Sundays aren't one of the doctor's days in Bran,' I said, which was more than a little nonsensical. Andrei said something in reply, but that I didn't hear at all.

Instead, I was on my feet. 'Can you show me the holes? In the stones.'

'See now?'

'Yes.'

'Come,' he said again, automatically tucking away the plate

and smoothing out the wrinkles in the tarpaulin. He led the way up the cluttered stairway, holding back a hand until he was sure the room beyond was clear, then led me rapidly through to the ugly unit and inside it. At his gesture, I pulled its door shut, taking out my torch.

I clambered over his bedding and up the claustrophobic passageway behind him, concentrating on the stairs underfoot rather than the press of stones on all sides. At the top, he pointed at a perfectly blank piece of wall, and stepped back, pressing against the wooden door.

So there I stood: at the top of a run of precipitous stairs, with a criminal whose secret I knew, who only had to give me a hard shove to avoid discovery. And then I turned out my torch.

Oh, if I survived this, Holmes was going to kill me.

But Andrei did nothing except breathe. My eyes slowly adjusted to the darkness. Finally, I became aware of a tiny stream of air on the side of my neck. Saying a prayer that I had not catastrophically misjudged this man, I bent gingerly to set my glasses against the stones.

The hole was, naturally, as long as the wall was thick, but its sides were smooth and it was wider at the far end than the quarter-inch of its inner diameter. It had also been cleverly angled so as to look down, rather than out at the far-distant hills. Through it, like a miniature telescope, lay the little crossroads at the centre of the village. A woman passed across my line of sight, right to left, carrying a basket. Father Constantin's wife.

Another faint breeze was stirring the hair on my left temple. This second hole brought me nearly against Andrei's rather fetid shirtfront. This one showed the road north towards Brașov. A cart was leaving town, a motorcar approaching, one that had the air of police department about it.

I pulled away. My eyes had adjusted enough that I could find the third hole by its line of dust motes through the dark. It was higher than the other two, and its tube considerably longer, since it cut through the wall at a diagonal. The end of it must also have been far larger, since the scope of this view was considerable – from the Bran crossroads, busy now with castle servants laying out trestle tables and food, to the line sketched in vegetation across the countryside that was the other north road out of Bran.

As I watched, the police motorcar appeared, turning up that road. It drove for a time, then stopped on the lane before the Stoica house. Perhaps half a mile short of the heavily used farm access lane beside the derelict barn. 'You said the barn with most of the roof missing?'

'Yes yes, very old.'

I pictured the place. Heavily grown about by trees and shrubs, a car parked behind it would be invisible to the neighbours. And on a Sunday afternoon, when no one was in the fields apart from Romany courting couples, a man might ride in on his remarkably silent motorcycle, and wait near the derelict barn until evening fell and a girl was walking home.

A toss of the blanket and a quick dose of chloroform, and he could bundle her away – into an oversized motorcar along with the cycle itself, scattering a few more oil stains on the floor. If he waited until full dark, and perhaps crept along the first half-mile by the light of the moon, he would soon be in open countryside, and could pull onto the road to Braşov as he had a thousand times before.

'Did you see the car leave?'

'No. Can only use holes for some time,' he admitted. 'Wind

316

coming through, it hurts the eyes.'

'I bet.'

'But later – lots later – there was car going along that road. Up to Braşov.'

'Any idea what time?' I asked, expecting a negative.

'Late. Maybe one hour before someone arrive, banging on door.'

That would have been Gabi's father.

That decided me. I pulled away from the stones and thumbed on my torch, raising it until it I could see his face, and he could see mine. 'Andrei, do you want to help Gabi?'

CHAPTER FORTY-TWO

ANDREI'S HEROIC DETERMINATION TO help find Gabriela, no matter what it cost him, was somewhat deflated when I explained that his role would be to sit behind a pair of locked doors with a book and wait for Holmes to return.

'I come!' he insisted. 'I help.'

'If you come, everyone will be looking at you, not looking for Gabi. And this is important.'

I could have left Holmes a message, coded or in some exotic language, but it was better to leave him an explanation and resource in one. Since I didn't actually know where I was going anyway, Andrei's person might put us on an equal footing when it came to finding me.

I drew my knife and poked around under the door to locate the wedge, then tapped it away. Andrei checked the peep-hole first, but there were no witnesses, and we got to the top floor without being seen. When we reached our rooms, I had to turn and yank

Andrei inside, so loth was he to sully its magnificence with his less-than-pristine self.

'You need to wait for my husband,' I told him again. 'He will not be here for at least two hours. You can sit, drink water, eat . . . well, there's not much, but eat whatever you can find. Read a book. Be comfortable.'

I went into my bedroom to fetch a few things I might need, and came back to find he had taken precisely one step further into the room.

Our door had a mere latch, no key. 'Lock the door when I go,' I told him. 'My husband, his name is Holmes. When he comes, he will find it locked. He will think, 'Ah, my wife is here,' and call to me. If you hear any voice not English, keep quiet, they will go away. They cannot come in. They will think I am sleeping. Yes?'

'Yes.'

'When you let him in, stand out of sight. Anyone in the hall will think it is me. Yes?' He nodded.

'Two hours,' I repeated. 'Or three. Anything you need?'

His eyes slid sideways to the adjoining door. 'You have water?'

'For drinking – oh, you mean, do I have a bath? Oh my dear young man, do I ever have a bath.' When I showed him the room with the porcelain tub and the actual geyser, he knew what he was looking at, and it might have been paradise itself. I grinned at him. 'Just not too long, yes?'

'One hour,' he confirmed, and gave me a grin in return.

What I could see of it under the shaggy facial hair seemed like a nice grin. Uncomplicated, not the brightest, but honest and open. I found myself looking at the rest of him, and thought of something. I went to Holmes' chest of drawers and took out the Roumanian costume. When I tried to hand it to Andrei, he would not take it. I looked pointedly at his much-mended and long-unlaundered garments.

'Andrei, you need clothes. People who see you now think, who *is* this? People who see you in these,' I held up the garments, 'will think, oh, it's some friend of the castle.'

Heaven only knew where he'd been for the past nine years – I had no time to find out now – but disguise was a thing Andrei understood.

I thrust the clothes at him. 'Lock the door. Have a bath. Eat the apples. And tell my husband what you saw through the holes.'

I waited until the latch sounded behind me, and flew away down the stairs.

The castle seemed deserted. Indeed, in the Queen's absence, even the entrance stood unguarded. Once away from the castle itself, I did not need to worry as much about concealment – I only needed the inside servants to think I was in my rooms.

I moved as quickly as I could without actually breaking into a run, but to my relief, the shiny prow of the shooting brake was in its place beside the village shop. I strolled into the shop, which was about to close. When the single customer had left, I purchased yet another assortment of hard sweets to justify my presence, and left. I poked through them, making a covert survey of the vicinity – I could hear the doctor's voice in the surgery, and a patient. A cart rattled past, the shop door locked behind me, and the instant I was alone, I ducked low and scurried to the narrow gap between the doctor's motorcar and the surgery wall.

I pulled open the back passenger-side door and found, as I'd thought, that the long bench built to transport patients was in fact a hinged box. There was a hasp, just inside the passenger door, but no padlock. I lifted the padded lid and looked in. Pine wood, seven feet long, two feet wide, less than eighteen inches deep. A couple of heavy boards lay in the bottom, one end bevelled and the other with a small crosspiece: ramps, for bathchairs, gurneys – or motorcycles. Chains at either end of the lid kept it from falling too far back and pulling out the hinges.

But for those chains, it might have been a coffin.

The thought gave me pause, literally. Staring into that bare wooden box, the very last thing in all the world that I wanted was to get inside. Visions of scraping fingernails, clawing at the wood . . .

I heard a voice then, and simply reacted. Dive inside, reach out to ease the door shut, then pull the knife from my boot and place it along the top edge of the box, to keep the hasp from accidentally fastening.

I let the lid settle over me – then thought of something else: check to make sure the sweets wrapper was securely twisted shut. The driver might notice a sound like rolling marbles, as we went around corners.

I shifted around so my right hand could hold the knife in place. I only needed enough of a gap to keep the latch from going down over its staple, while taking care not to let the blade stick out enough to be seen. Voices came, shockingly close – then doors opening, more than one. To my alarm, the car began to rock with the weight of many people climbing in. At least four bodies thumped down inches from my nose, amidst loud conversation and the sound of the engine starting. I felt the gears working beneath my spine, and the car set off.

There seemed to be three men and a woman, in addition to the driver. I caught the occasional word – they were talking about the Queen leaving, and something about the King, then laughter, which broke off abruptly to a voice from the front. It seemed to be a question, and although I couldn't decipher the words, their responses – in voices gone respectful – were about Gabi. I caught words here and there, enough to suggest that no one had any clue as to where she was or who might have taken her. The back-and-forth began to pick up.

And then a quick snap of a phrase from the front silenced them, but for a few apologetic phrases. There was no further talk.

It was both terrifying and absurd. My heart was pounding, my mouth dry as dust, and the only way I could keep from either bursting into panicked hilarity or shoving the lid up was to force my brain into a close and alphabetical review of Latin nouns. Masculine first declension. The *accola* sitting over my head started me: resident. He might also be an *agricola* – farmer – while another might qualify as *anagnostes* (a reader). The man behind the wheel was our *auriga* (charioteer). Fortunately, I had barely finished with my chosen Cs (*coprea, copreae, copream* – buffoon, a word that certainly described the occupant of the coffin) when the car swerved aside and braked hard. To my relief, we were not taking on more passengers, but getting rid of these. All of them? I couldn't tell. The juggling of the suspension was reversed, the doors slammed, voices called polite thanks, and the car ground back into gear and jerked away.

One sharp phrase, which sounded like a curse, then silence.

I lay still, but there was no further conversation. I seemed to be alone with the driver. Would he notice if my coffin lid rose, just a fraction? It would improve the state of my nerves, to have light and air, especially if we were driving to his house on the far side of Braşov.

A throwing knife like mine has no appreciable handle. Its thickness is uniform, other than the very tip, but the additional fraction of an inch would make breathing easier.

My head was towards the front and, this being an English motor, my right hand was on the side nearest the door, and thus, the lid's opening. I worked my left arm over – difficult, but just possible – to grasp the knife with my fingertips while my right hand pressed up.

The lid did not move.

I adjusted both hands and pushed harder, then hard enough that, if it had been open, the lid would have flown back and revealed me to the man in front.

Stop. Breathe.

In, out. Shaky, but controllable.

The weight of the passengers must have dropped the lid just enough to let the hasp catch over the staple. I could force it – I could try forcing it – but not without giving myself away.

I was strong. There was air – there was plenty of air, the stuffiness was in my imagination, and was not what was making me feel lightheaded. No, there was not sufficient height for me to bring my legs up, but my arms were strong. And it was only a wooden box, not a steel trap. I was not buried, merely inconvenienced. Really.

Breathe.

On the other hand, even my rational mind agreed that I did not wish to be trapped here any longer than I had to – not just because of the terror of being buried alive that was gnawing at my nerves. Because once the doctor stopped and got out, I needed to follow him, immediately. If I lost him, this entire fool's venture was for naught. Holmes would give me that look of mingled pity and disapproval, and Gabriela Stoica would still be missing.

So I took a deep breath of the stink of fear, and pulled away the knife.

I could always use it on my wrists. But before that, I would try something else.

The bench was simple, soft pine rather than finished walnut, but the man who had made it was a decent craftsman. He'd taken care to use the right length of screws, so they did not protrude and rip open an incautious hand. And while my skin was grateful for his care, just now I'd have appreciated a pair of identifying metal points to tell me where the staple of the latch was located.

Instead, I lay in the close, sweltering blackness and felt along the boards for any slight betraying rise in the surface. I found a bump, then another, but they were not a pair, and several inches from where I thought the latch was mounted. Down and up, back and forth, and – ah: one, then two minuscule strains in the surface texture, an inch and a half apart.

Cursing the dark, the low roof, and most of all my left-handedness, I drove the point of the blade into the wood, wrenched it around in a half-circle . . . and felt my whole body relax.

The wood was soft enough to give way. Carving a hole through it was just a matter of time and determination – and though the former might be in question, of determination I had plenty.

Sweat ran down my face and turned my palms slippery. I dropped the knife several times, but it made no sound on the deepening blanket of wood chips. The smell of pine was a pleasant change, although as it grew, I began to hope the open windows would keep the driver from noticing. And I breathed through my mouth, to reduce the chance of a sneeze.

We slowed, turned, turned again, paused – but I had heard the sounds of a city growing outside, and the man had told us he lived north of Braşov. Still, I redoubled my efforts, slicing my finger once when my hand slipped forward onto the blade – then suddenly the remaining millimetre of wood gave way, and the knife jerked forward to stop with a faint *tick*. I held still, waiting for a slowing or a swerve of reaction . . .

No. I pulled the knife from the hole and lay breathing for a while, as if that tiny hole was now letting in a flood of oxygen and daylight. I used the sawdust to dry my hands, let them rest for a minute, then shifted as far onto my right arm as the box would permit and went exploring.

The angle my digging had followed led straight to the side of the staple's upright section. I enlarged the hole, aware that now every fragment of wood risked dropping to the outside. At last, my exploring knifepoint found the line of the staple, and travelled up it until it caught on the hasp section that had fallen into place. I pressed outward, slowly, firmly . . .

The hasp came free. The lid went up a notch. I could breathe again.

I wrapped my aching fingers over the side of the box, in spite of the risk of giving myself away. I did not want the lid to drop shut on me again.

Hours after we had left Bran – subjectively, although

probably half an hour by the clock – the car slowed, turned left down a bumpier surface, then turned again in a near-complete circle. It stopped.

The engine died.

I tightened my grip on the knife.

I did not hear voices. No servants came out to greet the man, no passers-by carried on a conversation. Movement; the creak of the car's door opening; its springs rose a fraction. The door closed. Footsteps crunched in gravel around the front of the car, coming closer, then stopped – oh God, he was going to open the back door and look inside, see the curls of wood and the tips of my fingers. Hand tight on the knife, every muscle braced, eyes prepared for the dazzle of light, I heard the click of a door's latch and nearly – so nearly – flung up the lid and attacked.

But the light that seeped in beneath the lid grew no stronger and before I could make up my mind, the door slammed again.

This time, I did laugh aloud.

It was the *front* door. He'd been fetching something from his passenger-side floor.

Footsteps, receding. I edged up the lid, blinking against the light. Not too bad – night was near, and we seemed to be in the shade. I lifted my head slowly to peer out, just in time to see him disappear through the trades entrance of a once-grand country house.

When the faint sound of the wooden door closing reached me, I pushed the lid all the way upright against its chains, slipping the knife back into my boot.

Open the door, climb out of the coffin, drop onto a weed-grown forecourt. Lower the lid, ease the door shut – then a quick scurry to the house, bent over for fear of a careless glance out of a window.

I had brought my picklocks, but to my surprise, he had not locked the door behind him.

So I turned the knob and warily, braced for rapid flight, edged open the door.

Chapter Forty-three

THIS WAS, AS ONE would expect, the kitchen. At this time of the evening, pots should have been bubbling, footmen straightening their collars, the cook berating the tweeny for being underfoot.

It had been a while since this kitchen had seen a cook and footman.

The copper pans over the big cast-iron stove showed the first dull signs of tarnish. The stove was cold. The dirt on the floor would have been in itself a firing offence.

Not that there weren't clear signs of habitation: three saucepans in the outer scullery, plates and cutlery rinsed but unwashed beside them, and a small collection of basic provisions – bread, eggs, cheese, and a few tomatoes and onions – looking lonely beside a modern hotplate at one end of the twelve-foot-long countertop.

Was this the doctor's house? Even in its current state it seemed grand, for a country medic. Perhaps he was caretaking while the owners – and their servants – were away? It would explain the signs of a bachelor's life. Because there had been servants, until perhaps two weeks ago, to judge by the degree of patina on the copper.

I could hear no sound at all. Should I go out into the house itself, or down, into its cellars?

Following the theory that prisoners were kept in dungeons – and knowing his record of tucking women into dark spaces – I opened the nearest door, looking for a set of stairs. Instead, I found the pantry. It, too, had been active not long ago, with a bowl of potatoes in the early stages of sprouting and a small, dun-coloured moth, disturbed by the door's motion, that did not bode well for the grains and flour.

Then my eye caught on an object sitting on the floor – an object that would not be completely out of place in any country house in Surrey. Sides of woven willow, leather straps, a stencil declaring F&M: an actual Fortnum & Mason hamper, beloved of explorers and picnicking families the world around. The buckles were unfastened and a thread of excelsior dribbled over one side, so I lifted the lid.

Biscuits both digestive and iced, half a dozen wedges of cheese, and jars of relish, potted shrimp, and caviar. A small tin of Earl Grey tea, which had been opened. No wine – but two large bottles of Malvern Spring water (By Appointment to His Majesty the King) and one of commercial lemonade, with a hole in the excelsior showing where another had rested.

Not everything bore the Fortnum brand. A few of the items I'd have thought more appropriate for upper servants than the household itself – even a Marquis might hesitate to serve Carr's to guests – but the rest of it was clearly intended for formal use.

Oddly, the hamper contained the only English foodstuffs in

the pantry. There were tins, jars, and packets from Germany and France, some dried pasta from Italy, and a handful of things with Cyrillic or Turkish labels, but the majority of the provisions were Roumanian.

From alarmingly close came the sudden hard clack of heels on tiles, sending me into a leap behind the only possible hiding place, the half-closed pantry door. Had he been there all the time, lurking just outside the kitchen? Maybe not – and in case he didn't know I was there, I daren't move the door enough to get at my knife.

He came straight across the kitchen and into the pantry. It was a shock to see the shape cross the crack in the door, a foot away from my shoulder, and I braced myself for his 'Aha!' of confrontation. Instead, I heard a light slapping sound, followed by a rustle, then the tap of something hard being set on a wooden shelf. Another rustle, a slightly louder slap, then a tiny metallic jingle – the buckles on the hamper lid? A crinkling noise . . . and then he left – pulling the pantry door shut behind him.

Leaving me in pitch blackness, yet again.

More footsteps, the sound of a door.

Was he leaving? Or merely fetching something from the car before settling down to his snack of water biscuits and cheese?

A car started up, and I cursed my luck.

If I'd only stayed in my coffin . . .

Instead, I stepped into an empty kitchen, and saw that, yes, the car had gone. As for the hamper, it was missing the Carr's biscuits, a piece of cheddar, and one of the Malvern Waters.

It seemed a peculiar hour for a picnic. Perhaps he went somewhere to watch the sunset? Then I remembered the hospital – yes, he was probably checking on some patient there. Taking them a treat? That made more sense than serving them to a prisoner.

And if he'd intended some kind of perverted wooing of the girl, wouldn't he have taken her wine and chocolates?

I required more data. But if he had gone into Braşov, he might be away for an hour – and he could be heading for dinner afterwards, rather than face the dreary washing-up and near-empty larder. Even a short absence meant I could search the house without having to tiptoe through the halls.

The next door from the pantry held the stairs to the cellars. It smelt of damp, but there was an electrical light switch, which I turned on.

I found two locked doors. One held nothing but empty shelves. The other took me longer to open, and turned out to be a sort of strong-room. Here, too, the house's valuables may once have been stored, but now the shelves held only a few pieces of silver plate gone black with age.

I did not bother to lock either door, although I did wipe the soles of my shoes before crossing the kitchen, so as not to betray myself too blatantly.

On the other side of the service door, I could see why I had not heard his approach: carpeting, old and grey-looking in the early part of the hallway, newer and cleaner as it reached the dining room. This confirmed what I had seen in the kitchen, that the house had been maintained until fairly recently, the carpets swept and the fireplaces tidied for the summer. The windows were clean, the dust was not thick, and the cobwebs were in their early stages.

So, yes, perhaps two weeks of abandonment.

The long dining room table had the same dust over its polish, except for the end nearest the fireplace. Here, there were signs of a single pair of elbows sitting down to dine – although on closer examination, that area, too, had some dust, just not as much.

As if someone had started out dining in the formal room, but without servants, started to take his dinners elsewhere.

I found that elsewhere in the library.

The room bore all the signs of a long-time bachelor retreat, all dark colours, old paintings, leatherbound books, a couple of marble busts, and a very beautiful family tree produced some fifty years before. This room, too, had been recently abandoned by the cleaners, shown in the half-full wastebaskets, cluttered ash trays, and cups forgotten on tables. It was by no means disgusting, and the air smelt only rather stale, but it was clearly where the man had retreated, to simplify his solitary life.

A crumpled linen napkin on a table beside a well-used armchair testified to the occasional meal eaten with a plate in his lap. The rumpled travelling rug over the back of the settee suggested that he might occasionally fall asleep here as well.

I will be honest: I expected far worse. I expected a loathsome den, a place where an abductor of women could crawl to gloat and recall his foul deeds. I expected filth, not dust; depravity, not laptop dining and casual naps.

Perverts and degenerates are often quite good at presenting a genial face to the world, but when they retreat to a private space, it does not tend to look like this. The room was untidy, but frankly, it was nicer than one of Holmes' boltholes after he'd been there a few days. There was even an embossed leather bookmark in the German novel he had been reading. A quick glance over the shelves confirmed that many were old and few were in English, but among those was a three-year-old copy of *Dracula*.

I turned my back on the temptation of the large, leather-topped desk: before investigating its secrets, I had to be certain that Gabriela was not shut away in an attic.

Formal morning room, parlour, entrance hall, another larger parlour, a billiards room – all the usual fittings of a grand house, empty of life. This brought me around to the servants' realm, but just before that baize door was my first locked door outside of the cellars. I got it open, and found the estate office. There was a wealth of box files, although nothing more recent than 1913. The War had upended the orderly management of many estates, including, it would seem, this one. An ornately framed but somewhat faded map with a date of 1848 showed a considerable estate, with holdings all over the area, including several in the vicinity of Bran, and – yes, a crooked patch that might have coincided with the derelict barn near the Stoica house. Closer to the centre of the estate was a concentration of tenant farms and an expanse of wild land adjoining the forest, for generations of Mikó men to take their friends out for a day of slaughtering wildlife.

The explanation for the locked door stood on the shelves behind the old desk: jars, packets, and carboys, neatly labelled and arranged, containing drugs for his medical practice. Perhaps he had stopped leaving them in Bran after his surgery was broken into. In any case, the lock on the door was not new. Headache tablets, cough syrup, various ointments and the like, but also paregoric, morphine, ether, and – yes: chloroform.

This door I did lock when I left the room, then walked up the stairs in the gloom of dusk.

Bedrooms, bathrooms, dressing rooms, guest suites. And on the top storey, servants' quarters and attics full of old clothing and children's toys. The occupied rooms up here comprised a sort of suite, a bedroom and sitting-room, with cupboards suggesting a butler-valet and his cook-housekeeper wife.

Two servants for a house this size? Even considering the dust, they must have day help from nearby.

The doctor's bedroom suite went some way to explaining how two servants could manage: the modern toilet and hot-water geyser replaced a housemaid, electricity did away with the maintenance of lamps and candles, a stack of fresh shirts and linen testified to a laundry service in the town. A patent safety-razor in the doctor's cupboard said that he took care of his own grooming.

All in all, a house this size was a step above the salary of a Roumanian doctor, but enough corners had been cut to make life manageable – at least in the summer, without the cost of heating.

His wardrobe, too, was a notch above what might be expected, but the only extravagant touches were a beautifully tailored evening suit and a vicuña overcoat I wanted to steal.

A kind of sideboard in one corner of the dressing room functioned as the doctor's laundry room. On top was a stack of four crisply folded shirts. In the wastebin beside it was a crumpled-up sheet of off-white paper and twine, and a handwritten receipt for the week's laundry. Inside its doors were a pair of large canvas bags. One held three days' worth of shirts and linen – the smudged one I'd noticed on Saturday, and two others. If Saturday's was twice-worn, then he'd changed out of today's before going out again. Beneath that top shirt was the tan-coloured suit he'd worn when we met.

The other bag, smaller and lumpy, held a different kind of cleaning: shoes awaiting the polish brush.

One of them was a pair of slick-soled city shoes, approximately 300 millimetres in length, that bore a high-tide line of mud half an inch up their sides.

In the end, I left them there. The doctor had several pairs of shoes in the wardrobe. If he hadn't rushed to clean these four days ago when the stable yard mud was fresh, it was unlikely that he would worry about them the moment he returned home tonight.

I replaced the shoes and the canvas bags, looking over the room to be sure there was nothing out of place.

Cellars to attic, front to back, I had seen no sign of any woman under the age of sixty. I made my way back down to the library by the sheltered light of my torch, to settle in at the man's desk.

The centre drawer held the usual sorts of supplies, debris, and unfiled paperwork. He used a gold-nibbed pen from France, ink from Germany, and Italian paper for his correspondence. There was a piece of card stock similar to the one sent to the Queen, with the threat against Ileana, but without the original for comparison, I could not draw any conclusions. A pair of letters, their envelopes sliced open, appeared to be from friends, one of them writing to inform him of the death of a mutual friend from university, the other to give news of a daughter's impending marriage.

The top drawer on the left gave me pause: bullets, gun-oil, and a cleaning rag.

The doctor not only had a pistol, but had taken it with him.

It made the rest of the left-hand side somewhat anticlimactic, being mostly boxes of stationery and such.

The top drawer on the right-hand side revealed a bank passbook with a balance that made me blink. Father Constantin had said that the doctor came into money a few years ago, but I had not grasped the extent of that understatement.

So why would a man with that bank balance be camping in a house with no servants? I could understand if he'd been hiding a kidnapped girl in his attic, but unless this house had more secret rooms than Castle Bran, it held no prisoner. Perhaps the servants had caught on to his misdeeds, and fled? If so, they'd left their family photographs and winter coats behind.

The next drawer held further revelations: letters from his solicitor, with carbon copies of his own to the man. (I idly noted that there was no sign of a typewriting machine here, or in his Bran surgery. Did he have offices in the hospital? Perhaps with the use of a secretary? Yet another matter to investigate.) These letters illustrated just how much money he had at his command, and where it had come from.

For one thing, there was far more than the cash in his bank account. A French chateau that was in the final stages of being sold, stocks in several countries, half-interest in a yacht that was also being sold. It would take me the rest of the night to read all the long negotiations that the legal gentleman described, but I flipped through, to get a general idea, before returning them to their file.

The next one held business receipts dating back to the first of the year. There was nothing from 1924 in here – perhaps he turned those over to his accounting firm at the end of each year – but even lacking those, there was still too much to spend time on. It was quite dark, and headlamps could come up the drive at any moment. Again, I merely gave them a quick survey, hoping for any clue as to his wider interests – but then, pushed down and nearly invisible between a coal bill and one for the repairs of his surgery door (in June, though he'd told us the spring) my eye caught on a familiar font.

The letterhead would be familiar to anyone who had ever supplied an outdoor party, overnight rail trip, or sporting weekend in England: Fortnum & Mason.

Dr Mikó had received the hamper in July, having apparently specified that he wanted its contents to be both 'hearty' (a request I did not imagine Fortnum often received) and without alcohol.

Hence the potted shrimp, the surprising amount of cheese, and bottles of lemonade and Malvern Water.

And yet, there'd been a cut-glass tumbler on the table beside his well-worn leather armchair. I walked over and picked up the glass: yes, a clear aroma of spirits, probably *tuica*. I settled down in the chair, as if to absorb the man's intentions from his customary seat, and shut off the torch to think.

A doctor from an old Braşov family, who inherits a fortune. Yet instead of closing his surgery doors and setting off on a world tour – or even using some fraction of the money to restore the family house to its former glory – he orders a couple of nice suits, then continues his life as a village doctor. And when he buys a new motorcar, instead of something sporty or luxurious, it is a machine large enough to be converted into a combination of omnibus and ambulance, so as to better serve a smattering of agricultural accidents and problem births.

One might picture a mildly eccentric gentleman, comfortable with his life and happy to ignore the huge change in his status – except that at the same time, he has begun to convert as much of his new-found estate as he can into cold, hard cash.

Why?

He betrayed no signs of a terminal illness, that might be driving him to give away his possessions. He could be aiming to outdo Mr Florescu as a sponsor of village youth, except that schools could be built and scholarships established as easily from rental income and stock returns as money in a bank.

Was I in fact following a wrong scent? Andrei had seen the doctor's motor in an unusual place and at the key time, but what did that mean? The doctor was in Bran at all hours. He could have been taking a walk in the woods, and parked behind the old barn to discourage thieves – or even to avoid conversation with local busybodies. When it came to proof of wrongdoing, did we have a single blessed thing? Even if he had abducted Gabi and taken her away inside the bench of his motorcar, my subsequent occupation had now overwritten much of the evidence.

I looked across the dark room at the man's desk. If I removed that entire folder of communications with his solicitor, how long would it be before he noticed?

And more important: what on earth was delaying Holmes?

CHAPTER FORTY-FOUR

IT WAS NINE-THIRTY. I had been in the house more than two hours, and was no closer to finding Gabriela than I had been when the sun came up. The odds of the doctor returning increased with every tick of the big clock in the hallway. However, there was little point in leaving the house until either he or Holmes showed up. And there were certainly plenty of rooms to hide in.

I debated taking a few folders away to some upstairs room, but if he noticed them missing, it would be over. And I could look at them here, but it was too dangerous to show light, and drawing the curtains risked his noticing when the headlamps went across the house.

Instead, I slid open the library window a couple of inches, to give me warning of an approaching motor, and draped the travelling rug over a small table to hide my light. I considered taking one of the candles, but between the heat, the inevitable drips, and the chance of a betraying smell, it was better to wear down my batteries. I withdrew under the blanket with the solicitor's file, and settled in to read.

This time, I began at the back of the file-folder, although I found the sequence of letters more thematic than chronological.

The earliest correspondence was from January, 1923, when a German solicitor wrote to inform Dr Mikó that a distant uncle had died and left him his entire estate. Most of it was tied up in stocks and properties, but to judge by the doctor's grateful letters, the cash alone made for a huge windfall. The surprise, the questions, the letters that followed brought a sense of wonder. Mikó travelled to Hamburg twice, to see the solicitor, or possibly three times – some of the correspondence seemed to be missing.

The first trip was four months after the initial news reached him. A letter in June, written upon his return to Brașov, was filled with simple pleasure, his thanks, and a mention that the inheritance would make a considerable difference to 'my people here.'

Shortly after that, the doctor placed an order for the English shooting brake. That was also around the same time that Father Constantin said he had expanded the days of his surgery in Bran.

For the next year, the letters concerned the transfer of ownership and details of the properties involved. Then came a letter dated June 1924. After some detailed instructions on a problematic contract in Dusseldorf, Mikó wrote:

> In recent months, I have been considering this substantial
> change in my life, and I would like to come and speak with
> you in person about the possibilities it has opened. I also need
> you to find for me an expert in Roumanian and international
> property law, who can—

The remainder of the letter was missing.

Then in November, just under two years after the uncle had died, the doctor made another trip to Hamburg, although it was only referred to obliquely – 'As per our conversation last month,' said the carbon letters in German. During that conversation, he had apparently instructed his solicitor to sell as many of the properties as possible. One letter made passing reference to his Roumanian solicitor, so I made note of the name, but there was no hint as to what he was doing other than 'going forward.'

The entire folder, I thought, felt maddeningly incomplete. Almost as if the man had gone through and deliberately removed key documents.

'Doctor, what are you hiding?' I murmured aloud – and with that, two things happened. First, my eye caught on a phrase halfway down a page, and second, the creak of a floorboard had me fighting out from under the rug to confront my attacker.

'Holmes! Damn it, man, couldn't you have cleared your throat or something? How did you get here? I didn't hear a motor.'

'I had the Queen's driver drop me at the end of the drive, since I did not think coming all the way to the house would be the best idea. He seemed to think that the doctor had a telephone installed here, and gave me the number of a taxi service in Braşov, in case I got stuck.'

'We may need to ring them if the doctor doesn't reappear. But I'm glad to see you.'

The papers were spread across half the floor, the table now lay on its side, the travelling rug thrown off – it was a good thing I'd decided against the candle, or we'd be stamping out flames. I started gathering up pages and returning them to some kind of order. It took me a minute to find the one I'd been reading.

'Sorry?' I asked, realising he'd said something.

'Where is the doctor? His motor is not in the stables.'

'He was only here for a few minutes and then he drove off again, about two hours ago. I expect he's dining out, since he didn't have anything before he left. Did Andrei tell you where I'd gone? Oh,' I said, remembering the last thing he'd said to me before we parted ways. 'You said you'd realised that Florescu was hiding something from us. Could it have been Andrei?'

'To be honest, I suspected it had to do with the doctor. There is a great deal of history between them that Mr Florescu did not bother to tell us about. However, more immediately, yes: Andrei told me you'd been interested in how he'd seen the doctor's motor, so I knew you were going after him. However, it did take some time to discover the exact location of the Mikó house.'

'Huh,' I said. 'I didn't think of that.'

'No? How did you get here?'

'He brought me. Not that he knew it. I was under that seat he has in his motor, for transporting patients. Turns out it's a kind of box. There's a lock on the outside.'

I could see the many questions running across his face, but since any of them would have come out as accusations, he hesitated – just long enough for me to wave the page under his nose.

'I've found something, but we probably should move to a room that doesn't overlook the drive quite so openly. Oh – wait.

Does this look familiar?'

I had dug out the single sheet of card stock from the desk. He took it, felt it, tested its bend, even held it under his nose. 'It is very similar, but I should have to have both in a laboratory to see if it is in all ways the same as the other.'

'Do you want to hang on to it?'

He thought for a moment, then handed it back to me. 'For the time, let us leave it here.'

I put it back in the drawer. 'There's no one in the house, his servants appear to have been gone for a couple of weeks. We should hear when he returns, but it's probably best not to be right here. Bring that folder,' I said, and restored the table, woollen throw, and window to their original positions.

The billiards room had no windows and plenty of dust. I flipped on a lamp and took the folder from Holmes, spreading out pages across the baize surface. 'The Mikós have been prominent in the Braşov area for centuries. There's a family tree in the library that links the doctor's ancestors to the area's thirteenth-century Saxon rulers. This was their country house – they had another in Braşov itself, but the doctor's father sold it about fifty years ago. That seems to have marked the beginning of a downturn in the family fortunes. By the time the War began, the Mikó estate was in trouble, and when Transylvania went to Roumania in 1920, things became very tight indeed. The doctor appears to be the last survivor of the family, and inherited the estate when his father died in 1910. Between 1919 and 1923, he had to sell off several remaining farms from around the estate. Then two and a half years ago, he inherited a fortune from an uncle he'd scarcely known.

'And yet, he did not spend it on this house. He hired back a couple of the servants, bought that car and had it adapted as an ambulance, and had some very nice suits made – but he spent almost nothing on the family house. Oh, except a new hot-water geyser in his bathroom.'

'Yet he continued living here,' Holmes noted, taking the page I handed him. This showed the current boundaries of the estate – considerably reduced from those on the grand, faded map in the estate offices.

'Last November, he went to Hamburg to see the solicitor he'd inherited along with his uncle's estate. Since then, the main focus of their communications has been the process of converting real estate and stock portfolios into cash.'

'Any indication what he plans to do with it?'

'That's what I was searching for. But while I looked, I kept noticing that there were pages missing and references made to letters that weren't here. And yes, it could be poor record-keeping, but it could also be—'

'A deliberate attempt to expunge the record of some systematic crime or wrongdoing.'

'Exactly.' Holmes was bent over the fanned-out pages on the table, picking up one here, setting one atop another there. I let him be, since confirming the faint patterns I thought I had seen was even more important than hurry. Ten minutes later, he straightened, his grey eyes continuing to travel over the pages.

'Do you see it, too?' I asked.

'I see an outline.'

I held out the page in my hand. 'Because his filing system is somewhat slapdash, he left a couple of things that he might not have intended. One of them was an order from Fortnum & Mason – I'll tell you about that in a minute. But I think he also overlooked this letter in the culling process. That phrase, with the word *Familienschloss*?' I tapped the German lettering. 'It's to his solicitor in Hamburg. And my German's a little rusty, but it seems to me he's saying that his Roumanian property lawyer is looking for a way that he can take back the family castle.

'Holmes, I think he's talking about Bran.'

CHAPTER FORTY-FIVE

OLMES PROPPED ONE HIP onto the billiards table, head bowed over the carbon copy, thinking so hard I could hear the whir. I gathered the papers in something close to the order I'd found them in. Holmes finished, and set the key page on the top.

'The doctor should have returned by now,' Holmes said, without moving.

'He could be with friends.'

'Did he dress?'

'He changed his shirt, but his evening suit is upstairs. And Holmes? He has a gun. Something that takes 9mm bullets. There was a half-empty box in his desk drawer.'

'Probably a Steyer automatic,' he muttered. Then, in a typically abrupt change of subject, asked, 'Was that letter the only mention of a castle?'

'The only one I saw, although I haven't read everything thoroughly. But, the Roumanian solicitor his German lawyer found for him is an expert in international property law.'

'Couldn't it be another castle? This country seems to have more of them than Scotland.'

'True. On the other hand, the doctor has a large and dramatic painting of Castle Bran on his bedroom wall, where he would see it last thing at night and first thing in the morning. There are also half a dozen places around the house where paintings hung until recently. At first, I thought the gaps were where he'd been forced to sell off his valuables along with some of the estate farms, in the years after the War.'

'But you feel he took them down to conceal his monomania.'

'If he was planning something that would return Castle Bran to his possession, he might not want people to see how deeply interested, even fixated, he was on the place. That would also be a reason for removing the potentially incriminating correspondence from his records.'

'Because he intends to do something criminal.'

'If it's not criminal, why try to hide his tracks? He anticipates the attention of outsiders – the police. One painting of a castle on the wall is an innocent decoration. A dozen views of the same castle would create suspicion.'

'The servants would know, if he'd taken paintings down.'

'But would anyone think to ask them? Just like no one would think to ask . . .' My voice trailed away as a thought struck me. A small thing, seen out of the corner of my eye, but persistently irritating.

Holmes didn't notice my preoccupation. 'We need to speak with this Roumanian legal gentleman, although he may not wish to tell us anything. The doctor is a respected person in Braşov, and openly revered in Bran: no one would believe he would attack a woman and abduct a girl.'

'Even I find it hard to credit. He does seem honestly to care for the people. You and I have both met men who kill for pleasure, Holmes. Would you have thought Dr Mikó capable of it?'

'A doctor, a soldier, he has seen many things, and no doubt done his share of hard tasks. I will admit, I did not see corruption hiding in the man's soul. It requires very cold blood indeed to abduct a simple, hard-working village girl from her way home – a girl he has known all her life – and deliberately murder her.'

The word startled me out of the thought I was trying to hunt down. 'Murder! Holmes, do you think she's dead?'

'The longer he keeps her, the less choice he may have in the matter. Even assuming he performed the abduction itself in the same way he took you, and that she did not see him or his distinctive motorcar, once she is awake, she becomes a danger. She can be heard. She could see him, if he brings her food.'

'You're right. Although, once he had her imprisoned, he could just wear a mask, or slip her food under – wait.' Something I had seen . . .

More bits of the puzzle were clicking into place. Gabi's physical resemblance to Ileana. Taking her at night. The lack of a latch on my own prison. My fingers went to the high neck of my blouse, as I thought about this man who did not strike either of us as a killer. A man with a hamper of English goods.

'What if this is all one act?' I said.

'In what way?'

'Kidnap, threat, rumours . . . Holmes, you often note that the little things can be the most important.'

If he was surprised at the side-track, he did not show it. 'Certainly when it comes to an investigation.'

'Let me show you something.'

I led him through the dark hallways to the kitchen and the pantry beyond. I shut the door and turned on the electrical light, then flipped back the top of the Fortnum & Mason hamper.

'When the doctor left tonight, he took with him a packet of water biscuits, a piece of cheese, and a Malvern Water.'

I watched him pick up the packet of Earl Grey tea, check its contents, and decide – as I had – that all one could say was that the smell and general appearance were what we had found in the hex bundle. He returned it to the hamper, surveyed the remaining contents, then sat back on his heels to look at the shelves around us, with their basic staples and tins, packets from Italy and Germany, mineral water from France – and nothing from England other than what had been sent him in July.

'One other thing,' I said, when he had finished.

Back in the doctor's library, on the wall directly in front of the man's favourite chair, hung his family tree. I tugged the room's curtains shut again, that we might use our torches to examine it, and checked that my memory had been correct. Yes, it told a story within a story.

The tree itself was nearly four feet on a side and lavishly illustrated with gilt-edged coats-of-arms and portraits of the eminent. Two generations out of date now, the roots of the genealogical tree were in a fifteenth-century Voivode, or warrior-king, and included various princes of Transylvania. All the men were fierce of beard and intelligent of eye – and I noticed the name Báthory more than once. What had caught at the edge of my mind was a slight, nearly invisible break in the line between one of the last princes and the last shown Mikó, our doctor's grandfather.

If I remembered my European history correctly, around 1700

this part of the world had shifted from the Ottomans to the Hapsburgs, taking its title of Prince of Transylvania with it. The tree did include the Austrian emperors as far as Franz Joseph. They were, however, over at the very edge, so as to leave plenty of room for the full details of the Mikó family line.

Had it not been for that missing fraction of the boot – the only gap in the entire meticulously detailed tree – the line of succession between Voivode, prince, and doctor would be a direct one. Instead, a fact the artist had worked hard to obscure under decorative swirls and handsome portraits, the boot was broken, to indicate the sad truth of an illegitimate son.

That small gap meant that, as the decades went by, the doctor's family became increasingly distant cousins to the hereditary rulers of Transylvania.

I laid my finger on the small section of missing trunk.

'You know, I think the doctor may be creating a story,' I told Holmes. 'One in which he is the hero.'

CHAPTER FORTY-SIX

ONCE UPON A TIME there was a young man from the town of Brașov.

He came from a family of high-ranking boyars, Saxons who had arrived in the thirteenth century and built themselves into the highest levels in the principality of Transylvania. Unlike many of their class, the boy's family remained in their homeland, managing their own estate rather than leasing out the land and moving to a more fashionable home in France or Italy. The boy's father was a proud man and a patriot, adamant on responsibility and service – even as the changing world, a series of bad years, and his own disastrous habits of making poor decisions and placing trust in the untrustworthy whittled away the land that gave them status.

The father instilled in his son a love for the common people and a profound desire to do well for them. The boy decided to train as a doctor, and his father agreed, selling a farm so his son could study at the great universities to learn his trade, even if it only meant that he would come home to heal the ills of farmers and patch the wounds of those working in factories.

When the young doctor returned at last, qualified to practise in his homeland, he found his father bedridden. The son's life was beginning, the father's reaching its end, but his heart was eased by knowing that his son was dedicated to their people.

As the father faded, he told his son stories of the family's proud history. Of its treasure found and lost, of its sons sent off to conquer new worlds and invent new disciplines. And of the secrets of the family's past: how the Mikó family were not only of the aristocratic rank, they were in fact royal. Princes of Transylvania, not poor cousins.

Oh, the outer world did not take it as so: the record of a marriage had gone missing, a fire set by a rival so as to render an heir illegitimate. But royal the doctor's family was. More than the lands of the estate had been theirs, at one time. And perhaps, in a new day, their glory would return.

At long last, the father died. The doctor buried him, married a young woman of the town, had a son of his own. They lived in the family mansion, using her small inheritance and his slim hospital salary to eke out a life in the too-big, too-remote house. In the years that followed, more land went and fewer men remained to farm it, a terrible cycle of boundaries narrowing down.

Then the Great War plunged the world into chaos. The doctor went to war, his wife and son moved in with her parents, the house was closed up.

Four endless, nightmare years, battling disease and sawing off limbs, but all the while, all the long, exhausted, blood-soaked days, all the freezing sleepless nights, he held to himself the knowledge that he was a prince in disguise.

The War ended. Somewhat to his surprise, the doctor had not been killed by a stray bullet or one of the many outbreaks of cholera and typhoid. He went home to Braşov, to his wife and son in the tired house, with the few servants and farmers who had survived. He brushed off his medical bag, and went back to the quiet life of treating civilians.

A prince, in disguise.

And every time he went down to the village of Bran, he would look up and see the towers of the castle that should have been his. The place he had played in as a child, secretly regarding its derelict nooks and crumbling walls as his long before he learnt how true – how *nearly* true – that was. When they were boys, the caretaker's son, Grigorei Florescu, had seen his longing and used it to wield a child's power. Even after they grew to be men, Florescu kept the castle's rightful owner at bay.

All because of a four-inch-long iron key.

If he'd had money, the young doctor could have gone to the city fathers of Braşov and offered to take the derelict castle off their hands. They'd have been glad to unload it – but what then? His income was that of a country doctor, paid in chickens and coins, with a handful of rents from the estate's few remaining tenant farmers. Even if he'd sold everything he had, house, land, and furnishings, it would barely cover the cost of repairing the castle's roof.

His impotence was an ever-gnawing pain, even when his family brought him joy.

But in 1919, the Spanish flu swept the land, and he buried his wife and son in the same week.

The following year came the Queen.

The city fathers, seeing their chance at moving the growing

expenses off their books, drew up a magnificent deed and presented this foreign woman with *his* castle. And where another woman would have thanked them with the ill-concealed horror of a maiden aunt whose cat presented her with a dead rodent, this one promptly declared it a fairy-tale castle, and started pouring the riches of her English fortune into it.

For three years, whenever the doctor would pass through Bran to treat a broken finger or attend a breech birth, he was aware of the castle on the hill. He felt like a man who had lost his beloved to a wealthy rival: happy for her good fortune, grateful she was being given the care she deserved, and aching that he could not do it for her.

And then suddenly, out of the blue, he could.

That all but unknown uncle with his stunningly unguessed-at fortune and his intolerable sense of timing. The disbelief, the dawning realisation, and the terrible bitterness that followed.

Why hadn't the old bastard had the decency to die three years before? Why did he have to wait until the castle of their ancestors had been turned over to this foreigner, this dilettante, this *woman* . . .

He'd been handed the keys to the kingdom, only to find the locks changed.

He tried to make the best of it. He couldn't bring himself to use the money for his own sake, to restore the Mikó house to a thing of glory. He did turn some of his fortune to improving the lives of his people, and closed the part of his practice that had been primarily done for the income. But that only left more time to brood. He began to drink, he did not replace servants who quit, he found few pleasures.

Until one night after dinner, three glasses of brandy into

the evening, he looked up at the library wall and found himself studying the decorative branches of the family genealogy, that meaningless, all-important, ever-tormenting half-inch gap in the tree's branch.

What if it weren't there? What if everything wasn't as hopeless as he'd always assumed? Weren't there really only two barriers to reclaiming Bran as his own?

The first was that broken line, which rendered a son and heir illegitimate. But what if a record came to light? The official church records were gone, but letters of agreement might be . . . conveniently discovered. Long lost, joyously found, a marriage restored and a line of succession clarified. Once that was done, back-taxes could be negotiated, apologies made and accepted. He had no doubt that the city fathers of Braşov would be pleased to have one of their own inside those walls instead of a foreign woman.

But that left the Queen. Castle Bran was her beloved toy. The woman had turned all the years of offended pride and female resentments into making it a place that only grudgingly welcomed the men of her family, including the king himself. It was her playground, like a full-sized doll's house, that she could dress up and fill with silly decorations and frivolous guests.

But what if the castle no longer pleased her? What if that frivolous woman began to see its darker side – the dungeon in its cellars, the blood in its floorboards? What if the smiling peasants no longer pressed her outstretched fingers to their foreheads, and instead shied away as she came near?

How long would she overlook the cold shoulders, the lack of strewn flowers, the tugging of children out of her path? Rocks, even, thrown at her gleaming motorcar?

Not long at all, he thought. It would not take much to

undermine her enthusiasm for the villagers, and then for their castle. A few months, and she would begin to look around for another doll's house, and turn her back on Transylvania.

All it would take was a piece of paper, and a story. A story his people would react to like the pluck on a violin string. A story that could only be told by someone who knew them as intimately as he knew his own family.

The story of a woman who bathed in blood, whose perversions fed on the death of innocents, whose tastes and habits preyed on the people she treated as her possessions, as if they were part and parcel of the castle grounds. A woman whose wickedness stirred up other evil things, waking the dead and summoning the witches.

Only a fellow Transylvanian could craft a story that spoke to his people. And only a doctor would know how to bring it to life.

CHAPTER FORTY-SEVEN

'HIS TARGET IS not Gabriela,' I told Holmes. 'No more than it was me, or Vera Dumitru, or the chickens he tried to poison. His target is the Queen. And his weapon is a fairy tale.'

'When a doctor goes wrong, he is the first of criminals,' Holmes muttered.

'"He has nerve. He has knowledge,"' I added.

'Yes, I suppose – although I am not sure how much nerve has been required here.'

'I don't know, Holmes. I think it started with accidents: the girl who disappeared to Bucharest, then a few weeks later, the girl who cut her hand in the kitchen. Treating her may have given him the idea for an actual attack: frightening a child in the woods, and leaving a branch of lilac to tie it to the Queen.

'After that, when the Queen was away, he had months to work out his plans. The food basket, the drugs – oh, and the break-in at the surgery, to make it appear that there was someone else in the area with chloroform. He seems to have a motorcycle, as an alternative to that distinctive motorcar, and he figured out a way to conceal his comings and goings near to Bran – t hat old barn is a part of the family estate, according to the wall map. He let his servants go, took down the pictures on the walls. Then when the Queen returned, he started up in earnest: messages on walls, dead chickens. Though I bet he did have to work himself up for actually attacking me. I wonder if he practised somehow? And abducting Gabriela out from under the noses of her family? Careful planning only goes so far, when a man is doing everything himself.'

'A monomaniac is fanatically dedicated to his cause. It would take little push to go from theory to act.'

'So, he abducted Gabriela, and planted the pearl on the road where she was taken, to make it look as if the Queen had taken her. He is using proprietary food and drink to make it look as if an English person is keeping her prisoner, so that – what? When she escapes, like I did, she will tell everyone? Or when she . . .' I did not want to say it.

'Or when her body is discovered, the food and drink will be found with her.'

I stared at him. 'You think he would?'

'I think he's mad. I think he could. I also expect that when she is found, there will be another correlation to your own abduction.'

'What do . . . oh.' I touched my neck. Long, long ago, in another country and another state of mind, I had made a joke about Roumanians dying of exsanguination. There was no humour in the image of cheerful, vibrant young Gabi Stoica, pale and drained on a coroner's table.

'A doctor would not find it difficult, to drain the blood of a girl he has drugged unconscious,' he pointed out.

'And when she was found, the countryside would rise up against the Queen, and drive her from Bran.'

'Or so, at any rate, he would anticipate.'

In England, I might find it difficult to picture. But here? 'He's had her for a little more than twenty-four hours. She must have been alive this evening, since he took her food and drink. But even if he intends to use the rest of the supplies in the hamper, we have less than a day to find her.'

'So where would he put her,' Holmes wondered, 'if not in the house?'

'The map!' I exclaimed.

We hurried back through the corridors to the billiards room. The map I'd found in the folder was too small in scale to show anything but the general outline of the current estate. But when compared to the detailed map on the wall of the estate office, it gave us some ideas.

'Some of those buildings will have changed in the last eighty years,' I said, as Holmes applied a pencil to the small map, marking the location of various farmhouses and out-buildings.

'We want one far enough from here to justify motoring there, rather than walking, but without close neighbours who would notice visits from that distinctive motorcar.'

He had marked three. I compared them to the big map.

'If I were he,' I reflected, 'I'd want a place that people wouldn't necessarily connect with me personally, and that others knew about, too. Otherwise, how would the Queen think to imprison someone there?'

'He could plan on simply dumping her along a road – either dead, or alive but thoroughly drugged. However,' he added, hearing me draw breath to argue, 'you may be right. What about the hunting lodge, there in the edges of the forested part?'

'Off the road, a long drive leading in, and in August nobody's hunting deer but poachers. And witches. But it's a good six miles away. If we're going on foot, I am going to raid the pantry before we set off.'

He folded the map and slid it into a pocket, a distinctly smug sort of gesture. 'We could, if you like. Though it might be simpler to borrow transport from the doctor's stables.'

The options in borrowed transport were as follows: a landau with a broken axle, a child-sized dog cart with no quadruped in sight, a steam tractor without a steering-wheel, and a motorcycle. A gleaming, nearly new machine with a thin layer of road dust on its metal.

'That has to be the same one,' I said.

He dropped to his heels for a closer look at the long silver tube of the exhaust, tapping its side with a knuckle. 'This is a larger silencer than is generally provided. It explains how he could come and go without people noticing him.'

'There were oil stains on the floor of his motorcar – and two heavy boards made into ramps. He could hide the car, move around on the cycle, then load it up again when he needed to be on his way. Going out the back roads so no one in Bran noticed him.'

We studied the machine. A key rested in its ignition. A glance in the tank confirmed that it held petrol. A jacket, leather helmet, and a pair of goggles dangled from a peg beside the door.

It has always baffled me why, when a man and woman ride a conveyance on which one is seated behind the other, it is invariably the man on the controls. Surely it would be better to let the marginally shorter person go in front? Instead, the woman is left to the pillion position, where she might study the man's shoulders and the view to either side.

This might not be the time for a feminist discussion. And, after all, he'd been the one to find the thing, so – I waited until he had the machine running, politely declined the offer of our only pair of goggles, and climbed onto the hard metal luggage rack behind him.

He did give me the map, although we only required it once. We saw the gates leading to the hunting lodge but continued on past, along the unpaved road. After the next bend, he slowed, switched off our headlamp, then circled back.

He cut the engine as the gates came into view, and we pushed the cycle off the road, tucking it behind a tree, then climbed back onto the track.

I heard the rustle of his clothing, then the click of his pocket-watch opening. Its luminous hands said 11.15, almost four hours after the doctor had driven away from his house. Was the man here now? Did he plan to stop here for the night? Had he changed his mind about what to do with Gabriela? Was he . . . ? Would we find . . . ?

I shook myself, and followed Holmes' form, just visible in the light of the half moon. Down the road and through the gates, we found the drive's surface somewhat better than that of the public track outside. 'Do you see any sign of life?' I breathed.

'None.' I could see no shape of a building, no lights gleaming through curtains. Perhaps it was behind the trees.

On the big map, the lodge appeared to be half a mile back

from the road. We'd gone about half of that when we heard an approaching motor, and Holmes seized my elbow to steer me towards the verge. I agreed – best not to assume the motor would pass by. Unfortunately, either its engine was particularly quiet or it was travelling faster than it had seemed, because in seconds, its headlamps were swinging into the drive. Holmes gathered me up and threw our bodies at the nearest shape.

Fortunately, the shape was bushes, not the boot of a tree. We froze, other than slowly migrating downwards amidst crackles of wood and grunts of discomfort. The headlamps passed without slowing, so we scrambled backwards, with mild curses this time, and tore our clothing free of the barbs in time to see the distinctive shape of the shooting brake.

'That's the doctor's,' I said.

We ran after the tail lights, Holmes at the fore, me following as fast as I dared, being nearly blind. The headlamps turned, to reveal a building half-hidden behind the trees. We kept running for a bit, then returned to the verge and to as brisk a walk as the ground permitted. The engine shut off. I waited for a door to open, but oddly, he stayed in the car. No one came out of the building, and no lights burnt inside.

When both motor and lodge were in full view, Holmes and I came to a halt. The powerful headlamps, carving sharp designs of shadow over the front of the rustic building, seemed to be bouncing rhythmically: up-down, up-down.

'What is he doing?' I whispered to Holmes.

Still the driver remained where he was – and then there was sound as well: a man's voice, loud and unintelligible through the open window.

'He sounds angry,' I said.

'Very.'

It sounded like an endless string of curses – although that is not uncommon with a foreign tongue. The headlamps bounced, the voice chanted along with it.

'He appears to be pounding the steering wheel,' Holmes noted.

With that, the motor's door flew open. The driver climbed out and slammed the door with all his strength – so hard, in fact, that the latch didn't catch and the door flew back at him. This time the shout he gave could be nothing but a curse. It was followed by an even harder slam and a pound of his fist on the uncompliant metalwork, with a kick for good measure.

It should have been funny. It was anything but. I spoke into Holmes' ear. 'Something he learnt during the evening has sent him off the edge.'

'I imagine he discovered that yet another attempt at stirring up trouble has failed to raise so much as a rumour.'

Hex bags and poisoned grain were one thing, but to plot, plan, and carry out a pair of assaults, first on a guest and then on a maid – yet have no one talking about pearl necklaces and evil Queens?

'Holmes,' I said, 'a person held by an *idée fixe* can become truly deranged when he is thwarted.'

The doctor had left off his assault on the motorcar and moved to its back door, reaching inside for something. This door, shut with less violence, remained closed, and the doctor stalked through the light beams towards the lodge. Both of us strained to make out the object he carried, but only when he paused to unlock the door did it come into view: thin, long, rigid – sticklike, but with a gleam of metal at the end. Then the door opened and he was gone.

'What was that?' I hissed.

'It looked remarkably like . . . a carving fork.'

My hand shot up to the wound on my neck. 'My God, Holmes – we've driven the man to murder!'

Chapter Forty-eight

And then we were running again. Holmes drew his gun as he flew – around the motor, through the headlamps, towards our wild shadow figures on the front wall, up the steps and diving through the open door, ducking to either side in case the doctor was waiting there, gun out . . .

Nothing happened. Holmes reached out and eased the front door nearly shut, to block some of the blinding light. My eyes slowly adjusted. We were in a large room with heavy furniture and animal heads mounted on its panelled walls. Holmes moved on silent feet towards a door in the back wall. I followed, my throwing knife at the ready.

The corridor smelt of dust and mildew, but also of fresh spirits: the doctor's rage had been fed by drink. The dust was years thick on the hallway runners, testifying to the long abandonment of the hunting lodge. The doors on either side of the corridor were shut – then suddenly a low light gave shape to our surroundings, its source from around a corner. A rattle of keys came, and we broke into a run, gun extended as Holmes cleared the corner. The figure in the doorway was just taking a step forward. I shouted his name – but he kept moving, and Holmes' shot tugged at the tails of his overcoat.

Holmes darted to the far side of the doorway, but no return shots came. Instead, a shouted demand – in Roumanian, but the meaning was clear: Who is that?

I put my finger to my lips, telling Holmes that he should keep quiet. 'This is Mrs Holmes, Doctor. We, er, met the other day in Bran.' Twice, in fact.

Silence fell. Then, in a tone of wonder and exasperation, a low Roumanian mutter that did not require translation to interpret it as, *Dear God, some women don't know when to quit.* He then shifted to English.

'What the deuce do you want here? How did you find me?'

'Doctor, it is over.'

'Nothing is over. Not even this young woman's life, unless you want to be stupid.'

'I'm very glad to hear she's still alive,' I said. That much was certainly true.

'Of course she's alive, what do you think I am?' He sounded, of all things, offended. But perhaps the irony of the protest reached through the madness, because threat returned. 'And if you want her to remain alive, you will come in slowly and place the gun on the floor.'

Holmes shook his head, but I slipped my knife away, then sidled up to the door and edged one eye around the frame.

This had been a servant's room, small, minimally furnished, and with a tiny window, now boarded up. The walls were unpainted, the floorboards bare, yet the rusty metal bedframe was thickly draped with woollen blankets and feather pillows. A paraffin lamp hung from a bracket. Beneath it, a table held the room's comforts: matches for the light, a dozen or so English-language books, and food and drink with the Fortnum & Mason label.

The cheese was untouched, the biscuits had been opened, and the bottle of Malvern Water was half-empty.

But all that detail came via peripheral vision, because my gaze was locked on the man himself.

He stood on the far side of the narrow bed, bent over. His right hand held the object we had seen in the headlamps: it was indeed a carving fork, its curving prongs nearly six inches long, two sharp points that precisely matched the holes in my neck.

And, in the neck of Gabriela Stoica.

The girl was unconscious, drugged by the drink he had brought earlier in the evening. The doctor's left hand was beneath her lolling head, turning her upper body slightly towards him. On her neck, clearly displayed, were three pairs of stab marks, angry and smeared with dried blood.

A match for the marks hidden under the neck of my shirt.

Every one of which was well clear of any lethal vein or artery.

But not where the fork's prongs rested now.

'One small push,' the doctor said, 'and I puncture her carotid artery. She will die in seconds. Come in, and put down the gun.'

I studied his stance, the way his garments hung, and drew back into the corridor. Holmes was shaking his head vehemently, but he had not seen what I had. I mouthed silently the words *He has no gun*, then gave an emphatic nod at the one that he held. I stepped into view again, pausing in the doorway to prop my left shoulder against the frame. Out of his sight, I extended my left hand, palm up, towards Holmes. After a moment, I felt the touch of metal, and wrapped my fingers around the gun.

'Doctor, it really is over.'

'The gun.'

The man's hands were steady, despite rage and drink. If I turned the gun on him, even the tiniest jerk would open Gabriela's throat. So I took two steps into the room and set the weapon on the floor, nudging it away with my foot.

'And now your husband.'

'My husband isn't—'

'Please do not think I will not kill the child. I am, as you can see, a man who is running low on choices. If you wish Miss Stoica to live, Mr Holmes, you will join your wife.'

'I don't see a gun,' I said over my shoulder. Meaning that, even if the doctor had one, the brief delay of retrieving it would let us seize our own first.

Holmes stepped out beside me.

'Now, the two of you go into the next room and turn the key in the lock. When you have slid it back under the door, I will take this away from Gabriela's neck, and I will leave. By the time you break down the door, I will be gone. Before you reach help, I will be at the border.'

I eyed the door. It was narrow but sturdy, its lock old but recently greased. He saw me looking. 'I am afraid it will not smell very nice in there. I did not have a chance to empty the pot before you came.'

Having to shelter in an impromptu lavatory was the least of my concerns. His hand twitched, just a fraction. A trickle of blood started down the girl's throat.

'What's to stop you from taking the gun and killing us all?' I said.

I was mostly stalling for time – an automatic gesture, because no help was on its way – but to my astonishment, I could see him consider the matter. And what was more, he came up with a solution. 'You keep the gun. But remove the bullets first, please. Oh – and you have a knife, in that clever sheath in your boot. Leave that here, too.'

I looked at Holmes, and saw his face clearly for the first time. Another man would have been shaking with fury. He stood absolutely still, every muscle taut and his eyes like ice, and I knew that had it not been for those two sharp points of steel in the doctor's hand, he would cross the room and tear the man to pieces. Instead, he watched the thin scarlet line creeping down the white skin. Then he stood away from me, fixing me first with his gaze, then looking pointedly at the door we had come through. I read his message as if he had said it in words: *If the doctor pulls a gun, you are the one to flee and regroup.*

I took a deep breath, gave him a tiny nod of agreement, and we both dropped to our heels – me to pull the knife from my boot, Holmes to take up the revolver, loosing its cylinder to let the bullets bounce across the dusty floorboards. He then pointed the weapon at the wall and pulled the trigger eight times, to demonstrate its emptiness.

He stood. I flicked the knife across the room to leave it quivering in the wall, then stood as well.

The prongs of the fork pressed a degree less firmly, and he did not instantly reach into a pocket for a gun, so I decided to see if he would talk.

'Tell me why, Doctor. You care for your people, you have a lovely home in Braşov, you have money – why do you want to spend all your time and most of your money to repair Castle Bran?

369

You could build a hospital instead. A school – ten schools.'

I had not perceived madness in the man before, but it was there now, in the gleam of his eyes and the desperation in his voice. 'Because Bran is *mine*. Because my father lost what he had, and my grandfather lost most of his, and for generations the Mikó family has been cheated of what is ours, back to the days when my forefather was the Prince of Transylvania. It should have been mine – would have been, but for a lost marriage licence. And instead, the city fathers look at the cost of maintaining it and push it off on the first foreign harlot who will take it. Instead of offering it to me, instead of saying, "Some man who loves the people and wants only to serve them will make this a centre of life for our corner of the province" – instead of that, they throw it in the hands of a woman who plays with it and dresses it up as she would a doll's house. And when she tires of it, she will sell it to some wealthy playboy or give it to her worthless son, and the outsiders will come with their fast cars and their big noise, and the people of Bran will only suffer again.'

'The Queen does seem to love the people,' I ventured.

'The Queen!' he spat. 'The woman loves admirers, she loves the colourful peasants, she loves to look from her motorcar windows and see their farms and their children and their poverty.'

I kept a close eye on the two points, but despite his fury, they had not pressed further, so I did. 'Could you not educate her? Couldn't you—'

'To what purpose? They gave her my castle, and thanks to you, I will not get it back. Well, if I cannot have it, neither will she.' And with this chilling pronouncement, the doctor nodded at the side door. 'When the key has been slid out from under the door, I will leave.'

The fact that he had not summoned a gun of his own encouraged me to believe him – although if we had any other option, I would have taken that. But Gabriela was no longer in danger, and the door would give way eventually. Even if he had his gun in the motorcar and intended to come back with it, he would have to step through that narrow door to use it, giving one or the other of us a chance to overcome him.

And the man was too unbalanced for common sense. He might well kill the girl, if we did not give him some distance.

So we did. Holmes first, with the empty weapon, then me. Holmes closed the door and felt for the key. The mechanism turned. He pulled the key out, bent, and slid it under the door.

Instantly, footsteps crossed the outer room, followed by the sound of metal kicked across the floor. The steps continued, then seemed to stop. But there was no sound of Gabriela's prison door shutting, and the faintest of vibrations testified to his continued passage down the carpeted hallway. In a moment, more distant heels against wood, and a minute later the faraway noise of a starting engine.

Holmes' clothing rustled, and I heard the click of the gun's catch, followed by the faint rasp of brass against steel.

I recognised the sound, having loaded that gun a hundred times. 'You managed to palm one of the bullets?'

'The day Sherlock Holmes can't fool a doctor with sleight-of-hand is the day Sherlock Holmes retires to Monaco.'

'When we get out of here,' I said, 'I know you're angry, but don't kill him. You can hurt him, though. Hurting is fine.'

He shot me a glance of dark humour. 'Stand away, this could be messy.'

Blowing a lock mechanism from a door can be more than

messy – it can take off a finger, if done carelessly.

My husband is never careless.

The bullet damaged the mechanism enough that a few kicks sent the door crashing back. The noise half-woke the girl – she was fine, but for the new puncture on her neck, so I murmured reassurances until her eyes drifted shut. I tugged the blankets over her shoulder – although with thoughts of that motorcycle, I removed one of them and tucked it under my arm. Knife in boot, I headed for the door – then patted my pockets, found the handful of hard sweets I had bought half a lifetime before, and left them on the small table for her, grabbing up one of her pillows in exchange.

Then I ran.

The motorcar was gone and so was Holmes, but I followed him with my torch burning, through the lodge and down the drive, catching him up while he was still wrestling the motorcycle back onto the road.

'His tyre tracks showed him going back the way he came,' I told him. I placed the cushion on the hard metal rack, tucked up my feet and wrapped the blanket around us as far as it would reach, and held on tight.

Chapter Forty-nine

THIS LATE, THE ROADS were deserted – but only of cars, carts, and human beings. In the first two miles, Holmes swerved to avoid a large mouse, two rabbits, and a cat. At the same time, our headlamp bore witness to the motorcar's heedless progress, with one spray of glistening blood and the freshly flattened shape of something within a drift of feathers. A car as heavy as the shooting brake would sail blithely through anything smaller than a cow; for a motorcycle, a rabbit was dangerous, and a large fox could kill us outright.

Our speed edged off.

'Don't slow,' I shouted. 'We can't let him get away.'

He cocked back his head to call, 'He doesn't know we're after him. He has no reason to hurry.'

Isn't madness reason enough, I thought. But I shrugged down into the blanket and let the wind whip past. We were north of Braşov, therefore almost the exact centre of Roumania – a fact reflected on maps, with five roads coming together in the dot that was the town. Some of those were actual, metalled roadways, others largely aspirational, but since Bucharest was both the capital and the nearest city, its road would be well maintained. And it lay in the direction the doctor had chosen.

I spoke into his ear. 'Will he stop at his house first?'

The motion of his shoulders indicated that he was no more certain of the answer than I was. But because the mansion was just off this road, we took the risk of coming to a halt at the drive and turning off the motor.

No lights showing, no dust in the air over the drive. No sounds of an idling engine.

Holmes kicked our motor back into life and returned us to the road.

At the outskirts of Braşov, again I uncurled from the relative shelter of his back to shout. 'If the police department is open, we could ask them to wire ahead. Tell them a man is plotting to kill the Queen.'

He nodded, and slowed outside the building, but it was as dark as one might expect, from a small town in the still hours. He shifted up again.

'So,' I said. 'Where is he headed?'

'To the Queen,' he called back.

'He said he was going to one of the borders.'

'"If I cannot have it, neither will she."'

'He'd choose trying to get at the Queen over making a clean escape?'

'I believe so.'

I clung to him as the sleeping town flitted past, and considered the possibility of second-guessing a madman. I'd thought that as we spoke with the doctor, he'd seemed to regain some balance – enough to suggest he would choose a life forward rather than a final act and a blaze of glory. After all, his resources were enormous, the world at his feet. All he had to do was slip away from Roumania, and give up Bran to his enemy, the Queen.

What was the man thinking, there on the road ahead of us? Was he consumed by the need for revenge and the end of things, or had he seen the appeal of acceptance and a life elsewhere? Or was he simply speeding through the night, as blindly unaware of options as he was of the rabbits that dashed under his tyres? Waiting for a sleeping bullock to loom in his headlamps, or for the hands on the wheel to choose their goal . . .

Holmes was right: that all-or-nothing threat of his sounded more real than the idea of heading for a border. However, that still did not decide us.

'He knows she's in Sinaia,' I told him.

He sat back, letting the engine slow. 'Does he?'

'Pretty sure. He had passengers in the motorcar for a time, they were talking. But Holmes, that threat could be aimed at Bran itself rather than Marie.'

He drifted to a halt at a crossroads, beneath one of the town's streetlamps, and dropped his feet to the ground. There he sat, head bent, as deep in thought as I was.

Bran, or Marie? The Queen's beloved doll-house, or a direct assault on a royal palace filled with guards?

If I cannot have it, neither will she could also mean burning the object of his desire to the ground.

Castle Bran. Yes, it had stone walls, a ridiculously steep approach, and the tiniest of windows overlooking the drive – from the outside, an act of pyromania would require fire-arrows or an aeroplane. But considering that most of the servants would be out searching for Gabriela, a man with a match could walk through the door with little difficulty.

I felt Holmes come to a decision, but he turned on the seat and shoved his goggles up so he could look at me.

I nodded. 'Sinaia.'

He kicked the cycle into life again, and turned onto the Sinaia road.

As Brașov fell behind us, for the first time in hours, I spared a thought for Andrei Costea, well-bathed, but possibly growing hungry in our castle rooms. Should I tell Holmes what I'd learnt? No, better not to toss out any more distractions.

The road climbed, though its surface was good. Better yet, here it was more forest than farmland. Fewer chickens and cats, fewer henhouses to tempt predators, and wildlife more wary of engine noises than their more civilised brothers.

The drawback was, we saw no more bloody evidence of a motorcar's passage.

Grimly, Holmes took us faster, then faster yet. I tucked my head down, hoping to keep my spectacles from blowing off in the wind and became all too aware that the cushion had vanished from underneath me.

Two or three miles after leaving Brașov, I felt him react to something. I straightened, trying to see over his shoulder. 'What?'

'Headlamps,' he said. 'On the switchbacks ahead of us.'

Switchbacks were good. The road surface was excellent. A motorcyclist willing to take risks could gain on a car on the back and forth, especially at night when any oncoming traffic would warn with its lights. I let go of the blanket, allowing the wind to rip it into the night, and used the hand to pat at the pocket of Holmes' coat, to make sure I could find the revolver if I needed to. I then wrapped my arms around him and plastered myself to his back, going with his every lean and shift.

Our speed grew, terrifying and exhilarating. We clung to the road, leaning deeply left, and right, and left again, the surface closer to our knees with every turn.

The road hit its peak at Predeal, and started downwards, and I caught a glimpse of lights ahead – but . . .

Before I could speak, I felt Holmes' body go slack with disappointment, heard the slight reduction of speed as his hand ceased its full push on the throttle.

We went past the War-era Renault as if it were standing still, and flew on.

The road grew straighter, and any slight upper hand we might have had now lost ground to the powerful engine of the shooting brake. We joined a larger highway. Houses began to appear, and smaller lanes. A village, then another – and the occasional motor coming towards us, or ahead going south. We passed one of these, just before the town of Busteni, then another.

All of a sudden, Holmes reared back, setting the brakes hard and fighting to keep us upright. I had felt the shift of his muscles and reacted in an instant, but even so, his abrupt motion bashed my teeth and caught me off guard. We almost went down – if I'd been in his place, we would have – but he kept our wheels straight, and I felt the turn begin as soon as our flirtation with disaster was over. 'Sorry,' he said, and circled to take us back to the turn-off he had spotted just moments too late.

We were now passing through a series of expensive, locked gates with groomed trees and the occasional glimpse of formal gardens.

This must be Sinaia, the summer capital, where Bucharest moved when the weather grew hot.

It was a maze of small roads and drives, but Holmes seemed to know where he was going – or rather, to judge by the tension in his back, he had a picture of it by day, and was working to reconstruct the route by night.

Past some buildings, down a hill, across a stream – then lights appeared before us.

It could only be a royal castle, with sweeping entrance and guard house before a bulk that would contain hundreds of rooms – but in front of it stood the shooting brake, driver's door open and headlamps burning. As the cycle came to a skidding halt beside it, two men in livery were just crossing the internal courtyard, visible through a pair of archways. I clambered off the metal seat, as stiff as if I'd been on a horse all day. Still, I was in better shape than Holmes, who was struggling to uncurl his hands from the grips.

'Holmes, one of us has to move fast. Can you distract the guards?'

'Take the pistol,' he said, then raised his voice to call in his plummiest of tones, 'I say there, my good man, I wonder if you could help me? Terribly sorry, it's ridiculously late, but I'm looking for a gent who—'

The two men emerged from the right-hand archway. I pocketed the weapon and took off to the left as fast as my limbs would carry me. Which fortunately was faster than two hefty men with boots, overcoats, and ceremonial pikestaffs.

They shouted, but I made it across the courtyard and halfway up the grand internal stairway before the younger of the two had reached the doors. I was in a hall of some kind – this level would be entirely public and formal, thus far from the family's

378

bedrooms – but as I glanced up, I was startled to see the sky above open galleries. Lights burnt inside – not many, but enough to show me the stairs. As I launched up them, I began to shout.

'Guards! Protect your Queen! Stop the doctor – Ileana, it's Mary Russell – Mrs Holmes – Ileana!'

The two guards were shouting and clattering behind me, Holmes' voice joined the fray, and I was getting short of breath as I pelted along sumptuous corridors and grand stairways, shouting and cursing the solid sleep of the royal family. Where were the footmen – and how far had the doctor got?

Another set of stairs – and the living quarters at last, corridors with thick carpets and lined with busts and vases and paintings. One of the guards behind me was faster than I'd expected, I could feel him gaining on me and I thought of the gun, but who was I kidding, I wasn't going to send bullets flying here – and then from ahead of me came a man's shout. Halfway around a corner, I skidded on my heels and nearly went down, then ducked away from a large footman – who collided with the guard behind me in a pandemonium of curses, letting me dodge through the corner ahead of my pursuer.

Then everything happened at once.

On my first step inside the dim-lit corridor, I spotted a man with a doctor's bag standing hand raised from knocking at a closed door. At my second step, a door across from him came open. My fourth step, Ileana came out from it, sleep-tousled, arms full of fluffy white dog. I opened my mouth to shout – and at my fifth step, the door in front of the doctor drew back, revealing the Queen herself.

'He took Gabriela!' I shouted, but that was my eighth step, and the doctor's hand was shifting to straight-arm the Queen back into the room.

I pounded down the endless length of hallway, knowing I would never make it, unable even to pause and draw the gun – but then a white blur flew down the carpet, snarling and furious, to dive after the disappearing leg. The many-throated chorus of shouts was joined by screams, male and female, and the doctor reappeared, stumbling backwards, swatting at the white shape attached to the back of his thigh. Five more steps before I could tackle him – but I was ten feet away when a priceless oriental vase crashed down on his skull. He swayed, and collapsed.

The Queen and Ileana, wearing identical shocked expressions, looked from him to me. I slowed – only to go down under several hundred pounds of angry palace guard.

CHAPTER FIFTY

THEY DID GIVE ME a thick travelling rug before parking me in the formal great hall, under the eye of no fewer than four uniformed men. Minutes after I'd been placed there, a rush of traffic swept through, escorting a man with a doctor's bag. A few minutes after that, a sleepy maid appeared to light the fireplace beside me, which might not have been necessary, given that it was August, except for the odd fact that the room had no roof.

Thirty minutes went by. My bruises developed, my stiffness grew. Voices went back and forth from somewhere overhead, occasionally that of Holmes. The new doctor came back down – the king, in his sickbed, had apparently not even heard the disruption.

I could only hope that my brief message had reached Holmes; before the guards dragged me away, I'd managed to shout a few brief words over my shoulder – in Arabic, a language no one in the place would understand: 'Don't let her learn what the doctor wanted!'

Then I was hauled down here, while he was ushered into a private room for a conversation with Her Majesty.

Typical of men.

I got laboriously to my feet. The guards bristled as they watched me make a circuit of the settee, my attempt to keep the bruises from turning to stone. I hobbled like an octogenarian around the sumptuous, befringed silk, then winced as I attempted to raise my gaze upward at the odd ceiling. Was it not curious, to have such an ornate hall standing open to the elements? But this time I noticed a partial roof, an ornate glass affair that covered approximately a third of the space – and realised simultaneously that this must be some kind of retractable ceiling that had either jammed or been left open, and that the sky overhead was no longer black.

I came to a halt before the inadequate fire, whose warmth at least brushed the backs of my legs as it flew upward. I edged slowly about like a roast on a spit, and was considering the possibility of getting to my knees, so I could toast my shoulders as well, when brisk footsteps came up the entrance stairway, followed by the click of heels as the guards snapped to attention. I shuffled myself around to see who it was.

A tall, slim, dark man in his fifties, trim of moustache and intense of gaze: this could only be the Queen's advisor, friend, and purported lover, Prince Barbu Ştirbey.

'*Esti tu femeia . . .*' he began, then caught himself. 'Are you the woman they say was attacking the Queen?'

'I am the woman who was trying to save the Queen from attack. I believe you met my husband the other day. Mr Holmes?'

His eyes widened, and darted over my bruised and dishevelled figure before he turned on the nearest guard with a flood of crisply irate Roumanian. I unwrapped the wool from my shoulders and managed to drape it across the settee, then broke into his tirade.

'Sir, please, I should like to see that Her Majesty and the Princess Ileana are all right. And to speak to my husband.'

He shot a quick question at the terrified guard, who gave an equally brief reply. Prince Barbu then reached out for my elbow to guide me towards the stairs, a gesture that told me precisely how feeble I looked. I made an effort, and by the time we hit the second flight of stairs, I was moving like a fairly spry fifty-year-old.

'Sir, do you know if there is any news from Bran – about the girl who was taken?'

He made a sound of irritation and said, 'Yes, of course, I should have told you immediately. There was a telephone message from the exchange in Braşov, that the police went to the hunting lodge and found the girl. She is quite safe. Although, if I understood the message, angry.'

'That sounds like her.' I found I was grinning, at the thought of a furious Gabi Stoica. 'Does Ileana – does the Princess know?'

'She does. She was worried.'

'They are friends.'

My spirits were considerably lighter but that did not speed my pace any. However, our slow progress gave me time to take in the details – and detail there was in abundance. The palace itself – a castle in name only, despite the lorry-loads of decorative weapons and armour – was as new as its royal family. And the mind behind both the building and its decoration was of the 'If one is good, seventeen is better' school. Every balustrade carved, every wall covered by gilt-framed paintings, every door the result of weeks of a craftsman's labour. A Victorian sitting-room run amuck.

There could be no more different building from Castle Bran than this one.

Prince Barbu strode ahead of me, going straight to a door and flinging it open with the assurance of a man who lived here. He dropped to one knee in front of Queen Marie and raised her hand to his lips, a gesture that clearly came naturally to them both. He rose and turned to Ileana, who sat swollen-eyed but hugely relieved, her arms around the white dog on her lap. To her he gave a small bow, affectionate and slightly ironic. Her own tip of the head, despite the tension in her posture, held a similar trace of humour. He even patted the dog.

In less than five seconds, I knew all about the love and respect these three held for one another.

I moved over to Holmes, who looked askance at my swollen lip but said nothing.

'Does she know?' I murmured.

'What the doctor was after? I've not told her, and he wasn't conscious when we left him. I do not know if he is awake yet. You heard that the Braşov police found Gabriela.'

'I did – but look, we have to . . .' I started, but Prince Barbu came into earshot then, turning to Holmes and asking if they might speak. I watched them go, praying that Holmes had got my message, that he agreed with it – and that anything could be done to carry it out.

I gave the Queen and her daughter an encouraging smile. 'Your Majesty, I apologise that we could not keep Dr Mikó from disturbing your sleep with such a dreadful interruption. And Princess, congratulations on taking such decisive action. Bulldog Drummond would be proud.'

The girl's pinched face relaxed, just a little. 'You think so?'

'Absolutely! The only thing that will keep the Sapper from writing this up is the thought of offending your cousin's dignity.'

She considered for a moment the likely reaction of George V, when it came to such royal shenanigans as a young nightgown-clad Princess bashing an intruder on the skull with a priceless antique, and broke into a grin of pure pleasure. 'Someone ought to tell the Sapper about it, anyway.'

'If he does publish the story, he'll have to get the dog right.'

She tightened her arms around the sleeping creature. 'I'm so glad Gabi was found. But have you any idea what that man wanted? He's the Bran doctor, isn't he? I've seen him drive past in that extraordinary wagon of his.'

I could feel Queen Marie's warning look, but I was ahead of her in my caution. 'Princess, I'm sure that you know how irrational men can become when it comes to politics. I fear we will find that someone has turned the doctor's mind, and driven him to this act of lunacy.'

'But how did he get in?' she demanded. This time, it was the guard near the door who straightened sharply at her question.

'I would imagine that a man with a medical bag is a common sight here these days, with your father ill? Well, we are all fortunate that this Bedlamite met his match in a small dog and a student of Bulldog Drummond. And you can be very certain that the guards have learnt their lesson, and that it shall never happen again.'

CHAPTER FIFTY-ONE

SHERLOCK HOLMES FOLLOWED THE Prince out of the Queen's sitting-room and down a hall to a nearby room – a library, of a sort, although designed less for reading than to impress male friends with its solid expanse of leather spines. Prince Barbu pulled the doors shut in the face of the guard outside, then gestured Holmes to an armchair while he walked over to an elaborate drinks cabinet. He filled two glasses from a decanter of transparent liquid, bringing them back to the chairs. 'I don't know if it's time for a drink or morning coffee, but I imagine the latter will arrive before long. In any event, I need this first.'

Holmes took a generous, medicinal swallow, relishing the travel of warmth down his throat. It was *tuica*, but with a rich complexity that made the others he'd drunk taste like paint stripper. He took another sip, then both men reached for tobacco. When the smoke was rising, the prince flicked ash from the end of his cigarette.

'Tell me what happened.'

And Holmes did, from his arrival in Bran the previous evening, having accompanied the Queen to Sinaia, through tracing Russell to a country house on the other side of Braşov, to the motorcycle chase through the mountains. He kept to the main points, but even without the details, coffee had been served and the palace was about its morning business before he finished.

'I did not see what happened with Russell after we arrived,' he ended. 'Although I understand that she and Princess Ileana between them overcame the doctor. And I did see a revolver in his medical bag, afterwards.'

'Why were you not there?'

'One of us had to stay on the forecourt to distract the guards. Russell is quicker on her feet than I.'

'Although not fast enough to avoid the guards.'

'She'd done her job, and they were doing theirs. She saw no reason to hurt them.'

The Prince laughed; Holmes did not.

The Prince reached out to refresh their coffee cups, and sat back, considering. 'This Bran doctor. He honestly imagines that he has a right to Castle Bran? He's not simply a lunatic?'

'There does seem to be at least a fragile basis for his conviction that the family has a claim to the building. Inheriting his uncle's money made it appear to be within his grasp – at least, until Russell and I began to throw barriers in his way. Tonight's violence was a last, desperate act of fury and despair. No less dangerous for that, of course, but it was not what he planned at the start.'

'Is he mad?'

'*I* would call it madness. A psychiatrist might not.'

'I hate that he troubles the Queen, just now. There is too much on her mind as it is. The King. Their son. Ileana's English school.'

Holmes studied the other man, running his hand over his hair, as if smoothing away his own discomfort. 'Do you . . . that is to say, sir – do you love her?'

The Prince looked startled at the abrupt question. However, he did not protest, or declare it inappropriate. Instead, he gave a little smile. 'She is my Queen. I would give her my life. She, and her daughter.'

And Holmes nodded, as if this was answer enough. 'I don't know that self-sacrifice will be required of you, merely a degree of ethical flexibility. My wife believes that, were the Queen to learn of Dr Mikó's . . . delusions, it would taint her affection for Bran and its people.'

After a moment, the Prince nodded. 'It might. Not at first, but the thought would persist. She would find excuses to be elsewhere. Which would be a pity. Bran is the one place she can be herself.'

'I suggest you do not tell her. Don't let Mikó have his say.'

'Sir, are you suggesting that I have the man . . .'

'Not killed. Merely pull his fangs. He was found outside the King's rooms with a gun, after all. It would be easy enough to establish that his argument was with Ferdinand, rather than Marie. If he stands trial, it will come out – however, you may be in a position to find a doctor who will declare him mad. The poor fellow need not be hanged, or shot, merely put quietly away. The man could even be made quite comfortable, were the government to seize his considerable assets. He has no family, after all. But he must never communicate with the Queen or Princess Ileana. And you will need to be diligent that word of the man's claim never gets out. In fact, if you can arrange a day or two delay from the police in their investigations, I shall see that any corroborating evidence disappears from his house. After that, even if a rumour does get out, it will look like nothing but a sad dream.'

The Prince eyed the man across from him, then stood. He held out his hand. Holmes rose, and took it.

'I regret,' the prince said, 'that I will not have the opportunity to know you better, you and your lady wife.'

'Sir, the sentiment is mutual.'

CHAPTER FIFTY-TWO

BREAKFAST CAME, TO THE sunny morning room where I sat with Queen Marie and the Princess. On its heels came Holmes and Prince Barbu, smelling of tobacco, *tuica*, and satisfaction. The servants had brought large trays of bread rolls and fruit and a dozen other temptations that helped me forget the bruises darkening my skin. Ileana slipped bits of sausage under the tablecloth to the dog while she told the prince the adventure from her point of view. The Queen listened and smiled and tossed in the occasional remark.

And then it was over: table clear, servants gone, the Princess' eyes drooping a little in the warm air drifting through the window. Prince Barbu lit a cigarette for the Queen, then stood.

'I will telephone to His Majesty's doctor, ma'am, if you do not mind, then ask if His Majesty would like to see me before I go home.'

'I'm sure Nando would enjoy a brief talk.'

'Oh, and I forgot to say – Nadèja told me to ask you over for tea.'

'I would love to, but perhaps in a few days. Today Ileana and I will be returning to Bran.'

Ileana's eyelids flew open. 'Today? I don't have to wait?'

'I think our exile has gone on long enough. Can you gather your things?'

'Faster than you can!' She laughed and ran out of the room, the dog at her heels.

The Prince smiled at the door she'd flitted out of. 'It is a blessing she can still be so . . . nearly childlike.'

'Oh, you should have seen her in London – *quite* the young lady. But yes, here she can be free. She would love to see Nadèja, too. Why don't the two of you motor over to Bran? The gardens are spectacular, and they'll fade very soon.'

'We will enjoy that. Sir, madam,' he said, turning to us. 'It was a pleasure.'

He left. The Queen rubbed out her cigarette in the marble tray. 'I must let the servants know that I am leaving. I hope the two of you – but wait: you arrived on a motorcycle, I was told. Will it be necessary for you to ride it back again?'

'Oh, I hope not,' I said with feeling.

She laughed. 'Then you shall come with us. Although I imagine the conversation might be less than scintillating, following the much-interrupted night.'

'Madam, this is one time when I would choose soft upholstery over the wittiest of talk.'

It was just as well that I was not anticipating a compelling chat with Victoria's granddaughter. Even Holmes, though remaining bolt upright, allowed his eyelids to drift shut on some stretches of the road.

When we reached Bran, Ileana scrambled out of the car in a most unroyal fashion to confront Florescu.

'How is Gabi? Have you seen her? When can I go to her?'

The major-domo blinked at the onslaught. 'Good morning, Your Highness. Gabriela is fine. I was at the house when the police brought her back, two hours ago. They stayed to interview her, and when they left she was very tired. I expect she will sleep for a time. As for a visit . . .' The major-domo looked to the Queen for guidance.

'Not today,' Marie said briskly, and before her daughter's protests could rise up, she pointed out that Gabriela needed rest, that she could not rest if there was a royal princess in her house, and that arrangements would be made to bring her to the castle for a visit on the morrow.

It was, Ileana's face admitted, fair enough, although she continued to wheedle until the Queen fixed her with The Look. She subsided, and said that she thought she would have a nap herself.

The Queen watched her walk away, the expression of maternal command fading into simple affection. She then turned to us.

'When Mr Florescu has brought me up to date,' she said, 'I shall go for a ride. Would you two like to join me? There's sure to be riding outfits that would fit you.'

We thanked her politely and said perhaps another day, which did not fool her a bit. She went off across the courtyard towards her rooms – but when the butler made to follow, we waylaid him.

'Mr Florescu,' Holmes said, his voice silky. 'I believe we need to have a conversation.'

'Sir?' The man looked down his nose at the hand impeding his forward progress. 'Concerning what?'

'The shade of Bran,' I said. Seeing his lack of comprehension, I leant forward to make it quite clear. 'The ghost in your castle walls. By name of Andrei Costea.'

He didn't try to pretend. He gulped, shot a glance after the Queen, and said, 'I will come. When she is finished with me.'

'We will be waiting,' Holmes said, more threat than promise.

As we walked up the stairs, I finally had a chance to ask Holmes how much he'd learnt from our ghost.

'Only what he could tell me in approximately two minutes. I was taken aback when the door opened and it was his face rather than yours, but he seemed clear on his mission. Once he'd described how he'd got there, and what had so interested you, I left, hoping to catch the Queen's car before the driver returned it to the garage. The boy did say that you'd found him in a hidden stairway behind the walls, and that he had some kind of peep-hole overlooking the village. But he had no idea why you were interested that the doctor's car had been near Bran on Sunday evening.'

'I didn't get much more than that, myself. I felt that satisfying my curiosity was less important than immediate action. And speaking of which, I do apologise for going back on my promise to you. That I would stay in the rooms.'

'Understandable, Russell,' he said.

The doors to our rooms were still closed, and proved locked. I rapped on the wood. 'It's us, Andrei.'

The latch slid back. One step inside the room gave me the answer to one of my questions: yes, at least some of the castle's servants were in on the secret. He'd been brought food, drink, and a new shirt, one with considerably less decoration than the one from Holmes' drawer. And possibly scissors and a razor, since he was clean-shaven now and his moustache had been trimmed.

I fastened the latch. Something about the gesture brought a degree of wariness to Andrei's face – or perhaps it was the way Holmes and I loomed at him, looking like the word *interrogation* brought to life.

I touched Holmes' arm, summoning up a reassuring smile. 'Hello, Andrei. I hope you've been comfortable? I am sorry we were gone so long.'

He stopped backing up, although his face remained guarded. 'Is good. I slept on . . .' He gestured at the settee. 'Chair?'

'The settee? You should have used one of the beds.'

He looked shocked. 'No! Setter fine. Nicer than bed on stairs.'

'I imagine so. And I see they brought you some food.'

'Yes, I—' He realised what he had said, and shut his mouth.

'Don't worry, we're here to help,' I said. And though Holmes looked at me sharply, it was true. The least we could do, here in Bran, was solve the problem of one formerly dead deserter. 'Sit down, please.' When he stayed on his feet, even eyeing the door, I walked over to the chairs by the window and tempted him with, 'I need to tell you about Gabriela.'

'You found Gabi? Where? She good?'

'She'll be fine. We found her, and set her free. And then found the man who took her.'

The ploy worked. He followed me to the chairs, and plopped down on one of them, as ungainly as an adolescent. I did not understand the muttered phrases that spilt from his mouth, but I knew a prayer of relief when I heard one.

'Ah,' he said. 'Sorry. I say I happy she good. And I thank you. She good person, I think.'

'Oh, so she's a friend? Did you know her before you returned to Bran in January?'

'Not friend, not . . . how you say, open?'

'Directly?

'Direct, yes. I see her work, I hear her talk with others, always happy, never, er, complain. Friend of Vera.'

I nodded, but let the name go for the moment, and gave him a simplified and fairly misleading version of how we had found Gabi. He could follow English when spoken slowly, and he chuckled at the picture of Holmes and me on the motorcycle – then laughed aloud at the contribution of the dog and his royal owner. I admit I stretched things out just a bit, hoping that Florescu would arrive before the questioning turned around on his protégée . . .

Finally, a knock came, and I went to let in the butler.

With him, to my surprise, was Vera Dumitru.

Andrei shot to his feet and turned scarlet. Vera gave him one quick glance, then ignored him completely. He seemed not to know what to do with his hands. And when we brought in chairs for our new guests, again he looked longingly at the door, but in the end perched on the edge of his chair, head down, hands clenched together between his knees.

I let Holmes get things started. The two men would respond to his prompting more readily than mine.

'Mr Florescu, there are things you have misled us about, and facts that you have failed to put before us. To begin with, I would like you to explain how Andrei Costea came to be living behind the wall of Castle Bran.'

It took a long time, an hour or more of sentence fragments, interruptions, and translation from Mr Florescu, but slowly, the story emerged of the shade of Castle Bran.

CHAPTER FIFTY-THREE

ONCE THERE WAS A young farmer boy who lived in a quiet corner of an empire, barely aware of the great world in distant parts. He was not a particularly handsome boy, nor terribly clever when it came to witty remarks and the things held in books, for his family was poor. But then, everyone in the town was poor, so what did that matter? And yes, his father could be wicked when he'd drunk too much, but that, too, was not unusual. The boy loved the family's horses, and his neighbours found that beasts trained by the boy would work harder than most. His hands were clever, too, so that the carts he repaired and the shutters he built stayed together under hard use.

There was a man in the village – a man of some importance, paid a small stipend by the nearby city to watch over the derelict castle on the hill. He had once been a schoolteacher, or perhaps he'd merely gone to school, and had no sons or daughters of his own. Instead, he became an uncle to the children of others, finding tutors to help with examinations, helping to pay for books and uniforms and the occasional tuition. Not that the boy showed much promise when it came to school, but the man was kind, and sometimes when the boy's father raged, the man made up a bed before the fire, to let the boy sleep.

The boy had friends. One girl in particular, older than he and far more clever, brought him joy and teased him – gently – even while she said that the village would not hold her for long. But until she flew away, she let him stay close, let the boy bring her gifts and make her laugh.

As the boy grew, his father became harder and harder on him. What was worse, he took to hitting the boy's mother as well. Until one day the boy realised that he was no longer a boy – that he stood eye-to-eye with his father, and his work with the horses had made him strong. So he told his father that the beatings must stop. And soon after that, the father left, taking with him the leather pouch of coins kept under the hearthstones.

Not long afterwards, the mother turned her face to the wall, and died.

Around the same time, the war that had been growing on the other side of the world suddenly came near. The neighbouring country was now the enemy, and soldiers were needed. The boy's older brother had a twisted foot, their younger sisters were too small to work, so the boy signed the papers to be a soldier, arranging for his pay to be sent home.

His first battle was his last. It was close enough to home that, were the smoke ever to clear, he could have seen the shape of familiar hills in the distance. Not that the smoke and dust were ever less than choking. Not that he had the leisure to stand and search the ridgelines.

Once, years before, when the soldier was very young, he'd seen a neighbour pulled from a stall after the stallion inside had gone berserk. He'd had nightmares for years – still did, at times – about what it must have been like to be trapped inside that wooden space with a ton of kick and steel and fury.

That was what battle was like, only without the walls.

The blows came from all sides. Bones broke, blood flew – without pause, with no moment to think, to look around, to figure out which man was an enemy and which a brother soldier. He was hit, and bashed, and found himself on the ground and got up and was run over, and once a vivid scarlet bayonet came at his guts, and only missed disembowelling him by an inch.

When he woke, it was night. Everything was pain. The world groaned and throbbed. He went away, as many times as he could, but it was either still dark, or dark again, when he came around at last, and thirst drove him to his feet.

He couldn't quite think what he was supposed to do. There were men moving around in the distance, lights and noises, but he needed water, and there was a stream somewhere out there, he was pretty sure . . . and so he began walking.

Then it was evening, and there were other men on the road, but he kept clear of them, stepping into the trees. The forest was cool, and he was feverish. He dropped his rifle and equipment belt, then his coat, and his hat.

He woke to the sound of feet moving across a packed-earth floor. He hurt, but not as badly, and mostly in his head and in his belly. He was thirsty, but he felt as if he'd drunk not too long before. He was inside, but it was not a house he knew. He was pretty sure he'd know what he was doing there, after another sleep or two.

It wasn't exactly amnesia, for after his fever stayed down, and after the dizziness and headache faded, he did remember who he was and where he was from. But under that dust-thick knowledge lay the seething of battle, the horror of being trapped in a stall with a maddened beast that hated him enough to break his every bone and kick him to a pulp.

Why on earth would he go back to that? Germany and Austria were far away. He had done his part for their argument.

He stayed that winter with the old lady who had found him. He earned his keep, chopping enough firewood to keep her for years, digging a new toilet pit, repairing her roof. When the spring came, he laced on his boots and dressed in the clothes she had made for him, and he walked through the hills to his home.

He went by night, when the village was silent, and woke his older brother by scratching at the shutters until they flew open to chase away the gnawing rat.

There he learnt that he was dead and buried in the churchyard.

They talked, the two brothers. The village had found jobs for the elder, and for one of their sisters. The government had sent money to thank them for giving the army a life. There was no need, the older brother said, for the younger to return to his headquarters, possibly to stand trial for desertion.

'They shoot deserters, don't they?' he asked.

And the young soldier admitted that they did.

'So go. You don't need to stay here.'

'But . . . Magda?'

'Magda loves another. You are too young. Go away – far away, where no one is fighting and no one will wonder at a boy who is not in uniform.'

They did not know that there was no such place in all of

Europe. But a boy who had clearly been wounded, whose body was still an angry red mess, and moreover, a boy whose clever hands and strong arms were useful, in towns and villages that were bereft of men? A boy like that could slip in, find a place, and live quietly for a while.

He did return home twice in the years that followed: at night, and seeing only his brother. But the last time, his brother was about to marry, and told him not to come again. 'My wife won't understand,' he said. 'Her uncle is a policeman, and I won't ask her to lie to him.'

Sadly, the soldier left, and went back south, and settled into a village that needed a pair of clever hands. And he tried to be happy there, and he tried to fall in love with a local girl, but the growing need for his own hills, the sound of his own language, grew in him like an infection.

And so he went home, by night. Only this time he did not go to scratch at his brother's shutters. Instead, he sought out the man who had protected and encouraged him all those years before.

A man who was now in a position to offer a certain degree of shelter, but at a cost.

Namely: no one could know.

CHAPTER FIFTY-FOUR

'WHEN THE QUEEN IS not here,' Florescu told us, 'I live in the village. Andrei came to my door a week into the new year, half-frozen, and said that if he could not return to Bran, he would drown himself. I let him sleep before the fire until we could figure out what to do. But I have neighbours there, and in the spring, I move into the castle, to be here for Her Majesty. This year, it was earlier than usual, in March. If Andrei stayed in my house, he would be seen. So I brought him here.'

'How did you know about the secret stairway?' I asked.

'Madam, my family have been Bran's caretakers for a very long time. There is nothing about the castle I do not know.'

'I imagine you took care to encourage the Queen and her architect not to change the two places where doors are hidden? Not this year, at least.'

He blushed slightly – I couldn't blame him, considering the ugliness of that first-floor cabinet.

'So who else knows? The cook, her helper, the housekeeper. Vera. Not Gabriela?'

'No. And Vera has only known since yesterday.'

Vera herself spoke up at last, the first word she'd said since walking in. 'When I hear that it was you – you, Andrei, friend of my sister – who whusper at me from graveyard like some spooky! I so frighten, you scare the pants off a me.'

The startling colloquialism launched Andrei into a vehement Roumanian back-and-forth with Vera that I could only follow by their expressions and gestures: abject apology on his part and indignation on hers; a meek gesture to his wounded forehead followed by her declaration that could only translate 'It serves you right.'

Eventually, Vera relented – relented, too, in English. 'I would not expect that stupidness. My sister always say, Andrei was good boy.'

'You look like her,' he admitted to the floorboards.

'Ah – that why you stare at me through peepy-holes when I dusting and doing work? Good thing one of girls not have room near there. Not nice boy.'

His head snapped up. 'I not stare! I only look, see who out there.

Nothing to do. Long days, inside wall. I not stare. Not at girls.'

'Just at me?'

'Yes at you – I mean no, I always like you, and I like to see you, yes, you very . . .'

I thought I'd better cut this off before she went for his throat. 'To be clear, you're telling us that Andrei has lived inside the walls since March, shortly before the Queen arrived. A few of the servants knew, and would leave food down amongst the builders' storage on the ground floor. He would sleep during the day and come out at night, to retrieve his food and stretch his legs.'

Florescu resumed. 'When the Queen is away, there is no problem for Andrei to come and go at night. Only one guard, and I can send him to kitchen, or tell him I can't sleep so I will take his watch. Then Andrei can walk, out in the open. At night, through the village a little, mostly through the forest. This is not perfect, not permanent, but until the Queen goes again, back to Bucharest when it grows cold, this is all I could think of.'

'Your fear is the charge of desertion, is that right?'

'He could be shot.'

I looked at Holmes. 'Do you know the law here?'

'I imagine it is much the same as ours.'

I explained to the others. 'Roumanian law may be different – or I suppose, that of the Austro-Hungarian empire – but if it's anything like England, yes, desertion is a crime, but no one is interested in prosecution any more. A confession usually results in discharge and an annulment of any awards or medals. But that raises a question – Andrei, how old were you when you enlisted? When you became a soldier?' I added, since his face was a study in confusion.

'How old? I think maybe fifteen, sixteen.'

'You lied about your age?'

He shrugged. And it was true – even English regiments tended to keep mum about soldiers they discovered were underage, merely deploying them in areas less likely to see active battle. I remembered reading about a twelve-year-old boy fighting with a Balkans regiment, in the early days of the War. By 1916, the Central Powers would have been desperate enough to turn a blind eye to the age of those in uniform. Nine years later, a certain amount of shame might have entered into their view of desertion.

'Andrei, you were underage and badly wounded. You nearly died, and you walked away *after* the battle was over. I doubt that in 1925, any military court would want to prosecute you. And if it does, well, my husband and I know many powerful individuals.'

He stared at me, uncomprehending. I opened my mouth to try again, with words of one and two syllables – but Florescu got there first.

As the Roumanian phrases rolled out, those almost-comprehensible bites of near-Italian and almost-Spanish, the soldier's face went from confusion to scorn, to disbelief, then open protest, before verging into astonishment. When Florescu went silent, the young man sat frozen for a time before his dark eyes swung over to Holmes and me. We gave him an encouraging nod.

He leapt out of his chair to seize my shoulders and kiss my cheek soundly. He did precisely the same to Florescu, and would have embraced Holmes but for an outstretched hand, pointedly stuck into his face. That he grabbed and shook, hard.

As he did so, he grinned, wide and incredulous from under that recently trimmed moustache – and with that, a jolt of recognition hit me, explaining many things.

The young man had the same long, distinctive incisors that I had seen beneath the edges of Florescu's moustache. God only knew what had led Florescu to marry a mad wife and forced the other woman into marriage with a wife-beater – or indeed, when those two nuptials had taken place – but clearly, some twenty-six years ago, the future major-domo had had an affair with a village girl.

The boy did not yet know that his protector was something much more than that to him, but Florescu did – I could see the awareness in his eyes. Here was the last secret Florescu had kept from us.

While this realisation was reverberating through me, Andrei had turned to Vera, and froze. In the end, she broke the impasse, rising from her chair to step forward, as dignified as Queen Marie, to bestow on her admirer a decorous kiss on the cheek – only to let out a loud 'oof' as he flung his arms around her and swung her in circles across the floor.

The three of us watched the laughing couple. Florescu looked startled, Holmes had a pleased expression on his face, and I – I was thinking: some weeks . . . no, five *days* ago, I arrived here feeling that I was stepping from a fever dream into a sun-dappled fairy tale. One with a Queen in a castle, a witch in the woods, and an honest peasant boy in disguise. A story where maidservants planned their own future and the Princess got to vanquish the evildoer. One where ghosts came out of the shadows, and true love came out of the air. This tale had everything but a talking cat.

I leant over to rest my shoulder against my husband's. 'And that,' I told him happily, 'is about as close as one can get to a story-book ending.'

END NOTES

By Miss Russell's editor,

Laurie R. King

As Miss Russell said, in some fairy tales, happily ever after is where things end; in others, happiness is where the problems begin.

There was indeed once a Queen by name of Marie, and a Princess by name of Ileana – but the tale in which Ileana grew up was the kind with darkness at its base. The kind of story where a little girl is surrounded by forces out of her control, with disease taking her baby brother and enemies driving her family from its home, with guns and bombs and assassins coming far closer than any child should see, and ending in betrayal by her own family.

Queen Marie died in 1938, so she did not see the Communist era devastate her beloved country. She had many problems with her wayward son, Carol II, but she could not know that he would take revenge for imagined slights by banning Prince Barbu Ştirbey from her funeral, and by driving his sister Ileana from her homeland.

Ileana survived, serving her country in any way she could.

She married twice, and died at the age of eighty-two in an Orthodox monastery in Pennsylvania, where she had been Mother Superior for many years.

Prince Barbu Ştirbey, who also served his homeland in spite of its government, died under the Communists in 1946, the day after attending a party at the Russian Embassy.

Romania's huge economic problems under the Communist dictator Nicolae Ceauşescu woke a desire for tourist money – which led to the reinvention of Bran Castle as Dracula's Castle. This makes for a colourful visit, although there is, as Miss Russell realised in 1925, a notable lack of evidence, historical or architectural, that Bram Stoker had this particular Carpathian castle in mind.

Those familiar with the village of Bran and its castle may notice that the author occasionally plays fast and free with certain details: the location of churches, the progress of the castle plumbing in 1925, Queen Marie's social calendar, and Ileana's location during that summer. As her readers know, despite being Miss Russell's literary helpmeet, I am not always able to ascertain when various aspects of the Russell Memoirs have undergone a transformation, whether through Miss Russell's creative memory, her taste in storytelling, or some arcane matter of national security.

Please don't blame me for Miss Russell's deliberate imprecisions.

Acknowledgements

This story's correspondent of *The Times*, Mr Alan Broder, takes his name from the generosity of a certain professor of computer sciences at New York's Yeshiva University, during a 2020 fundraiser for Second Harvest Food Bank in central California.

Thanks are due, now more than ever, to the fabulous ladies and gents of Penguin Random House, who battled for this book through stressful weeks of pandemic lockdowns and election turmoil. That it exists at all is due to their dogged determination that life will go on, and stories will be told. Thanks, Hilary, Allison, Kim, Melissa, Carlos, Emma, Caroline, and a thousand others. I love you guys.

And when it comes to love, my buds and supporters, without whom I just can't imagine this past year: Zoë, Bob, Alice, Merrily, Karen, Sabrina, Erin, John, Mary Alice, Anna, Angela, Clio, and all you Beekeeper's Apprentices, I feel you at my back, pushing hard.

Thanks, too, to the folk at Bran Castle, Romania, who cheerfully replied to odd questions from the other side of the world – and who have one of the best websites out there. And to Olga, who corrected my Roumanian spelling.

In books, as in life, it takes a community.

About the Author

Laurie R. King is the award-winning, bestselling author of seventeen Mary Russell mysteries, five contemporary novels featuring Kate Martinelli, and many acclaimed stand-alone novels such as Folly, Touchstone, The Bones of Paris, and Lockdown. She lives on California's Central Coast, where she is at work on her next Mary Russell mystery.

LaurieRKing.com
Facebook.com/LaurieRKing
Twitter: @LaurieRKing and @MaryRussell

If you enjoyed *Castle Shade*, look out for more books
by Laurie R. King . . .

To discover more great fiction and to place an order
visit our website
www.allisonandbusby.com
or call us on
020 3950 7834